# Silver Enigma

An *ISCFleet* Novel

The first book
in the
*Preeminent War*
Series

# Rock Whitehouse

*With gratitude
for those who stand the watch
in the real world,
whether near or far,
in the heat, the cold, the dark, the depths.*

*And for those who await their return,
constrained to love them from afar.*

# Table of Contents

# Prologue

War isn't usually a surprise. Governr
prepare. But you know it *might* happen. /
the gloves off, so, there's usually a lot o
before the shooting starts.

Technology, on the other hand, does s
flash of intuitive insight, pushing itself irre
Forstmann's development of the faster-thar
lifetime, as in the lifetime of men like the `
his inspiration move from small eng
realization.

For Forstmann, his choice to never reve
have Forstmann Propulsion Incorporated (
system would also mean progress from r
comprehension.

The Drive created economically viable
the nearby stars. Asteroid mining and in-
conceivable but highly profitable. The cor
organized as the International Space Cour
governments to create a navy capable of
valuable assets were now traveling. The I
Fleet by treaty in 2061.

Exploration at the star 40 Eridani A brou
who call themselves the Inori, meaning, the
Inor, is a beautiful, warm, quiet, almost per
home, and they are peaceful, friendly, and
humans. Their lives reflect the tangible
everywhere and part of everything they see,

The Inori were very different from us in
requisite carnivores, compulsively enamorer
in art and architecture.

But these all turn out to be small differer
welcoming to their new human friends. The
ways to both sides, supported by a growing s

This pretty place, ironically, is where the
destruction.

# Chapter 1

Space Fleet University
US Campus
Friday, October 2, 2076, 1740 EDT

Senior Cadet Carol Hansen stood very still, crying as she stared out the window. David Powell's heart stung when he caught sight of her as he left the Navigation Lab on his way home. *Rick again*, he thought as he approached her. Saying nothing, he stopped and stood next to her in front of the full-height windows that helped light up the long brick halls of the University. She closed her eyes after a moment, then spoke without turning to David.

"It's just so hard sometimes," she said, not quite a whisper.

"It doesn't have to be." He spoke the words evenly enough, but inside he was furious over Rick Court's lousy treatment of her. This was one of those times he wished he could tell her how much he cared for her himself.

"I know," she said quietly, "But..." the words trailed off in a combination of pain, frustration, and resignation. *But I care about him,* she meant to say. David silently nodded his understanding. He'd seen this scene before, many times. He felt intensely connected to her, a feeling that went beyond desire, beyond any need to possess. As intense as that feeling was, at this moment he held his silence. In this place and time, he decided the most loving thing he could do for her was to be her closest ally, her best friend, to literally stand with her. Not much later, he would regret letting this opportunity pass, but in truth, what he did was just who he was, and he really could not have done otherwise.

Rick Court had his issues, for sure, not least of which was a shitty childhood with a single father for whom 'bastard' would be praise by faint damnation. David knew Carol thought she could help him, could be good for him. Whether Court could possibly be good for her was an entirely different question.

David stood with her for what felt like a very long time. In reality, it was only a few minutes. Outside the tall and broad windows just in front of them, a robotic mower was moving silently left and right, trimming again the already-neat lawn. The fall colors were vivid in the trees in the distance, and behind them, the sky in the west was a heroic mixture of blue, purple, gold, and pink. Dark clouds framed in gold leaf moved across the sky, changing moment to moment as if something were alive in them. David and Carol were silent. She didn't sob; the tears just flowed down her cheeks. As she turned to say something to David, a door slammed, and Court came strutting down the hall.

"Carol! Let's GO!" he yelled at her. Carol looked at David, meeting his eye for less than a second, then smiled slightly and turned to follow Rick out of the building, wiping her tears as she went.

David didn't move at first. He remained at the window alone, trying to fix in his memory the fine details of her face; her shoulder-length dark hair, her brown eyes, the curve of her nose and chin, and the few scattered freckles that punctuated her fair complexion. She was a beautiful woman now, not at all the girl of eighteen she was when he had met her the first day of freshman year. Three years plus of training had trimmed all of them down in some ways and built them up in others, but with Carol, there was just a hint of softness that reflected the woman beneath the strength. He imagined he could still smell her fragrance beside him, almost as if she had left an aura behind.

Then, at last, the emotion drained away, and the moment faded back to normal, the electric tension so palpable just minutes before now dissipated.

He moved down the long dark hall, through the massive double-doors and out of the university. The air outside was crisp, with that flavor of fall David loved. He took his time walking to the 'subcar' transport station, allowing himself time to decompress from the encounter by the window.

By the time he was pressing the button for the elevator down to the subterranean tube system, he'd reconciled himself to his choices. It was the right thing to do, he knew. Meantime, Monday would start a week of exams, and he had plenty of work ahead of him to get ready.

## Chapter 2

ISC Fleet Destroyer *Liberty*
In orbit above Inor (40 Eridani A (b))
Saturday, January 15, 2078, 0700 UTC

Ensign Carol Hansen flopped into her preferred spot in the last row in the shuttle headed down to Inoria. The gray faux leather seat was firm but comfortable. The five-point safety harness was a different story. She pulled it down from her shoulders and snapped it together at her waist as usual, and as usual, when the harness' servo motors auto-adjusted to her, it felt a little too much like an over-confident second date when she was younger. As she squirmed slightly in response to the harness, she pulled the *Fleet Guide to Inoria* out of the left thigh pocket of her slate-gray uniform and began to read.

The windowless, narrow spacecraft started to fill with other crew members headed down to visit the planet's only large city. The shuttle's seats were four-across, with an aisle down the middle. The small talk among the passengers sounded strangely muted in the confined space of padded seats and well-insulated bulkheads. Her Fleet University classmate Ensign Marty Baker squeezed through the crowd and sat down across the aisle from her. Carol looked up from the *Guide*.

"Good morning…Marty." For more than three years, that had been her friend David's spot. As the memory flashed to mind, it made her reflexively look to her right, seeing an empty seat where Rick would have been back in those same years. But Rick was, thankfully, elsewhere.

Baker didn't miss the momentary delay in her voice. He held her eye for just a second before responding.

"Morning, Carol."

She looked up as a tall, thin, balding man with large glasses and an oversized nose came down the aisle. Senior Lieutenant Rich Evans, *Liberty's* Intelligence Officer, nodded to Carol as he sat down a row ahead of Marty. She had spoken to Evans several times recently as part of her duties leading ship visits for the Inori. She found him smart, witty in his own Kiwi way, and as respectful of subordinates as he was of superiors. She instinctively liked and respected him in return.

"G' morning, Hansen! Finally getting downstairs?" he asked, pulling down on his own seat harness.

"Yes, lieutenant. captain says no ship tours for the Inori on Saturday, so I'm taking the day off." The ship visits had been a pleasant experience for everyone, and Carol seemed particularly adept at relating to the visitors.

"So, you doing the tour?" Evans asked, seeing the *Fleet Guide* in her hand.

"Yes," she answered, pointing to Baker. "Marty's tagging along for comic relief."

"Excellent! You both deserve a bit of a break."

"What about you, sir?"

He smiled broadly, his blue eyes lighting up behind the large lenses.

"Carter and I are headed up north into the countryside. Small tour — supposed to be very unique up there."

In a few minutes, the shuttle's large square split hatch swung closed with a distinct thump. Once the shuttle moved into the ShuttleLock for launch, they heard a couple clicks and felt one heavy push, and they were heading down to the surface.

An hour later, the hatch swung open again, and the star we call 40 Eridani A, which the Inori call "Rorina," flooded the passenger compartment with the warm light of dawn. The usual disembarking chatter quieted as they filed out and met the requisite Inori greeting detail. Nine two-meter-tall Inori, with their smooth, hairless, sand-colored skin and their large, impenetrable black eyes, greeted each visitor in turn. They shook hands awkwardly, with both forelimbs, each human hand disappearing inside the Inori's large, smooth palms, which have a long opposing digit and five webbed fingers. The Inori were similar to humans in overall design, bipedal with two arms and minimal neck. The Inori were unclothed, with no visible sex organs or waste elimination structures.

Once clear of the line, as Carol retrieved the guide map from her pocket, she saw Evans and Carter jump into a waiting vehicle — an open-sided beat-up thing that looked vaguely Jeep-ish — and pull away, heading north. Looking around as she unfolded the map, she could see that the shuttle landing pad sat on a small hill at the eastern edge of the city. To her left, she saw only a few structures in the mostly open, rural countryside. Inoria rose quickly to her right. Ahead of her, she saw the large bay beside which it stood, the tall enclosing mountains split by the narrow mouth just visible in the hazy distance. The map in the *Fleet Guide* reflected Inori street design: all oblique angles and complicated intersections. No right angles, ever. The pattern reminded her of the folded-paper snowflakes she had made as a child. Marty caught up with her, looking over her shoulder at the map.

"Remember paper snowflakes?"

"Yeah, doesn't look much like Omaha," he observed, one eyebrow up. Marty had known Carol only slightly at the University, but they had become better acquainted as shipmates. While he had come to appreciate her, and she likewise to enjoy his company, his role was very much that of a sidekick. He knew it, he enjoyed it, and he wanted nothing more from her. His heart would find its home elsewhere someday, he knew.

Carol had planned to walk the city alone, but at dinner last night, Marty had invited himself along, and now that he was here, she was glad for the company. They started roughly southwest, towards the first site on the tour. It was good to be walking real ground and breathing real air, even if it wasn't home. The crushed stone Inori pavement crunched pleasantly under their Fleet-issue nonskid shoes, and they liked the solid, natural feel of it.

"So, Carol, if this is your first time here, what's been keeping you upstairs?" As he spoke, Marty's eyes followed an attractive Warrant Officer as she passed by in a group going in the opposite direction. Carol pulled him back around by the arm.

"Roskov asked me to be available for the Inori visits, and anyway, I wanted time to study for the L-T exam."

Now re-focused on Carol, Marty replied, "You're too dedicated, Hansen. You're a bad example for the rest of us."

"Thanks!" She took a few steps before continuing. "And stop ogling Long."

"I wasn't *ogling* her," he said defensively, "I was *noticing* her."

Carol gave him a smile and a small shove, and they continued on to the first site, the Inori Foundations Museum.

The star was full up by now, fueling a warm, cloudless day, and the taller buildings glowed with reflected light and the subtle colors of the masonry. The Inori built with a material that resembled stucco but was harder and smoother. The iridescent flecks in it reflected a variety of colors, depending on the angle of the star's light from the observer. As Carol and Marty moved along, buildings changed smoothly from red to blue to purple, each one emphasizing a different shade at any given moment. The Inori weren't much for other colors on the outside of buildings, but the windows, six-sided of course, looked much like human stained glass with bright, vibrant hues lit from within. Carol was gradually aware that she was squinting, her eyes naturally resisting daylight unlike what they were designed to handle.

"Got your shades?" she asked Marty as she pulled hers from the zipper pocket on her right sleeve.

"Yup!" he replied as he dramatically produced his own Inor-specific sunglasses and put them on.

"Much better!" he said with relief.

"Yeah, it's weird how this light gets to your eyes after a while; it doesn't feel that bright at first."

As they walked the tour, they found themselves enthralled with the city and began to understand at a visceral level what others had tried to describe. It was an ethereal, ephemeral experience; the colors constantly changing around them, reflecting both the complexity of the city's layout and the shapes of the buildings themselves. As they went along, one moment of beauty would smoothly morph into another: the same but different. The Inori Council building was Carol's favorite, just three stories tall but quite broad and nine-sided. Nine was a recurring theme in the city, perhaps even more than three or six.

They walked the first half of the published tour in an hour and a half. It conveniently ended at a small tourist café. The Inori had adopted tea but could not tolerate coffee. There was a small selection of baked goods for their frequent human customers. Marty found two surprisingly comfortable Inori wicker-something chairs near the back wall of the café. They rested their feet and drank properly brewed tea with fresh English biscuits as they talked quietly about the city.

Then their NetLinks went off.

Marty looked in surprise at his wrist and then at Carol, confusion obvious on his face. "Combat Recall?"

A heavy rhythmic vibration came through the floor, some distance away but clearly getting closer. Carol beat Marty out the door by just a step as the deafening sound caught up with the muffled rumbling in the ground. They looked towards the noise and saw debris rising into the air in the distance.

"Oh, shit!" Marty said, fear sneaking into his voice.

Carol quickly turned back northeast, and they started running toward the shuttle landing area. They made a few dozen strides, Carol a couple meters ahead, when they heard a new sound very close behind them, a shower of something moving very fast and smacking the stone pavement. As the sound came closer, running ahead of the more massive vibration, she felt more than saw something strike very close to her, throwing up stones, and she heard a wet crunch just behind her, followed by Marty's cry of pain.

She stopped and turned around as he was falling to the pavement, blood flowing in a red flood from a gash that stretched from his collarbone to his thigh. She ran back to kneel at his side only to see the color draining from his face, the life fading from his eyes as he looked up at her. Carol held his gaze as he slipped away until there was nothing more to hold. Fighting back rising tears, Carol looked to her right and saw a line of holes leading up to and past Marty's mangled remains.

"Lazy Dogs?" she asked herself aloud, looking again at the trail in the street and recalling the mid-twentieth century anti-personnel darts. The weapon had laid Marty wide open, nearly cleaving off his right leg mid-thigh. Further along to her left, she could see the line led to two Inori, bent over another flailing in pain. The flails faded quickly as the helpless victim's life drained away.

The deafening drumbeat finally caught up with her, and the building behind her took an impact, pummeling her back with small rocky debris. The shockwave and sonic boom lifted her and then slammed her to the pavement. As she looked up, the fine dust that was starting to fill the air sparkled with bits of Inori masonry, and she had the sudden impression of being trapped in some kind of hellish snow globe.

She got up, reluctantly leaving Marty where he was, and moved away from the building, fearing it would collapse on her. Her Ground Combat instructor's voice echoed in her head as she ran: *Get your ass down, Hansen, and get under cover. You're no good to anyone dead!* There were impacts all around her now, and she looked for some kind of shelter, finally crawling between two large piles of rubble that had fallen from a small building. Shoving her growing fear to the side, she got down as low as she could to wait it out. She said a prayer for Marty. She said another *Liberty*.

Aloud she said to herself, "Oh David, you're going to be so pissed you missed this."

The Countryside North of Inoria
Saturday, January 15, 2078, 1000 UTC

After a bumpy ride north out of Inoria, while Carol and Marty were enjoying the city, Rich Evans and Matt Carter had followed their guides into the rolling countryside along a well-worn path. After an hour of hiking, they had stopped just past a grove of what passed for trees on Inor, where a small stream flowed into a lake. The trees were short, compared to Earth, no more than three or four meters tall. A single patchy white-and-black stem rose a meter or so from the ground and then spread out into several main branches, each of those splitting quickly into numerous sub-branches. The leaves were darker than most trees on Earth and far more complex in their structure.

They sat on the bank and watched the creatures in the stream, which on the one hand were obviously fish and on the other like nothing they had ever seen before. As they sat together by the stream, Rich asked the Inori a question that had been on his mind for some time.

"May I ask about Ino?"

"Yes, RichEvans, what is your question?"

Rich sat up straighter, a subconscious expression of respect. "In human religions, there are books — collections of stories really — that tell us about God, that teach us what a religion means, its traditions, its morals. Are there stories of Ino? Is there a book of Ino?"

The Inori made a low rumbling growl that Rich understood was laughter. It went on for what seemed a long time. Rich felt slightly silly now, hoping he hadn't offended them with the question. Finally, they stopped, and one spoke.

"Yes, we have heard of this practice among humans. We do not understand it. The world, RichEvans, is the book of Ino. The sea, the sky, the land, we sitting before you, are all the stories Ino requires. So, no, there are no stories, and there is no book. Ino is present everywhere."

Evans nodded his understanding, thought a moment, then asked again. "How are the young taught about Ino? Do any ever refuse to believe in Ino?"

Again, laughter.

"Ino does not need to be taught, RichEvans. The young know the presence of Ino in their teachers, in their food, in their litter-mates. As to your second question, it is even stranger to our ears than your first. To refuse to believe in Ino is to refuse to believe in the sunrise, or the stars, or ourselves. Ino is as tangible for us as the ground we sit on, as the water flowing before us."

They rested there, taking time for tea and talking to the Inori about the animals of the countryside, their habits, and how similar animals behaved on Earth. It was a pleasant, nearly idyllic scene, one the NetLinks' shrill alarms shattered.

Evans looked at his in disbelief. He looked over at Carter, who said, "Combat Recall? What the hell?" Evans acknowledged the message on his NetLink but was unable to raise the ship by audio.

"We gotta go. Now." As Evans stood, he could see bright streaks in Inor's deep blue sky, leaving thin lines of smoke as they headed towards the city.

"What the hell, indeed," he said to Matt.

They watched for just a moment as hundreds of streaks passed over. Shortly after, they heard a whistling sound followed by a rapid sequence of sonic booms. Evans and Carter and the two Inori moved as quickly as possible back the way they had come. Hills and creeks and ponds that had been pleasant diversions on the way out had transformed into unwanted obstacles on the return.

Evans had only a vague idea of what was happening, but the smoke now rising in the south could not be good, and *Liberty*'s Chief Intelligence Officer was impatient to get back into the city and back on the job.

The Streets of Inoria
Saturday, January 15, 2078, 1015 UTC

It had been several minutes since Carol last heard an explosion nearby. The attack, whatever it was, had moved off to the east. Carol crawled out of the rubble, covered in dust and bits of masonry from the buildings. Fire crackled and an acrid, unpleasant smoke tainted the scent of the breeze. She brushed the dust off as best she could. Her hair was getting in her face, so she pulled out the band she kept handy and shoved it into a ragged ponytail. Her earlobe stung where a shard of something had cut her, but she was otherwise unhurt. She pulled the guide map from her thigh pocket, slightly surprised it was there as she had no memory of putting it away. She could feel heat on her back, so she moved west, away from it, and toward the central north-south thoroughfare, Meridian Street, a few hundred meters away. She soon encountered the remains of *Liberty*'s Chief Navigator, the gregarious Nicolai Roskov. He had been her direct superior, a very good man with a touch for teaching that Carol doubted he knew he had. He looked worse than Marty, almost unrecognizable but for his uniform.

"Oh, sir, I am so sorry," she said as she looked down at him. She marked his position on her map, Marty's too. They would need to be able to find them again later.

"Ensign?" called a voice through the smoke and dust ahead of her. She looked up from the map in surprise at the sound of a human voice.

against what remained of the wall behind her and closed her eyes. *Think! Think! Teresa! What do you do next?*

As Carol looked around their location for the first time, she saw that they were on a small side street to a large intersection. The southeast portion of the intersection was behind them. The northeast area was more or less intact, damaged but not flattened. There was rubble all around, but some parts of what must have been a café remained intact. It was time to check their perimeter: she'd feel a lot safer with more information. This little group was still her command, as far as she was concerned. She decided it was time to get them moving, doing something useful, and get their minds off home.

"Johnson, Smith, Sanderson; get up and circle this block. Roberts, Alvis; go across the intersection and try to get around the southwest corner. Cornell, Phillips, Glass; you three take the northwest. Stay together, no heroics. If you find more crew, bring them back if you can. If you can't, make sure you have a positive ID."

She paused, looking from face to face to make sure they understood her meaning.

"OK, get going." The groups got up, brushed off the dust and ash that kept settling out of the smoke overhead, and moved out as she had directed. Her assignments left four young Marines behind. Their tall, dark-skinned corporal spoke up.

"You have other plans for us, Ensign Hansen?"

"Corporal Jackson, I need you and your men to stand by Commander Michael."

This got Terri's attention. She jumped up and pulled Carol a few steps away, speaking quietly but directly into her ear.

"Ensign, you are overreaching your authority, and what's more important is that you're overreacting. I do not need—"

Carol looked Terri hard in the eyes and blew right through her objections.

"Commander Michael—ma'am—you are the senior surviving officer in a combat situation. For the moment I am your de facto deputy, and that makes *me* responsible for *your* safety."

Slowly, Terri smiled just a little, trying hard not to let Carol see it. *This one has some real backbone*, she thought. She decided to let it go.

"Very well, Ensign. Until Commander Davis returns, at least."

Carol nodded and then walked out into the intersection to wait for her crew. *Her* crew. The thought came to her so easily that she was startled by the clarity of it. *These people will follow my commands, and I am now responsible for their lives.* The reality of combat leadership now weighed on her mind. With death in the air all around them, she wanted very much to keep it off herself and her people. She prayed silently *Please, God, don't let me get them killed.* Still, next to her worries and stress, another part of her felt calm and confident. Her training had prepared her well for this day, and she had thought enough to pay attention when it counted.

Terri Michael watched her go, seeing the sensitive, naïve ensign fading and a real officer beginning to emerge. She put her head back and closed her eyes. *So, Abuelita Santos, what would you think of your little girl now?* she wondered. *I would think your friends are very lucky to have you!* her inner Grandma answered. *Maybe,* she responded, *I hope so*. Setting the pleasant side conversation with her memory of home aside, she forced herself to consider what might happen next and how she would react. Her thoughts were not restful or pleasant, but they were necessary, and she would not shrink from the contemplation of such violence as that which she might need to defend her people and the Inori.

## Chapter 3

Meridian Street
3 Kilometers North of Inoria
Saturday, January 15, 2078, 1205 UTC

Lieutenant Commander Len Davis, *Liberty's* Weapons officer, was at that moment scrambling down the remains of a fifty-story tower that had fallen across Meridian Street with his small detail of one young ensign, Stevens, and two chiefs. He was actually doing much better than Terri's estimate, making around three klicks an hour through the destruction. Inor's marginally smaller gravity didn't hurt, and neither did its higher oxygen content. They pushed hard, and about three kilometers north of the city, he saw Evans and Carter heading towards him at a crisp pace.

Davis greeted them grimly, his dark face seeming even darker with the weight he felt.

"Welcome to hell, Mr. Evans, Mr. Carter."

"Do you know what happened, sir?"

"We're at war, Rich. Don't know who, got no damned idea why, but most of Inoria is in flames, and *Liberty* is gone."

"Gone?"

"Gone, Rich, as in destroyed in combat."

"Can't say I'm surprised, sir. I saw three explosions but couldn't be sure what they were."

"Three?"

"Yes, two to the north and then one back more over Inoria."

"So, we must have hit something," Davis said hopefully.

"Yes, sir, that would be my slightly uninformed assessment," Evans said with irony in his voice.

"Ever the skeptic, lieutenant?"

"Just a humble slave to verifiable facts, Commander."

Davis managed a wry smile, and the six survivors started to trudge back south. The increasing destruction wore deep furrows in Rich Evans' face and mind as he began to appreciate the breadth and depth of the disaster unfolding before him. As they walked, Rich saw the crushed stone pavement perforated from place to place. He asked Davis to stop so he could take a better look. He stuck his finger in the hole but was unable to touch anything.

"Anybody got a knife?"

Ensign Stevens produced a Marine KA-BAR combat knife from a holster on her right calf. She smiled as she passed the weapon over.

"Just sharpen it when you're done, sir."

"No promises," he responded as he started digging. As he struggled to move the soil aside, he spoke without looking up. "Looks like Lazy Dogs to me, Commander."

Davis looked puzzled. "Say what?"

Evans leaned back to look up at Davis, shaking the dirt off his hands as he did. "You need to brush up on your mid-twentieth century military history, sir. I know it's been a while. Lazy Dogs are anti-personnel darts dropped from high altitude."

Evans finally hit something with the knife once he was down a quarter of a meter or so. He dug around the hole until thin fins were visible. "Unbelievable," he muttered as he proceeded. He finally exposed enough of the dart that he could wiggle it free from the gritty, light-brown Inori soil, cutting his finger on the edge as he did. He pulled out a dart that was perhaps a quarter of a meter long, with a round body maybe three centimeters in diameter. The leading edges of the fins were razor sharp, swept back at an acute angle.

"These things are sharp as hell, Commander. I've seen what they do, and it's pretty horrible."

He returned the KA-BAR back to Stevens, who frowned at its condition, but cleaned it best she could and stuffed it back on her leg.

"So, you think the rest of this is, what, RFGs?" Davis asked.

"Yes, it could well be an RFG attack. We'll need to dig some up to be positive. Did you see the streaks in the sky?"

"Yeah, I saw them. They were coming right at me."

"Wow. Scary."

"No shit. Would these be guided or dumb or what?"

"Good question, sir. My guess is that they're guided, but we need to look around. There may be evidence in these holes that will help us."

He stepped off, and they were back on the move south. Davis and Evans walked well ahead of the others.

"Rich, I don't have the brief on dispositions. Where are our ships?"

Evans thought a moment, then consulted his NetLink for the time.

"Well, let's see, it's January 15, 1255, UTC. *Antares* is on a shakedown to Proxima Centauri, just enough distance to give the drive a workout. *Stoykiy* is en route to Sirius for a quick recon of the system. Somehow nobody's flown by to see what's there. Now that's a real secret, sir, both dangerous and embarrassing as hell."

Davis nodded his understanding as Evans continued.

"*Bondarenko* is at Epsilon Eridani, the *Dunkirk* group is at Tau Ceti. *Stalingrad* is at Earth, I believe. That's all I can recall offhand."

"What do you expect them to do?"

"Well, sir, you know how the brass is; they'll all be doin' the headless chicken dance."

"True, but what would you expect?"

16

"If I were there, I would grab *Dunkirk* and send her here to secure the area. They're relatively close. Then, I'd throw *Stalingrad* out of Earth orbit and send her here, too, secretly, to cover the evacuation."

"But, will we be here to evacuate?"

Evans took several steps before responding. "Thinking invasion?"

Davis nodded. "This sure looks like Normandy early on June the sixth, doesn't it?"

"Yeah, I suppose it does, sir." Evans looked all around him, pausing a second to study the smoke rising from Inoria. "Could also be Dresden."

They took a few steps as Evans paused to think.

"Still, I think while an invasion is a possibility, it's unlikely."

He stopped, turning to Davis.

"The best inhibition to an invasion is biological. If they're really alien, they might not want to risk it. They could destroy the planet just by coming if they bring some monster bug the Inori, or we, can't defeat. Or get one that *they* can't handle."

They resumed walking.

"An odd thing about a space war, sir, which you never see in the movies, is that a poorly prepared peace delegation can obliterate the race you mean to make friends with."

"But they were able to hit their Inori targets pretty well, right? Wouldn't you think that means they know a lot about Inor?"

"No doubt they do. And taking that a step further, knowing a lot about Inor would tell you that these people are not a threat. No weapons, no warships, not so much as a militia. Their space technology is 1970's at the latest. So why trash the place? It makes no sense to destroy an undefended society that poses no threat. Even the planet isn't unique. There are two other habitable planets in this system that don't happen to have any intelligent life on them. If they needed a base, they could have one for free and in secret. No, sir, this is different. Must be real thugs, these guys. Can't wait to kill some."

Len Davis smiled grimly at Evans' attitude. Rich Evans, despite his thin six-foot-three-inch frame, was tough as old shoe leather underneath. He had thick glasses, a shy demeanor, and a wry grin with which he hid the steel of his character. He hardly looked the warrior, and those who counted too much on appearances might find themselves surprised by someone they had severely underestimated.

They turned their faces back to Inoria and resumed their descent into Hades. The rest of the trek into the city passed mostly in silence. Evans stopped from time to time to examine the holes in the street, taking pictures and measuring them best he could. It became clear to him there were at least two sizes, and he marked the larger ones on the guide map he had purchased to plan his outing. *Some outing*, he thought, hacking their way deeper and deeper into the hellish fire, disgusting

17

smoke, and horrible scenes of pain and death.

The Hexagon
Inoria
Saturday, January 15, 2078,1650 UTC

Len Davis sighted Terri Michael atop the ruined fountain just as she was spotting him from a distance of about a kilometer. The night was approaching, and his small group of men and women was moving at a brisk, nervous pace to get to a secure place before dark. By the time they reached the intersection Carol had secured, they were tired and leg-weary despite Inor's lower gravity and higher oxygen.

"Good afternoon, Commander Michael. Damn glad to see you." Len said with a wry smile.

Terri returned the grin. "Damn glad to be seen, Len. All well?" There was real relief in their handshake.

"Aside from being frightened out of our wits, we're OK. A couple of shrapnel wounds on folks who were closer to Inoria than I was, but nothing serious. What's your status here?"

"With your group, we've got sixteen crew here of thirty-five on the planet. I've got five confirmed dead, including Roskov."

"Well, I guess that leaves you as the senior surviving officer, Commander Michael."

She nodded. "It does. And you are now the Deputy Commander of ISC Forces, Inor."

She pulled him aside a few feet. "Did Dean get to you?" she asked quietly.

"No. You?"

She nodded.

"And?"

"Not much…he was already in the fight and had to cut me off. NetLink went down right after that. Wished us luck."

They stood there a few seconds, thinking of Carpenter, then she took him further aside.

"We need to make some plans. Get Evans and Hansen and let's take a walk."

Davis' face showed his surprise at the mention of Carol Hansen's name. "Hansen?"

"Len, that girl is all steel underneath the velvet. She's kept her head, took charge when she had to, assigned me a guard, secured the area, so yeah, she's in."

"Yes, ma'am." He turned to his group. "Lieutenant Sanders, you're in charge while we're away. See if you can scare up some food. Looks like a café or something there. There should be something edible around. Rich, Ensign Hansen,

18

the Commander and I would like you to join us."

Len Davis turned around and walked the twenty yards or so to where Terri stood. Rich and Carol joined them momentarily.

Carol spoke first. "Commander Michael, ma'am, Sanders is a lieutenant, and Coleman and Stevens are the same rank as me, and—"

"Ensign Hansen," Davis interrupted her.

"Sir?" she asked warily.

"Nobody standing here gives a crap about seniority, especially among ensigns. Commander Michael wants you here, so you're here."

"Yes, sir." Carol turned quickly, catching Corporal Jackson's eye and lifting her head just a bit. He nodded in response and got his men up.

Terri turned from scanning the southern horizon. "Let's walk. We've got a lot to talk about. Mr. Evans, where are our ships?"

Rich repeated the recitation he had already given Len on the locations and his expectations of the ISC Fleet.

"So," he concluded, "I think we have at least two weeks, probably more, before we see anyone from Earth. By SLIP, CINC will have the word about a day after we send a message."

"Sounds right. OK. We've got to discuss scenarios and options. Ensign Hansen, what will the enemy do next?"

Junior officers speak first, Carol knew, so she expected the question to come to her. Shrugging, she answered, "Hard to say, Commander. We have so little data to work with. We don't know why they attacked, their goals, their capabilities, or what their social structure is. I don't have a clue."

Terri turned and put her hand on Carol's shoulder. "Good. Carol, always tell me you don't know when you don't know. I hate having to figure out for myself that someone is just talking and not really saying anything. Mr. Evans?"

Rich smiled. "Really, Commander, I can't improve on Ensign Hansen's assessment. Except, maybe, as I was saying to Commander Davis on the walk south, these guys are real thugs. I mean, Inor is this sweet little planet of industrious but harmless people. They're no threat to anybody. To hit a planet like this makes no sense."

"All right, we don't know what these bastards will do next. What should we prepare for?"

Len spoke next. "We can't prepare for much. The biggest gun we have on hand is a KA-BAR."

There was nervous, cynical laughter at that statement. There was silence for perhaps twenty yards of walking.

"If I may, Commander?" Carol started.

"You may."

"I was thinking about the rescue question. As Mister Evans said, *Bondarenko* and *Dunkirk* are fairly close. There is a SLIP transmitter in the Embassy. We could call them ourselves. It will be two days for them to get the word from Earth, and it would be only hours from here. Plus, if these assholes are as good as they seem to be, both are in some danger—"

Rich smiled as he cut her off. "Giving orders to other ships? I don't think we—"

"No, Rich, she has a point." Terri interrupted. "We signal them both as a warning and a notice of our situation."

"We copy CINC," Len added. "And maybe we've called in our own cavalry."

"Yeah, that about covers what I was thinking. But if they come, it's their call." Carol finished.

Terri suddenly stopped and looked behind her at a shadowy figure about twenty meters behind them. Night had finally come, and the smoke overhead, eerily lit by the fires, made it feel that much more sinister.

"Who's that?"

Carol responded immediately. "Corporal Jackson, ma'am. There is also a Marine about thirty yards ahead of us and another over on our right." She paused for effect, smiling slightly. "The corporal is really very good."

Michael looked at Davis. He nodded slightly. They exchanged a second, more intense look, and then Terri started moving along the street again.

"Hansen, I would love to have a talk with your profs at the U. Who the hell taught you all this?"

"Excuse me, ma'am? Taught me what?"

Terri turned and pointed to the corner behind which the other survivors were waiting. "There are a lot of experienced crew, including officers, back there trying very hard not to shit their uniforms they're so scared. Here you are, having won your first argument with your new commander, set a watch for the officers, and maybe figured out how we might call for help and not all get killed."

Carol paused for a moment, looking off into the distance, then turned back to Terri. "I had a friend at the university, Commander, he was maybe the smartest one in our study group, and we used to sit up and argue about what we would do if we were in some situation or another. He was really good at tactics and evaluating a situation, and he taught me, well, taught all of us, a lot about setting aside the stress and thinking our way through the problem."

"Where is he now?"

"He never graduated...he...uh...he had a personal problem Senior term and dropped out. I sort of lost track of him after that, but he's in the service somewhere. Warrant officer."

Terri Michael shook her head. "Senior Term? Must have been some problem."

"It was," she said quietly.

"Was it you?"

Rich's blunt question took Carol back a step, but she recovered quickly.

Ignoring the blush burning in her cheeks, she replied, "No, sir, it wasn't me. It was worse than that."

"He as good as you?"

She nodded.

"I want his name when we get back home, Carol. If he's down in the bowels of some ship, he's wasted." She paused a step and then continued the discussion at hand. "We need to get someone to the Embassy. We need to evaluate and secure the landing zone. Is the shuttle still there? I doubt it. Rich, how do we get all our people together? We still have several unaccounted for."

"Well, the Embassy has a NetLink node. I've got the network prefix settings for *Liberty,* so I could get a NetLink loop set up. That would let us recall everybody."

Davis stopped to pull out his NetComp tablet. Looking around, he matched the map to the streets he could see. "Embassy is about four and a half blocks south. Maybe a klick. The shuttle landing zone is about four klicks east. Lucky thing Inoria isn't large, as cities go."

"OK, Rich, take Carol and whoever else you need and head for the embassy. Len, take Carter and about a half-dozen and get to the shuttle. Hopefully, by the time you get there Rich will have a NetLink running, and you can give me the bad news."

Len shook his head. "Terri, it's getting awfully dark. The crew that came down from the north is pretty tired, not to mention beat up. Should we split up now, or would it be better to wait until the morning?"

She paused to reconsider her plan. "Rich, think you can get the NetLink up tonight?"

"Sure."

"OK, then you take Hansen and whoever you think you need and go do that. The rest of us will bed down where we are tonight, and then, Len, your group will leave in the morning. I still need to know if we have a shuttle or not, but I can wait a few hours for that. It will be safer in daylight, too."

As she finished this statement, they rounded the last corner of the section they had been walking around and came into view of the ruined fountain and the shattered café in which the rest of the crew waited. Michael stopped.

"Time to clarify our responsibilities. Davis is XO. Rich, you're Comms and Intel. Hansen, Operations. We get a ship again, you're done in Navigation. Any objection to making Hansen a lieutenant? She'll need that to deal with the others."

They all agreed.

It was time to get back to their ragged but unbowed group in the shell of the little café.

The Hexagon
Inoria
Saturday, January 15, 2078, 1745 UTC

Evans, Hansen, and three technicians left shortly after the walk, escorted by PFC 'Lockup' Lochner and Private 'Dumbo' Dobo. The Marines walked ahead of the group, with Evans just behind and Hansen following in the rear. It was dark and smoky, the street dimly lit by distant fires reflecting off the haze hanging over the city. They were about halfway there when Lochner signaled for the column to stop. He pointed to some bodies in the street.

"Dumbo, check that out." They had come on two more *Liberty* crew, killed in the street, with two Inori next to them. As Dobo moved to verify their NetLinks, he heard a noise nearby. He drew his flashlight like a sidearm and fired the intense beam at the source of the sound. In the bright light, he saw another crew member, recoiling as if it had physically struck her.

"Dumbo! Cut the light!" Lochner commanded.

He flicked it off.

"Lockup, get over here," Dobo said quietly. He and Lochner moved around the bodies in the street to where the survivor was cowering in a doorway. Lochner switched to low-intensity red light so he could see. It was Denise Long, a young Warrant Officer who had earned her degree in physics at Dalhousie University and then signed up as a nuclear applications engineer, managing the ship's reactors. She had been aboard *Liberty* for only a few months. Lochner could see her still trembling, face and uniform splattered with blood and dust. She stared, wide-eyed, at the mutilated bodies in the street, their torsos laid open, and the red and purple blood mingling in the low spots, sinking into the pavement. Blood and slabs of human and Inori tissue littered the street. Lochner moved to place himself between her and the bodies, and as he did, she looked up at him, still shaking, barely able to speak.

"Is...it...over?" she asked, her voice shaking like the rest of her.

Lochner spoke quietly, "Yes, Ms. Long, it's over, at least for now."

Her eyes came back down as if looking through the Marine at the carnage behind.

"We were walking, and then—" her voice barely audible, she continued, "Their heads just...their bodies..." Her voice trailed off, and her body shook again. She doubled up as if to vomit, but there was nothing left in her.

"I understand, Ms. Long. We've all seen things like that today. Are you hurt?"

"No, I don't think so." she seemed to look at herself for the first time in the dim red light of Lochner's flashlight.

"Can you stand?" Lochner asked her.

"I...I...don't know. Is it really over? I can't hardly breathe," she gasped, "I am so afraid. Is it really over?"

Lochner and Dobo looked at each other. Then Dobo leaned over to her.

"We're all afraid, Ms. Long," he said gently. "It's time to get up now. Time for you to be brave."

She nodded slightly, and they each took an arm to raise her up to her feet. She took a moment to steady herself, then walked with the Marines back across the street.

"Hello, Long," Rich said, "It's good to see that you are unhurt. Come along to the embassy with us."

She fell in line with the technicians, and they moved on south. Dobo verified the casualties' NetLink identities and trotted to catch up. In the four blocks to the embassy, they found about twenty human dead. The last section of Meridian Street before the embassy seemed devastated, but the building was intact.

The same could not be said for the nerves of the inhabitants. The tall, fat, silver-haired and flush-faced former southern governor was in full panic.

"Lieutenant!" the ambassador yelled as Evans entered the embassy. "What has happened? Why didn't you stop it? What…what…what are we going to do?"

Evans held back most of his anger, but not all. "Ambassador Johnston, sir, we did not just let this happen. *Liberty* was destroyed trying to stop it. Now with your permission, Ambassador, we have work to do." Johnston visibly retreated before Evans, who just looked him in the eye and waited for him to wilt.

"Of course, Lieutenant, of course. Whatever you need."

Evans watched as Johnston's face went from indignant to horrified as the Marines brought Denise Long through the front doors. Covered in blood spatter, dirt, and bits of, well, never mind what else, Lochner and Dobo walked her through the lobby and into a restroom. Johnston stared at them all the way until the door closed. Only now, as they went through the door, did Evans notice all three wore the Canadian maple leaf on their left sleeves.

"That is what a war looks like, Mister Johnston, the good part, anyway. The living."

"Oh, dear God," Johnston mumbled. Evans thought for a moment the ambassador would throw up. "So, who exactly is in charge now?"

"Of the embassy, you are, sir, of course. But with *Liberty* gone and with her Captain Carpenter, Lieutenant Commander Michael is the Senior Surviving Officer. She is now in command." He let the ambassador absorb that fact. "We need to re-map the embassy NetLink, sir, so that we can communicate and organize our people. And we'll need to send a SLIP message immediately."

The ambassador nodded faintly and retreated to his office with his young assistant, chattering nervously to her as he went.

"You always lop off their heads first?" Carol asked quietly.

"Only the fat stupid ones."

They shook their heads at the politics of the appointment of ambassadors and started up the stairs to the NetLink equipment near the roof.

"Lieutenant!" Evans turned to find a young embassy officer hustling across the lobby. "Brown, sir, communications."

Evans nodded.

"I sent a FLASH SLIP message reporting the attack as soon as we realized what was happening. What else do you want to send?"

Rich was surprised at the initiative shown by a junior member of the incompetent ambassador's staff. "Where's the communications office?"

"Across the lobby, sir, down that hall, second door." Brown was starting to get his breath.

"Very well. Thanks, Mister Brown, we'll be right there."

Brown headed back across the lobby to his workspace.

Rich turned to Carol. "Go see Brown. Report the loss of *Liberty*. Report the attack as RFG with Lazy Dogs. Use exactly those words. Report the number of known living crew members. Report that we have almost no weapons and no prospect of finding any. Ask for instructions and an ETA on rescue."

"Yes, sir. Anything else?"

"As you suggested, send something similar to *Bondarenko* and *Dunkirk*, make it actual—just for the captains—don't ask them to come, just advise them of our situation."

"Understood. Anything else?"

"Not for the moment. I'll catch up with you after I'm done upstairs."

Carol nodded and walked towards the Comms office. As she crossed the lobby, she noticed for the first time the twenty or more civilians who had sought refuge there. They were in chairs, on the sofa, or on the floor, leaning against walls. She tried to ignore the fear-filled eyes locked on her as she walked across the lobby, her uniform filthy, blood and soot-stained, and into the communications office of one Darrell Brown. He looked up as she entered.

"Ensign Hansen! That was fast."

"Well, as of a few minutes ago, it's *Lieutenant* Hansen."

"Congratulations, I suppose?" he said, unsure of what a sudden promotion really meant.

"Well...whatever...How do we proceed?"

He handed her a plain pad of paper. "Just write it out, and I'll get it into the SLIP transmitter."

She wrote quickly in her delicate, neat script. Nearly as fast, Brown transcribed the message into the SLIP transmitter and gave her a copy for confirmation.

```
FLASH 2078011151850UTC
TO: CINCFLEET
FROM: HANSEN, CAROL, LT, FOR MICHAEL, TERESA, LCDR, SSO INOR
INORIA ATTACKED 207801151000UTC RFG WITH LAZY DOGS
BY UNKNOWN ENEMY.
```

```
LIBERTY DESTROYED IN ORBIT.
MULTIPLE ORBITAL EXPLOSIONS SEEN.
TYPE AND NUMBER OF OPPOSING FORCE UNKNOWN.
SEVERE DAMAGE TO CITY AND SURROUNDINGS.
WEAPONS NIL. REQUEST INSTRUCTIONS AND ETA FOR RELIEF.
19 KNOWN SURVIVORS INCL LCDR DAVIS SLT EVANS LT SANDERS
ENS COLEMAN STEVENS.
7 CONFIRMED KIA ON SURFACE INCL LCDR ROSKOV ENS BAKER.
9 MIA.
END
```

"RFG?" he asked, curious.

"You need to read more sci-fi, Mr. Brown. After all, you're living in a world of faster-than-light-travel and friendly and now, some not-so-friendly aliens. RFGs are 'Rods From God.' Pournelle and Heinlein used them, as I recall. We think that's what this was — high-speed inert metal projectiles."

"OK. And, Lazy Dogs?"

"Little-used mid-twentieth century anti-personnel weapon. As Lieutenant Evans put it to me, think oversized darts falling from the sky."

"I see. Copy correct?"

"Yes, looks good. How long?"

"It should be home in right around twenty-four hours."

"So, a response is at least forty-eight hours away."

Brown nodded. "That's correct, lieutenant. Anything else?"

"Yes, we need to warn *Bondarenko* and *Dunkirk*."

Again, she wrote, and again Brown worked quickly to get the message transmitted.

```
FLASH 207801151855UTC
TO: BONDARENKO ACTUAL
       DUNKIRK ACTUAL
CC: CINCFLEET
FROM: HANSEN, CAROL, LT, FOR MICHAEL, TERESA, LCDR, SSO INOR
INORIA ATTACKED 207801151000UTC BY UNKNOWN ENEMY.
LIBERTY DESTROYED IN ORBIT. MULTIPLE ORBITAL EXPLOSIONS SEEN.
TYPE AND NUMBER OF OPPOSING FORCE UNKNOWN.
SEVERE DAMAGE TO CITY AND SURROUNDINGS.
THREAT TO OTHER FLEET ASSETS SEEMS LIKELY.
19 KNOWN SURVIVORS.
7 CONFIRMED KIA ON SURFACE. 9 MIA.
END
```

"Good. That's it," she confirmed.

"Anything else, lieutenant?"

She smiled. "Not at the moment. Thanks, Mister Brown."

She turned and left the Comms office.

Embassy of Terra
Inoria
Saturday, January 15, 2078, 1930 UTC

Messages sent, Carol headed up to the roof of the embassy to get a better look at the city. As she walked out onto the flat, gravel-covered surface, she saw the two Marines and Denise Long looking out across the destruction. Seeing Carol, Lochner left the railing and came over to her.

"Lieutenant, did you need us?"

"No, Lochner, just coming up to have a look."

"Yes, ma'am."

She looked over at Long, seeing her now upright, alert, and looking out at the damage. "Lochner, you did wonderfully with Long."

He nodded in acknowledgment. "Well, she's just a college kid in uniform, Lieutenant. She could be Dobo's little sister or mine. She wasn't ready for this, but I think she's OK now."

"And, college kids, as you call them, don't crawl through trenches with rotting pig guts while live ammo zips overhead, do they?"

He shook his head. "No, ma'am, I really don't think so. Did they do that to you, too?"

"Twice."

He winced. "I see. So maybe our officers aren't all the candy asses we like to think?"

She smiled in response, but Lochner's comment sent her back to the time she crawled up out of the trench, exhausted, wet, cold, and wearing a disgusting stink, to find Dan Smith and David Powell standing over Rick Court, down on all fours, vomiting profusely. Dan and David just looked at her and shook their heads. The trench gunk stuck to their hair wiggled as they did that, an image which made Carol smile inside, in spite of what was happening around her. She remembered hearing Dan say something like 'Get up, candy ass...' as she walked by and headed for the showers. Court's snappy f-bomb-laden reply was cut off by another blast from his belly.

She put that memory aside, and looking back at Lochner, she said, "Well, some could do it without losing the big fat lunch they gave us right before. Some couldn't."

"Somehow, Lieutenant Hansen, I expect your lunch and you made it to the end together."

"Roger that, Marine."

Lochner walked back to his countrymen, and Carol moved to the other side of the roof. It was as close to a vision of Hell as she ever thought to see in real life. There were craters everywhere, it seemed, with large gaps left in buildings, many still smoldering, some still in flames. A dark pall of smoke hung over the city, reflecting the yellow and red light from the fires. Bodies lay in every street she could see, dark pools of blood surrounding and accentuating the deaths, some still wet and reflecting the light from the sky. She could hear the sound of pain and the sound of those trying to give aid. The Inori language sounded gruff and coarse to human ears, but she could hear the echoes of alarm and haste as they worked to get the injured down to the temporary hospital on the beach. Then, there was the stench of death and burning buildings, which attacked her nostrils and sinuses and engraved itself on her memory.

As she looked out on this disaster, she wished David Powell were there with them. Or, with her. His calm presence and intensity of purpose would be welcome tonight.

She thought about that last day when he had stood at the window beside her as she struggled again with her relationship with Rick. He had walked out the wide university doors like it was any other Friday, only to find it was unlike any Friday any of them had ever seen. His father's suicide that day and his mother's subsequent collapse derailed David, splitting him away from his career and his friends. Carol thought of him daily, sometimes wondering why, but she had not heard from him in a very long time.

## Chapter 4

Frigate *Bondarenko*
Epsilon Eridani
Sunday, January 16, 2078, 0306 UTC

Lieutenant Commander Anna Nonna was sleeping restfully in her cabin, just behind the ship's Bridge. Their investigation of Epsilon Eridani was proceeding as expected, the few significant planets were located and mapped, and some of the larger asteroids were cataloged for a future survey. Before bed, she had read her weekly SLIP message from her husband and son back in Odintsovo. The baby boy was doing fine, now walking and jabbering nonstop, but Daddy wondered if he wasn't in a little over his head. She smiled as she recalled the child, his tiny voice, and the quiet, sweet warmth as he slept in her arms. He had blond hair like his father's but dark eyes like hers, and everyone commented on what a beautiful child he was.

And, of course, they were right.

The FLASH message alert on her phone interrupted her gauzy dream about them. She snatched the device from her desk and entered the security code. "Good gracious God..." she whispered to herself as she read Carol Hansen's message. She reached for the ship phone on her desk.

"Conn... this is the Captain. Assume Alert Status One." She could hear the alert alarm ringing in the ship.

She closed the connection and opened another.

"Nav...yes, this is the Captain. I need a course and time to Inor best speed...Yes, from our current position...as soon as possible...yes, wake him up...very well."

She clicked off the Nav connection and opened another.

"All officers in the wardroom in fifteen minutes."

She reached for her tablet, checking her recollection. Yes, Inor was about 5.5 light-years away - nearly six days! She pulled on a uniform, ran a quick brush through her short dark hair, grabbed her tablet, and headed out the door, not forgetting to take one last look at little Artemiy's picture next to her bunk.

The wardroom was alive with conversation as Nonna walked in and sat at the head of the table. The room was immediately quiet.

"Ensign Vasilescu, please close the door." A young Slovenian ensign was standing at the door. This was her first trip into deep space, and she was nervous enough without all these alarms and emergency meetings, in the middle of the night no less! Now, she trembled just a little. The door closed, and Nonna looked out at two dozen sets of wide eyes.

"*Liberty* has been destroyed at Inor," she said flatly. "I don't know how or by whom, but it was a deliberate, hostile act. There are twenty or thirty survivors on the surface. My intent is to go to Inor immediately."

She turned to her supply officer.

"Lieutenant Cook, we planned to be here another two weeks, then home. We will need to go six days to Inor, and then it would be over two weeks back to Earth from there, possibly with additional personnel. What about stores?"

Cook thought for a moment. "We have a week in reserve, per regulation. So, really, we have five weeks' stores on board. We'll need to keep track, but I think even if we spend a few days at Inor, we should be OK. Nothing we can't manage."

"Weapons?"

A dark-haired woman leaned forward. "Usual stock, Captain. Twenty Spartans, fifty Lances. We were planning a live-fire drill into the star in a few days, so all the ordinance is still aboard." *Bondarenko* was, after all, a frigate, not a cruiser or even a destroyer. Her size limited her ability to carry weapons.

"Very well. Does any officer here have a material objection to proceeding to Inor forthwith?"

She looked methodically at each member of her staff, and each met her eye with confidence.

"OK then." She picked up the phone. "Conn....set course for Inor best possible speed."

She hung up the phone, rose, and the meeting was over. It was 0345. She went directly to the Bridge, to the Communications station.

"I have a FLASH for you."

The crewman nodded his understanding.

"To...CINCFLEET, SSO Inor, *Dunkirk* Actual...one...Departing Epsilon Eridani for Inor best speed, ETA 207801211300...two...alert status one in effect...three...full weapons load on hand...that's it."

"Yes, ma'am, I have it. It will reach Inor in about eight hours and twenty minutes. Earth is eighteen hours away."

Nonna turned around to find her Executive Officer, or XO, LCDR Watson, next to her.

"The brass at Fleet will be going nuts. In command but unable to really control anything."

Nonna nodded her agreement, hands on her hips. "That, Dick, is why they taught us to think for ourselves."

Cruiser *Dunkirk*
Tau Ceti
Sunday, January 16, 2078, 0928 UTC

Captain Kieran Barker was standing the first watch Sunday morning, as was his habit. It kept him in touch with the Bridge crew and gave his junior officers a small weekend break. His mug of tea was nearby on the Conn workstation. He also took this usually quiet time to work through his backlog of reports to read and paperwork to manage. He had a very capable XO in Captain Andrew Sackville, but some things the captain just had to do. The detailed survey of Tau Ceti was dull and routine, as he had hoped. His small task force had 'invaded' the system from three sides, surprised its imaginary defenders, and vanquished their feeble opposition. Or, so the simulation went. Destroyer *Aurora* and frigates *Gagarin* and *Grissom* had performed as planned. But, truthfully, there was no good reason for it to be otherwise, there being no actual opposition. Once they secured the system, the survey of the planets and other small bodies around Tau Ceti began. He visibly jumped when his phone screamed. He scooped it up and read the message.

"Bloody hell..." He picked up the ship phone.

"XO...Andy, I need you on the Bridge immediately."

He hung up, and after thinking for a moment, he picked it back up.

"Lieutenant Edwards...Angela, this is the Captain. So sorry, but I need you to take the Conn as soon as you can get here. Yes, that will do fine." He stood at the captain's workstation and spoke in a loud voice that rattled off the walls and windows.

"All stations set Alert Status One."

The watch-keepers began raising the ship's combat readiness, calling in additional personnel, and increasing the level and number of external sensors operating. He then turned to the Communications station.

"Comm... send a message to all vessels to set Alert Status One. Tell them this is no drill. Nav! I need time to Inor best possible speed."

As he finished those commands, Andy Sackville arrived on the Bridge.

"You won't believe it, Andy. *Liberty* has been destroyed at Inor. There is something like thirty surviving personnel on the surface."

"Attacked? By whom?" Barker shrugged and passed the phone over so he could read the message. "*Bondarenko*? Where is she?"

"Epsilon Eridani. They're about four light-years closer."

"So, they got this, what, six hours ago?"

"That would figure, yes...they're five and a half light-years from us, so we won't hear a response from them for several hours."

Sackville looked across at the CO. "You planning to go?"

Barker nodded. "Yes...we have to go. Besides *Bondarenko,* there is no one even close."

"Close? Good Christ, we're *nine days* away!"

Barker shrugged. "So, what, Andy? We have to go. I know Commander Nonna. She'll go."

"OK, sir, orders?"

"All staff meeting thirty minutes… say…1000. I want a Logistics, Weapons, and Nav report. I need to talk to the other captains before then."

"Yes, sir. Interesting times."

Barker grunted. "Interesting, indeed."

At about that time, Lieutenant Angela Edwards arrived on the Bridge. Captain Barker briefed her on the *Liberty* report and ordered her to maintain course and status pending a move to Inor. He then left the Bridge for his office.

Captain Barker held a voice conference with the other three ship commanders, advising them of what had happened at Inor and his intent to go there. He asked them for Logistics and Weapons availability, although he was quite sure he already knew their status. He gave them an hour to be ready to depart for Inor.

A short while later, Captain Barker entered the conference room and faced a scene not unlike what Anna Nonna had on *Bondarenko*. The staff quickly quieted down. An emergency meeting on a Sunday morning?

"Ladies and Gentlemen, *Liberty* has been attacked and destroyed at Inor." He waited a moment for the gasps and cuss words to subside. "There are on the order of thirty *Liberty* personnel on the surface, or rather, there were when this message was sent some fifteen hours ago. Nav, what is our best time to Inor?"

"Sir, that's about nine-point-seven light-years, so nine days, maybe a little more at best speed."

"And from there back to Earth?"

"Plan seventeen days - might be a little less."

"So, we are looking at a minimum of twenty-six days, plus whatever time we spend at Inor. Very well. Stores?"

"Yes, Captain. By the original exploration plan, we would leave here in five days, then a thirteen-day run back to Earth. Add the one-week reserve, and we have about twenty-five days provisions on board." He paused a moment. "I expect you will get similar reports from the other ships."

"So, if we were to spend one day at Inor, we would not exhaust our supplies before we return home?"

"Correct, sir, but I think that would be optimistic, and if we are bringing back survivors, we will run short."

"Yes, I see. Tell the galley we need to reduce our food consumption by twenty percent. That won't hurt too badly, and should stretch our supplies to accommodate any passengers."

The staff murmured general, if grudging, agreement.

"Weapons?"

"Full load still aboard, sir."

"Very well. We will depart for Inor at 1045. That will be all." He turned to the Communications Officer. "Comms, I have a message for Inor and CINC."

```
FLASH 207801161030UTC
TO: SSO INOR
        BONDARENKO
        CINCFLEET
```

```
FROM: TF DUNKIRK
TF DUNKIRK DEPARTING TAU CETI FOR INOR ETA 207801260230
END
```

The Hexagon
Inoria
Sunday, January 16, 2078, 0600 UTC

As 40 Eridani A, 'Rorina' as the Inori call it, rose, its naturally orange light now appeared quite red and angry looking through the pall of smoke over Inoria. The sky had been lighting up all night with falling debris, but fortunately, nothing fell within the city. There were bright flashes out to sea, doubtless from large masses of wreckage striking the planet. If they hadn't known what it was, people might have thought it the best meteor shower ever.

Rich Evans and Carol Hansen spent the night at the embassy, mostly on the roof, some in the friendly Comm office where there was a spare couch, and some outside the front door with the Marines. Rich reset the NetLink to access *Liberty* devices, and immediately they had communications with all the *Liberty* personnel.

Back at the shattered intersection, it had been a difficult night. Bringing up the NetLink node gave them communications, but it also added one more death to their list. They now knew that there were twenty-six survivors and nine dead. Luckily, none of the survivors had severe injuries, but the deaths were hard news for all of them. The whizzing sound of wreckage falling, some hitting the ground, disturbed sleep and raised anxieties.

Terri Michael woke early, about 0500. Today, like yesterday, UTC would roughly correlate with the apparent solar time in Inoria. It happened from time to time as the rotational rates of Inor and Earth cycled in and out of synchrony. Len Davis was up at about the same time and got his group ready for the four-kilometer walk to the shuttle pad. The streets were still a mess, so it would be slow going. They raided the wrecked cafe and split the limited amount of human-consumable food they found. In Inoria, there was usually plenty of good food around, but not in this cafe, which was off the usual tourist paths and did not cater much to humans. Davis' group left about 0630.

With the NetLink up, Terri could now send SLIP messages herself through the embassy's facilities. Her Fleet-issue NetComp tablet had somehow survived in her side pocket. Slowly she pecked out an update:

```
PRIORITY 207801170600
TO: BONDARENKO, DUNKIRK, CINCFLEET
FROM: MICHAEL, TERESA, LCDR SSO INOR
STATUS REPORT
(1) NETLINK RESTORED CONFIRMED 26 ALIVE 9 KIA
(2) CONSTANT SMALL DEBRIS REENTRY OVERHEAD
(3) NO FURTHER EVIDENCE OF ENEMY ACTIVITY
(4) NIL WEAPONS NIL SUPPLIES
```

```
(5) WILL CONSOLIDATE POSITION AT EMBASSY TODAY
(6) NEXT UPDATE 12 HOURS
END
```

That sent, she regrouped with her officers to discuss their next moves.

"So far, no invasion," she told them, "But we can't rule that out."

Not that they had any weapons to repel one, they all knew.

"Let's get together what we have and head for the embassy. Once we get our situation stabilized, we'll need to get back out here to recover our people."

The group of twenty or so officers and crew gathered what they had brought or found and organized themselves into a rough column of twos. Ensigns Coleman and Stevens took the rear of the column, with Commander Michael in the front with a couple FPI engineering officers. Corporal Jackson took the point.

As the dawn grew and daylight came up full, moment by moment the city looked worse and worse. Terri guessed that two-thirds or better of the buildings had been damaged, most severely. There were bodies all over the streets, mostly Inori but some human as well. Inor had become a place for the moderately well-to-do to visit, famous for its unusual beauty, the welcoming Inori, and their exotic cuisine. Businessmen were here as well, trading limited kinds of technology or space-mined metals for Inori spices, art objects, and foods. It had been a beautiful place but now appeared battered and scarred. Hopefully not permanently, but Terri thought the healing might take a long time.

The kilometer-long walk south on Meridian Street took over an hour as they worked around debris and tried to quiet the fear and alarm in those human survivors they encountered. One portly salesman in a cowboy hat and matching accent demanded to go back to Earth immediately. She explained to him that there was no ship, and even if there was, he wasn't getting on it. He was demanding and arrogant, and finally, he just swore at the officers and stomped off. Terri shrugged it off, and the group continued their trek south.

"Strange days!" she said to no one in particular.

Embassy of Terra
Inoria
Sunday, January 16, 2078, 0800 UTC

True to their welcoming nature and their preoccupation with water, the Inori had constructed the 'Fountain of Earth' in front of the Terran Embassy. It was a two-meter-diameter globe, with the oceans recessed so that as water pumped out at the top, it ran through them and drained into a wide pool below. It was a nice touch. But North America and Siberia had both taken a hard hit in the attack, likely a couple of Lazy Dogs. An RFG hit would have demolished it altogether. As Carol looked at it idly, as she waited for the rest of the survivors, the water was dripping off in all the wrong places.

It was nearly 0800 as the ragged group approached the embassy. Carol, seated atop rubble in front of the embassy sipping her coffee, watched them approach. Evans was up on the roof. She touched her NetLink.

"Rich, they're almost here."

"Roger that, be there shortly."

Carol was still atop the rubble pile when the group arrived.

Looking up at her, Terri asked, indignant, "Hansen, is that coffee?"

"Yes, ma'am," she responded brightly.

"So, I spend the night under the stars, ducking falling God knows what ship shit, cold, hungry, and here you are like a princess on a throne with hot java?"

"Well, Commander, I did spend most of the night on the roof and some out here with the guard, but otherwise, yes, ma'am, that's about the size of it." She paused briefly for effect as she climbed down. "Shall I get you some?"

"Yeah, twenty cups, I think."

"Tea for me," Simmons called.

"Got any soda, Lieutenant?" came another voice.

Carol just grinned and looked at Terri. "Breakfast is ready for you, ma'am."

The crew moved on into the embassy and down the hall into the commissary. It was warm and smelled fantastic, so much better than what they had been inhaling all night. Terri held back and kept Carol with her.

"How's the Ambassador?"

"Stuffed shirt with smelly diapers, I think, Commander. Lieutenant Evans smacked him down pretty hard last evening, which he deserved. I beat him up pretty well this morning to get the supplies for a meal for the crew. It took some convincing, but he eventually gave in."

"Did you leave a mark?"

"No, ma'am. Plausible deniability and all."

They laughed briefly, and Terri moved into the commissary. She was the last to eat, with Carol just in front of her. As they were finishing up, the silver-haired fat politician came through the commissary door. He caught sight of Carol on the other side of the room and headed straight for her. She looked across at Terri, who had her back to the door.

"Diaper alert six o'clock."

Terri suppressed a grin and nodded her understanding. He came on at full speed, blundering through the chairs.

"Lieutenant Hansen, where is your commander?"

Terri Michael pushed her chair back, rose, and turned to the man. "Good morning, Mister Ambassador. I am Lieutenant Commander Michael. Thank you for this breakfast for the *Liberty* survivors, sir. It was very kind of you."

Taken off guard by her soft but firm voice, he gladly took credit for what Carol had done.

34

"Of course, Commander, the least I could do. I am Sidney Johnston."

He managed a smarmy, insidious politician's smile and reached out his fat ruddy hand, which she took and returned a firm handshake to his limp offering.

"Commander, the Inori Council has asked me to meet with them and asked that I bring a senior military representative with me. They did not exactly say what it was about, but one should assume that it is in relation to the current situation with respect to the, uh, tragedy of yesterday."

She looked at him blank-faced. "A tragedy, sir, is when a young person dies too soon or someone suffers needlessly. Yesterday, Mister Ambassador, was an aggression, a deliberate act of war, and I believe to euphemize it as something less than that is not helpful."

He inclined his head and oozed condescension. "In diplomacy, Commander Michael, we must be more guarded in our discourse. We must be sensitive to our counterparts' needs and feelings."

"I don't see how reciting an obfuscated line of crap and not the truth is somehow being sensitive. But fine, ambassador, I will go with you."

She turned to Rich Evans, seated next to her.

"Rich, mind the store until Commander Davis gets back. We should be hearing from him pretty soon. Hansen, you're coming too."

Carol almost spat coffee. Johnston leaned back in alarm.

"Me, ma'am?" she asked in surprise.

"Hansen, did I stutter or something? Yes, you."

By now, Johnston had recovered himself. "Really, Commander, we need to keep our delegation small. Young Hansen, while obviously quite competent and also quite loyal to you, is, well, perhaps too direct for our purposes?"

Terri looked at him and then back at Carol. She turned to her left.

"Perhaps you're right. On second thought, Rich, how would you feel about a walk over to the Inori Council with me?"

The ambassador, shocked, replied, "Lieutenant Hansen will be fine, Commander. Really, I'm sure she'll be fine."

Terri smiled a little to herself, having forced the old politician into an option he clearly couldn't accept.

Len Davis did check in shortly after that. The shuttle was indeed destroyed. Terri instructed him to come into the embassy and get his group a meal. They would make more plans from there later.

Meantime, she told him, she would be off not being a very good diplomat.

ISC Fleet HQ Communications Station
Fort Eustis, VA
Sunday, January 16, 2078, 0416 EST (0916 UTC)

Communications Chief Mark England hated the long and tedious overnight shift. Tonight, he only saw a few routine messages, nothing urgent. Get, verify, record, deliver. They told him this job would be exciting. They lied. He leaned back in his chair in the darkened room, half-surrounded by monitors showing the incoming and outgoing messages as well as the overall system status.

He was just getting up to go fetch yet another cup of coffee when the SLIP receiver alarm went off. He slammed himself back down into his chair and pulled up the message.

```
FLASH 207801151020UTC
TO: CINCFLEET
FROM: LIBERTY ACTUAL
UNDER ATTACK ABOVE INOR. ENEMY UNKNOWN. PROGNOSIS GRIM.
END
```

England reached for the red Command Center phone as he instructed the system to forward the message to the Fleet Operations Center's Officer In Charge (OIC). The OIC picked up before the first ring finished.

"Operations Center, Commander George."

"Commander George, this is Chief England in the Comms room. I have a FLASH for CINC." James George, a sturdy-looking former athlete, saw the message indicator in his display and opened the content.

"Anything more, England?"

"That is all, sir. The message is twenty-three hours and fifty-six minutes old."

"Shit."

"Roger that, sir."

"CINC gets this automatically?"

"Yes, sir, it will be on his personal device already. Meantime I wanted to get it to you directly. "

"Very well. Let me know if there is any more."

"Yes, sir."

England hung up the line. *Under attack? By whom?*

CINCFLEET Personal Quarters
Fort Eustis, VA
Sunday, January 16, 2078, 0417 EST (0917 UTC)

Fleet Commander Admiral Connor Davenport was, as one would expect, asleep at home when his phone screamed a siren tone announcing the arrival of a FLASH message.

His wife jumped up, cursing the damnable device. "Dammit, Connor, that thing drives me crazy!" she whined.

Davenport nodded sleepily at his agitated wife and picked up the phone to read the message.

"Are you listening to me?" she demanded.

Davenport's eyes opened wide as he read the message. "Oh no, oh God no...."

His wife continued her rant. "Here it is, Connor, four o'clock—"

"Marian, please, please, be quiet for a minute. I can't think!" he interrupted her. Shocked at his words, Marian was quiet.

"What is it?" she finally asked.

Davenport could not think of a nice way to say it.

"War. Goddamn space war." He thought for a moment, then said, "I'm going in. I need you to pack me a bag for a week and bring it to HQ later today."

He turned back to the phone. "Get me the Operations Center on a secure line."

The phone quietly made the connection, displayed the correct security status, and connected his call.

"Operations, Commander George."

"This is Davenport. You have the flash?"

"Yes, sir. I am drafting a general message to all vessels to raise their alert levels, pending additional information. I'll instruct the ships in our immediate vicinity to report their readiness and condition. "

"Very well, Commander. I will be there in a half hour."

"Understood."

Davenport dropped the call and dressed. There was not much he could do right away other than what George had already started. But questions swirled in his mind about *Liberty*, her crew, her captain, what had happened, if there were survivors, and what was happening *now*. 'PROGNOSIS GRIM,' Carpenter had said. He finished dressing in a few minutes and started out of the bedroom. Marian was standing in the way.

"War, Connor? WAR? I need to know, right now, Connor, *right now*, I need to know if we are safe or what I need to do. Someone has to look out for this family!"

Davenport just looked at her.

"I don't know," he said finally, deciding to tell her the truth. "This happened very far away, but I don't know if we're safe here or not. If we're not, there may not be much we can do about it. Keep all that to yourself, Marian. I'm sorry, but I really do have to go now."

She turned and walked into the bathroom, slamming the door behind her. The CINC went down the stairs and out the door. His assigned autonomous electric vehicle delivered him to the ISC Fleet Operations Center in less than 20 minutes.

ISC Fleet HQ Communications Station
Fort Eustis, VA
Sunday, January 16, 2078, 0428 EST (0928 UTC)

England was considering what all this could mean when the SLIP alarm went off again.

```
FLASH 207801151032UTC
TO: ISC PRESIDENT
    UN GENERAL SECRETARY
    CINCFLEET
FROM: TERRAN EMBASSY AT INOR
INORIA UNDER ATTACK
NUMEROUS EXPLOSIONS AND FIRES IN CITY
ORBITAL EXPLOSIONS REPORTED
EMBASSY SECURE AND UNDAMAGED
END
```

He went ahead and forwarded it to the Operations Center, then picked up the phone.

"Operations, Commander George."

"There's a new message, Commander. You should have it by now."

George checked, and indeed there it was. "Thanks, England," George said and hung up without waiting for a response.

So, not just a conflict in space, the attackers had struck the planet itself as well. Shortly after that, Admiral Davenport arrived. James George was ready for him.

"Sir, I think we should issue a general warning to the fleet."

"Yes, Commander. I agree."

Davenport then outlined what he wanted in the text. George prepared it and had the Admiral's approval before sending it.

```
FLASH 207801171100UTC
TO: ALLFLEET ACTUAL
FROM: CINCFLEET
TOP SECRET
THIS IS NOT A DRILL
LIBERTY UNDER ATTACK 207801151020UTC AT INOR
INORIA ALSO UNDER UNSPECIFIED KINETIC ATTACK
WITH EXPLOSIONS AND FIRES REPORTED
ALL SHIPS ASSUME ALERT STATUS ONE AND REPORT POSITION AND READINESS ASAP
END
```

*Holy crap*, George thought to himself, *we've gone from just another quiet night into a war in what, forty minutes?*

Vice Admiral Stanimir Arkadiy Yakovlev arrived in the Operations Center not long after Davenport. The Deputy Commander of the ISC Fleet was a stocky, handsome Russian with an impressive dark mustache and gray hair. The incongruity was a source of general amusement to the staff. Yakovlev was tough, even prickly, but quite competent. He greeted Davenport with a nod.

"Ordinarily, I would say 'Good Morning,' Connor, but this is no good morning."

Davenport gave him a wry, sad kind of smile. "Indeed, Stan, this is no good morning."

Davenport briefed his deputy on what they knew and got his agreement on the warning message.

"Well, if I may, sir, we need to get someone to Inor. There may be additional attacks, and there may well be survivors on the planet." Davenport indicated his agreement. "We may also need to assist the Inori with rescue or medical assistance on the planet as well."

"Commander George?" Davenport called.

"Sir?"

"What do we have in the area of Inor?"

James George had already made a quick check of ship locations. "Nothing, sir. I checked that first thing."

The admirals both turned to look at George.

"Define nothing, Commander," Davenport demanded.

"No ships within five light-years, sir."

"But, Commander George, it's not even sixteen light-years *from here!*"

"Correct, sir."

The admirals now looked at each other. Yakovlev spoke first. "They're either very lucky or very good."

"Don't count on luck. Shit. Commander, what's in orbit?"

"One moment, sir." He swiped and poked and checked his status display. "*Stalingrad* is here, due to leave in a week or so with *Friendship*. Their next assignment is Wolf 424. Several others in lesser states of readiness."

"Who is closest to Inor?" Yakovlev asked.

George went back through his screens. "Frigate *Bondarenko* is at Epsilon Eridani, sir, five and a half light-years away. She could be at Inor by maybe seven or eight days post-attack, considering the SLIP will take fifteen hours or more to get to her."

"Who's next?"

"The *Dunkirk* task force is at Tau Ceti, nine-point-seven away. She has *Gagarin, Aurora,* and *Grissom* with her. So, again, that's twelve from here, so maybe eleven or twelve days?" He paused to check another screen. "They're near the end of their tour, due back here in just under twenty days, so they might be short on supplies if we keep them out too much longer."

"What else?"

"*Freedom* and *Vostok* are at the new Kapteyn Station starbase. They ferried out some staff and supplies. So, that's, lessee, ten point seven."

Davenport grunted in frustration. "So again, we're looking at twelve days to get them to Inor."

During this exchange, more Operations personnel were arriving, responding to the alert George had issued. Chief of Operations Rear Admiral Hans Gerhard had quietly joined the discussion.

"I don't think *Freedom* and *Vostok* could be considered combat-ready after that ferry mission, and whatever capabilities they do have, we're going to need at Kapteyn."

Davenport nodded his agreement. "Yes, Hans, that is correct. The other implication of what you say is that we need to get someone else out to Kapteyn soon as we can."

"Yes, sir, I would agree with that assessment."

"Speaking of bases, what about Tranquility?"

Again, James George flipped through the screens on his NetComp tablet. "*Eagle* is there, sir. She's in good shape for defense. *Canberra* is en route there now, so I think that is covered about as well as we can."

"Very well, Commander."

Davenport stopped a moment to look at the officers gathered with him.

"Gentlemen, it is now 0515. We got the first message less than an hour ago. The politicians will be waking up soon, and I expect the news will start to pick up on all this activity around HQ. The diplomatic cables will be leaked soon if they haven't been already. I need to have something to tell them."

James George spoke first. "Well, sir, we have to do what we can do. *Stalingrad's* Captain Petya told me he has too many crew members ashore. He needs 24 hours with top priority on all travel assets before he can go. That means he's seventeen days away." George waited for the Admirals to respond.

"Continue, Commander," Yakovlev prompted.

"Sir, I believe we should send *Bondarenko* and the *Dunkirk* group to Inor right away. Even with the delays we've talked about, they're the best we can do."

"What about their supplies?" Gerhard asked.

"They'll make do, sir. They have the required extra week of consumables aboard, and they'll have to dip into that, but I think they'll manage."

"And then?"

"And then send *Stalingrad* as soon as she can get her crew back aboard. In fairness to Captain Petya, they were not expecting to go back out for another week or more."

The admirals agreed.

"You know, sir," George said finally with some bewilderment, "I never figured a space war would be fought in slow motion. The other thing we need to keep in mind is that the battle at Inor is really long over. We're just learning about it, but we can't affect the outcome of something that happened yesterday. So, let's not think like we can."

"Yes, Commander, I agree. But, as you said, we do the best we can at the moment, right?" Admiral Yakovlev asked.

"Indeed, sir, that is really all we can ever do."

George went to the communications desk and issued the orders in Davenport's name. The Fleet would respond, but given the distances and time delays involved, none of them were sure how much good it would actually do.

## Chapter 5

Inoria
Sunday, January 16, 2078, 1000 UTC

They walked to the Inori Council building with two Marines in escort, a distance of perhaps a kilometer and a half. On the way, Terri received *Bondarenko*'s message.

"*Bondarenko* is coming. She should be here in five days. I expect the *Dunkirk* to come, but it's too early to have heard back from Captain Barker. Best case, they will be a day or two behind. I expect more from Earth after that, but we won't know for a couple days."

The RFGs had struck the Inori Council building twice. Fresh craters marred the broad, beautiful, curved granite staircase. But it was passable, and the central atrium just inside the entrance was undamaged. Carol's heart sank at the destruction. Only yesterday — *how could it have been only yesterday?* — she and Marty Baker were talking about how this was her favorite site on the tour. The council chose to meet with the human representatives in the atrium as their regular chamber was in ruins. The nine Inori sat in their usual half-circle, with the humans seated at the open end in a smaller half-circle.

The Inori language had frustrated all human attempts to tame it. There were just too many sounds that human vocal cords could not quite duplicate, and close just wasn't ever close enough. The Inori spoke very good but accented English. They had also learned Russian, which seemed more natural to them, and French, which was a challenge. An early pioneer in communication with the Inori once joked that they should all just meet in the middle and speak Klingon.

The Inori seated at the center spoke. "We welcome you, Mister Johnston, and express our thanks for your attendance."

"We are welcomed, sir. We are grateful for your invitation. May I say at the outset that we are saddened by the events of yesterday, and we express our sympathy to you and your people."

Terri found herself surprised at Johnston's smooth delivery. He actually sounded sincere.

"We are comforted, sir. And we express our condolences to you, Mister Johnston, for we know many humans were taken away as well. We know Ino does not wish this to be so. May we know who you have to accompany you?" The ambassador rose and motioned for the officers to do the same.

"This is Lieutenant Commander Teresa Michael, Council. She is the most senior military officer here on Inor." He turned to his left, "This is Lieutenant Carol Hansen, her able assistant."

"Welcome to you both."

Taking her cue from Johnston, Terri answered. "We are welcomed, sir." She started to say more but held back.

When Johnston sat, they sat.

The Inori seated to the left of the first speaker then began. "Human friends, we find ourselves at once grieved and frightened. We have no protection against such horrible acts. We would be grateful for any reassurance you can offer us that we might calm our protectorates' fears."

Johnston motioned to Terri to respond.

"Sir, as you know, our ship was lost yesterday. We have nothing above us at this time should another attack come. However, there is already one warship coming to our assistance, which will arrive in about five days. I believe a group of four more will arrive a day or two later." The Inori who had spoken nodded in acknowledgment, and then there was a lengthy exchange among the council members. The three humans sat quietly and waited for the outcome of the discussion.

"Human friends, we have limited knowledge of these things. We have never seen such events. We have been traveling in space for a long time, some five hundred years of Earth. As you know, the two other worlds of Ino around his star are rich with delicacies and spices which are highly prized by our protectorates and which we cannot produce here on Inor. Our charges will suffer greatly if we lose access to these." The Inori then went on. "Already, we have lost contact with several of the vessels which move between the three worlds of Ino, and we fear they have also been lost."

"Sirs, we will hope that your vessels are not lost, but we have little ability to help until the warships that Commander Michael has reported to you arrive. Once they do, we could attempt a search for the missing if that is the council's desire."

Carol spoke up, her inner strategist hard at work.

"Sir, if I may ask the council a question?"

Johnston had a look of barely hidden terror.

"You may ask," the first Inori responded.

"Have any of the crews of your vessels traveling the worlds of Ino ever encountered other vessels? By that, I mean spacecraft not from Inor or Earth? Might the crews have seen things they could not identify or explain?"

The question set off a furious discussion among the council, which went on for several minutes. As the Inori talked, Johnston drew Terri and Carol closer.

"Very interesting, Lieutenant Hansen. You've set off a lovely firestorm. Let's hope they're not going to toss us out. What are you getting at?" Carol, as usual, unable to hold back, offered her opinion.

"Well, Ambassador, if the answer was just 'no,' we would have heard that long ago. I was thinking if this enemy had reconnoitered the system like we would, it's possible they were spotted. From this discussion, I think maybe so."

Terri nodded, then shrugged. "Or they don't know and don't know what to tell us."

The conversation finally died down, and the Inori on the left nearest the three humans spoke. "Human friends, we ask your pardon for our delay,"

Johnston stood and addressed the speaker. "And we grant you pardon, but it is no imposition, sir. We are content to await your answer."

"We appreciate your patience. What you have asked did occur, perhaps ten Earth years ago. Three crews in succession told tales of large ships following them. We dismissed these as fantasies or 'space dreams' induced by traveling far from Inor. Perhaps we were mistaken."

Carol thought for a moment. "Sir, thank you for sharing this knowledge. Are you aware of any documents of that time, records, or images of what was seen?"

There was another small flurry of discussion among the Inori.

"We do not create or keep images as humans do. There are no records, as you would think of them."

That seemed to end the discussion, but Carol's hunch had been right — the enemy had been here not all that long ago.

"Are there other matters you wish to discuss?" Ambassador Johnston asked.

"We are concerned about the humans who have died on Inor. We understand your customs and practices with respect to the end of corporeal life are much different than our own, but we must collect the remains quickly, or the city will become foul and unhealthy. We ask of your intentions in this regard."

Johnston looked at Terri and Carol, neither of whom had considered this question. Carol had made notes of where victims could be located, but there had been no discussion of what to do about them.

"We were not prepared for such a disaster as this, and so we are unsure of our course of action at this moment. We, of course, share your concern for the city and the sea, and we shall work expeditiously to resolve them."

Carol got the ambassador's attention. "Mr. Johnston, we need options. Would they allow in-ground burial, even temporarily, or would they permit humans to be buried at sea like Inori?"

"Aren't you getting ahead of the plan, which by the way, we don't have yet?" he hissed at her.

Terri shook her head. "No, sir, she's asking for the information to support creating options. Whatever we can't do constrains the plan we might want to develop. There's no point in planning to bury the dead unless the Inori will permit it."

Johnston nodded, somewhat reluctant to admit that they were correct. "If I may ask the council a question?"

"You may ask."

"Would this wise council permit the burial of human remains here on Inor, or would you permit human remains to be buried at sea as the Inori do?" Again, a flurry of discussion. A different voice, about halfway around the right side of the semi-circle, answered.

"Human friends, we honor your work beside us and your sacrifices yesterday to defend us. We do welcome any lost human into the sea with our own lost ones. The land is for the people of Ino, and we cannot bury remains in it, human or Inori. We are also aware of what you call 'cremation,' although you have not asked about it. Such incineration is also not possible, as the people of Ino would breathe the human remains from the air. That cannot be permitted."

"Thank you, sir, for your considerate responses."

He turned back to the chairman. "Is there anything else the council wishes to address with us?"

There was a moment of silence before the chairman replied. "There is nothing, Mister Johnston. You are welcome to return to your embassy."

"We are welcomed, sir, and will do so with your kind permission."

At that point, the Inori rose as one and filed out of the atrium. The three humans turned and headed out the entrance and down the broad, pockmarked granite stairs. The Marines got themselves up off the pavement, took a careful look around, and made themselves ready to head back to the embassy.

"That was interesting," Carol said quietly. "We didn't speak in quite this way during the ship visits. I was more or less pointing and describing and taking questions. But do they actually think like that?"

Johnston nodded. "They really think like that, Lieutenant Hansen. We would say to a visitor, 'welcome, come in,' and the person would respond with 'thank you.' The Inori expect a response in the same manner as the opening. So, when they say 'welcome,' the response is to acknowledge that we feel welcomed, not to express generic gratitude. If they say 'pardon us,' the response must express explicitly that they are pardoned."

"Five hundred years," Terri said quietly. "No one had any idea they have been in space that long."

"I thought they were new to this, backward, using crude and simple technology." the ambassador commented.

Terri thought for a moment and then replied, "Well, replace crude and simple with cheap and reliable, and you might be closer to it. Still, wow."

"You only said 'sir' to them?" Carol asked.

"I think you know, Lieutenant, that the Inori have three sexes, not two. In diplomatic discussions, we use 'sir' to convey respect, but to them, it carries no gender connotation as it does in regular English. It feels strange at first, but since none of us can tell the difference between the three sexes anyway, it seems to work adequately."

As they stepped off for the Embassy, Carol wondered about the enemy, who they might be, and what they might do next. There was no way to know; that much she knew. But like any good officer, she hated the lack of information and the uncertainty it created in all of them.

ISC Fleet HQ Communications Station
Fort Eustis, VA
Sunday, January 16, 2078, 1146 AM EST (1646 UTC)

Mark England's shift was over at 0700. His supervisor, Technical Chief Diana Aviles, having received the alert, arrived early to assist and eventually relieve him. He went for a quick breakfast, then was back on the console. She assured him it wasn't necessary, but England wanted to help, and mostly, wanted to see what was going to happen next. Aviles knew this and let it go. After all, she might need the extra hands, and England was a good operator, fast and reliable. Just before her lunch break, she did. The FLASH alarm went off for the third time that day.

```
FLASH 207801151850UTC
TO: CINCFLEET
FROM: HANSEN, CAROL, LT, FOR MICHAEL, TERESA, LCDR, SSO INOR
INORIA ATTACKED 207801151000UTC RFG WITH LAZY DOGS BY UNKNOWN ENEMY.
LIBERTY DESTROYED IN ORBIT. MULTIPLE ORBITAL EXPLOSIONS SEEN.
TYPE AND NUMBER OF OPPOSING FORCE UNKNOWN.
SEVERE DAMAGE TO CITY AND SURROUNDINGS.
WEAPONS NIL. REQUEST INSTRUCTIONS AND ETA FOR RELIEF.
19 KNOWN SURVIVORS INCL LCDR DAVIS SLT EVANS LT SANDERS
ENS COLEMAN STEVENS
7 CONFIRMED KIA ON SURFACE INCL LCDR ROSKOV ENS BAKER.
9 MIA.
END
```

"Look at that, Chief Aviles, survivors!" he yelled. A few minutes later the alarm went off again. Now, *this* was interesting.

```
FLASH 207801151855UTC
TO: BONDARENKO ACTUAL
    DUNKIRK ACTUAL
CC: CINCFLEET
FROM: HANSEN, CAROL, LT, FOR MICHAEL, TERESA, LCDR, SSO INOR
INORIA ATTACKED 207801151000UTC BY UNKNOWN ENEMY.
LIBERTY DESTROYED IN ORBIT. MULTIPLE ORBITAL EXPLOSIONS SEEN.
TYPE AND NUMBER OF OPPOSING FORCE UNKNOWN.
SEVERE DAMAGE TO CITY AND SURROUNDINGS.
THREAT TO OTHER FLEET ASSETS SEEMS LIKELY
19 KNOWN SURVIVORS
7 CONFIRMED KIA ON SURFACE. 9 MIA.
END
```

In the Operations Center, these messages provoked some short-lived cheers, followed by the full realization that they had suffered an awful loss. Davenport stood with the other two flag officers, reading both messages and trying to understand their implications.

"Clearly, someone out there has a working brain." The old admiral smiled, tapping his finger on the message displayed on his tablet. "*Bondarenko* and *Dunkirk* have this message already — long before our warning. Michael doesn't say 'come get us,' but that's what she hopes will happen."

"Pretty shrewd, don't you think, Connor?"

"As we used to say, Stan, well played."

"Yes, she may have played this well enough to save what's left of her crew when we could not."

"Sir, we should get out an update to the fleet," Commander George suggested.

The three admirals agreed. Again, Jim George drafted and sent the message.

```
FLASH 207801161630UTC
TO: ALLFLEET
FROM: CINCFLEET FLEETOPS
TOP SECRET
UPDATE ON SITUATION AT INOR
(1) LIBERTY LOST IN COMBAT AT INOR 207801151035UTC
(2) CONFIRMED 19 SURVIVORS 7 KIA 9 MIA ON SURFACE.
(3) SEVERE DAMAGE TO CITY FROM RFG
END
```

The message sent, George called over his relief, LCDR Harold Torres, and they began looking at the day cycle correlation between UTC and Inor. Torres had arrived hours ago, but James George, like Technician England, was loath to leave while events were still unfolding. And, like England, the extra hands and minds were useful. The Operations officers walked over to the CINC and his deputy.

"Sir, the attack seems to have come mid-morning in Inoria. We're in those days where UTC and the solar time in Inoria are somewhat in sync. So, the time of Lieutenant Commander Michael's message is about dusk. If the city is as badly damaged as she seems to be saying, they might just hunker down until dawn. We should not be surprised if we don't hear from her for a while."

"Makes sense, James. Harold, you have the picture?"

Torres nodded.

"OK, very good. Commander George, go on home. Are you on tonight?"

"Yes, sir."

"Good. Get some sleep, and we'll see you in a few hours. I need you rested."

CINC sounded sympathetic but firm. He wanted James to get some time off. Truth was, the CINC was expecting some long shifts in the next few days, and men like George and Torres had to be fresh and alert.

Torres took George aside.

"RFG with Lazy Dogs? Hard to believe."

"Yeah, this was a bloody, awful attack, meant to kill and maim and destroy."

"Planning to get any sleep, James?"

George looked around the room, shaking his head. "I'll try but probably not. I feel like sleeping in the basement, but it wouldn't matter."

"See you later."
"Yeah, later."

ISC Fleet HQ
Operations Center
Sunday, January 16, 2078, 1300 EST

After James George had left, the admirals called in the Plans chief, Captain Fiona Collins.

"Fiona, what do the savants in Plans think at this point?"

She frowned at Yakovlev's comment.

"I hate that term, Admiral, as you well know, but I do have some pretty smart folks over there."

"And?"

"And, there are no existing contingency plans based on a Pearl Harbor at Inor, sir, or anywhere else for that matter. The team is currently working through some basic ideas, sometimes at the top of their lungs. I almost had to separate a Senior Warrant and a full Commander this morning."

"Well, spirited debate means they're invested, right?" Davenport asked.

"Investment is not their problem, sir, data is. We don't have enough, and in arguing hypotheticals, you can take near any idea and make it either plausible or ridiculous."

Fiona paused, looking at each Admiral in turn, before continuing.

"But, for now, since the 40 Eridani system has been pretty well surveyed, we think they aren't local. Which means it is a near certainty that they have some kind of FTL drive. Both the Embassy message and Commander Michael's report refer to *multiple* orbital explosions. To us, that means it is likely our weapons are effective against them at some level."

"So, what was the altercation about?"

Fiona smiled. "Whether the Inori know the enemy or not. The commander said they must; the warrant said that was a stupid assumption. Commander took offense."

"So?" Yakovlev led her to continue.

Fiona shrugged, overcoming her reluctance to get into details about something that happened within her section.

"So, Mister Price was correct — it is an unfounded assumption — and I made Commander Henderson apologize. She was not at all happy with me."

Admiral Gerhard had joined the conversation.

"Well, tell Joanne Henderson that we all respect her dedication. We will all likely find ourselves wrong about a lot of things as this goes on."

"That is true, sir. I will tell her."

"Very well, thank you, Captain Collins. Let us know when you have more."

Fiona turned and headed out of the Operations Center, down a flight of stairs and back a long, poorly lit hall to her noisy and now very unkempt Plans Section. She saw scattered pizza boxes, cold slices still visible here and there. Coffee cups and other drink containers were everywhere.

She was surprised to see Joanne Henderson and Ben Price seated together at a worktable. Henderson and Price looked up at her, acknowledged her return, then returned to their very face-to-face conversation. It ended with some small nods and smiles, and then they got up and went back to work. Fiona worked her way over to Price. She looked into his eyes, which were a little moist around the edges.

"Ben?"

"Yes, Captain?" he said, delaying.

"Ben!"

He put down his tablet and looked at her. "I told Commander Henderson I was sorry, too, ma'am. We're all pretty stressed down here, you know? I was gonna play hockey tonight. Instead, I'm planning a space war while my wife packs to go home to Montana."

He paused and looked across the room at Henderson.

"She is so smart…I thought we needed to be back on the same team. I told her, yes, I was right this time, but next time I might be wrong. And I told her just because I am calling her stupid in front of everyone doesn't mean I don't respect her opinion. She finally laughed at that, a little anyway."

Fiona took a moment to digest what he had said. "Mister Price, you are a wonder."

"No, Captain Collins, I am just shit scared like everyone else, and we need all of us if we're going to survive."

"So, what are you working on?"

He picked the tablet back up. "Well, we were working while you were off hobnobbing with the big brass."

He smiled at her look of disgust.

"Yeah, that's what we call it. Anyhow, between FPI and the miners and the Fleet, we've surveyed a lot of star systems in the last twenty years. Oh, by the way, we want FleetIntel to review all the previous system data available, but we think it's unlikely they came from anywhere we've been."

"Sounds reasonable. Go on."

She pulled herself up to sit on a table across from Price.

"Well, there seems to be a gap, Captain. We've done really well in the northern hemisphere, but in the southern sky, except for Proxima and Barnard's and a few other close-by stars, we haven't really looked very hard." By now, Henderson, the tall and dark-haired former soccer player, had not-so-casually wandered into the conversation.

"Gerhard sends his best regards," Fiona said to her.

"Asshole," she said sharply. The response surprised both Fiona and Ben. There was a moment of awkward silence. Fiona looked from Henderson to Price and back, then finally to Price, who defused the moment.

"Roger that, Commander, it's Admiral Gerhard Asshole from now on."

Fiona turned back to Joanne. "You up to speed on Ben's observation about the southern sky?"

"Yes, we were discussing that when you came back."

"Of course you were," Fiona said skeptically.

"Well, that and some other issues," Henderson responded tentatively.

"Uh-huh." Fiona was now in full skeptic mode.

"Price, get me the hell out of this."

"Really, Captain, we were. It was something that hit us both as we started to look at the sky in the general direction of Inor."

"OK, so —"

"So, we need to get the hell out there and plug this gap, Fiona," Henderson responded. "We'll go over it with the full team, but Price and I think it's obvious that first thing, we need a recon effort to find this species."

"How sure are we that they are in one of these systems we haven't checked?"

Henderson shrugged. "Well, taking that to a logical extreme, they must be in a system we haven't checked because we're pretty sure they aren't in any that we *have* surveyed. Whether they are from a system reasonably close by is another question. It's a big universe, but we have to start somewhere. They could be from very far away, which would multiply the problem by God knows how many orders of magnitude. If they are, it might be lifetimes to find them, even with the Drive."

"Or they could be here tomorrow," Fiona commented, looking away.

"Or that, yes." Price agreed.

"Or we could be wrong. They could be from Polaris," she continued.

After a second, Price responded. "Well, Polaris is F class and over 400 light-years away, so I don't really think—"

"OK, I get it," Fiona said, cutting Price off with a laugh. "Get the team together and get me a position paper on this concept. See if you can prioritize which systems to check first. Some are not habitable—"

"At least, we think they're not." Henderson interrupted.

"—so, let's wait on those," Fiona finished.

Joanne and Ben consulted for a few minutes, then began gathering the rest of their eight-person Plans team to go over the idea.

Fiona went back to her office and picked up the phone, dialing Ron Harris, Chief of FleetIntel.

"Hey, Ron, it's Fiona. How's *your* day going?" She let the barrage of expletives go by unanswered. When he finally stopped, she continued.

"Yeah, I love you, too, pal. I have a job for your guys."

She explained the idea of a knowledge gap in the southern stars and the request to re-examine systems they had already surveyed.

"So, what am I looking for in this old data, Fiona?" Ron asked skeptically.

"The bastards that hit Inor."

"Oh, well, if that's all, no problem."

"Shit, Ron, I don't know what to look for! We just thought it would be smart to examine what data we already have before we go all over the goddamn universe trying to find them."

"I get it, Fiona. We'll run the check. I'll review the detection criteria with my data miners and see if there is something we can tweak. I don't think it will take all that long. Give me a couple hours, and I'll call you."

"OK. Call my personal phone in case I'm not in the office."

"Will do."

She hung up the phone and took a moment to think about the day and about where they were going with this plan. This had to be a very advanced culture. Would they inhabit multiple planets? Multiple locations? Once they found them, what would, what *could*, they do about it? Could they find them without revealing themselves? She'd been in the Fleet for a while now, ten years — or was it twelve — sometimes she couldn't remember — but it had been an academic exercise. They talked about conflict and war-gamed it, but they had never seen real action. Now, a real war was upon them, and she found herself in a critical, highly visible position. She took a moment to say a prayer for the dead, for her team, for her superiors, then herself. Guidance, wisdom, and insight would be sorely needed if they were to prevail.

It was mid-afternoon when she returned to the conference room battlefield. Now it was Ben and Joanne arguing against the other six, pointing at the sky chart, over to the electronic whiteboard, and back to the other sky chart. The questions, the challenges, the back and forth of if, what, and how. Moments like this were why she loved this job: her team had the relentless, ruthless ambition to get it right.

Fiona thought it was fun to watch.

ISC Fleet HQ Intel Section
Fort Eustis, VA
Sunday, January 16, 2078, 1530 EST

Good to his word Captain Ron Harris worked with the data analysts and the few biologists he had access to in an attempt to broaden the criteria for their review of existing planet data. That process was now in the works, and he didn't have much hope that they would indeed find anything new. But it was worth a try.

Ron sat down with his cadre of analysts to talk about what they knew about this enemy and what they needed to know. Excluding himself, he felt he had ten of the brightest minds in the Fleet. He had only a small HQ Intel section, mostly because there was so little military intelligence to process, but also to maintain a collegial environment, free of silos and limited vision. Everybody in Ron's shop had access to the whole picture. Beyond his core of ten analysts were about twenty support personnel: the data miners, communications, and technology resources able to find or create the information they needed. But the real brain trust resided in the ten individuals in front of him. He took a moment to look around "The Table" as it had come to be known. The Table itself was nothing special, just an old, well-worn maple library table, but it was large and solid enough to absorb the pounding fists and occasional refreshment flood that came with their intense discussions. Today, Ron could see coffee cups of several sizes and designs, containers of various carbonated beverages, small notebooks absorbing notes, and tablet computers taking a beating. There were several side conversations going on, all at once.

"I had a good conversation with Captain Collins in Plans," he began, calling the meeting to order, "and we agreed that we know at least three things. First, they're not local to 40 Eridani A; Second, they probably have FTL travel; Third, our weapons are effective against them at some level."

"Keen grasp of the obvious there, boss," Lieutenant Ann Cooper commented.

"Well, it may seem obvious, but it's still what we have as a starting point."

There was general agreement on that.

"RFG's with Lazy Dogs. Somebody paid attention in their Theoretical Weapons class," LCDR Elias Peña observed,

"Yep, that's for sure," Harris answered.

Warrant Officer Kelly Peterson looked up from her tablet. "Isn't that the one where all you do is watch old movies?"

Harris sat up straight, feigning offense. "It's not the movies that are hard, Peterson. It's the writing up of what you would do if you were faced with whatever the movie threw at you that's difficult."

"So, that's a yes?" she followed up, pushing the boss just a little.

"Yes, but to be fair, in the second semester, we read old sci-fi books, too," Harris answered. "Does their use of these weapons tell us anything? I doubt they've read much Pournelle."

Frances Wilson, the oldest and perhaps most hardened member of the analysis team, spoke first.

"Well, they're as ingenious and vicious as we are, I guess. It will be interesting to see the RFGs. Pournelle suggested tungsten, but you'd probably have to bring that up from a planet. If you were satisfied with some cheap nickel-iron rods, you could make a thousand from any modest-sized iron asteroid you might have handy."

"OK, so, what do we really know?" Harris asked again.

Elias Peña spoke up. "Not much beyond what you've already said, Captain."

Peña was, without the title, the apparent second-in-command of FleetIntel. He had been on several consecutive tours in space and was now doing his first HQ tour, which he hated. He thought it much easier to be single aboard a ship where he could focus his thoughts and emotions on the critical tasks at hand. Back on Earth, either on leave or in this HQ assignment, he found he was less professionally focused and more personally stressed.

"Anything else?" There was silent agreement as he looked around the table, so Harris went on to his next question.

"OK then. What do we need to know?" Harris asked. The answers came quickly from all around the room.

"What kind of FTL drive are they using? Have they independently found the Forstmann technology?"

"How their anti-ship weapons work and how we might defend against them."

"How are they communicating? If they have a Forstmann Drive, do they also use SLIP?"

"What do they *want*?" The strident voice brought all eyes again to Frances Wilson, seated opposite Captain Harris. Physically, she was a fairly small and unremarkable well-past-middle-aged woman. But her mind was as keen as it was quick. "If we can figure out what they want, the rest may be irrelevant."

"And if all they want is to kill us?" came the sharp reply from Peña.

"Then that would be a useful fact, would it not?" was her calm response. They locked eyes for a moment, with Peña finally acknowledging her insight with a slight nod as they disengaged. Ron found himself smiling slightly at this exchange. The intellectual competition seemed to make them all smarter somehow.

Ron nodded his agreement. "OK - we could go on and on - but I think our immediate requirements are for technological intelligence, specifically weapons, communication, propulsion. I would add sensors to that - it would be useful to know from what range they can detect us. So, what are our challenges?"

"Damn laws of physics are stacked against us," Ann Cooper said flatly. "We want to find them, but the distances and the delays are incredible, even with the Drive. This isn't the North Atlantic. We can't lay out a line of sonobuoys and catch the Russians as they blunder by. It's huge beyond comprehension."

Kelly Peterson leaned forward. "They must have a home. We're building starbases - geez, I hate that term, it's so sci-fi - so I expect they would as well. There must be outposts, depots, and service and repair facilities. All of those are essentially stationary targets. Unless we want to theorize they live entirely on ships."

"But even if that's true, they could be anywhere. Their depot could be hanging out halfway between their two least favorite stars," Frances responded.

Peña replied, "Correct, and any facility like you're talking about would just be a large ship. To be in a useful position, it would have to be capable of FTL. Otherwise, the supplies would take lifetimes to get to where they're needed. That's what we're doing. Drape it in stealth like we do, and it's damn near invisible."

"We still need to know how they're moving and communicating," Scott repeated.

Harris nodded. "To answer the first question: no, we can't detect a ship moving FTL under Forstmann Drive. You all know the basics of how it works, or how they've told us it works, anyhow. Ships under Forstmann Drive exist in an isolated area of space-time around the ship. As explained to me, the drive bends space-time in front and behind, and the ship falls into the void, pushed from behind. Once the drive is off, they're back in so-called normal space with the rest of us, and we can see them. I don't know about SLIP. I could try to ask."

"Well, sir, just because *we* can't detect a ship in the Drive, we should be at least open to the possibility that *they* can." Ann Cooper pointed out.

"There's no reason to assume that!" Kathy Stewart argued.

"Not assume. Just remember that we may not be the top dog here. They may have capabilities we aren't aware of."

Harris retook the direction of the discussion. "OK, let's think about action items. We need a SLIP technology briefing. That'll take some doing."

"Forstmann invented the drive. Could we ask them if there are any other methods that they know of to achieve FTL speeds?" Roger Cox asked.

"Oh, sure, no problem. Let's ask the biggest company in our part of the known universe for its deepest secrets," Peña commented sarcastically. Harris gave Peña a glance of disapproval but didn't push it any further.

Roger Cox ignored Peña's condescension. "They also invented SLIP. Are there alternative methods?"

Harris decided it was time to wrap up the discussion. They needed more information, and they weren't going to get it sitting there. "We didn't cover the gap that Captain Collins' group pointed out. Any dispute on that?"

"Ugly thing, sir. Needs to be checked out." Peña agreed, speaking for the group.

"So, can we agree that our first tactical priority is to cover these nearby systems? Besides simple checks for intelligent life, giant repair depots, and alien starships, we should task them to look for answers to the other questions we've raised."

"OK then, I will confirm with Plans that we agree that the recon they have proposed should go forward immediately. I will also outline these other needs for them." Harris was wrapping up, and the group knew how this went. He took one final look around the table. *Good people trying hard*, he thought.

"OK, that's it."

They stood when he did, and he was quickly out the door and headed back to his office. Once there, he called Fiona Collins again and gave her the Intel endorsement of the need to look at the gap systems. He gave her the high points of the discussion: weapons, communications, propulsion, sensors, home planet, depots, and the rest. Hanging up, he leaned back in his chair and thought about the next call he had to make. He had CINC's confidence, but it was not without limits, and if he asked for something like he was about to ask for, he really needed to be sure he really needed it. As head of FleetIntel, he could make the call. CINC would pick up. He picked up the phone and called a member of his team instead.

"Frances, can you come to my office? Thanks." In a few seconds, the thin, graying, mid-fifties woman arrived, closing the door behind her. She sat across from him, notebook in hand, pen at the ready.

"After the discussion today, the Drive and SLIP and whatever, who should we be calling to get the information we need?" She looked surprised. She took a moment to reply.

"Not the question I was expecting, Captain, but there is only one answer: Randy Forstmann. He did the original FTL research; no one knows the internals of both technologies like he does."

Ron paused, looking across the desk at his most senior civilian analyst. She had been at this since long before he joined the Fleet, having come over as a much younger woman after time at the NSA, where she worked on Chinese ICBM assessments. Scary stuff. She was almost old enough to be his mother, but one thing she was not was matronly. Her husband now commanded a mining ship and so was gone for long periods, just as he always had been. They were childless, but Ron knew she doted on her small collection of nieces and nephews whose pictures decorated her desk. She was hard-headed, demanding, critical of sloppy thinking, and thin-skinned at times. She commanded respect from all around her, and she could throw a wicked verbal elbow when necessary. Her dedication to his Intel shop, he knew, was beyond question.

"OK, I'll call CINC." After a moment, he continued, "I hope you weren't planning retirement, Frances, because you're here for the duration."

She smiled slightly. "Wouldn't think of it."

"Good."

"Good luck with CINC." She rose and left, closing the door behind her.

He picked up the phone, dialing the Operations Center.

"CINC, please...Captain Harris in FleetIntel...Yes, I will wait...Sir...Admiral, FleetIntel has a request...Well, sir, we need to talk to someone, and we're going to need your help...Randy Forstmann...Yes, we're serious...There are questions about FTL propulsion and communications that we need answers for...I'd rather not be more specific, sir...I know they're guarded about their technology, but we're in a war here...Thank you, sir." He hung up, feeling that it was almost too easy. But maybe Forstmann would refuse. More likely, Ron thought, his lawyers would refuse.

He got a message that the data miners had nothing new to report. He called Fiona Collins back and then headed back to the Operations Center to see what else might happen that night.

# Chapter 6

*The Drive Pub and Bistro*
Just off Fort Eustis, VA
Monday, January 17, 2078, 2030 EST

Ben Price had done what he could with the information available on the second day of the war. It wasn't much. They were still arguing about which stars to prioritize, and he was getting tired of it. *But at least it was an honest argument*, he said to himself, *a fight worth having*. Fiona Collins had sent him home a few hours earlier. He finished up his work and went to his now sparsely furnished apartment just off the base to shower and change. Skipping dinner for lack of appetite, he headed out for a walk in the cold evening, hoping the chill would clear his head a little, and eventually found himself wandering into *The Drive*, a pub favored by Fleet HQ personnel. It was a safe place for Fleet folk, where they could unwind, let off a little frustration, and easily get back to their quarters.

Ben walked into a warm, noisy place, media screens covering almost every wall with all five major news channels and several sports channels going all at once. He found it strange to recognize the nondescript HQ building he worked in daily as the backdrop for various talking heads, looking all serious and sincere over the WAR IN SPACE or DISASTER AT INOR headlines at the bottom of the screen. He saw clearly how little they knew as they stood there chattering away, pretending to be the experts. Huge pictures of Teresa Michael and Carol Hansen frequently replaced the HQ image as the anchors prattled on about how little was known about them. Ben thought the images looked like ID pictures, and he doubted either woman would have been pleased to have those plastered all over the planet. He avoided the crowded dining room to the left of the entrance and headed into the large oak-paneled bar on the right.

Looking down the long bar packed with patrons, he saw Joanne Henderson seated alone in a corner booth at the far end of the room. After their dust-up yesterday, they had made a decent peace, but he suspected that Henderson was still stinging from their initial exchange. Almost without thinking, he made his way along the bar, pausing to greet some acquaintances, and ended up standing at Joanne's table. Dressed down in jeans, an SFU hoodie, and walking boots, she was drinking something dark with ice. He couldn't tell just what.

"May I join you, Commander?"

"Sure, Price. But you'll have to stop calling me by my rank. Sounds strange in a bar."

Ben sat in the other corner of the booth, a spot that gave both of them a good view of the room.

"What would you prefer? We do have this whole military chain-of-command structure to deal with."

She shrugged and was about to answer when the waitress appeared. "What will it be?"

Ben looked over at Joanne. "What are you drinking?"

"Glenlivet 15 on the rocks."

Ben gave a fake shudder and looked up at the waitress. "Dewar's, double, neat."

As the waitress left, Ben looked back at Joanne, who was now looking at him as if she had just seen him for the first time, one eyebrow pretty far up.

"Took you for a beer man."

"And I took you for a wine woman. I guess this time we're both wrong."

She gave in and smiled at that. "I guess so," she said with a wry but growing smile.

*Issue settled*, Ben thought.

"So, this-is-me-not-calling-you-Commander-Henderson, what would you prefer?"

She leaned back against the booth, slowly turning her drink as she looked into it as if to find an answer. "Look, Price, we've both been at this for what, ten years? Maybe more? We've been working together for a while now. Off-duty, like this, how about we just do first names? At the office, yeah, we need to be military."

"Well, Joanne, calling you Joanne will take some practice."

"As will calling you Ben, Ben." she took a sip of her drink. "Did you get your wife off to Montana?"

Ben suddenly had a pained, desperately unhappy expression. He squirmed in his seat a little. Henderson didn't miss it.

"Spit it out, Ben."

He wondered if he should confide in her, their friendship being just seconds old. But something about her told him he could. He decided to risk it. "Well, I didn't tell the whole truth yesterday. She wasn't just moving. She was leaving. I got the papers from her lawyer today."

"You have children?" She was a little unhappy with herself that she didn't already know the answer since she'd been working with Ben Price for months. But she had always kept a distance between her personal life and her work, it hadn't come up in conversation, and she would not have asked about it herself.

"No, which does simplify the problem, I guess. She said she'd had enough of wondering what would happen next, where we would go next. Her folks never thought I was up to the job, anyway."

"So, what happened?"

Ben smiled sadly and nodded as the waitress set his drink on the table. "Oh, it was quite the scene. How I don't do this, and she does all that, and she doesn't deserve this f-ing fleet shit life."

He paused a second.

"And then I got hit in the face with her rings."

Ben looked up from his drink at Joanne. "And she just stood there, glaring at me."

"And then?"

"So, I'm looking down at those rings on the floor, you know? Goddamn engagement ring was like three months' pay. But really, I didn't care. I still don't. I looked at the rings, took a last look at her, picked up my coat, and walked out."

"Where did you go?"

"BOQ. I had to beg, but the clerk found me a room. I didn't sleep much. She left this morning, so I went back to the apartment after work today. Not much left, but I'll get by."

"Well, it's her loss—"

"No, Joanne, it isn't. It's mine," he interjected. "I loved her enough to marry her and mean it. I still do, I guess. Now, well, she's westbound somewhere around Iowa, and now all I have left, I guess, is the Fleet."

His second drink came. He took a long sip and then found himself turning the glass and looking into it for answers, just as Joanne had been when he walked up to her table. After a moment, he looked across at her, his eyes slightly narrowed as he considered how to ask her the question on his mind.

"What?" she asked, seeing his expression.

"Admiral Asshole."

She frowned and looked away. She turned a little and switched right leg over left for left over right. She was several years older than Ben, but with her hair down, it was easier to see that she was an attractive woman. He wondered why she tried so hard to hide it. *Then again,* he thought, *maybe it was just the lighting in the bar*. She turned back to him.

"Let's just say the Admiral has a degree in foreign relations."

"Oh?"

"Russian hands and Roman fingers."

Ben leaned back and looked at her sympathetically. "What did you do?"

She sat up very straight, obviously proud of herself. Then she leaned over and spoke quietly, close to Ben's ear.

"Crushed his left testicle with my knee. He was off for two weeks. Flu, they called it."

Ben nodded his understanding, then leaned in closer. "Joanne, just for the record, I am not coming within six inches of you without a written invitation with witnesses, OK?"

She pulled back and laughed. "Ben, you would never do what Gerhard did. You're a man. He's a child."

"Thanks to you, he's damn near a boy soprano!"

They laughed pretty hard at that. When it faded, she looked back at him, and her face softened.

"I really am sorry about your wife. I know that will make things harder for you. Have you told Fiona?"

Ben shook his head. "No, but I will, sometime soon. It's a little embarrassing somehow."

"Bullshit. I realize you might feel that way, but what, Ben Price, have you done wrong? You cheat on her, mistreat her?"

"No, of course not."

"Right — listen to yourself — *of course not*. You can be a real pain to me sometimes. But you're smart, you have integrity, and you can be trusted. Don't be embarrassed if you didn't do anything wrong."

"A pain? *I'm a pain*? And here we were getting along so well."

She made a face. "Oh, and you haven't thought *I* was a pain in the ass?"

He feigned shocked surprise. "No, ma'am, at least, not since I came in the bar."

She smiled, took a deep breath, and leaned back. "Jesus, Price, you make me laugh. That's really dangerous."

"I meant what I said about the invitation, except now I think it should also be notarized. Can't be too careful."

They watched the room for a while, exchanging a funny, mostly unkind commentary about the patrons as they came and went.

"So, Joanne, I'm about to be divorced. Wow, that sounds strange. What about you?"

She hesitated, looked away, looked back, and finally gathered herself to tell him her story.

"Divorced, long time now." She took a sip of her drink. "He was my coach, and I thought he was a lot more than he really was." She paused, then continued, the pain still echoing in her voice. "And he thought I was a lot less than I really am."

"Ouch. That had to hurt."

"Yes, it was a hard time, but it was necessary. I'm glad to be on my own."

"You don't find it lonely?" Ben was really asking about his own fear of the future.

"It can be, but I have the Fleet to distract me." She stopped to look directly at him. "You may find it harder than I do, Ben. I've seen people who do fine and others who really hate it. Me, I am free to serve as I want and to think and do as I want without having to weigh anyone else's feelings or needs. That works for me."

"I see," Ben responded.

There was a long silence as they sipped their Scotch and watched the blizzard of activity in the bar.

"Ben, I haven't had a friend to talk to in a long time. I come in here from time to time. Some of the drunker townies will try to pick me up; the Fleet people mostly just stay clear. Fiona will sit with me sometimes, but not that often. I do love the Fleet, but it can get quiet at night. When it's too quiet, I wind up here."

"Well, Joanne, it seems we can both use a friend right now."

He reached out his hand, and she shook it, sealing their deal.

A little later, Ben finished his second drink, picked up his parka, and went back out into the cold night, heading for the sofa in his living room. The bed that had been his was now somewhere out west.

*The Cookie Factory Bar*
Near Space Fleet University Campus
Northern Ohio
Monday, January 17, 2078, 2100 EST

About the time Ben Price and Joanne Henderson were toasting their new friendship, an average-height, average-looking young man in jeans and a plain hoodie slipped out of the freezing, snow-less evening and into *The Cookie Factory* and sat at the end of the bar, two stools removed from the next patron. He carefully curved the bill of his ISC hat to give himself the illusion of being alone in a crowd, his eyes hidden within.

David Powell was less than happy to be in the Advanced Intelligence Analysis Class to begin with. Now, of all things, there was an honest-to-God war on, and there up on the media screens was a really lousy picture of Carol Hansen. He looked at it almost in spite of himself, his gut twisted itself near in half to see that face, one he loved and missed so much, on such display. She was in the middle of it, right where she belonged. *Right where he belonged, too*, he thought. But David was stuck back here in Ohio, finishing the Intel school, after which he'd probably be the lead Intel tech on a ship. Not in command, not the boss, just the brains. It didn't help that he could look across the campus every day and see the main SFU building, the one he had spent over three years in, had excelled in, and in which he had last laid eyes on Carol one Friday that seemed an eternity ago.

He nursed his tall draft IPA, looking up occasionally to see who else was around. He dismissed the offer of a menu with a wave, and the bartender frowned at him as she turned away. *The Cookie Factory* was a place, something like *The Drive*, which catered to Fleet students. He saw three others of the eight in his class seated in a booth. They would glance his way from time to time, but their faces made it clear that none of them were interested in a conversation with him. David knew he had only himself to blame for that. He'd come in not knowing anyone and really not caring, at least at first. The other seven had come together right out of Warrant Candidate School, which he'd been able to skip. Fleet bumped their eighth classmate to make room for David. So, in their minds, he was an outsider from the start.

He had an obligation to fulfill, but it was no secret to anyone that this was not his first choice, and he'd really rather be somewhere else. *Somewhere with Carol,* he admitted to himself. His classmates were all excellent candidates, smart and dedicated, and he knew they'd do fine. But he was clearly first in the class, slapping down every unit check and final exam with far too much ease. That he didn't seem to care what the others thought about him only exacerbated his separation from them. *If it's going to be so damned easy for him,* they said among themselves, *the asshole could at least be friendly about it.*

The instructors knew his history. SFU had denied his request to return and finish, so the best possible second alternative was this Intel school. But no one let on about why he was there to his new classmates. As far as they knew, he was just a jerk.

On another level, he knew he was being distant and cold to them. At some point during the course, he'd hoped to break out of that funk, to let himself just be where he was, but something held him back. *Selfishness?* he asked himself. *Self-pity? Anger? Grief?* None of those really felt entirely accurate, but bits of each seemed to fit his dark mood. He felt as locked in place as someone in a bad dream where the freight train was bearing down, and they couldn't get their feet to move them off the tracks.

*So,* he asked himself, *what the hell was he doing here in a bar full of people when he thought he only wanted to be alone? Good question,* the other part of him answered.

Leaning over with his elbows on the bar, he was about halfway through the draft and crafting an exit when he was aware of someone sitting next to him. Sneaking a look over, he saw the lead instructor, an older Senior Warrant named Ray Salazar, looking down at him.

"You know Powell, you're a real pain in the ass," he said flatly.

"Yes, Mister Salazar, I suppose I am."

"I mean it. Your attitude is screwing this up for everyone, including yourself."

"Really, Mister Salazar, I'm just trying to do my job."

David looked up again at Carol's crummy picture. Salazar looked up at the image and then back at David.

"Stop looking at her, Powell. She's there, and you're here. Get your head back where your ass is."

"Sir?"

"I know all about Hansen, Powell; wonderful girl, shitty boyfriend. But you're not going to get any closer to her by locking out everyone around you."

"OK—" David was about to object to this line of the conversation, but Salazar wasn't opening that door.

"You can't keep this up, Powell. It's not like you. I checked with a couple of your old instructors."

"Oh, great," he said sarcastically.

"Actually, they used that same word, but without the snarky attitude." Salazar picked up his dark beer and turned to face Powell directly. "This shit is easy for you, Powell, I know that. But you know what? It isn't for everyone." He took a swallow and set it back down. "Last time you were in that situation, you were the first one to help, the first to lend a hand."

"So?"

"So, where the hell is THAT guy in MY class?" he demanded.

David had no answer.

"See the little dark-haired one?" Salazar asked.

"Margie Nixon."

"So, you know her name? I'm surprised." Salazar took another sip. "Yes, Nixon. She's getting by, but she doesn't have the Physics background that most of you do. And Browning—"

"Gregg."

"Holy crap, Powell, two names? Do you know them all?"

"Yes, Mister Salazar, I do. I'm not—"

"Good," Salazar interrupted, "Browning is doing better than Nixon but not what he could be."

"Why are you telling me this?"

"What would the old Powell, you know, the one who was like *second* in his Cadet class, what would he do?"

David thought about it a moment before replying.

"He'd form a study group and try to bring them along. Coach them."

"Helluva idea, Mister Powell, genius!" Ray Salazar drained the rest of his Porter and pushed the glass away, standing up off the bar stool. "Tomorrow, Mister Powell. Tomorrow, you start the road back to being yourself." He was smiling now. "Good luck! You're going to need it."

"Mister Salazar, is this all about me or them?" David asked, puzzled. What had started out as an off-the-record dressing down had suddenly turned into a counseling session, then a pep talk. All in five minutes.

Salazar looked at him for a few seconds. "Everything is about everything, David. You help them, and someday they will help someone else, and helping them helps you. Meantime you'll all be better analysts and better people."

"Yes, Mister Salazar, I guess so."

"No guessing required, Powell. Just get it done." Salazar turned, pulled on his parka, and headed out the door, leaving David to consider just how he was going to break down the brick wall he'd built between himself and his classmates. It might not be easy, but the more he thought about what Salazar had to say, the more annoyed he became with himself for not being ready to be fully engaged where he was. After all, he was in the Fleet, where he always wanted to be, and he had a chance to do interesting work. He smiled at the older man's advice: *Get your head back where your ass is.*

He finished his beer and got up to leave, surprising the bartender with a smile and surprising her even more with a generous tip.

ISC Fleet HQ Intel Section
Fort Eustis, VA
Thursday, January 20, 2078, 0900 EST

The meeting with Randy Forstmann was surprisingly easy to arrange. Davenport hardly had to begin asking before Forstmann enthusiastically agreed to sit down with FleetIntel. In only a few days, the FPI Executive Shuttle arrived at Fleet HQ, and three men made their way to the Intel Section, where Ron waited for them at the front desk.

The first two were large, nondescript, but carefully groomed. Ron took them for engineers or executives or, worse, *lawyers.* They wore expensive suits and shoes and carried expensive briefcases. The third man, his face instantly recognizable, was shorter, thinner, dressed informally in cotton and denim, good but not extravagant leather boots, carrying only a tablet computer case.

They arrived in the midst of a heated argument that they were unsuccessfully trying to keep from being overheard. The words 'NDA' and 'limits' and 'sir' leaked out of their intense but quiet argument. Finally, the two suits shook their heads at the smaller man.

"Sit down here and wait for me," came the exasperated but clear tenor voice of Randy Forstmann as he pointed to a few chairs in the waiting area. "Try not to make a nuisance of yourselves." He turned to Ron.

"Captain Harris, I presume?" he said with a smile, extending his hand.

"Yes, Mister Forstmann. Welcome to FleetIntel."

They walked to the full but quiet FleetIntel conference room. Forstmann looked a little older than his years, but the active hazel eyes and short gray hair were just as they were in the documentaries and sensational media shows about him. The Fleet personnel rose as one when he came in, the sound of old chairs skipping over the tile floor disturbing the peace. Randy Forstmann moved to the foot of the table, opposite Ron Harris, and took a seat. The Fleet personnel sat when Forstmann did.

Ron opened with a respectful appreciation for the man's willingness to even talk to them. "Mister Forstmann, thank you for meeting with us today. We hope you are aware of how vital this is to our efforts here."

"I am indeed aware, Captain, and I am glad to be able to assist," Forstmann paused briefly. "But I do actually have a few ground rules, if I may?"

Ron indicated that he should continue.

"My name is Randy. I don't really like to answer to 'mister' or 'sir' as it makes me feel even older than I already am. I want to know each of your names — beyond what is on your uniform — so that we may talk more freely."

"Anything else, Randy? No subjects off limits?"

"My personal life is the stuff of media obsession and fantasy, so let's stay off that if we could. Otherwise, fire away!"

The room relaxed noticeably as they came to realize that Randy Forstmann wasn't some Howard Hughes-ish recluse gazillionaire remote from the world. He was a regular guy, direct, an engineer like several of the Intel staff, a little shy maybe, unassuming, who also happened to be a gazillionaire. They went around the table doing introductions. Randy took notes on his tablet, typing quickly without looking at his hands. It was an amazing thing to watch. He made eye contact, he acknowledged what they said, he laughed at all the right places and asked the right follow-up questions. By the end, the staff found themselves completely taken with him.

Introductions completed, Randy opened the discussion.

"So, Ron, you have questions for me?"

"We do. Let's start with this: during your research, either before the discovery of The Drive or later, have you become aware of an alternative method for FTL travel? We're trying to gauge the likelihood that this culture has separately discovered Forstmann drive or are using something else."

Randy responded immediately.

"I am not aware of any such method. The graviton/anti-graviton approach is the only one I know of. But I have to add that this has not been a major area of research for us. Once I devised a workable drive concept, we concentrated on scaling it up, optimization, control, electrical efficiency, things like that, not on alternative approaches."

"But in your research, you did not see another path to FTL?" Ann Cooper asked.

"No, Ann, I did not."

"Are you aware of a method by which a ship running Forstmann Drive FTL could be detected?"

"Under the Drive, ships are in their own, uh, segment of space-time. The space in front is bent towards the ship, and the space behind is bent away. I don't see how that can be remotely detected. If a ship passes nearby, with the right equipment one might detect some excess gravitons, but it should not be detectable from any distance."

Frances had her doubts about the certainty in his answer. History was full of disasters where scientists or soldiers were sure they knew something that turned out to be false. She decided to follow up on his statement.

"How close is close in your mind?"

"A few thousand kilometers at most."

Unsatisfied, she continued, "Randy, does the drive emit anything besides gravitons and antigravitons? I'm interested in anything that might give our opponents the ability to find or track our movements."

"We have tested the Drive in a variety of ways, Frances, measured the net output versus power input, and monitored it across a range of EM frequencies. I am certain that it emits nothing harmful and confident that no unintended energies are being radiated."

Frances inclined her head a bit, one eyebrow raised as she wrote in her notebook.

"You are unconvinced?"

She set down her pen, leaning back in her chair.

"It is my job to be unconvinced, to doubt, and to probe. Part of your answer is that you are *certain*. In the other part, you are *confident*. Those are different concepts. If there is one thing that modern technological war has taught us — right up to the Second Korean War in 2033 — it is to be skeptical of our own abilities and respectful of the enemy's."

"Yes, I see." He spent perhaps a minute typing on his tablet. "I will talk to my engineers about this question to see if, even after twenty years of experience, there is any potential for detection that we have not considered."

"Randy, can we talk about SLIP?" Roger asked.

"We can talk about anything, Roger, but what about SLIP interests you?"

"We're trying to work out how this enemy culture might communicate. We sort of assume that they have FTL propulsion and that they also have FTL communication. So, the question is, if they were also using SLIP could we detect it?"

"SLIP is a very sensitive technology. The easiest description for outsiders, which is not technically accurate, is that we communicate by phase modulation of vibrations in what we think of as the layer below normal space-time."

"How is addressing handled? Can SLIP receivers see messages not intended for them?"

"Good question. Yes, they can. Addressing is handled within the structure of the message."

"You mean, like TCP/IP?"

Forstmann smiled. "I didn't think anyone still remembered that. Yes, exactly like TCP/IP."

"If that is the case, if a SLIP message recipient is offline at the time the message arrives, it will be missed?"

"Yes. It behaves like radio to some extent."

"Does a SLIP signal radiate in all directions like radio?" Frances asked.

"Yes."

"Could one build a SLIP receiver that would copy all SLIP traffic, regardless of destination? Like a network sniffer?"

Roger Cox was now on a roll. Randy looked surprised and thought for a few seconds.

"Yes, such a thing could be built, but I never thought of doing that."

Randy began typing as Roger continued.

"If I had such a generic SLIP receiver or several, I could triangulate the source of a SLIP transmission, could I not?"

"You could, yes, based on time difference of arrival," Frances interrupted.

"Time difference?" Randy asked, puzzled.

Ron indicated that Frances should explain.

"Any message that is radiated outward, like a radio wave, can be intercepted. If the same transmission is received at multiple locations, given accurate enough timing, it's a straightforward math problem to calculate where the transmission came from."

"But that means..." Kelly Peterson started, then stopped, as a cold realization made a sudden change in the atmosphere in the room. Dark clouds now covered the early sunshine of the meeting.

"Shit," came the quiet word from somewhere around the table. Several heads nodded, and the room became very quiet.

"Why?" Randy asked.

Ron looked across at Randy, realizing that while he was a technological wizard, he had no experience in military history or the application of technology to military intelligence. He tried to speak kindly, without condescension, as to someone who could understand but had not yet learned what they needed to know.

"If they're any good at all, as Frances has explained, they could triangulate the sources of SLIP messages and figure out which are ships or headquarters or whatever based on analysis of the transmission patterns, even if they can't read them." Ron paused a second to think. "Traffic analysis has been used very effectively since before the Second World War. Plus, our encryption may not be as absolute as we think. The Poles and Brits cracked the Enigma when the Germans were sure it was impossible. It wasn't."

"And if they are any good and they do have SLIP, it seems distinctly possible they already know about us," Frances added. "That's very bad news."

Roger picked the discussion back up. "Randy, if the enemy were using SLIP, would we know it? Are there multiple, uh, channels, or frequencies that they could be using that we would not normally see?"

Randy picked his tablet back up and began searching through it. "I think that is possible. I would need some time to consider it."

"If they do, could we intercept those communications?"

"I am not positive, but if there are other channels, as you call them, then we would likely be able to receive them."

"In SLIP, is the sender aware of the receiver in any way?"

"No."

Ron asked, "How much time would you need, Randy, to see if there are other channels in SLIP?"

Randy thought for a few moments. "A week, at least. I will need to assemble a team at FPI to look at it. But now I have a question."

"Please, go ahead."

"If SLIP is as potentially dangerous as you say, surely we should be making changes to the transmission methods and encryption to try to obfuscate the messages. We must do something."

Harris smiled. "No, Randy, even if everything is just as the worst case we've described, we do nothing."

"Again, I don't understand. If they could be reading our mail, we need to act!" Forstmann insisted.

Frances leaned forward, turning her head to look directly at Forstmann. "No, sir, we don't. If we make an obvious change, the enemy will know that we know our communications are vulnerable and that we know they are on SLIP."

"Which will tell them their own communications are at risk," Roger continued. "And if it really does turn out they are onto our SLIP technology, we can use that to tell them what we want them to know."

"And then use some alternate method, maybe another channel, for our real communications," Ann said.

"But for now, nothing but nothing changes." Ron finished.

"Ron, may I never play poker or chess with this crew. Amazing."

The meeting seemed to have been completed, but Forstmann didn't move. The staff had started to gather themselves to leave but settled back into their chairs. Ron looked across at Randy.

"Randy, was there something more?"

"Ron, I have the finest technical minds that money can buy, and as everyone knows, for me, that's saying something. What I don't have is nasty, sneaky, wonderful minds like these." He pointed around the room, then waited as if still thinking about what he wanted to say.

"Yes?"

"I would like to borrow two of your most annoying staff to come to FPI as my guests. I need their viewpoints on this. I will pay for everything. They can come back to Jackson Hole with me on my shuttle. I will put them up on our dime. I would want them for, say, two weeks?"

"Did you have someone specific in mind?"

Randy smiled. "Well, Frances would be wonderful company for my wife and me, but I think Ann and Roger are what I need." They both gasped. "They have young, sharp minds and are not afraid to tell the old buzzard the truth."

"I see. Well, what of it?" Ron asked.

Ann looked at Ron, "I will need 24 hours, sir. I have to make arrangements for my family."

"You have a family, children?" Randy asked.

"Yes, a husband and a two-month-old baby boy."

Randy smiled. "Bring them," he said in a matter-of-fact tone.

"Excuse me?" she asked, incredulous.

"Bring them. There is plenty of room on the shuttle and plenty of room in the residence I have in mind. I can get you whatever help you need, nanny or whatever. This is one time, Ann, where finances are no object."

"I still need a day to get us ready. Stan will need to work it out with his job, too."

"Agreed." Randy turned his head to the other side of the table. "Roger, can you join us?"

"I am just a junior officer, single, living here on base. I think I can make it. But since you have to come back for Ann anyhow, I would like a day to let the family know I will be out of touch for a while."

Ron nodded his agreement. "But that raises another point: your destination is classified. Ann, you'll have to tell Stan, but he will have to keep it to himself."

"Yes, I understand. He'll be fine."

"I am sure he will." Harris looked across at Randy. "That cover it?"

"It does. Thank you, Ron, for allowing me to borrow them."

"Well, that's not so hard. I agree with you that their viewpoints will be useful to your team. Plus, since it doesn't cost me anything, I don't have to fight with the budget people for approval."

Again, the meeting seemed to be over. Warrant Officer Kelly Peterson had been mostly quiet throughout the interview, taking copious notes, but now leaned forward. She was also a young mother who had joined the Fleet partly to get away from her dysfunctional family, partly to serve, and partly for the adventure. She found a soulmate in her basic intelligence analysis class, and now, just into their second five-year service commitment, they'd had their first child about six months ago.

"Randy, might I ask a question of a more personal nature?"

Randy looked over at her. "No tabloid scoops, Kelly," he said, waving an index finger in mock seriousness.

"No, of course. But Randy, you are a man wealthy beyond comprehension; your name and your accomplishments are known by everyone on the planet and always will be."

She stopped as he waved off her comments. "Oh, do stop all that nonsense, but please go ahead and ask what's on your mind, Kelly. I'd like to hear your question."

"Everything I said is true, but here you are comfortably seated with us motley Fleet people, modest in your person, kind and patient and inclusive in your conversation, open and generous with your knowledge and resources. How is it that you have remained so, well, normal?"

Randy leaned back, smiling in a shy, thoughtful way. "Dear Kelly, you have paid me a great compliment. My wife hasn't referred to me as normal in some time!"

He let the laughter die down.

"But, my friends, the answer is that true wealth is not to be found in possessions or monetary success. If it were, none of you would be here, but you *are* here. So, real wealth is something more, is it not?"

The room became quiet again, all eyes on Randy.

"I will tell you what my grandfather told me. He was a man of modest accomplishments, comfortable enough in his retirement but not rich. He was a bright fellow who always claimed his father was the better intellect. I don't really know, but I have my doubts about that."

He paused and looked again directly at Kelly.

"But Kelly, what my grandfather said is really very simple, and he would be glad that I shared it with you. He said: Tell my grandchildren, to tell their grandchildren, to bring light, not darkness; to give to life, not take from it; to leave every thing, every place, every person, every moment, *better* for their presence. I will not be there to be proud of them, he said, but they will live lives they themselves can be proud of. And that, dear Kelly, is real wealth."

Ron waited a moment, not wishing to rush him out.

"Thank you, Randy. You have been everything Ms. Peterson described. For my money, your grandfather would be very proud."

Randy nodded. "Today, perhaps. Yesterday, not so much. Tomorrow, well, we will just have to see."

Now, the meeting was really over. They stood; Randy took his leave with handshakes or embraces as necessary and left the room.

Chapter 7

ISC Fleet HQ Intel Section
Fort Eustis, VA
Friday, February 4, 2078, 0900 EST

Ron Harris gathered his crew around The Table to hear what Lieutenant Ann Cooper and Ensign Roger Cox had learned at FPI. To keep security tight, he had told them not to report while they were there unless it was really a matter of life and death. He did have them check in daily to confirm that they were well and that work was progressing. The usual casual talk and chattering across the table died down as Harris closed the door and took his seat.

"Welcome home, Roger and Ann. We've been anxious to hear what you've learned. So, Ann, what's new?"

"Well, sir, my assignment was to look at the FTL drive and see if there was a way to detect FTL ships. My written report is about twenty pages, showing what has been investigated and various theories about it."

She looked down at her tablet, then back at Harris.

"The short answer is that FPI does not believe a Forstmann Drive ship can be directly tracked. On the other issue, alternative FTL drive technologies, FPI's engineers and physicists agree with Randy that there isn't an alternative to the graviton/anti-graviton drive for FTL travel. That said, however, I did get them to admit to the possibility that the Forstmann Drive is not the only way to do it. They don't know of any other way, but they were not willing to absolutely rule it out."

"How confident do you feel about these conclusions?"

"Well, sir, I remain skeptical, and I am not at all sure how helpful this report is. They are very smart out there, and they were working hard to be open-minded, but since we're dealing with an alien culture of unknown capabilities, I have to say I am not convinced that we have a final, exhaustive answer."

She finished with more than a little disappointment in her voice.

"I agree. Roger?"

"Sir, regarding SLIP, we had two questions: do there exist multiple channels, and can we tell if the enemy is using it. The news here is somewhat better. Turns out we can change the modulation frequency to create individual channels. It's rather amazing to me how much this technology acts like radio waves."

"What about the enemy?"

"While we were there, we, well, I should say, they, built a generic SLIP receiver, something analogous to a network sniffer. We were able to copy all the fleet SLIP traffic for a day. Scary, really. But that was only possible because the modulation frequency was known."

"If it's like radio, then there would be bandwidth requirements? Are there constraints on the possible modulation frequencies?" Tim Jackson asked.

Roger nodded. "There are. They chose the current frequency for maximum distance, and it seems they picked one in the middle of the practical range of frequencies. Considering bandwidth and the limits of range, they figure there is something like a thousand available channels."

Ex-NSA analyst Frances Wilson spoke up. "So, if we had a thousand SLIP receivers..."

"Or a fast SLIP scanner," Kelly Peterson interjected.

"...we could monitor the entire usable SLIP communications system?" Frances finished.

Roger shook his head, amazed. "That is what they are saying, yes. And, they've already started designing a channel-selectable generic receiver and, as Kelly anticipated, an automated scanner."

Harris sat back in his seat, then looked over at Frances.

"This is starting to sound like an NSA COMINT project, Frances. Do you have any friends over there that might like to join the Fleet?"

"I've been here for a long time now, Captain, but I can make a couple calls, maybe have a cup of coffee or two."

"Good. Please do."

Harris looked again at the closed door, then squirmed uneasily in his chair.

"There's more. We now have two significant projects: SLIP and FTL technology. But there are more on the way."

"What else?" Ann asked.

"I can't say at this point. The next is at least a week or two away, anyhow." He paused. "There are some other matters."

"Whatever it is, sir, just tell us." Senior Lieutenant Charles Anderson was getting nervous seeing his steady, reliable boss look uncertain.

"CINC is sending us help, and I have to admit we're going to need it. We're getting Rich Evans from *Liberty* when they get back." He turned to the tall, handsome New Mexico native officer at his right. "Elias, you've been the deputy here, in practice if not in title. We're going to make that formal. Rich is getting promoted, but he will be junior to you."

"Really, Captain, if you'd rather saddle Evans with being your bagman, be my guest," Peña said, laughing.

"Not a chance. We're about to double or triple in size, so I need someone I don't have to teach how we work. You've got it, like it or not. There will have to be divisions of projects, but we are not going to lose the integrated, small-group approach we have had up to now."

"What is it that you need from us?" Scott Morgan asked.

"Nothing that you haven't given me before. The leaders of all these so-called special projects are in this room. We will have to add Evans, but, you know, he's earned it. You are all cleared for everything we know, so in here, there will be no holding back, right?" They all agreed.

They left the room with a mixed mindset. They had plenty of work to do at the moment but felt disconcerted at what might be just over the horizon.

Fleet HQ Shuttle Landing Area
Fort Eustis, VA
Friday, February 11, 2078, 1100 EST

The large transport shuttle carrying the *Liberty* survivors down from *Dunkirk* set down on the mark directly in front of the temporary stands put up for the media. It had been a long trip back from Inor, and they were all relieved to be home again. *Circus* would not be too strong a word for what they saw outside when they arrived, nor would *chaos*. Once the shuttle was down, the hatch opened, and the *Liberty* survivors filed out. Teresa Michael came first, with Len Davis, Rich Evans, and Carol Hansen right behind. The other twenty-two survivors gathered behind this foursome as they approached the line of brass assembled to greet them. Admiral Davenport was first, delivering a crisp salute to Terri Michael and receiving likewise in return. He then extended his hand, grasping her right hand with both of his, taking his time so the media could get plenty of good footage.

"Commander Michael, welcome home! We are all very proud of you."

The roar from the crowd made it hard to hear. Terri was almost shouting in response. "Admiral, as the Inori would say, we are welcomed. We just did our jobs, sir. We're very happy to be back. I know you wanted a statement."

"Yes, Commander, just step over to that mark. They can hear you from there."

Terri walked over to the mark on the pavement across from the massed media, clearly reluctant. As she did so, the cheering and whistles from the crowd died down. Her crew silently assembled behind her just as they had come off the shuttle, her three deputies immediately at her back. She looked around for a moment, grateful for their presence. Terri Michael was still a young woman, but the stress of the time on Inor was plain on her face. There were lines at her eyes that no one would have seen before, now evident as she squinted in the sunshine. She had lost perhaps ten pounds off her already-trim frame. Her short, very dark hair was ruffled a little by the breeze, and a few new flecks of gray shined through here and there.

Fleet had sent them fresh uniforms up on the shuttle. She wore the slate gray Fleet daily work uniform, her name in white over the right pocket, and new gold oak leaves shining on her collar. Her command wings in silver, blue, and white over the 'ISC FLEET' in white above her left breast pocket, the stars and stripes at the top of her left sleeve, the *Liberty Bell* ship's crest at the top of her right. It was a simple, functional design that evolved from what armies, navies, and air forces had worn since the mid-twentieth century. It fit perfectly, but it was almost too new. It itched a little at the collar. She looked out at the mass of people and cameras, twenty or more red lights shining back at her. *Oh, Abuelita, are you watching?* she asked her late grandmother silently. *Can you even believe it?* She looked around for a moment, giving herself a second to prepare. *Of course I can believe it. I told you they were lucky to have you and I was right!* Terri smiled again, her inner Grandma so confident in her, then she took a deep breath and began

"Good morning. I am Lieutenant Commander Teresa Michael, and it is my privilege to command the survivors of the *Liberty*." There, got that out. *Just keep going.* "We are delighted to be home, but our happiness is tempered with the memory of those who could not return with us." She took a deep breath. "Captain Carpenter was an excellent officer, a respected mentor for me and others. Lieutenant Commander Roskov was a reliable, knowledgeable, incredibly funny associate, and I miss him every day." She smiled slightly as she recalled Roskov's kindness to her. "Chief Scranton was a daily example of the ideal shipmate; his dedication, integrity, and work ethic won the admiration of all aboard. I am a better officer, a better person, for having flown with people such as these."

She paused a moment, still working to control her emotions as she recalled these friends she had lost.

"There are too many for me to name individually. Eighty-four crew members were lost either on board or on the surface. But you must also understand that some thirty-five thousand Inori died that day. This kind, courteous, welcoming culture has suffered an incredible loss. Even so, they cared for us, fed us, and helped us in every way possible. We are most grateful to them."

She paused again to catch her breath. This part would be the hardest.

"I was fortunate to have with me a marvelous group of officers and crew who met every challenge, overcame every obstacle, managed every fear. Lieutenant Commander Davis led the difficult victim recovery operation with grace, respect, and care that was inspiring to watch. Senior Lieutenant Evans restored our communications, allowing us to locate and organize ourselves. He also gave me honest assessments of our situation, especially when they were not what I wanted to hear. Ensign, now Lieutenant Hansen, displayed maturity, courage, and command awareness well beyond her time in service, and I dread what this would have been like without her at my side. The rest of the survivors followed our lead in every way imaginable, working difficult hours in terrible conditions without hesitation or complaint. I am completely in their debt."

She took one more break to breathe and get her gut back under control.

"I would be remiss if I did not also thank our cavalry. Commander Nonna and Captain Barker did not hesitate, did not wait for orders, but took the initiative and came to our aid and the Inori's despite the danger. They are some of the best we have." *Time to wrap this up*, she thought.

"Again, we are most happy to be home. This is the only statement we will make. The crew has decided they do not wish to speak individually with any media. We expect you to respect that decision. Thank you."

Her speech complete, she walked back to the line of brass, their welcoming committee, the crew following behind in rank order.

"Excellent, excellent work, Commander," gushed the CINC.

"Thank you again, sir. May I introduce..." each officer and crewman went down the line. It was like the worst wedding receiving line you ever saw. CINC, Deputy CINC, Director of Operations, representatives from the Space Council, various country representatives, and FPI executives each had a moment with the crew. One had to give Davenport credit, though. He had taken the time to learn every survivor's name. It seemed to take forever, but finally, they worked their way to the ground transports and headed towards the quarters where they would stay for the next few nights. For Terri and her crew, it was finally over. There were a lot of tears on the transports, relief sinking in that they were finally home. They would have a couple days for rest and interviews with FleetIntel and then four weeks' leave. *Stalingrad* and her group were still at Inor, guarding the planet and looking for more evidence about the enemy.

The media were all over the survivors and their families, but not one broke rank. They had held a meeting on the way back, and they all agreed that there would be no media interviews on the return. If anybody wanted to write a book, fine, go for it. But no circus acts for the masses right after losing so many friends. It would be disrespectful. And they knew Captain Carpenter would not approve.

Just about the time Terri Michael was addressing the media, a small shuttle from *Dunkirk* was quietly setting down on the other side of the ISC Fleet HQ building. Ron Harris was there to meet it.

ISC Fleet HQ Intel Section
Fort Eustis, VA
Friday, February 11, 2078, 1130 EST

Ron Harris carefully placed the package in his office safe, locking it carefully and locking his office behind him as he left. He had called a meeting for 11:30 AM and was now hustling to the conference room.

When he entered, everyone was already there, as usual. As he sat down, they were quiet, well, mostly. He wondered how they would take this. Clearing his throat for attention, he spoke quietly and thoughtfully.

"*Gagarin* found *Liberty*'s flight data recorder. It's in the safe in my office."

The room was immediately silent. They thought the FDR had been lost in the ship's explosion. If intact, all communications, sensor data, weapons conditions, and ship status for the last 24 hours would be available to them.

"What kind of condition is it in?" asked Elias Peña.

"It's fine, maybe a little soot, but intact. Now, folks, let's remember that the fact that we have this is exceptionally sensitive."

"And exceptionally lucky!" Elias Peña added.

"Indeed. As I said last week, we have another special project over our usual fleet intel support duties."

"We need to get into that thing right away, sir." Roger Cox said, intrigued.

"I know. I have the access code."

There was a 'what are we waiting for' atmosphere in the room that Harris could feel. Every eye was on him, and every face had an expectant excitement about it.

"OK, OK, we'll open it. We will start with the scan data. I don't know that we should be reading out the communications yet. There are going to be a lot of familiar voices of friends and former shipmates on those recordings. Let's concentrate on who, or what, we're up against, OK?"

"What about the RFGs? Or the Lazy Dogs?" asked Frances.

"Less success with those, but what they have is still on *Dunkirk*. I know Evans dug up a Dog the first day. They'll bring them down when we can figure out where they should go. The Lazy Dogs are much bigger than the ones used in Vietnam, something like a quarter of a meter long and sharp as Hell. The RFGs are huge - maybe five meters, and they went in a long way."

"But we have one?"

"Most of one, I think. I am not sure what condition they were in - Intel on *Dunkirk* did not want to get into detail, which I understand. I would have thought they vaporized on impact."

They got up and moved into a larger workroom. Harris opened his safe and brought the package into the work area. He unzipped the duffel *Dunkirk* had sent it down in and placed the recorder on a worktable in the front of the room. It was smaller than one might think; perhaps two loaves of bread laid end-to-end. It wasn't high-visibility orange like an aviation data recorder, but a low-visibility flat black, designed to be located only by those who knew exactly how. Each FDR had a radio receiver, listening on a unique frequency for a unique activation code. If the FDR heard the right code on the right frequency, it would transmit a homing signal. *Gagarin* had picked it up the second day at Inor. On the front of the device was a recessed access door, just four screws holding it in place, and behind which was a numeric keypad.

Then came the tricky part. The FDR required a ten-digit access code. There was only one code that would open it, and you only got one chance. Enter the wrong code, and the device would irretrievably erase its contents. They'd get nothing. They looked at each other for an uneasy moment. Harris smiled slightly as he made up his mind, handing a small screwdriver to Scott Morgan.

"Mister Morgan, this one's yours."

Scott sat down in front of the FDR, easily removed the cover, and set it aside. He saw the keypad: ten numbers, a 'Start' button, a 'Del' for corrections, and a

'Submit.' Once you hit 'Submit,' you were done. It would either open or self-destruct. Captain Harris produced an orange envelope with 'LIBERTY' hand-written on the outside. He opened it carefully. Inside was a bright yellow card with the ten magic digits. He handed it to Scott.

"Don't you want to do it, Captain?"

Harris smiled. "Nope. If you screw it up Morgan, I'll just pretend I wasn't even in the room."

"I appreciate your confidence, sir. Lieutenant Stewart, could you please read the numbers?"

"Sure. Captain, could you read it with me, sir? One five six nine one zero one three five eight."

Harris read the numbers along with Kathy Stewart.

"Those are correct, Lieutenant."

"OK, Scott, you ready?"

"Yep. Pressing Start." Kathy repeated the numbers slowly as Scott pressed the keypad and verified with the display on the FDR.

"OK, Lieutenant Anderson, could you please take the card and check the display on the FDR?" Scott wanted yet another independent set of eyes to check his work. Ron Harris appreciated how careful Morgan was, getting others to verify the entries but remaining in control and responsible for the process.

"The numbers match, Mister Morgan."

"OK — here goes — Submit." As soon as he pressed the button, a tone sounded, and they heard the locks unlatching. They had gotten it open.

Scott gently opened the now-unlocked access door and found the data cable inside, right where it was supposed to be. Pulling out his regular Fleet issue NetComp tablet, he inserted the connector, and the flight data recorder application came up. They could now access all the data stored on the FDR. The first display indicated that they had the full twenty-four hours of data, which was good news. From there, he could select which data group to look at: Communications, Sensors, Weapons, Engineering.

He chose a few options on the tablet to display the image on the large monitor on the wall.

Now everyone could see what he was looking at. He leaned back, took a breath, relaxed slightly that the device was working, and looked at Harris.

"OK, sir, what would you like to do first?"

Harris took out his own tablet. "What time was Carpenter's message?"

"1020," said Chuck Anderson.

"OK, let's open the Engineering logs. He would have been idling in orbit until they saw something. Start around 0930 and see."

Scott swiped and poked until he had the engine data displayed. Slowly he advanced it until..."There! At 1003 the engines go online and start pulling at one-quarter power, probably moving away from the planet."

Kathy Stewart touched him on the shoulder. "OK...keep going...he goes to one half at 1015...wow...at 1019, the engine data stops."

"Stops?"

"Yes, sir, it just stops. The data ends at that point."

Scott looked again at the display, but there was no mistaking it.

Harris frowned. "OK, open the scan data and let's start at 0930 again."

Scott opened up three data streams: IR, visual, and radar. He skipped the UV and gamma-ray detectors for the moment.

"0930....scanning...wait...what are *those*?"

On the screen at 0952, six IR targets came over the planet's horizon.

"What the hell? OK, keep going. Normal speed." Harris kept his eyes locked on the monitor.

"Can we zoom the visual?" Kelly Peterson asked. Scott switched the large image display from IR to visual. There were a few dots visible where the IR targets had appeared.

"Starting to see something, just at the edge of the resolution."

Harris rubbed his chin absentmindedly, eyes still on the monitor. His crew knew he did that when puzzling over something he didn't understand.

"OK Scott, let's continue. Can you show me visual and IR side by side?"

Scott split the screen left and right so they could directly correlate the IR and visual data. The visual screen now displayed six very obvious dots.

"Those are really bright," Frances observed.

"I see that. Scott, do we have a radar range on those?"

"Yes, sir, radar just came online, two thousand three hundred kilometers."

Harris took his eyes off the screen to look at Scott. "What?"

"Two thousand three hundred kilometers."

"Jesus Christ those are huge," someone mumbled.

Harris turned his attention back to the screen. "OK, let's go forward in normal time, try to see what they saw."

"Lots of small IR traces down close to the planet, Captain. Look here...and here...and here. Time is 1001."

"This is the start of the attack on Inor?" Frances asked.

"We will need to study this in more detail, but yes, that's what I would say," Anderson commented.

"Radar?" Harris asked.

"Yes, sir, numerous objects reentering and more in a long line behind."

"Weapons status?" Ron asked.

It took a minute for Scott to navigate to the Weapons Status data and get it displayed. "Weapons are not quite ready. At 0959, they have just commanded the rotaries to open."

They continued to watch the data as it moved ahead in time.

"Now...1001 still...there are IR flashes on the lead ship....at 1002, we have radar showing objects heading for *Liberty*."

"Which explains engine start. He's been fired on." Harris said sadly.

"Makes sense," said Scott. He held the data at 1002, looking closer at the radar display.

"OK, here's the first launch; eight Lances fired on the lead enemy ship."

"Four inbounds, sir. There are IR plumes, so these are rockets, not using Drive. Sensor status shows that *Liberty*'s surveillance monitors were tripped. There would have been an alarm at the Surveillance station."

"Let's move ahead...wow this feels creepy," Ron said.

As the time moved ahead, they could see that the first four shots would miss. *Liberty* was still accelerating away from the planet and the oncoming enemy. He let the data run in real time.

"It's 1010 now. More flashes from the lead ship, or what I think is the lead ship. IR plumes again."

"Radar shows eight incoming missiles...faster than the last ones, I think...and they are tracking on *Liberty*."

They let the data flow for a few more minutes, watching the enemy missiles close in on *Liberty*, saw the last-minute call for power, then, finally, they understood why the engine data stopped.

"Looks like maybe six or seven hit the Drive. The Nav status loses Drive state at this point."

"So, he has no propulsion?" Harris asked.

"Doesn't look like it, Captain."

"Incredible." Ron just stared at the screen for a few seconds, wondering what it had been like to feel that: to know you were finished, you just weren't dead yet.

"OK, Morgan, let's continue."

"At 1020, he fires eight Lances, four at that lead ship and two each at those big suckers behind it." The data ticked forward. "Wow! Where did that come from? The ship just took a hit at 1022, and I didn't see it coming in the data." Morgan was surprised, and it showed in his voice.

"Battle damage?" Ann asked.

"Maybe, but the Comms data ceases at that point. I've been watching as we go along to see what data is still there."

"Continue," Harris said, dreading what was coming.

"At 1022, he fires another six Lances at the two in back. "

"IR flash on the lead ship at 1023, sir. A Lance. More on the two larger ships right after. Then there is a huge IR blast from that direction. We'll have to go frame by frame to see it all."

"What's in the radar data?"

"Looks like the big boy on the right blew up, sir. The big boy behind and to the left was also hit just after and blew."

"What the hell are they carrying that is so volatile? And in space no less?" wondered Ann.

"Where are we, Morgan?" Harris asked, sounding tired.

"1023, sir. The two big guys have exploded. The lead ship took a Lance hit but is still coming on. There is so much heat the IR display is totally saturated."

"Radar?"

"Lots and lots of pieces flying around. I'm moving ahead." After another minute, Morgan stopped the data. "Oh, crap."

"What?"

"In the radar data, I can see, uh, eight incoming missiles. See?" He got up and went to the large monitor, pointing to the computer's display of eight tracks headed in the general direction of *Liberty*.

"Time?"

"1025. He fires again at 1026, four Lances, at the lead ship."

"Wait — Carpenter was no fool. Why did he never fire a Spartan?" Roger Cox asked.

"No Spartans on board." was Scott's quiet response.

Harris was shocked. "None?"

"No, sir. The loadout is in the weapons status data. We'll have to ask Operations why that was."

"Wait!" Lieutenant Anderson stood and walked to the display. "*Liberty* was ship number three. I seem to recall that she needed a magazine overhaul to be able to take Spartans. She has the old four rotaries, too. After overhaul, she'd have two rotaries twice the size."

Harris grunted. "Oh, right, I remember that now, so he had no defense at all. How awful...OK...continue."

"OK, sir, 1028, and there are more inbounds, looks like another eight. The enemy seems to like even numbers. *Liberty* fires again, four Lances at the back ships."

"1029 now. Lance hits on two ships. In the visual looks like pieces coming off."

"Can we zoom in on the visual? I'd like to see what we're up against." Elias Peña asked.

"Sure, sir...there." Displayed on the monitor was a shiny, almost polished surface of a cylindrical vessel.

"Morgan, which one is this?"

"Lead ship - you can see the Lance hit to the upper right."

"Can you tell how big it is?"

"*Liberty*'s computer says five hundred meters. It said the bigger ones were eight hundred meters long, maybe one seventy-five across."

"What the hell were they carrying? And why did it explode?" asked Cooper.

There were no answers.

"OK, let's finish the run. Go ahead, Morgan."

"Sir, at 1030, there are now sixteen inbound missiles. *Liberty*'s computer is screaming alarms. At 1035 the radar loses track at about a kilometer, and then the data goes offline. All of it."

They stared at the frozen last images from *Liberty*.

"Ugh, I think I'm gonna be sick." Scott Morgan mumbled sadly.

"Get in line, man, get in line," Jackson said, still looking at the display.

They were quiet for a full minute. Ron then sat down, indicating to Scott to turn off the display.

"OK, folks, we will get the full report off the recorder tomorrow. Elias, I'd like you to work with Kathy and Scott on the enemy vessels themselves. See if you can tell what they're made of and what the hell blew up."

Peña nodded his agreement. Ann Cooper got out of her chair and walked to the front of the room.

"Do we all understand what we've seen here? *Liberty* was at rest, half asleep, really, expecting nothing, but in a half hour from a standing start she destroyed at least two enemy ships and damaged three more."

"And if that was an invasion force," Frances added, "the battle at Inor was not the disaster we've thought but was actually a victory."

"With a heavy cost." Kelly Peterson added.

There was another long silence, broken by Elias Peña's quiet voice.

"You have to tell them, Ron, you have to brief the survivors."

Harris nodded slowly, leaning forward in his chair, head in hands.

Elias continued, "Everyone thinks Carpenter lost the battle. He didn't."

"Yeah, after we debrief them, we'll get them together and let them know what happened. Speaking of which, Elias, I want you to run the debriefs with Tim and Kelly. I don't think they really know much, but get their stories on the record and anything else they might think would be helpful. We're obligated to talk to them but make it easy. Get with Terri Michael and get started tomorrow. I want them done by Monday so we can cut them loose."

Harris leaned back in his chair, suddenly feeling very tired. He had just watched how his friends and some Fleet University classmates had died a violent death. They were all very quiet.

"OK, enough for now," he said, finally. "I'll put it back in the safe in my office."

"It's painful to look at, sir, but this is a goldmine for our defense." Kelly Peterson said thoughtfully.

"And for our offense," Elias Peña's anger was plain in his voice.

"Agreed," Harris said, finally. They closed the FDR, and accompanied by Peña, Ron locked it back up in his safe.

Chapter 8

ISC Fleet HQ Main Conference Room
Fort Eustis, VA
Monday, February 14, 2078, 0900 EST

Ron Harris stood nervously at the front of the room as the *Liberty* crew filed in, Kathy Stewart next to him. Terri Michael was one of the first to arrive, with Rich Evans and Len Davis not far behind. Lieutenant Hansen and Ensign Stevens worked the lobby, greeting the crew and moving them into the large, theater-style conference room. The officers said 'Hello,' commented on the crappy Virginia winter weather, Valentine's Day, and generally made polite small talk about not much while they waited for the meeting to start.

"Captain Harris, can you tell me what this is about?" Terri asked quietly, pulling him aside, concern clear in her voice.

"Well, we wanted to take a moment to say thanks to the crew and let them know how much we appreciate their help," Ron said evenly, noncommittal.

"Bullshit, Ron. I know you have the FDR," she said, looking him hard in the eye. His small smile gave it all away. "You're not going to—"

"Play the audio?" he interrupted. "Give me a *little* credit, Commander. Besides, I haven't heard it. I may never hear it." He looked at her steadily and shook his head. "Remind me to never be interrogated by you."

Harris had spent much of Sunday arguing with CINC about if and what to tell the crew. CINC finally agreed that they should know the basic facts, a victory, not a defeat. And they could see the better images of the enemy ships to appreciate what Dean Carpenter had done. But no details on strikes, misses, the damage to *Liberty*, or her final moments. He broke away from Terri and was talking to Kathy Stewart about microphone volumes and checking the slides when Carol Hansen appeared at the front of the room.

"All present, Commander," she said to Terri.

"Thanks, Carol. Please call the crew to attention." Carol hesitated a second. ISC Fleet was not as formally military as some, so this was an unusual request. She turned and gave the command, and they stood as if one person, each straight and as tall as they could be, eyes ahead, chins up. Ron quickly glanced around the room and was pleased to see that his people had come to attention with them.

"Captain, the floor is yours," Terri said.

"Thank you, Commander." He looked over at Carol. "Lieutenant Hansen, please place the crew at ease and ask them to sit." She did so, and there was a murmur among them, something good about being a crew again and not a collection of survivors. Harris went up the steps onto the stage.

"Good morning, *Liberty*. I am Captain Ron Harris, Chief of Fleet Intelligence." He waited for the buzz that generated to subside. "I first want to thank you all for your time over the weekend. Lieutenant Commander Peña and his interview group appreciate your participation and tried very hard to get this over as quickly and painlessly as possible. I know many of you thought your experience at Inor insignificant, but I assure you all of the interview data will be correlated, and we may find something interesting in it before we're done."

He nodded to Scott Morgan at the back of the room, and the red 'TOP SECRET' banner appeared on the screen. Another buzz rose, and he again just waited for it to die down. *Let them have these moments*, he told himself.

"I really don't care if you have a documented clearance or not. What I am about to show you both I, and CINC, believe you need to see. But it is *classified,* and you must, and I do mean *must*, not reveal anything that you see here. I don't tend to be heavy-handed, but if there is a leak, we will find out, and there will be consequences."

He waited just a moment. "Fair enough?"

There was a unified 'Yes sir!' from the entire group.

"OK. As most of you know, there are flight data recorders on all Fleet ships. *Gagarin* recovered *Liberty*'s recorder, and we received it on Friday about the time Commander Michael was speaking to the press."

He turned to look directly at Terri.

"Thanks for the diversion, by the way. That came in really handy," which got him a few laughs.

"We did an initial exam on Friday afternoon and then worked over the weekend to dig more into the details. So, next slide, please, Mr. Morgan."

The slide was a 'beauty shot' of *Liberty* in orbit.

"Ladies and Gentlemen, from a dead start on a quiet Saturday morning, your captain and your shipmates went into Earth's first ever space combat and dealt this enemy, whoever they are, a *decisive defeat.*"

There was a long moment of shocked silence, then cheers and applause that went on for a while. This crew had believed their ship, without them, had lost the battle above Inor. This was a welcome revelation for them.

"I must also say that all of us here at HQ: CINC, Operations, Plans, Intel, are in awe of what *Liberty* did that day. The price was steep, but it seems obvious to us that a far greater disaster was avoided."

He turned back to face the screen.

"Next slide, Mr. Morgan."

The screen dissolved into a visual image of a large, silver, generally cylindrical object, some stars visible around it. The end nearest them appeared convex, with what might be windows or openings. There were no apparent markings. They were seeing it from just right of end-on.

"This spacecraft is about eight hundred meters long. Damn near half a statute mile. It is perhaps one sixty in diameter. *This* is what your shipmates faced up and beat."

He waited a few seconds. "Next slide."

The image was a long-range shot of six cylindrical ships, four smaller and two larger. They looked the same except for scale. Ron walked from the podium to the screen, where he could point out details directly.

"This is what appeared over Inor. Six crazy huge ships. A couple points about these. First, look at how bright they are. They're almost like polished stainless steel. The enemy makes no attempt to conceal themselves. I don't know what that means, but I do think it's significant. At this range, *Liberty* would have been nearly invisible visually. Second, of course, is the size. They are enormous, even compared to what we have planned. *Enterprise*, for example, is to be only five hundred meters long. Finally, they seem to be somewhat brittle. These two behemoths were demolished by about six Lances."

There was another murmur in the crew.

"I can't go into too much detail about the battle, but let me just say that *Liberty* fought valiantly, outnumbered, outgunned, and right to the last. You should remember that with pride. I sure will."

Ron stepped back from the screen to the podium.

"That's what I wanted to tell you this morning. I'll take questions, but I can't guarantee any answers."

Terri spoke first. "How was *Liberty* destroyed?"

Ron looked at her from the stage with a 'did you really have to ask me that' look on his face. He looked away, then turned back to the crew.

"I can't — no, I won't — go into detail on that. *Liberty* was outnumbered six to one. Hard to win a gunfight with those odds. They hit all six, we think, killed two, and took a chunk off the lead — that first image we showed you."

Len Davis was next. "What was the enemy's armament?"

"Again, I can only say so much. But, that said, the enemy used very high-speed chemical rockets with explosive warheads. Not that different from our own weapons except for propulsion."

Rich Evans leaned forward in his seat. "How likely is it that we just got lucky with those big ships, and they aren't as brittle as you say?"

"It's possible. Can't say what those odds are."

The next question came from someone in the crew. "How many shots did *Liberty* absorb?"

"I am not going to get into details about *Liberty*. Some of that is still being parsed out of the FDR data, and, frankly, it's not important for our purposes here. I'll just say she took a lot of punishment before she was destroyed."

"Where did the enemy come from?" Terri Michael asked.

"The initial IR data indicates that they came in from the south, as viewed from Earth. That may be significant, or it may not."

"Where did they go?"

"No clue."

The questions died down after that, the crew asking mostly minor items that Harris wasn't able to address. It was time to wrap up.

"Nothing more? OK, please remember the classification of this briefing. Good day, all." As he walked down the steps, Terri Michael stood, and the entire crew stood at attention with her. Harris stepped formally before Terri, exchanged a salute, something rare in the Fleet, and took his people out of the room.

This was the last time the *Liberty* crew would be together as such. They might serve together on some other ship or see one another from time to time, but this was their final time together as a crew. They were in there for more than an hour after FleetIntel left, and when they came out, there were a lot of tears and red eyes, warm embraces, and firm handshakes, promises for coffee or lunch dates that might or might not ever happen. But none of that mattered. They, this small group of 26 individuals, would always be a singular: *Liberty*. They would each carry a piece of it in their hearts forever.

ISC Fleet HQ Office of the Commander in Chief
Fort Eustis, VA
Tuesday, February 15, 2078, 0900 EST

CINC invited Terri Michael to meet with him and his deputy for an informal discussion of the events at Inor. She instinctively translated 'invited' as 'ordered' and 'informal discussion' as 'inquisition.' Having no choice, she went. Admirals Davenport and Yakovlev met with her in Davenport's office just off the Operations Center. While on Inor, she sent daily status updates to CINC and kept detailed notes of meetings, news, and decisions. On the long trip home in *Dunkirk*, she had written a report of their ten days on Inor. That report had gone to CINC as soon as *Dunkirk* was in laser range, sometime the previous Thursday.

"Good morning, Commander. Coffee?"

The admirals took seats on one side of a conference table. She moved to the opposite side, across from the two senior officers. She politely declined refreshments and sat.

"You are well? Your crew also?" asked Yakovlev.

"They are responding well, sir. The crew debriefs are done. Captain Harris' presentation yesterday really lifted their spirits. Most are on leave starting today. I have held the officers back until after this meeting." Her tone was firm and direct, even a little chilly.

Davenport took notice. "You see this meeting as, well, adversarial?"

"I do," she answered, perhaps a little too honestly. "Everything I could remember is in my report. I don't know what else there is to say. You have the FDR, so I don't understand what more you need of me."

Davenport leaned forward a little, hand folded under his chin as if in prayer. He spoke quietly, gently. "This is a hard loss for us, Commander. We're not here to interrogate you. There are some things we'd like to ask about, so we have your first-hand view."

"Yes, sir." Her cautious guard remained up, but she was now more open to their questions.

"Tell us about Hansen's talk with the Inori. Does she still believe the enemy was there?"

"I would not phrase it in quite that way, sir. Hansen thinks it is more likely than not, based on the Inori reports, that the enemy did a recon on the system something like ten years ago."

Davenport remained skeptical. "She is convinced this 'Historian' on the Council is truthful?"

"Again, sir, she would say, and for whatever it's worth, I agree, that the Historian is accurately retelling the story as he knows it. We asked him a couple times to go back over it, and each time was entirely consistent. The lack of written documentation is troublesome, for sure, but that's how they are."

"You were not kind to the Ambassador in your report," Yakovlev said evenly, changing the subject.

"Yes, in the future we should choose diplomats with less ass and more brains," she said with contempt.

"Excuse me?"

"He had to be pushed, prodded, and begged to do what obviously needed to be done. He had little or no ability to think effectively in a fluid situation. He was good at talking to the Inori Council, that's true, but otherwise, he was in way over his head."

"I see. I will pass along your thoughts to the ISC Board," Davenport said evenly.

Terri doubted that her opinion would ever leave the room. "Fine. He was a complete jerk. Feel free to quote me."

"I should tell you that Ambassador Johnston was effusive in his praise of you and your crew," Davenport responded.

"Of course he was. We're famous Fleet heroes, at least, according to the media. He's just grabbing a little reflective glory."

"Diplomats are a way of life, Commander," Yakovlev said, "and while we're driven to specific solutions and measurable results, they are sometimes looking at softer criteria. Relationships are important, after all."

"Yes, sir, I do understand that. One must, however, be ready to react in a useful manner to unforeseen circumstances. He did not display that talent while we were there."

The admirals looked at each other, appearing satisfied with what they had heard.

"New subject, Commander Michael. We've been thinking about your next assignment."

That perked up her ears. She was already long past tired of being *Lieutenant Commander Teresa Michael The Heroic Commander Of The Liberty Survivors*. She never felt heroic, and neither did any of her crew. The whole media business disgusted them: so much ignorance paraded as insightful commentary.

"What did you have in mind?"

"First, promotion to full Commander. We feel you've earned that."

She failed to keep the surprise off her face. "Thank you, sir." But she knew to be a full Commander meant more than silver oak leaves. She was getting a ship!

"Second, how about *Antares*?"

No way she was going to conceal her feelings about this. *Antares* was a brand-new Unity Class Destroyer. A little bigger, a little faster than *Liberty*, with better sensors and a lot more firepower. She gave up a broad smile.

"Well, sir, *Antares* would be fine, to be sure." She thought for a moment. "I have some requests."

"Commander. I've just given you silver oak leaves ahead of half of the promotion list and the newest ship in the fleet!"

"Indeed, you have, sir, and I appreciate all of it. But if I don't ask now, when should I?"

Davenport smiled. "OK, then, go ahead."

"My crew goes with me."

Yakovlev leaned back in his chair, considering the request. "Mostly, yes, that's fine. She already has a pre-commissioning crew, so we'll have to see how the skills line up and who we move off. Nice statement for the public, though, and good for the survivors' morale as well. But Evans is going to FleetIntel with a promotion, and Davis is getting a promotion and *Sigma*."

"*Sigma*. Really? Very nice. One last request?"

"Of course."

"Hansen. I promoted her in the field, sir, but FleetPers has not confirmed it. I need that to stick."

"Yes, we can do that. Don't make a habit of it, or FleetPers will be giving me a headache, which means I will be giving you an even bigger headache."

"Also, sir—"

"You said one more. Is there one more one more?"

Terri Michael was taking Davenport to the cleaners, and he was enjoying it. At least she was open about it.

"A small one. Hansen told me about a Fleet University classmate, Powell. He had a family emergency senior term and did not graduate. He basically dropped out of sight after his father committed suicide. She feels strongly that he got a bad deal, was nearly done with his courses, was an exceptional student, and deserves to be commissioned. Since the University denied him re-admittance, he's serving out his commitment as a warrant. I'd like that looked into."

Davenport was writing down the name. "First name?"

"David."

"I will have Lieutenant Peters look into it."

"One more question, sir, not a request."

"Certainly."

"Who did you have in mind for XO?"

"We'll send you a list of eligible O-4s. Pick who you want."

"Oh, well, that's very generous. Thank you, sir."

Yakovlev leaned forward, preparing to get up. "So, this meeting was perhaps not so painful? No rack? No hot lights? No inquisition?"

Terri smiled. "No, Admiral, not at all what I expected." As she stood, she extended her hand to Davenport. "Thank you, sir, for everything. I appreciate it, and I know the crew will be very grateful to you."

As she left, she had to admit to herself that it really was no inquisition. CINC and his deputy needed to hear some things from her, not from her report. She had satisfied them and was walking out with a promotion and a new ship. *Not a bad deal,* she thought to herself. She just wished Dean Carpenter was there to congratulate her.

Terri left CINC's office, and as she walked through the Operations Center, a thick-set, dark-skinned Lieutenant Commander waved her down.

"Commander Michael, ma'am, James George. I was on watch when *Liberty*'s message came."

He reached out his hand, and Terri took it.

"I was also here for your first two updates."

"Both? Were you not getting any sleep, Commander George?"

He smiled. It was a genuine smile, and she could see the cheerful soul that powered it.

"James, please."

"Terri."

"Well, I hung around for a while after Captain Carpenter's FLASH, then went off after your first and was back for the second. Great work you did, Terri. Tough situation."

"I got lucky with the crew."

"Yes, I saw your statement when you got back. Well said."

"So, if you were the watch officer at that time...the war warning, the rescue op order...that was you?"

George was suddenly shy, looking down at his shoes for a moment, then recovering.

"Yes. Word is your oak leaves will be changing color soon," he said with a sly smile.

"Indeed? How is it that everyone knows before me?"

"It's Fleet Headquarters. Hard to keep any decent secrets around here."

She laughed. An idea was forming in the back of her mind. She wasn't sure it was a good idea, but it was looking better and better.

"Any time in space, James?" she asked, trying to sound not too curious.

"Yes. I did a turn as Maintenance officer on *Freedom* and then Weapons on *Aurora*. I was the XO on *Chaffee* and then back here."

OK, it was now a really good idea.

"Excuse me, James, I need to ask CINC a question."

"Yes, of course."

She walked back into CINC's office, blowing past a startled Lieutenant Peters in the outer office.

"I want Commander George."

"Will you never stop?" he asked, exasperated.

She shook her head.

"He's on the list. If you want him, you can have him. It's a solid choice Commander Michael, but there are other good officers on the list as well."

"Something about him. He's it. When can I get him?"

"First of the month? You won't need him until then."

"Done. Can I tell him?"

"Sure."

She closed the door behind her and walked back to Jim George, working away at his console.

"James, how about you come with me on *Antares* as XO?"

His mouth dropped open a little, then closed. Then he didn't move for a second. "You're serious?"

"Yup. CINC agreed. He said first of the month, but we'll work it out."

She reached out her hand, and George took it.

"Welcome aboard."

"You always hire XOs off the street like this?"

She shrugged. "First time. But if it works out well, I won't promise not to do it again."

George smiled as if he had just found a new friend. "Commander Michael, that is, Terri, I think we're going to get along very well."

ISC Fleet HQ Main Conference Room
Fort Eustis, VA
Monday, February 21, 2078, 0955 EST


Plans Chief Captain Fiona Collins paced impatiently at the front of the room, her long reddish-brown hair flaring out each time she reversed course. Her pale cheeks grew pink along with her frustration level. Ron Harris had not yet arrived with his FleetIntel crew, and neither had the catering. *Nothing like no coffee to kill a meeting,* she thought. The invited Fleet personnel were slowly filling the room, including the famous Commander Terri Michael, an appellation Fiona knew Terri despised, now commanding *Antares*, and nearly-as-famous Len Davis, who would soon be taking over *Sigma*. Newly promoted Lieutenant Commander Rich Evans would come over with his new FleetIntel assignment. Lieutenant Carol Hansen was also present, standing with her new XO, James George. Anna Nonna of *Bondarenko* was there as well, with her XO Dick Watson. Captain Barker of *Dunkirk* sat quietly in the second row, reading, sipping the proper tea he'd brought with him. Americans, he always said, couldn't make tea worth shit, so he brought his own.

Also sipping tea were Captain Nobuyuki Kawaguchi and First Officer Noboru Nakahara of *Nippon*, the largest cruiser yet built. Weapons officer Hotaru Oshiro, the lone female representative from *Nippon*, sat nearby with coffee. Not far from the Japanese officers were the Koreans from *Tong-il* (Unification). Captain Yong Sook Man and Executive Officer Hea Jung Jun were looking at a tablet, reviewing again together the material FleetIntel had provided ahead of the briefing. The commanding officers of about a dozen other destroyers and frigates were there, making a crowd in the theater-format room.

A minute or two before 1000, the FleetIntel crew followed the catering cart into the room, which resulted in a scramble for coffee and the usual bagels and other accompaniments. As she looked around the room, Fiona thought *One would think we could do this all with a virtual meeting*, but security issues and plain old human nature made it far better to hold this gathering in the real world, not on fifty separate screens. As the chatter and congratulations and mini-reunions started to die down, the coffee, soda, water, bagels, and donuts distributed at least somewhat evenly, Fiona moved to the front of the room with Ron Harris.

"Good morning, everyone. I know many of you, but for the rest, I am Captain Fiona Collins, Chief of FleetPlans. This is Captain Ron Harris, Chief of FleetIntel. Both sections have been working hard over the last month to learn what we could, try to figure out what we don't know, and then devise an approach that will allow us to find, assess, and kill this enemy."

Ron took over. "We do have some interesting information for you. Kathy, let's have that first image."

The same image of the enemy ship he had shown to the *Liberty* crew earlier appeared on the screen. There was an audible gasp in the room. *Gagarin's* captain looked over at Kieran Barker and smiled. The work of locating the FDR had indeed been worthwhile.

"Here is our enemy, as seen by *Liberty*. Thanks to *Gagarin*, we have a wealth of information from the flight data recorder. This is one of the smaller of six ships that *Liberty* faced. You will have full briefs in your ship Intel shops but let me make a couple quick points."

The screen dissolved into a list of bullet points, and Ron indicated each as he went through them.

"First, the appearance. They are shiny, like stainless steel or something. This enemy is not concerned about being seen. I personally find that very interesting, but I honestly can't tell you what it means. Second, the scale. The larger ones are nearly a half statute mile long. Shocking, really. Finally, they're brittle. *Liberty* destroyed two ships with six Lances."

Ron waited a few seconds, then continued.

"Beyond that, *Bondarenko* and the *Dunkirk* group looked extensively for useful artifacts around Inor, but aside from a few bits of small debris, they found nothing. We don't know if it all burned up on re-entry to Inor or if the enemy is that good at cleaning up after themselves. They had the area to themselves for several days. The debris we did find indicates an advanced space-faring culture, likely using asteroid metals for construction. The important takeaway from this is that this is not some hyper-advanced society. Their construction is not like ours, but it is consistent with our own abilities. The second takeaway is that this is an enemy we can kill, and that's important."

"Good 'cause I want to kill a lot of them. If you'd seen Inoria..." Len Davis said.

"Well, Commander Davis, I am sure we'll get that chance." Anna Nonna added.

The murmurs of agreement and a sudden blizzard of side-conversations told Fiona this gathering could be quickly sliding out of control, so she stepped in to get it back on track.

"Hopefully, we will all get our chance. We're here today to brief you on the search framework we've devised. Let me give you the high points, and then we can dig into whatever details we need to."

"We are going to swarm these stars. Each of you will receive a list of stars to investigate. Ships will receive different but overlapping schedules, so they will be visiting systems at different times. There is no specified number of days to recon each system. You'll need to see what's required to get the data we need and then move on. FleetIntel has outlined what the data collection protocol should be, and you will have that on board. But you are in command, and you can implement the protocol as you see fit. We can't anticipate every scenario. You know what we need. The rest is up to you. Now, for the details..."

As Fiona dove into spectral types, distances, limits, chances of habitations, known planets, and all the essential ideas her very bright group had worked out,

Carol found herself thinking about how she had come to be there. She was just another ensign on just another ship less than six weeks ago, and now here she was suddenly already a lieutenant, a famous one at that, and assigned as the Weapons officer on a brand-new ship. She caught herself wondering where David was at that moment. Despite what she had said to Terri Michael, she was quietly keeping track of him and knew he had just completed his Advanced Intel Analyst school, first in his class, as usual.

A gentle impact from Terri Michael's toe on her shin brought her back to reality, now in full attention to what Captain Harris was saying.

"...there are risks here - no denying that. Not only is there a risk of contact with the enemy, but there is also a possibility we will encounter yet a different culture. I know I don't need that right now! Three is plenty, so try to avoid that, OK?"

He got the polite laughter he deserved.

"Finally, we still don't know what the attack at Inor was really about. There is the invasion theory, and there is also the genocide theory. But we don't really know. Hopefully, this search will result in some kind of revelation that clears that up for all of us."

He sat down as Fiona stood.

"Regarding the potential for contact with new cultures, we are not the United Federation of Planets, and there is no 'prime directive' for you to follow. We should, however, avoid contact whenever possible for operational security reasons. We don't know what we don't know, and any culture could potentially be an ally, or a subject, of the enemy."

She turned to Ron Harris. "SLIP?"

He nodded in response and stood. "About the SLIP system. We don't know if the enemy is listening on SLIP or not. We think it is at least possible that they are. I can't say 'probably listening,' but that's how we'll work. Make your status reports *right before you leave the system.* If they are listening, by the time they've figured out where you are, you'll be gone. Whatever you send, keep it short, again assuming the enemy is listening. Also, given all the uncertainties in these schedules, if you are detected or fired on, get a SLIP message out immediately. There will be long periods where we really don't know where you are, so if they get onto you, call for help. Now, any questions?"

"On SLIP, the transmissions are all encrypted, are they not?" Len Davis asked.

"They are, as were the German U-boat transmissions in the Second World War. Let's not repeat that experience."

"I assume FleetIntel has looked into whatever data we already have on these systems?" another captain asked.

Fiona nodded. "Yes, I asked them right after the Inor attack to review everything, even back to SETI in the early part of the century. We have some remote images, Hubble and Spitzer and Webb and their successors, but nothing that rules these systems in or out as the source of this enemy species. This general plan is based on the latest information we have, Commander."

Again, Ron and Fiona traded places.

"I do have a couple of surprises for you, new arrows in your quivers."

Ron suddenly had dozens of curious eyes on him.

"We've been working on a ship-deployable probe since well before the Inor attack. We realized that a Lance was most of what we need in a probe, but they tend to explode when they get near an enemy ship."

He waited for the polite laughter to subside.

"So instead of developing a whole new vehicle, we've devised a kit that you can use to convert a Lance into a probe we're calling a Sleuth."

"Cute name," Kieran Barker commented.

"The process involves removing the warhead and replacing it with sensors and communications equipment."

"But a Lance isn't stealthy, Captain Harris. Won't it be seen?"

"Part of the kit is a stealth cover that you put on the vehicle after the conversion is complete. Your Intel and Weapons people will be getting complete briefings and written instructions before you leave. Each ship will have six kits. The second surprise is a new weapon."

More rumbles of approval for this came from the audience.

"Normally, FleetWeapons would brief you on this, but he is unavailable today, so I get to give you the good news. The Lance is like a rifle bullet. We decided we needed a sawed-off shotgun to go with it."

Now there was real excitement in the room.

"It's called a Bludgeon, and as its name implies, it is a large, crude weapon. It contains four hundred kilograms of explosive. But the shotgun part is the hundred tennis-ball-sized steel spheres expelled when it detonates. We're hoping that wide areas of the target will be negatively impacted by their arrival."

"When will these be available?" Len Davis asked.

"Immediately. They'll be delivered before you go."

Terri Michael immediately saw the value. One of these beasts might be far more effective against these brittle enemy ships than a dozen Lances. "How many can I get?" she asked.

"FleetWeapons can give you about one-quarter of your weapons load in Bludgeons. Production is not quite at full speed yet."

"One more thought," Ron said, taking the podium, "is that we should expect this enemy to be looking for us as well. They knew enough to fire on *Liberty* before she had taken any action against them. Beyond that, we have no idea if they are aware of us or not. If they aren't, their experience at Inor should make them start looking. I would not be surprised to run across their vessels as we search these stars, even if they don't actually inhabit the system."

There were a few more questions on process and messaging, and then the meeting wrapped up. There were more greetings, farewells, handshakes, and collegial embraces as the officers worked their way out of the room. It was all very courageous, on its face, but there was an undercurrent of anxiety about the risks they faced and the hard fact, known to all, that some would never see this place, or these colleagues, again.

Henderson watched them leave with Ben Price.

"How many, Ben, will be with us a year from now? How many have we seen for the last time?"

Ben crossed his arms and thought for a moment.

"Some, I am sure of that. But it's our job to help as many get back as we can, right?"

She nodded, then picked up her tablet and headed up the incline to the back of the room. As she got to the line, her arm went around the shoulders of Carol Hansen. It was a brief, reassuring gesture.

Ben remained for a minute, watching the queue at the door slowly dissolve into the outer lobby. Having spent the last nine years in Intel and Plans, he had never felt so deeply connected to the fleet before. For him, it was no longer just a collection of ships but a living population of commanders, officers, and crews. Having recently spent so much time talking to them, the loss of a ship was no longer a conceptual thing but the painful prospect of losing real people he knew and respected. He stood there feeling a dark dread, then, realizing he was the last man in the room, hustled himself into the lobby to greet whoever he could before they were gone.

Fleet Shuttle Landing Area
Fort Eustis, VA
Monday, February 28, 2078, 1300 EST

It was cold, with a sharp wind blowing down out of the north that somehow smelled like snow. Newly promoted Commander Len Davis carried his duffel from the ground transport, pushing against the bitter bite on his face. He wrestled his way into the shuttle waiting facility, pulling off his knit cap and tossing the duffel on an empty chair. He walked over to the desk to check in. A young crewman stood as he approached.

"Commander Davis, headed for *Sigma*."

The crewman checked his manifest, poked the screen to confirm Davis' presence, and looked up.

"About a half hour yet, Commander. The warrant officer over there is also headed for *Sigma*."

He indicated a young warrant officer sitting not far from Davis' duffel. His face buried in his tablet, headphones in his ears, his uniform looked fresh, his double Rings of Saturn bright and new. He looked up, sensing Davis looking at him, and Davis saw green eyes, light brown hair and a pleasant, if not overly handsome, face. As Davis walked in his direction, the warrant stood. As he got close, he could read the name tag.

"At ease Mister Powell. I'm Commander Davis. You're headed for *Sigma*?"

Davis pulled his bag over and dropped into a chair one removed from David.

"Yes, sir, as are you."

"First trip out?"

David nodded twice. "Yes, Commander. I understand it's your first command."

"Worried, Mister Powell?" Davis asked comically.

"Not at all, sir. Congratulations."

"Thank you. What's your assignment?"

"I just finished the upper Intel school, sir, so I'll be Chief Tech of the Intel section."

"Good. I can cross that off my list of worries."

Davis was sincere but with a humorous edge. David liked him right off. He seemed like a man who could listen.

"I hope so, sir."

*Powell,* Davis thought, *where have I heard that name? Hansen!* She said he was a warrant somewhere. At that moment, Len realized he had Carol Hansen's lost classmate on his Intel staff. He decided to probe just a little more to see what had actually happened.

"So, tell me about yourself, Mister Powell. How did you come to join the Fleet?"

David squirmed uncomfortably. He knew Davis had been at Inor with Carol. Davis might know about him. Then again, he might not. He decided he might as well tell the truth since, in any case, it was easier to remember.

"Well, sir, it's a long story. The short version is that I was at SFU but had to drop out — family reasons. I'd been there long enough that I had a commitment to fulfill, so when I was able to come back, they made me a warrant."

"I see, and how do you feel about that?"

David frowned. "Like when your fondest ambition is one step from your grasp, then it just disappears, like a mirage. Sir."

"I'll bet it does. Still, you're in an important job on my ship, and I'll be counting on you."

"I know my duty, Commander. I will do my job best I can, have no worries about that."

David's voice was firm and even, and Davis was confident that he meant what he said. "Very good, Mister Powell, As I said, I will cross off the Intel section as something to worry about."

David smiled and went back to his tablet.

Davis sat back in the chair, closing his eyes as he mentally reviewed his assignment. *Sigma* was a good ship, older but solid and with a creditable crew. It was a choice first command. The search would soon be on, he knew, and he had ambitions for finding and killing as many of the enemy as possible. They would pay for Carpenter, he vowed silently, and for all the rest, they would pay a hundred-fold.

*Sigma*
Earth Orbit
Monday, March 7, 2078, 0930 UTC

As *Sigma* floated quietly above the mid-Pacific Ocean, a typhoon brewing right below her, Len Davis looked around his new wardroom for a moment before starting the discussion. He was mostly pleased with what he saw, lots of good people with a few that, well, needed further attention.

"OK, ladies and gentlemen, our first target is GJ 3622, an M6 dot 5 variable, 14.8 light-years away. You all have the summary. It seems to have a large, close-in companion."

He paused to take a sip of coffee, then continued his discussion of how he wanted to enter each star system and what his priorities would be. At the end, there weren't many questions, which didn't surprise Davis that much. The officers had all the briefing materials in advance, including Len's thoughts on how to perform the actual investigation of each system. But it was useful to him for them to sit and look it all over together. He could see questions in their eyes much more easily than in any kind of electronic message.

Even in an age of FTL travel, space mining, and friendly and hostile alien species, leadership was still a personal skill. In a ship carrying over a hundred souls, he felt it essential to know the crew and that they know him. He would then be better able to see what they needed to be confident in their work. He was their commander, not their friend, but he wanted them to know he was with them and would give them what support he could to help them get the job done.

"OK, it is now 0950. Commander Rodriguez, are all visitors off and all crew aboard?"

"Yes, Captain. All present. The ship is in all aspects ready to proceed." Linda Rodriguez, *Sigma*'s executive officer, answered in the expected manner.

"Good. Nav, let's get underway at 1030."

"Yes, sir, 1030 it is."

After the briefing with the officers, Len worked his way around the ship. He stopped at the Intel section, partly to check on David Powell, partly to keep an eye on Lieutenant Todd Boyd, one of the officers he had some concerns about.

"Powell, got a minute?" David was surprised to see the captain's head leaning inside his small work area. He stood, managing not to trip over his chair in the process.

"Yes, of course, Captain."

Since David happened to be alone, Len stepped in and closed the door. Davis motioned for David to sit back down, and he took a seat, backward, in the next chair over.

"So how is it going? How are you adjusting to the ship?"

There was genuine concern evident in his voice and posture.

"Just fine, Captain. Sally and Abe are excellent to work with. We're working on improving our process and trying to understand how to get actionable data to you more quickly. That part may take a while."

Len nodded his understanding, then looked at David more directly. "How is Lieutenant Boyd? He was a year ahead of you at the University, was he not?"

David frowned, thinking about how to answer. Since it was a private conversation, he thought he might as well show the man some respect and be direct. "If you're asking if he's been a complete shit about me not finishing the university and now working for him, well, yes he has. But I expected no less."

"Some history there?"

David nodded. "Yeah, there was a survival overnight I led with a mixed group of upper and lower classmen, including Boyd. He couldn't light a fire to save his soul. I did it by the manual right in front of him in about fifteen seconds."

Davis smiled. "Ouch."

"Yeah, but, sir, the weird part is, only he saw that. It's not like I stood up and pointed out what a dork he was."

Davis shook his head, wondering how egos and brains seem so often to miscommunicate.

"If it gets to the level of interfering with the work, I need to know. Short of that, I will leave it to you to deal with him. I can give you a bit of leeway, Mr. Powell, but don't put me in a position where I have to side with that jerk."

David was surprised the captain would say that about an officer. Davis continued as if he had heard what David was thinking.

"I couldn't say that to just anyone, David. For my money, you're an officer in every way but rank. I am going to get Boyd more involved in what he really wants: weapons and comms. You'll have more freedom of action down here than usual. I know you're up to it."

"Thank you, sir. We won't let you down."

"I'm sure you won't."

David wondered just what 'leeway' meant and whether Boyd was going to be as big a problem as he thought. On the other hand, if Boyd wanted to be elsewhere, that was fine with him.

## Chapter 9

Fleet HQ Grounds
Fort Eustis, VA
Tuesday, March 8, 2078, 1045 EST

Lieutenant Ann Cooper took a long walk around the Headquarters Campus. Last week's snow and wintry cold had broken, and today there was sunshine, not much wind, and a little warmth. Early flowers were beginning to show themselves in the gardens around the buildings and along the walkways. Fort Eustis was well forested in some areas, and as she looked around, she thought she could see the first hints of green in the groves. She had been doing a lot of reading about the Second World War since the Inor attack, and she found the parallels with their current situation interesting. She wondered what lessons she might learn from that conflict that would help them win this one. After all, this was the first genuinely existential threat the world had faced since that time. Only now, defeat might well mean death for all, not subjugation for some.

She let her mind wander over the issues they were working on. The SLIP team, which Roger Cox was leading, was developing hardware for scanning what they thought were the practical SLIP channels. The lack of radiation associated with the enemy ships intrigued her. If they weren't using nuclear power, what were they using? Fuel cells? Something really dangerous, like a hypergolic? *Liberty*'s sensor data did not have fine enough resolution to give them a spectrum of what had exploded, just that it had generated a lot of heat.

*So much space to search*, she thought. *This could take years*. Or, as they were likely to say to each other, the enemy could be here tomorrow. She had been in the room as a resource when Fiona Collins and Ron Harris had browbeaten the CINC and Chief of Operations to establish a defensive position close to Earth. The enemy had appeared just a few thousand kilometers from Inor. Very close, really, and if they did that here, there would be no time to pull a ship back from Mars or the asteroid belt or where the hell ever else they might be. They still kept a picket line just outside the orbit of Uranus, just in case. There were six ships, with three in the plane of the planets and three in orbits perpendicular to the plane. It was a dreary assignment that drones should be doing.

*Drones!* She thought suddenly, *if we built an IR surveillance drone, gave it a SLIP receiver, and a SLIP scanner...* She looked up to realize she had stopped in the middle of the sidewalk, and other people were walking around her, giving her amused or puzzled looks, wondering what was wrong. Realizing where she was, she turned on her heel and headed back into the FleetIntel offices.

"Roger! I need you!" she yelled across the office.

"Yes, ma'am!" Roger, amused, smiled and shrugged at Scott Morgan, with whom he had been discussing the SLIP problem.

Roger followed her into a small workroom off the main area. "What's up, Ann?"

Her nose and cheeks were red from being outside, her hands a little white. "I have an idea…How much does a SLIP transmitter weigh?"

Roger sat across from her. "Not sure, a hundred kilos maybe?"

"And what would this new SLIP scanner weigh?"

"A little more, say one twenty-five. What are you getting at?"

"How much for a 360-degree IR scanner?"

"Well, that's out of my area, but they're big...hold on a sec..."

He worked on his tablet for a minute. "The last IR telescope launched was 2045. It was about a metric ton. What are we talking about, Ann?"

She was also pounding away at her tablet but looked up when he asked. "A drone, Roger, a stupid boring drone. IR detector, SLIP scanner, and SLIP transmitter to send data home. If we could get such a thing, we could build them by the dozens—"

"Or hundreds…"

"...and we could leave them like little info-mines all over the place."

"Info-mines. Cute. I like it. Let's get Scott and Kathy in here and see what they think."

Roger went out and dragged the other two into the workroom. Ann began drawing blocks on the electronic discussion board, adding questions, numbers, then more questions.

They had gone in there around 1100. It was after 1300 when Rich Evans walked through the workroom, coming back from lunch. He couldn't help noticing the animated group in the small room. Through the glass, he could see a little of the board: SLIP, SLIP SCAN, and IR SCAN scrawled pretty plainly. They did not notice him watching. After a moment, he walked over to Elias Peña's office and knocked gently on the closed door.

"Come in! Oh, hi, Rich. What's up?"

Evans looked at Peña, then back across the room, then back, as if he wasn't sure what to say. Finally, he asked Peña warily, "So, Elias, should we worry that we have four of our people holed up in the little workroom, working on I got no idea what?"

Elias got up and came to the door to see for himself.

"Huh. Yeah, I've seen that before. Wait until the hands get down below their shoulders, and they are nodding their heads more than shaking them. And if they sit, that's a good sign, too. Once that happens, it's safe to go in. For now, whatever it is, just let 'em run with it."

Evans chuckled. "Understood. I'll check on them in a little while."

"Or they may come to you before that."

It was almost 1430 when Rich took another look at the crew in the small room.

There was now evidence of lunch: fast food bags and drinks on the table. They were all seated, with Ann appearing to review what was on the board, which had the appearance of having been erased and re-written several times. Deciding that Peña's criteria were satisfied, he wandered over and tapped on the door. Kathy Stewart opened it as the other three scrambled to their feet.

"Oh, please sit," he said, slightly disgusted. Rich was always a little uncomfortable with military formality in an office setting like this. *We're here to work together,* he would say, *not to bow and scrape just because of rank.*

"So, what's up?" He closed the door behind himself, then leaned against it, arms crossed.

"Info-mines," Kathy said brightly.

"Yeah. For the record, Ann came up with the name."

Rich looked around at four young faces, all pretty happy with themselves.

"Info-mines...so...OK...tell me more."

Ann pointed to the board. "Well, we have a lot of space to monitor, and we can't possibly do it all with ships, not with any persistence. It will always be hit-or-miss. Besides, we have better things for our ships to do than sit around looking into empty space—"

"Like killing the bastards," Kathy interrupted.

"Right, like that. Drones are good at doing boring shit," Ann finished.

"OK, keep going," Evans said.

Roger picked it up from there. "We also have the SLIP project. Once we have a working scanner, we'll need to place some number of them around to watch for enemy transmissions. The more, the better, and the wider the dispersal, the better our location ability is."

Rich was intrigued. "We've sent a good part of the fleet out to check the nearby stars. What you're proposing, assuming I get it, is to replace that effort with these Info-mines."

"Not quite, sir. Ships, people, need to check for immediate dangers, like a ship or a depot or some other enemy facility. But these drones could remain behind to give us a continuing presence. It would let us keep watching long after we've left."

Rich shifted his back against the door, hand on his chin, thinking. "Based on their appearance at Inor, I think this enemy is arrogant, or maybe just ignorant, and the idea that we would keep watching after we're gone might not occur to them. I like it." He thought for a few more seconds. "So, what about the time delay problem? If they come out of FTL far enough away, it will be a while before we see it at the IR sensor, right?"

"True," Ann responded, "but in this application, I don't think we care. We were thinking each mine would call in on an irregular schedule, maybe once a day or once a week or so, to report any SLIP messages or IR hits it has seen. We could always include an interrogation function so we could ask it what it's seen since the last data dump."

"I'd rather know right off, but I take your point. And keeping the drone—"

"Info-mine," Scott interrupted.

"OK, Info-mine, as quiet as possible is a good idea."

"So, what do we do now, Commander?" Scott asked.

"Well, you could see if you have a few billion dollars lying around."

"We already checked the cushions on the chairs, no luck," Kathy responded.

"This is a good idea, folks. Ann, write it up and send it to Elias Peña, Captain Harris, and me. Set up a time for us to talk it over further."

And so, the Info-Mine was created.

The next day, Ron Harris and Fiona Collins brought CINC down to FleetIntel to talk to Ann and her group. He was impressed and got funding for a pilot run of twenty units. But he insisted on a slick new name: *Sentinel.*

Ann's group was disappointed. To them, they would always be InfoMines.

Bachelor Officers' Quarters
Fort Eustis, VA
Thursday, March 10, 2078, 2330 EST

The resident officer's quarters were small, with just enough room for a bed, a minimal closet, a sink with a mirror, and a desk. It was actually not much larger than a captain's duty cabin on a ship. Two rooms shared a shower and toilet. It was close living, but the price was right, and for single officers and warrants spending a great deal of time on duty, it was a good deal. Scott Morgan had returned to his room late this night after working on the design requirements for the Sentinels. It was a lot of work for the growing but still-small FleetIntel shop, but he was glad to be in the middle of the action.

He had also spent time today reading over the *Liberty* timeline based on the sensor data. Several issues nagged at him, including how the enemy targeted her so quickly. As he stood in the shower, trying to make the steaming hot water rinse away the stress of the day, he replayed the timeline over and over in his head. The IR flash, the bright dots on the visual so far away, the radar images of...wait...radar? *RADAR??* He grabbed his head with both hands. *How the hell did we miss that?* he thought. He quickly finished his shower. Still dripping, he picked up his phone and called Captain Harris.

"Morgan, what the hell are you doing on my phone at this hour?" Ron said with equal parts annoyance and concern for his team member.

"*Liberty.* They turned on the radar."

"Yeah, so what...oh hell. Morgan, you're thinking that's how they saw her?"

"Yes."

"How did we miss that?"

Scott smiled. The boss was no slouch. "Exact thought I had, sir. It's so obvious we never thought of it."

"If that's what happened, then our stealth may not really be compromised. Carpenter advertised his position." Ron's mind was racing forward.

"Yes, that's how I see it."

There was a short pause as Harris considered what to do next. "OK, Scott, set up a meeting at 0900 with the group, and we'll talk it out. If we think this is right, we'll have to get an update out to the fleet."

"Yes, sir, will do."

"And, Scott, good work. This has been driving a few of us pretty crazy over the last few weeks."

"Thank you, sir."

Morgan was able to set up the meeting using his phone and then managed to get to sleep, but much later than he had planned.

The next morning there was a louder buzz than usual when the FleetIntel core staff met at 0900. Scott went into the office around 0600. After all, he was awake anyway and began looking again at the engineering and surveillance logs from *Liberty*. It didn't take long. The radar had been engaged almost immediately after the IR detections and never turned off. The group finally sat and quieted down.

"OK, as you already know, Scott woke me up last night. Go ahead, Mister Morgan."

Scott leaned forward to speak. "Yes, it's pretty obvious now. Right after the IR contacts, *Liberty* turned on her radar, and they continued to run it until the end. If this culture understands radio and radar, that would explain how easily she was targeted."

"I agree as far as that goes," commented Rich Evans, "but that is only one possible mode of detection. Have we looked at the potential for stellar occultation? If *Liberty* was blocking some bright stars, that might be how she was seen."

"It is possible, Rich, but since we know for sure the radar was left on, and we don't have a substantial reason to think that a significant occultation occurred, I think we need to act on what we think is most likely," Peña said, putting an end to the occultation argument.

Scott Morgan spoke up in response, glad for the deliverance. "We should get a message out to the fleet, something like how further analysis of the *Liberty* data shows that the enemy may be aware of radar and to keep use to a minimum?"

Harris nodded his agreement. "Draft it up, Scott, and send it to me and I'll get it out."

It didn't take him long since he had been writing it in his head all morning.

```
PRIORITY 207803111500UTC
TO: ALLFLEET
FROM: NAVINTEL
FURTHER ANALYSIS OF LIBERTY DATA GIVES STRONG
INDICATION THAT ENEMY IS AWARE OF RADAR.
RECOMMEND ALL SHIPS MAINTAIN RADIO SILENCE UNTIL
```

```
IN OPINION OF COMMANDER THE REQUIREMENT FOR
RADAR DATA OUTWEIGHS RISK OF DETECTION.
END
```

*Antares*
En route to Lacaille 8760
Tuesday, March 15, 2078, 1130 UTC

*Antares* was late leaving Earth due to some shakedown issues but was now en route to Lacaille 8760, a dim red dwarf not quite 13 light-years away. A week out, newly-minted Weapons Officer Carol Hansen was again crawling up a magazine of Lances to figure out where the stack was stuck. Her Chief Tech, Emilio Guzman, was beside her as they worked their way to the top of the missiles, eventually finding a bracket bent slightly, just enough to hang the mechanism. A well-placed mallet strike from the chief put the bracket back where it belonged. They crawled back out and re-ran the rotary pre-load.

"Smooth, Lieutenant Hansen, looks good."

"Seen that before, Chief?"

He nodded. "Yeah, if you're not real careful when you load them, that bracket can flex, almost like it's just a little too thin."

"I'm just glad this is the only one. Go ahead and offload the rotary and then re-load and offload again. If all that works, I think we can sign it off."

"Yes, ma'am. But, Lieutenant..." he hesitated.

"Yes, Chief?" she said, inviting him to say whatever was on his mind.

"Well, not really my place, but I would have thought the Weapons Maintenance Officer would be back here dealing with this."

She smiled slightly. "I have a lot to learn, Chief, and the best way is hands-on, don't you think?"

"I do."

She left the weapon storage area and headed back forward. She took a quick lunch in the wardroom and then went to her quarters. At 1600 she'd have the Conn for four hours. She pulled her brand-new Bible down from the bookshelf, and it crackled as she opened it. Her old one, its cover worn smooth, pages covered in handwritten comments and bulging with notes and long use, had burned up with *Liberty*. She missed it like a lost friend. It had been her companion since she was eight. She often thought about how she could reconcile her faith, its history, stories, and legends, with what she now knew of other worlds. Was the Inori's Ino the same God as hers? If so, had Christ died for the Inori, or even the enemy, as well as all humanity? She didn't know, and thinking about it didn't really make it any better.

In her old Bible she had highlighted a passage from John: *And I have other sheep, that are not of this fold,* which some people thought meant souls on other planets. Carol was skeptical that was what Jesus had in mind, and she didn't see that it mattered much to her own faith. *There were things that people just could not know,* she thought, *and I can have faith without complete understanding.*

She felt the faithful warrior's conflict: the competing commands of mercy and humility against the obligation to forcefully defend herself, her home, and her friends against a dangerous enemy. She had seen first-hand the wretched deaths at Inor, and she could not, faith or no, allow that to happen again if it were in her power to stop it. That much, she was sure of. She would fight this enemy with a clear conscience, without hesitation or remorse. She was neither sheep nor wolf, rather the vigilant sheepdog dedicated to protecting the flock to the point of death. She and David had debated this very dilemma at length, long into the night, and he had eventually come to see, respect, and adopt her view.

She leaned back in her chair, arms crossed and looking at the ceiling. She thought a moment more about David, their 'spirited discussions,' his sincere, pleasant presence, and how his eyes had a soft intensity, an openness to her, that allowed her to just be herself, her feelings flowing openly. It was so different from Rick's hard stare. She thought about that last time before he disappeared, how David had stood next to her for so long. He asked nothing of her, just gave his support and caring when she needed it. Was there something there she was missing? She never felt small around David like she did with Rick. She and Rick were no longer a couple. She had tried to care for him, thinking she could bring out something positive she thought she saw deep within him. But if it was there, she never reached it, and now she doubted that there was much deep down inside Rick but more Rick.

She was sorry to have wasted so much time on him, but there was no undoing that now. She felt restless in her heart, like something she didn't know was trying to emerge, something important trying to be heard, or felt. But in these quiet moments, when she had time to search her own heart, over and over it was David who appeared there.

*Sigma*
GJ 3622
Tuesday, March 22, 2078, 2120 UTC

*Sigma* came out of FTL about 10.5 Astronomical Units (AU) from GJ 3622, coasting to the desired 10 *AU* distance and adjusting speed so she would passively orbit the star. As soon as they were back in normal space, her full complement of sensors opened up, and they started looking at the system. GJ 3622 is small, perhaps a tenth of the mass of Sol, a typical red dwarf, with an occasional flare. It didn't seem likely to have any indigenous life. In a few hours, they identified the Jupiter-class close companion and two other smaller but still sizeable gas planets. It took a little longer to recognize three small rocky planets, all bare of atmosphere and well outside any habitability zone. There was an asteroid belt of sorts as well, orbiting just outside the primary companion.

Sixteen hours later, David got up from his workstation in the Intel section and headed for the Bridge. It was now midday Wednesday, and after a double shift examining data, he needed a break. He also wanted to sit with the Surveillance workstation on the Bridge to see how they were doing. It wasn't a very long walk, and when he got there, he found the Surveillance officer, Senior Lieutenant John Sanders, observing behind their position. They exchanged a silent greeting, and David took his place standing next to Sanders, leaning against the raised command workstation which all the other stations half-encircled. Two techs were working the sensor arrays, one a senior chief and the other a relative newcomer, but as David observed them, he could see that they were doing a credible job. Sanders leaned over to David.

"Anything interesting in the re-processing?"

David shook his head. "No, nothing new. I was getting a little glazed-over back there, so I thought I'd come up and see it from the pointy end."

"Still hoping for that high-albedo object?"

David smiled. "Well, Lieutenant, I'm not sure 'hoping' is the word I would use, but we are here to find the bastards, right?"

"True."

They continued to watch the process for another half hour. The Surveillance crew were methodically detecting and identifying orbiting objects, then examining them individually more closely with higher resolution detectors. They could then break out the reflective spectrum of each object, which gave them a general idea of what it consisted of. David was looking for shiny, or high albedo, objects with a narrowly defined spectrum representative of a particular iron-nickel-carbon steel alloy. That was the best theory of what enemy ships and facilities would look like. As they watched, Lieutenant Todd Boyd came on the Bridge to take a practice watch at the Weapons station. When he saw David standing with Sanders, he came striding over. He grabbed David by the arm and pulled him over to the right corner of the Bridge.

"Powell! What the hell are YOU doing on the Bridge?" he hissed.

Taken slightly aback by Boyd's aggressive tone, David responded evenly. "I was observing the Surveillance crew's process, getting a better idea of how they actually collect our data. It's really pretty interesting."

"How about you get your ass back to your little gnome-hole and do your own job? If you wanted to be on the Bridge, you should have damned well stayed in school."

David, holding his temper better than usual, remained calm and even in his response. "Lieutenant, I am doing my job. Understanding the source of our data helps inform its analysis." He said nothing of the sixteen hours he had already spent in the Intel Section, a double shift in which he had never laid eyes on Boyd.

"That's a matter of opinion, asshole," Boyd shot back, "and since I am your boss, it's only my opinion that matters. Get lost."

Sanders overheard a little of this and started to turn towards Boyd to respond, but a quick glance and slight headshake from David stopped him. While they couldn't hear what he was saying, Boyd's aggressive body language was unmistakable, and now half the Bridge crew was looking at him. He was making something of a fool of himself, and David saw no reason to detract from that effort.

"As you wish, Lieutenant."

David stepped past Boyd and moved off the Bridge. Boyd caught Sanders staring at him.

"Little shit needs to know his place," Boyd said bitterly as he walked by.

Sanders said nothing, and Boyd finally took his place at the Weapons console. David went back to Intel and checked on Abe Jackson and Sally Gray. Satisfied they were up to speed, he headed for his cabin to get some rest.

*Sigma*
GJ 3622
Wednesday, March 23, 2078, 2230 UTC

After twenty-four hours of lazing in a 10 AU orbit around GJ 3622, Len Davis gave the order to start closing in on the planets. They started with the gas giant that happened to be nearest to them. The planets were all around the star, some off to their right or left, some on the opposite side. Since the Drive made all of them easily accessible, Davis decided to check them out in random order.

"Better to be unpredictable," he said.

The first rocky planet they explored was about half the mass of the Earth. They settled into a thousand-kilometer sun-oriented orbit, each revolution about two hours and forty-five minutes. Having determined there was nothing interesting in the moonscape below, Davis broke off after two orbits and headed for the next planet, one of the gas giants. This one was perhaps half the mass of Jupiter and nearly featureless, like Neptune.

David was at his station in the Intel work area, validating and reviewing the data as it came in. Sally, Abe, and David had worked up alert criteria to back up what FleetIntel had provided and, with the help of the Surveillance group, had automated the process of reviewing Surveillance data. They had determined conditions for objects worthy of a second look, objects they wanted to examine in detail, and objects that should set off alarms. They were now in the validating phase, both continuing to manually inspect interesting data as well as checking the alerts that their post-processing routines generated. It was tedious work, but if they were going to be betting their lives on it, it was necessary. David was pretty sure they had a good handle on what not to alert on, but they had no actual enemy hardware to verify that the process would kick off an alert when it should. He fed it the data from *Liberty* as a test, which worked, but the lack of additional samples troubled him, and so he kept up a review of all data that met even their most minimal criteria. They just could not afford to miss anything.

The Weapons Officer had initially rejected Boyd, a situation which Boyd blamed on poor instruction and faulty assessments. He complained bitterly to the XO, LCDR Linda Rodriguez, that Briggs and Fleming had not given him an even chance. The fact that as the Intel Section Chief, he reported to the Weapons Officer, whom he had just accused of bias, didn't seem to register with him. Rodriguez spoke separately with Briggs and Fleming and the senior Fire Control Tech, Chief Tripp Dodson. She then directed Boyd would get a second chance and run through the process again. It was essential to Boyd's career that he succeed, and the XO wanted him to have every opportunity. If he failed, he would not make Senior Lieutenant and would be out of the service in less than twenty-four months.

The little Neptune — which the crew named Nepi — had several significant moons and a couple dozen small ones, all rocky and dull. In fact, the entire GJ 3622 system turned out to be as boring as one could hope, but it took several days to determine that.

David had slept from midday Wednesday late into the evening. By 2300 he was back in the Intel Section. Just before 0700 the next morning, he was still monitoring and post-processing the surveillance data when Lieutenant Lisa Briggs appeared at the workroom door. He was again alone in the workroom. Jackson and Gray were at breakfast and would be back on duty soon.

"Mr. Powell?" she inquired quietly from behind him, trying not to startle him.

David turned to the door and stood when he saw who it was. "Yes, Lieutenant Briggs, something I can do for you?"

Briggs, seeing that no one else was in the room, stepped in and closed the door. She hesitated as David sat back down.

"Lieutenant?" he asked, wondering what this visit was about.

"You can call me Lisa."

David shook his head, then gestured for her to sit. "Can't. What's on your mind?"

Lisa sat, her face looking a little pinched, clearly unhappy. Her long ponytail swung side to side as she talked. "I heard about Boyd's little performance yesterday."

David raised his hands as he shrugged, a gesture of 'nothing I can do about that.'

Lisa continued, a tone of worry in her voice. "I have to tell you, David, that little shithead's ego far exceeds his abilities. Weaps doesn't want to certify him; he thinks he'll choke in the clutch. XO is pushing to let him sit anyway."

"Why are you telling *me* this, Lieutenant? It would be better for me if he made it in Weaps, and I would not have to deal with him."

"So you know you're not the only one who sees this jerk for what he is. Jake — Senior Lieutenant Fleming — is about to give the XO the bad news. And what's wrong with Lisa?"

"We're not cadets anymore. I'm no longer a half-year behind you, and I just feel that I need to avoid anything that looks like I am stepping out of my lane. Most everybody knows the story now and if they start to think I'm using old connections for, well, whatever, I'll lose all credibility."

"You wouldn't."

"Maybe not, but you were taught like I was that leadership is perception as much as reality."

She nodded in response, her regret evident on her face. "I just can't get over that you didn't get back into the University. You should have, you know."

David smiled weakly, a reflection of the pain that wasn't exactly fresh but wasn't wholly over, either. "Perhaps, but I didn't, and that is the reality we live in."

She reached across and touched his shoulder. "We admired you back then, David. Anyone who knew you then still does. You were always a step ahead, but so generous with your help. I, for one, appreciated that more than I can tell you. Something will happen, I am sure, to get you back where you belong."

He thought for a moment before answering. His voice sounded resigned but clearly not satisfied. "Who's to say this isn't where I belong?" he said, pointing to the deck. "For now, at least, I have work to do, and I am going to keep doing that until something else happens."

She shrugged, mostly agreeing with him. Then she smiled, held his shoulder firmly, pulled him closer and kissed him on the cheek. "For luck."

Then, she was up and out of the room. David took a moment to process what had just happened, then got back to the work in front of him. *Something will happen,* she had said, *to get you back where you belong.* It made him hurt anew that he wasn't where he might have been, and he wasn't sure the hope she encouraged in him was really a good thing. So often he had seen hope 'spring eternal' only to be followed closely by reinvigorated despair. He shook off the feeling and went back to work.

Finally, early on March 25, they left GJ 3622. Davis was satisfied but also disappointed at having seen nothing of the enemy nor of anyone or anything else. As they left, they sent the required no-contact SLIP to HQ, and David took the transit time to continue to study their surveillance process, refine what he could, and add where he thought necessary.

Lisa Briggs turned up twice during the transit, inviting him to come along for meals in the wardroom. He went, glad for some friendly company, but was still wary of her attention. In his mind, they could be friends, even close friends, but he could not let her think that there might be more to it than that. They had the shared experience of the University to draw on, and they were, after all, shipmates.

But at some point, he might have to push her back, as gently as possible, to keep everything clear. For David, there was no Plan B, and he believed that Lisa deserved to be someone's Plan A.

ISC Fleet HQ Intel Section
Fort Eustis, VA
Monday, March 28, 2078, 1030 EST

It had been a couple weeks since Ann had hatched the idea of the persistent surveillance drone that started out as an 'InfoMine' but wound up a 'Sentinel.' She grudgingly admitted to herself that Sentinel really was an apt name, and it was far more important to her that her concept became a reality than it retained her somewhat silly name.

She headed to Ron Harris' office for her regular update to him on the progress. She waited at the door a minute until he opened it from the inside. A woman sat across from his desk, blonde hair pulled back, thin, with hard, severe features.

"Thanks for coming in, Susan," Harris said, dismissing her. "I will talk to CINC and get back to you."

She stood, shook Harris' hand, and left, not appearing to notice Ann at the door. After she was gone, Ann took her seat.

"Who was that?" she asked conversationally.

"Exobiologist." He looked at the door as if to make sure she was really gone. "Wants a direct commission to Commander and charge of the project she has in mind."

"Wow."

"She may get it. OK, so how are we doing on the Sentinels?"

"Fine. The factory is planning to add a small line to generate the fuselages if we go into full production. For the first twenty, they'll have to hand-install the sensors and antennas. They feel it's too small a run to set up a whole new assembly line to do the completion work."

"And the power units?"

"Radioisotope Thermoelectric Generators. They say they can give us RTG units they already had for some kind of exploration probe. They weren't too specific, and I didn't ask a lot of questions."

Harris nodded. "Agreed. Never look a gift horse in the mouth."

Ann looked at him, slightly puzzled.

"Never mind."

"OK, then, the SLIP scanner and transmitter are the biggest payload mass, but the design seems to be able to handle it. We agreed on ion thrusters to keep it oriented."

"The RTG is up to that load?" Harris asked skeptically.

"Actually, the load is pretty small in the overall context of the vehicle. It's fine."

Harris nodded his understanding. "OK, then." Harris took a sip of his coffee, expecting Ann to get up and head back to her own desk, but she didn't move.

"Something else on your mind, Ann?" Ron didn't use first names much, only in private and only to indicate that the more junior person was free to express themselves.

"I want to go."

Harris shook his head. They had already had two conversations about Ann's desire to go out with the first batch of Sentinels.

"I need you here. You will write up all the procedures, but it has to be left to the regular fleet personnel to get these things on station."

She was clearly unmoved and sat there staring at him.

"I expect the first deployment trip will be a long one, several months. All of that will be under the equivalent of radio silence. No, you're staying."

"I really think I would be a valuable resource for those initial deployments and that I could help the Fleet personnel get those procedures right. "

"No doubt you could," he replied, "But I need you here, and they need to take ownership of the process."

"Really, sir, I think—" she stopped as he shook his head.

"No, Ann. No."

He was in command. It was his decision. She stood and left without another word. Ron could have called her on her breach of etiquette, but he let it go. She was deeply disappointed, he knew, but he wasn't going to change his mind.

ISC Fleet HQ Intel Section
Fort Eustis, VA
Thursday, March 31, 2078, 0945 EST

Frances had taken delivery of the first SLIP scanner on March 22. It came with a bearded, short-haired, barely middle-aged hippie-geek named Lloyd. No last name, just Lloyd. His intensity as he introduced the instrument to Roger Cox and her reflected both his pride in having invented SLIP in the first place and his affection for this newest innovation. He was constantly after Roger for more information and to share the latest update with him.

Lloyd didn't quite know what to make of Frances. She was maybe twenty years older than he was, and while she seemed pleasant enough at first, she had a wicked tongue when you stepped over some line you didn't know was there. Adding to his unease was a growing realization that she was maybe smarter than he was, something Lloyd hadn't encountered since Forstmann. As the week went on, Frances began to see through the younger man's swagger and, almost in spite of herself, to like him. He, on the other hand, absorbed several verbal broadsides before he started to see the value of her insights, her questions, and her skepticism, that had at first baffled and angered him. Forstmann had told him, 'These people don't think like we do, and that's good,' but Lloyd was only now realizing just what the old man meant. You couldn't just tell her. You had to show her. You had to prove it to her. He started to see that this might be a useful exercise, not the pointless waste of time he had thought at first.

The scanner would cycle through the entire thousand channels twice a second, which was faster than Frances had anticipated. It had a second SLIP receiver attached, so if it detected anything on a channel, it would command the slave receiver to tune and record it while the scanner continued to search. She had to admit it was a pretty slick setup.

After a week, they had seen only Fleet traffic, nothing they could not identify. Frances sat dejectedly in Ron Harris' office with Rich Evans and Elias Peña.

"So, Frances, are they quiet, or are we wrong?" Elias asked.

She raised her hands in frustration. "I don't know. The fleet does maybe a dozen messages a day, less now than before Inor. Maybe we're just out of range. Maybe they're not talking right now."

"We'll just keep at it," Evans said encouragingly, "until we hear something or we come to some other conclusion. But don't be discouraged, Frances. We all thought this was plausible, and we still do."

She smiled wanly, clearly tired. Ron took notice of her fatigue. She had been working at least two shifts a day, sometimes as much as twenty hours.

"Let's take a break, Frances. Go home for a long weekend and get some sleep. Roger and the team will keep an eye on it and let you know if anything happens."

Frances shook her head. "It's my job, Captain. I can manage."

"It is your job, but it is also Roger's and everyone else's as well."

He looked at her steadily, forcing her to look him in the eye. Finally, she relented.

"You'll make sure they'll call me?"

"I will."

Slowly she nodded her assent. "OK, then. I could use a couple nights..."

Harris waited to see if there was more, and when she didn't continue, he answered.

"You are as dedicated as anyone I've ever seen, Frances. But get some sleep and come back on Monday, and we'll see where we are."

After she left, Rich Evans spoke.

"We all agreed the SLIP scanner idea was plausible, but that doesn't make it correct. Could we be just out of range?"

Ron leaned back in his chair. "The miners have sent SLIP messages from a distance of at least twenty or twenty-five light-years. If the enemy is anywhere within that range, we should be hearing them."

Evans shrugged. "Unless they're not talking, or we're off on what a SLIP channel means. Or they have some other technology we aren't aware of."

"Or those, yeah," Elias agreed.

Ron looked away. "I've never felt so stupid and helpless since I joined Intel. Weird."

After Ron's comment, they sat for a moment, digesting their situation. Finally, Ron shrugged, stood, and left the room. Peña was right behind him. Rich Evans sat a few more minutes, searching in his mind for what they might have missed. Suddenly aware he was sitting in Harris' office without Harris, he got up and headed back to his own space, still suspicious they had missed something.

Chapter 10

*Antares*
GJ 825
Saturday, April 2, 2078

Originally known as Lacaille 8760, discovered by the 18th-century French abbot Nicolas Louis de Lacaille, GJ 825 is the brightest red dwarf in Earth's sky. Unfortunately, that honor does not extend to being visible to the naked eye. Only 12.5 light-years away, it's just over half the size of the Sun, is much older, and generates only a small fraction of the Sun's light. As Terri looked out her bridge windows at the star, it *felt* old to her. She knew full well that was irrational, that she was projecting something onto an inanimate object, but still, there it was. It felt as if the universe was looking back at her in idle curiosity, having long ago seen wonders far greater than one small spaceship from an uninteresting planet orbiting a nondescript star.

*Antares* came in well inside one AU, slightly above the plane of the system. They anticipated that there would be no planets, as all previous efforts to find them had failed. And indeed, there were no planets of any significance. They found a few large rocks, the largest about half the size of the Moon, but it was mostly oversized gravel.

This was her first stop on her first command, and Terri was determined that they do the search correctly. FleetIntel had provided them the reflection spectra of the ships that had attacked Inoria, and the expectation was that other enemy ships or facilities would match those spectra.

They were so brazen, according to FleetIntel, that they likely would not be hiding themselves. Terri found that logic tenuous at best. Terri had read the after-action report of *Dunkirk*'s recent encounter with the enemy at GL 674, which supported this opinion, but she still thought there wasn't enough data to make such firm conclusions.

She was happy with the Surveillance Officer, Lieutenant Ryan Lewis, who had been a member of *Antares*' delivery crew. A *plank owner* in the old Navy parlance. He had taken time to brief her on how he would apply the *Liberty* spectra to the search at GJ 825, with appropriate corrections for the differing emission spectrum of each star. She hadn't thought of that, but as soon as he pointed it out, she realized it made sense.

Carol Hansen, to whom she had handed the Weapons Officer position, something usually held by a more senior officer, was crawling all over that department, literally and figuratively, becoming a reliable resource on both the weapons on board and their delivery systems. Her Weapons Maintenance Officer, the tall, blond Dane Warrant Officer Jon Swenson, complained once to Michael that with Hansen on board, he might as well stay in his bunk. But it was a good-natured complaint, reflective of how hard Carol was working to get up to speed on her new assignment. Everyone had questions about the young woman who got the battlefield promotion at Inor. Was she the real goods, or did she just happen to be with Michael when she needed someone?

The conclusion among the Weapons crew, so far, was that Hansen was the real deal. Her unassuming manner let them like her, and as she dove into the systems and weapons, sometimes literally, they came to respect her energy and her ability to listen to them and absorb new material. Terri Michael watched all of this with a sense of satisfaction, her initial impression of the young woman now confirmed.

So far, the only smudge on this pretty picture was an argument Hansen had gotten into with her Chief Tech, Emilio Guzman. Guzman was easily ten years Hansen's senior, another *Antares* original. He had come over from the US Air Force five years ago and was a master technologist on the weapons, the magazine system, and the rotaries. It had become an open shouting match in the magazine as Hansen pushed for a procedure change that Guzman's experience told him was not a good idea. The team watched in amazement as they fought.

"This would save us reload time, and that might save the whole damned ship," Hansen had said, her voice becoming strident.

"I am sorry, Lieutenant, but I can't agree with those changes," Guzman replied.

"Who's in charge here?" she blurted out.

Guzman's eyes flared in anger, and he shot back at her, "You are, Lieutenant. Start acting like it!"

She stepped towards him, the anger rising in her voice. "Just get it done, Chief." Guzman held his ground but lowered his voice just a little.

"As I said, Lieutenant Hansen, I can't agree to this. I don't think it's safe." She stared at him for a few very long seconds, pivoted on her heel, and left the Magazine. Guzman went to the captain shortly after this exchange, knowing that this conflict could not remain unresolved. He spoke firmly but with obvious respect for both the captain and the young lieutenant.

"She's very smart, Commander, but she's new. What might make sense to her on a theoretical level doesn't always make sense in practice." He went on to explain what Hansen had proposed and what his objections were. Michael took his point and called Hansen in to talk to her.

"Carol, if you raise your voice, you've lost the argument. You can have strong opinions, you can have disagreements with subordinates, but in this service, we have some of the smartest Chiefs and Techs that have ever put on a uniform."

"Yes, ma'am, I am aware of that."

"So, don't act like you're smarter than they are, better educated, whatever. You may well be, but that's not the point of leadership with this kind of crew. You can't force them. They have to want to follow. It's hard, and it's hardest when you're new."

"What is it that you want me to do?"

Terri was going to let Carol come to her own conclusion. She wasn't going to dictate the solution.

"What do you think is necessary?"

Carol deflated a little as she thought about it. "I need to repair the relationship with the Chief and the crew. I need to go down there, look them all in the eye, and apologize. I've always said if someone can't ever admit they're wrong, I can't trust them when they say they're right. "

"I agree."

"I really am sorry, Commander Michael. I lost my temper a little."

Terri smiled at her. "Fix this and move on, Carol. They're a good group, and you're a good leader. It'll be fine."

The next morning, she showered, put on a clean uniform, and walked to the tech's working area in the magazine. It felt a little strange, almost as if she was going on a date. But she knew she had to show them that she was serious and appearance mattered. As she entered, they snapped to attention, and she wilted just a bit.

"Oh, please don't do that."

They relaxed. She looked around at them, her eyes finally landing on Chief Guzman.

"I am sorry, Chief, for how I behaved yesterday. I still have a lot to learn about many things. It seems when and how to have a disagreement with someone of your stature is one."

She turned to the rest of the crew.

"And I apologize to you, as well. I really do aspire to be a better officer than I was yesterday."

Guzman smiled slightly, then walked up to her. "Thank you, Lieutenant. May I have a word?"

They walked out of the work area into the passageway.

"Yes, Chief?"

"If I may, Lieutenant? I've been at this a long time."

Carol found herself dreading what he was about to say, but she knew she should listen anyway. "Say what's on your mind, Chief."

He spoke quietly, sincerely. "Your argument was with me. Settle up with me, and I'll take care of the rest of the team."

"I wanted everyone to hear it. They all heard what happened yesterday."

"Yes, they did, which is regrettable. Remember, we're a team, too, you and I."

She nodded her understanding.

"Your mistake was letting yourself get so invested in something that you didn't think you could take no for an answer."

"I hadn't thought of it that way."

"Well, try to. This crew already respects you, Lieutenant, you don't have to try to impress them. Fact is, the less you try, the more they'll be impressed."

"I see."

"Up to now, you've been doing the right things, getting into the guts of the systems and learning from both the books and the equipment. You already have them in the right frame of mind. Keep that up, and they'll do anything you ask."

"And their Chief?"

Guzman gave her a wry smile. "Well, he sees plenty of good things in this new boss. She may yet work out."

"You'll let me know?"

"If she doesn't, you'll be the first to know."

"Thank you, Chief, and I really am sorry about yesterday. I'm not sure what happened."

Guzman smiled and shrugged. "That's easy. You're eager, you're smart, and you want to make things better. But you're not experienced enough yet to have that gut reaction that something that sounds good is a really bad idea."

"Commander Michael said something similar."

"Well, she's a very smart woman." He paused a second, then said, "I am not one to oppose you just to be difficult, Lieutenant. You're not the first sharp young woman lieutenant I've ever worked for. I get what you're trying to do. But if I say 'No,' I've got a reason. If you don't understand, then let's talk it out. In private if necessary."

"I appreciate that."

Guzman smiled. "Good. Done?" he said, extending his hand.

She took it. "Done."

She went back to her small office, and Guzman went back to his group of techs.

ISC Fleet HQ Intel Section
Fort Eustis, VA
Friday, April 15, 2078, 0900 EDT

Ron Harris was already on his second cup of coffee as he listened to Frances Wilson and Roger Cox report on the progress with the Sentinels and SLIP scanning. By this time, FPI had built about twenty-five SLIP scanners. Along with the one at Fleet HQ, three more were at Inor, Tranquility II, and Kapteyn Station. There would now be as many as four reference points to work with if they detected any enemy transmissions. The rest of the scanners were on their way to the asteroid belt ship factory for use on Sentinels.

Ann Cooper's team had finalized the hardware design requirements a few weeks earlier and were about to complete the software requirements. It was an inelegant thing, she thought, looking something like a six-sided coffin with google eyes, legs, and antennas that looked like cobwebs. They had initially planned for a massive supercooled IR detector, but after reviewing the *Liberty* IR data, they decided they could install six basic IR detectors and get the needed coverage at a fraction of the mass and cost. Now it was time to finish the behavioral requirements. Rich Evans and Elias Peña were also there.

"I am really concerned about operational security," Rich began. "Have we included a self-defense or destruct mechanism?"

"There is no explosive self-destruct, but if there is unauthorized access, the memory, controllers, and SLIP electronics will be destroyed," Ann replied.

"How, exactly?"

"Thermite capsules, initiated by a signal from the master controller," Roger answered.

"We can instruct it to do this remotely?"

"Not as currently designed. There's no technical reason we could not do that, but it was not part of our discussion."

"I think a remote kill capability would be useful. We can't know all the circumstances in which we might need it, but it won't cost much to do, and it might just save us," Elias agreed.

"Yes, sir, we will add that," Ann replied.

"What have you decided on the data dump schedule?" Elias asked.

"We had a couple of discussions on that, and we decided to make it weekly, with some random adjustment plus or minus."

Ron looked up from his notes. "How much of an adjustment?"

"Up to twelve hours."

Rich shifted in his chair. "Does that schedule reveal anything to them about us?"

Roger Cox answered for the group. "No, sir, we don't think so. A week is a human construct, seven rotations of the planet, but doesn't immediately correlate to anything observable from outside the solar system."

Frances then picked up the explanation. "We concluded that the schedule would not give them any information that would be helpful in finding us, which was the most critical question in our minds. Once they found us, they might make the connection, but even if they do, so what? Knowing what a week is doesn't give them a strategic or tactical advantage."

Satisfied with that, Ron Harris was ready to move along. "OK, sounds right to me. What about the alarm logic?"

"Those criteria are programmable from here; regular IR events, SLIP, and radio detections are recorded and sent weekly. There are criteria we can set for intensity and time where it will send the report sooner."

Elias looked at Frances. "Define sooner. Shouldn't it be immediate?"

Frances shook her head. "Strategic security. We don't want them to know what we think is important. It will send the data within twelve hours if it matches the alert criteria. That number is also remotely adjustable."

"And the poll logic?"

"We can ask any Sentinel to send a summary of events since its last report at any time. We can also ask it for the details of a particular event."

Evans still seemed unsatisfied. "How much of this is flexible?"

"Most all of it, sir. We're using the Fleet's standard hierarchical transaction processing engine so we can define conditions for events and actions to take on those events as necessary. That also means we can update criteria remotely."

Rich looked at Elias and nodded. "OK, good enough. Let's get it done and get these things moving."

Discussion over, Rich and Elias left the room. Ron Harris looked around at the team.

"Good work, all of you." And then he was up and gone as well.

ISC Fleet Officers' Quarters
Fort Eustis, VA
Friday, April 15, 2078, 1730 EDT

Meredith Harris stood at the stove, fretting over the lasagna. She could buy a decent prepared version in the store or online and, in a pinch, have it delivered by drone or autonomous surface vehicle in less than an hour. Lots of people she knew did that. But she never thought food like that tasted like anyone actually made it, and for Meredith, the work and care of preparing were as much of the loving of family and friends as the sharing of the meal itself. She remembered her mother's glowing stories of family gatherings at her great-grandparent's big house in the woods, and she wanted that warmth, that welcome, to radiate from her home, too. Even if that home was a cookie-cutter house on a former army base. While the house itself didn't matter very much to her, the feeling of being home with those she loved surely did.

Fiona had been there the night Meredith and Ron met while he was at the University, and she had watched, almost shared, as they fell so quickly and deeply in love. Ron made no secret that he wanted a full career, and Meredith unreservedly signed on as the wife of a Fleet officer. There were many weeks spent alone, time she used to finish her Master's or to work on whatever house they were living in at the time. Fleet being what it was, and until recently no war to fight, even when assigned to a ship Ron was usually gone for only a few weeks, then back for about the same time, then out again. When they were assigned to FPI in Idaho or HQ in Virginia, or he was teaching at SFU in Ohio, she saw him nearly every day. For a military wife, she knew this was pretty soft duty, and she was grateful for it.

Unlike many of his peers, Ron had no interest in 'man-toys' or other amusements, and so his paycheck went to the home and the family, less a few percent for his day-to-day expenses. She, likewise, had no need for expensive clothes or possessions or whatever the current fashion trend might be. They lived well but absent of extravagance. Meredith knew there would be a long life after the Fleet, and she was putting savings away every month, except when the kids or the house needed something right away. She and Ron talked about money just once a year when he got his raise or a promotion. She would let him know what was where and what it had done that year. The rest of the time, he didn't think about it much because Meredith had it covered.

She was tall, nearly six feet, just a couple inches shorter than Ron, and broad-shouldered for a woman. She had light brown hair, not quite blond, and unusual green eyes with flecks of brown that always seemed to have a glint of joy in them. She wasn't classically beautiful, but her smile could flood a room with light. She was expressive and open, and when Meredith cared about you, there wasn't much question in your mind about it, and when she hugged you, you surely knew you'd been hugged. The way she was, to be inside Meredith Harris' circle was a life-enriching experience.

She finally decided the beef and Italian sausage and marinara mix was acceptable and went on to layer the filling with seasoning, pasta, and cheeses. She gave it a final embellishment of herbs, and into the oven it went. She was pouring herself a tall glass of a favorite local red when Fiona arrived. If you were expected at the Harrises', you didn't dare ring the bell or knock: you just came on in and navigated yourself to the kitchen.

"Hi, Meredith!" Fiona called.

"FIONA!" Meredith yelled like she had just seen a long-lost sister. Meredith held the smaller, slightly-built Fiona for a few seconds, then released her with a kiss on the cheek.

"Jesus, Meredith, you're gonna crush me one of these days."

Meredith laughed. "Hmmm...no...break a rib maybe...wine?"

She poured generously, and they walked out of the kitchen onto the deck at the back of the house, into the warm but fading sunshine.

"No kids?"

"No, Mom took them for the weekend."

"How is G'amma these days?"

"She's doing well. Since Dad died, she's been able to see the kids more, and I think that helps her."

"No doubt. It was sad to see him gone so soon."

"Too soon. I miss him so much. But she loves chasing those three little kids around."

"And, indulging them?"

Meredith laughed again, almost spilling her wine. "Oh my God, let me tell you..." she went on to describe her mother's latest extravagance for her grandchildren. She had eight, but she never seemed to have trouble finding time for any one of them. They were the joy of her life, and she was a bright light in theirs.

Ron came out of the house somewhere in the middle of the second glass of wine, carrying a beer. Meredith held him perhaps even closer than she had Fiona, and he sat between the women.

Meredith looked at each of them in turn.

"You're both experts at covering your feelings, so, anything new today?" Fiona looked at Ron, who shrugged.

"Nope. Still nothing on the SLIP scanner. The Sentinels will be getting out there in a few months, but we haven't seen anything yet."

At the outbreak of the war, senior officers at or above the rank of Commander could request security clearances for their spouses. The theory was that they could talk more freely, including with colleagues, if they didn't have to exclude those nearest them from the conversation. This was one more issue where ISC Fleet differed from most military services, which would see this as a severe security risk. But, since the ISC Fleet's opposition was alien and unlikely to be present on the planet, there was minimal risk to operations. Some officers questioned the wisdom of this policy, but Ron didn't. For him, the benefits far surpassed any reasonable downside.

"But you still believe in these ideas, right?" she asked.

Ron looked out at the sunset a moment before he responded. "I do. But I do sometimes wonder if it's only because we couldn't think of anything else."

"We all bought off on it," Fiona pointed out, "even Forstmann. So, if it's wrong, there are a lot of people who were wrong with you."

"Yeah, I know. For once, failure can't be an orphan 'cause this one has a major paper trail. But it might be a bad case of groupthink."

"Which, of course, could get us all killed." Fiona finished coolly.

Now Meredith looked from one to the other. "I have known you both so long. I can't imagine two people I love and admire more. I mean it, but I still don't understand how you do it."

"Do what?" Ron asked.

"You talk about how millions, billions maybe, could be killed…sometimes you say it could happen tomorrow…so calmly, like this was a normal thing to talk about."

"For us, it is," Fiona answered evenly. "This is our job, Meredith. We work these problems because we can and because the world has, in effect, asked us to. We have to stay calm."

Ron nodded his agreement.

"And, to be fair, we've lost *Liberty* but no other casualties for us yet. We've met them twice now and kicked their proverbial ass both times. The Inori have suffered terribly, but most of us have never been there. Never even spoken to one.

They're a remote, intellectual construct for most of us, just slightly unreal. That distance helps. If I had seen a shipmate of mine killed there, like Terri Michael and Rich Evans and Carol Hansen and the rest did, I would probably feel more emotion about it."

Meredith was unconvinced. "Still...such a fearful risk...so many people..."

Fiona took another sip, then responded. "I am not as sure there is such a risk. Inoria is about the size of a large-ish city, something like Richmond or Cleveland or Des Moines. They sent six ships and still failed to completely destroy it, maybe because of *Liberty*, maybe not. But there are hundreds, if not thousands, of such cities all over the Earth. It would be a frightful effort for them to be able to make a significant attack on us."

Ron was less sure. "Unless they switch to nukes," he responded skeptically.

Fiona looked at him. "Hey, pal, try to remember it's *your* wife I'm trying to reassure here."

"Oh, in that case, please do go on!"

They laughed at themselves a little. It *was* hard to process sometimes the idea that they were in a real space war with friendly, if non-combatant, aliens and an unseen, unknown alien enemy. Fiona was no Polly-Anna, and for Ron, the sky wasn't falling, but at this moment, she was more hopeful about the eventual outcome than he was. For Ron, the lack of information on the enemy was an enormous and seriously dark cloud from which all manner of evil might fall in the next few seconds. Fiona saw the same cloud, but she also saw the swarm of ships around it, trying to hem it in and understand its size and real danger. They understood each other well, and together they made an effective and efficient team that CINC could count on.

With the growth of the Intel department, the rumor was that a star was in Ron's near future. Fiona had no comparable increase in her Plans group, so to her, it seemed unlikely that she would see one anytime soon. But really, she didn't care. The work was good, her staff was good, and to see her friend promoted said only good about him, not less about her.

*Antares*
En route Epsilon Eridani
Saturday, April 16, 2078, 0240 UTC

Carol awoke with a start, sitting straight up in her bunk. "Shit!" she said, a little too loud.

Her roommate, Medical Officer Doctor Marcia Soto, woke up, looked over at her, and turned back over.

"Not here, Hansen. It draws flies and lifers."

Carol didn't hear Marcia's version of the old soldier joke. "I may have blown

120

it, Marsh. How the hell could I be so *stupid*?"

"Hansen, I'm trying to be asleep right now, you know, like I was, like, *a minute ago!* What are we talking about?"

Carol had awoken from a nightmare about David and Rick Court. She couldn't quite piece it all together now that she was awake, but she still felt fear in her gut.

"Me, Marsh, we're talking about me being a complete idiot."

Soto rolled over to face her roommate. "You? An idiot?" she said incredulously. "Carol, again, what the hell are you talking about?"

Carol was awake now but still within the shadow of the nightmare and not yet fully adjusted back to reality. She flopped back down on her pillow, trying to catch her breath. She felt cold and realized suddenly that she was drenched in sweat.

"Never mind, Marsh. Go back to sleep," she said quietly.

"Oh, sure, no problem. You wake me up calling yourself names and expect me to just roll back over and float off?"

"Sorry, Marsh. Just a bad dream, I guess."

Dreams, she knew, were just dreams, not revelations. They were something the brain did every night. The intracranial drama we perceive is only one part of the brain trying to interpret what's happening elsewhere. She knew all of that, but as she looked around in the darkness, a few images flashed back to her mind. She could see hope in David's face and anger in Rick's. They stayed with her as she walked to the bathroom for some relief and a change of nightwear. When she flipped on the light, the images were suddenly gone, and reality snapped back into focus. Even so, the emotions flowing from both men, and herself, were hard to ignore. She looked at herself in the mirror.

"That thing you thought was trying to get out?" she said to her reflection. "Remember that? Well, honey, it's out now."

The message from her subconscious seemed clear: break free of her regrets about Court and take the risk to reach out to David. Her NetLink said 0245, but there would be no more sleep tonight. She dressed, grabbed her earphones and tablet with her books and music, and headed for the wardroom lounge. She could curl herself into a couch there, and no one would think anything of it. She needed time to think, but at least now she knew what it was she had to think about.

ISC Fleet HQ Plans Section
Fort Eustis, VA
Monday, April 18, 2078, 0730 EDT

Fiona had just arrived in her office when the phone rang. CINC's assistant, Noah Peters, was asking her to come to CINC's office. She dropped her jacket on the chair, picked up her tablet, and headed upstairs. She ran into Ron Harris on the way. They looked at each other with curiosity.

"Going to see CINC?" Ron asked.

"Uh, yeah. Noah call you?"

"Yup. Something's up."

They hustled into the CINC's offices. Noah Peters was standing outside the door, waiting for them. As they entered, CINC was at his desk. His assistant, Captain Patricia Cook, sat across from him. Deputy CINC Yakovlev was there, as was FleetShips Admiral Miles Sloane, FleetWeaps Captain Garrett Velasquez, and FleetSupply Captain Kathleen Barton. Fiona looked around as she entered, and it was clear that everyone was as puzzled as she was about why they were there. She heard the door close behind her.

"That's everyone, sir," Noah Peters said before taking a seat near the door.

"Very well." CINC took a deep breath. "Admiral Gerhard has been relieved," he said flatly.

Fiona could not help raising an eyebrow at the name. Gerhard had a reputation for borderline behavior with both peers and subordinates, but she hadn't heard of anything recently.

"I won't go into the details, but let's just say some aspects of his character have become a distraction."

*Well*, Fiona thought, *that's telling me without telling me.*

"There are issues in the Operations Section that I need to be addressed. I'm promoting Captain Cook and assigning her to run it."

Patty Cook sat very still in her seat on the left of the rest of the gathered officers. Fiona snuck a glance at her, wondering if she had just heard this herself.

"I made this decision last night. I informed Gerhard immediately and Captain Cook just this morning."

She had not seen CINC seething with anger like this before. The staff waited for him to finish.

"I brought you all here so you could hear the news directly from me and to ask for your support as Patty does what may be a tough job over there." He leaned back in his chair. "Are there any questions?"

Sloane, the most senior of the collected staff officers, spoke first. "Sir, we will all give her whatever assistance we can."

"Good choice, sir," Fiona heard herself saying.

She could see Patty Cook relax just a bit in her chair.

"Thank you. That's all for now," CINC said, dismissing them.

They stood, congratulating and commiserating with the new Admiral, wishing her well and offering any help she might need. Ron and Fiona headed back to their divisions together.

"Oh, man, who did Gerhard fondle this time?" Ron wondered.

Fiona smiled. "Long past time CINC dispatched that creep. Joanne will be pleased."

Ron was surprised. "She had a problem with him?"

Fiona leaned in, speaking into his ear. "He put his hands where they didn't belong, and she gave him a knee where it counted. He left her alone after that."

Ron smiled. "I can see that. Well, he got a knee to the career today. It's over."

"Yup."

As they arrived at the stairs, Fiona headed down to the Plans area, pulling Joanne into her office. She wanted to tell her personally before it became news.

*Sigma*
En route Rana
Monday, April 18. 2078

It was thirty-five light-years from GJ 3622, a red dwarf, to Delta Eridani, GJ 150, also known as Rana, a red giant. It was over a month in FTL, a dull, boring transit that would take the last week of March and virtually the entire month of April. David took the first couple of days off to catch up on sleep and then was back in the Intel workroom.

David completed his review of the GJ 3622 data by mid-April. They were all satisfied that there was no significant enemy presence there, at least, nothing on the scale of what *Liberty* had encountered at Inor. He had mixed feelings about the end of the review. Sure, it would mean less work for him and his team, but it also meant he'd have more time to think about other things that he'd been avoiding. His Father. His Mother. Carol. That jerk Rick Court. That local jerk Lieutenant Todd Boyd. Lisa Briggs seemed to be making a project of him, pulling him into card games or movies with other young officers, people who knew David from SFU or, at least, knew of him. Those times were a welcome relief for everyone from the boredom of the transit.

With the GJ 3622 data put to bed, the Intel crew started studying Rana. It is a red sub-giant, a bit more than twice the diameter of the Sun, with a mass about thirty percent higher. Years of remote examination had found no evidence of planets, but given that it was a giant, it was entirely possible that Rana had planets far enough out to be too small for remote detection. He was no astrophysicist, but he had his briefings and instructions, and he knew that as a by-product of this search, the Fleet was producing several lifetime's worth of observational data for real astrophysicists and astronomers back home.

## Chapter 11

*Antares*
Epsilon Eridani
Friday, April 29, 2078, 1030 UTC

Carol stood behind the Surveillance console, watching Ryan Lewis and Jayvon Dean search for a target. Commander Michael had specified an iron asteroid, at least a hundred meters in diameter (or length, they tend to be irregular at this scale) but not more than three hundred, as the subject of their first live-fire exercise. She didn't give them any reasons for her criteria because, well, they were arbitrary, and she had just kinda made them up on the spot. She really wanted to test the team's ability to find whatever she might ask them to find. Epsilon Eridani has two asteroid belts, and typically the irons are more prevalent closer to the star, so they chose to focus on the inner belt at around three AU. There was a Jupiter-class planet just outside the belt, so they confined their search to an area on the opposite side of the star. All of this was more or less part of the exercise: *find what I asked you to find in the area I said to look.* The odds were small that there would not be a target that met the criteria, but neither would it be quick or straightforward to locate. It would take some searching, and that was also part of the point.

They had spent the first few days at Epsilon Eridani looking for the enemy, as usual, but did not find anything suspicious. The initial search completed, Terri Michael had sprung the exercise on them, giving them twenty-four hours to find and strike the target she described. Ryan and Jayvon were now closing in on a few candidates that Intel Officer Jack Ballard had given them from their earlier search for the enemy. It felt slightly like cheating to exploit their pre-existing data, but hell, Michael had said 'find it' she didn't say 'find it without using the old data.'

So, they did.

Finally, Jayvon leaned back from his screen, pointing.

"OK, here is an iron. Computer says it's one-fifty long. It looks pretty lumpy, so it might be an aggregation."

"Solid or rockpile, Mister Dean, we'll kill it," Ryan answered.

"OK, designate that Alpha-one."

"Alpha?"

"Yeah, Alpha as in asteroid."

Ryan laughed. "Crap. I should have thought of that myself. OK, Alpha-one it is."

"There is another one, here—" he pointed to another dot on the display. "It's about two-twenty-five and looks less like a rockpile to me. Designate Alpha Two."

"Looks like there are a couple more..." Ryan began, then stopped. "But we have two good targets."

Carol walked back over to the Weapons station and had her techs select the two targets and designate preliminary weapons for each. At that point, all she needed to know was which target to strike and with what. When she returned to the Surveillance position, Ryan was hanging up the ship phone.

"Carol, you ready?"

"We are. Just need her to tell me which one and with what."

"OK, good. She's on her way now."

A minute later, both Commander Michael and XO James George arrived.

"Show me."

Jayvon looked at Ryan, expecting the senior officer to respond, but Ryan indicated that Jayvon should give the update.

"Yes, ma'am. We've located two targets which meet your requirements. Both are irons. One is about one hundred fifty meters long and looks to us like an aggregation. See here," he pointed to the display, "the surface is pretty lumpy."

"And the other?"

"Another iron, about two hundred twenty-five meters. To our eyes, that one looks more solid, but as you know, that's guesswork much of the time."

"Yes, I understand."

She walked back to confer with XO George and then came back and turned to Carol.

"Lieutenant Hansen, you have thirty seconds to execute an attack on Lieutenant Dean's target Alpha-two. I want two Lances and a Bludgeon. Go."

Carol hustled the thirty feet back to Weapons and gave the instructions to her techs. In twenty seconds, all three weapons were on their way.

"Not bad, Lieutenant." James George, standing close behind her, commented.

"Yes, sir. We did have the rotaries out with a variety of weapons, so we saved that time."

George walked back over to the Surveillance position to see the results of the attack. After about ten minutes, the asteroid lit up with the detonations of all three weapons. Carol was surprised at how bright the Bludgeon explosion was — several times brighter than the Lances.

"Wow, that was intense," she said to herself.

"Yeah, good word for it,'" XO George said to her quietly as he turned and left the Bridge.

ISC Fleet HQ Intel Section
Fort Eustis, VA
Monday, May 2, 2078, 1025 EDT

Frances usually spent the first couple of hours in the office reviewing the SLIP scanner results from the previous night. She wasn't quite sure why she did it, but it was something they used to do at NSA sometimes, and it just felt necessary to her. *Somehow, maybe,* she thought, *I might see something the computers don't.* As the channels moved in a steady flat line across her screen, a few Fleet transmissions appeared, all normal, well recognized, entirely routine. As she lifted her tea to take a sip, there was a small interruption in the steady line of the last two channels. It had been just a rumble on the line, nothing to trip the scanner to record. Static? Some other kind of interference? She ran the data back and replayed it twice, zooming in on those two channels. No, she wasn't imagining it. Frances picked up her phone and made a secure call to Jackson Hole. A sleepy voice answered.

"Good morning, Mrs. Wilson."

"Hello, Lloyd. I have a question for you."

She had never called him before, so Lloyd pulled himself out of bed, trying to get himself fully awake.

"What is it?"

"I've seen some interference, maybe static, on two channels. I can send you the data if you—"

"No, Mrs. Wilson," he interrupted, suddenly fully alert. "There is no such thing as static on SLIP. Any signal in any channel is artificial."

As Frances thought about the implications of that, Lloyd continued, "Send me the data, but if it's showing up in two channels, then maybe our channels are wrong: too wide or too narrow. I will get over to the office right away. Send me the data."

She hung up the phone and packaged up the scan data for transmission to FPI. That gone, she walked to Ron Harris' office.

"Hello Frances, good morning."

She skipped the pleasantries, as she often did when she had something else on her mind. Harris had long ago come to understand this was just how she was. She didn't mean to be rude.

"We might have something in the SLIP scan."

Harris looked up hopefully. "Really? When?"

"Last night. I thought it might be some kind of interference, but Lloyd says that can't happen. It has to be artificial."

"So, what now?"

"I want to get the other stations to look for this in their scans as well and report the time it was seen."

"You think it's a message?"

"Well, if it isn't natural and isn't ours, we need to process it and see."

"Proceed. We won't know anything for a couple of days, I know, but keep me posted."

She went to the Intel communications office and drafted a message to the SLIP scanners at Inor, Tranquility, and Kapteyn.

```
PRIORITY 207805021530UTC
TO: SLIPSTATION T, SLIPSTATION I, SLIPSTATION K
FROM: FLEETINTEL/WILSON
POSSIBLE MESSAGE NOTED HERE IN SCAN DATA CHANNELS 998 999
AT 207804302131 UTC.
REVIEW SCANS IMMEDIATELY FOR ANY CORRESPONDING ACTIVITY AND
REPORT TIMES TO ALL.
END
```

She stopped back at Harris' office.

"It's sent, Captain. As you said, it will be a couple days before we hear anything."

"Very well. Thanks, Frances."

She left his office and returned to her own small space. She looked again at the signal the scanner had detected. It really wasn't much more than a pebble in the smooth line of the scan data. An hour later, her phone rang.

"Hello, Lloyd," she answered.

"Mrs. Wilson, I think we may have something here. I'm getting the engineers that did the channels work with me back in, and we're going to see what we can figure out."

"Can you tell anything from what I sent?"

"Not really. We can use what we have to get a location, but if we want to get inside the message, we need to catch the content on a regular receiver."

"Yes, I understand that."

"But Mrs. Wilson, this means that we were right about SLIP. They are using it, and so we can use that against them."

"Well, Lloyd, let's not go too far. This could be some other species we are not aware of. It isn't necessarily an enemy signal."

There was an audible sigh on the line. "Really, Mrs. Wilson, you can be so discouraging sometimes."

Frances smiled. "I've had more time to make more mistakes than you have, Lloyd. I've had enough egg on my face over the years to make a thousand omelets, so I've learned to remain skeptical until the data is really in."

"A thousand omelets. Did you have to remind me I missed breakfast?" he said, laughing.

"Well, go get some because we won't know anything for a while unless the stations report on their own."

"Goodbye, Mrs. Wilson."

"Good day, Lloyd. Let me know if there is anything I can do for your team."

They hung up, and Frances went back to reviewing the scans.

ISC Fleet HQ Operations Section
Fort Eustis, VA
Saturday, May 7, 2078, 0900 EDT

The new Fleet Chief of Operations, Admiral Patricia Jane Cook, had already been in her office for several hours, weekend or not, and her third cup of coffee was cooling on her desk. Her close-cropped silver-flecked hair contrasted with her dark skin as she stared at the daily ship status report on her tablet. Her round face, with its pleasant, soft features, was a lie. She was as hard and demanding an officer as any in the Fleet, with a well-known intolerance for errors and delay. But on this day, she was more worried than angry. Unity Class Destroyer *Otbara*, her name the Russian word for 'Valor,' was overdue. She had made the required call leaving GJ 54.1, heading for her next stop, GJ 1061, just 3.8 light-years away. But that was ten days ago, and they had heard nothing more. Cook dropped her tablet on the desk and got up, headed for the outer office. Her assistant, LCDR Mark Rhodes, was working at his desk, also heedless of the weekend. Mark was still adjusting to his new Chief, who had been on the job less than a month. She dropped into the chair across from him. Rhodes had become accustomed to these unannounced arrivals, knowing they generally signaled an incoming salvo of problems for him to address.

"Ma'am?" he asked, inviting her to express what was on her mind.

"*Otbara*," she said flatly.

Rhodes leaned back in his chair, still looking at the admiral.

"I was looking at that yesterday. Ten days, is it?"

Cook nodded.

"In that case, ma'am, she's officially overdue."

Cook closed her eyes for a moment, thinking, then re-opened them.

"What do we have?"

Rhodes checked the current ship dispositions on his tablet.

"*Columbia* and *Antares* will be at Kapteyn later today. They would be the closest. Beyond that—"

"Never mind. Order them to proceed immediately to GJ 1061."

Cook stood as abruptly as she had arrived and disappeared back into her office, the door closing with a noise that was not quite a slam but far louder than the usual gentle thud. She sat for a moment before picking up the phone and dialing the Operations Center.

"CINC, please, this is Cook...Yes, sir...Sir, *Otbara* is overdue. I am ordering *Columbia* and *Antares* to GJ 1061 to investigate...no, sir. Nothing since the routine exit message from GJ 54.1...Yes, sir, I will...thank you, sir."

Mark Rhodes issued a short, direct, alarming message and sent it immediately.

FLASH 207805071400 UTC

```
TO: ANTARES, COLUMBIA
CC: CINCFLEET
FROM: FLEETOPS
OTBARA OVERDUE ENROUTE GJ 1061 ETA 207805011800
PROCEED IMMEDIATELY GJ 1061 FOR SAR
ADVISE OPS, CINC ON DEPARTURE
REPORT STATUS ON ARRIVAL
END
```

It would arrive at Kapteyn Station in fourteen hours and six minutes, just after 0400 UTC.

ISC Fleet HQ Intel Section
Fort Eustis, VA
Saturday, May 7, 2078, 1030 EDT

The data from the three other SLIP scanning stations had come in late Friday. Two had seen the same signal. Tranquility II had been offline at the time they would have seen the signal. Frances carefully entered the intercept times into the analysis program that FPI had provided. It spun for a few seconds and then displayed a location for the source of the signal. The display showed the likely position in Right Ascension, Declination, and distance in light-years. The astrophysicists tried mightily to get her to think in galactic coordinates and parsecs like they did, but she just looked at them and kept saying, "A parsec, that's what, 3.6 light-years, right?"

She looked at the coordinates on her tablet and carried it with her to the stellar position reference board outside Harris' office. She could hear him talking to the Chief of Operations, Admiral Cook. It was not good news, she could tell as he finished.

"Yes, Patty, we'll hope for the best. Thanks."

He hung up. She looked at the board, and her heart jumped when the location of the message corresponded to a single star. She was still smiling inwardly when Harris noticed her and came out.

"Something up?" she asked him.

"*Otbara* is overdue. They were headed for GJ 1061."

Frances' mood went from joy to pain, from the light of confirmation to the dark of dread.

"Oh God," she said, and Harris, who had started to leave, turned around.

"What is it?"

She looked at him, pain clear on her face.

"The message we talked about on Monday?"

"Did you get the other station's data?"

"Yes."

She was still just looking at him.

"And?" Ron was getting impatient, not understanding what was happening.

"GJ 1061."

Ron's face suddenly matched hers. They had an unknown message that correlated to the possible loss of a Fleet ship. His stomach suddenly a heavy stone, he walked back into his office and dialed Operations.

"Commander Rhodes, it's Harris. Is Cook still there?" He waited a few seconds for Cook to pick up. "Patty, stay put. Frances and I are coming over."

He hung up and took her arm. "Let's go."

"Cook?" she asked, surprised.

"Yep, we're going to read Admiral Cook in on our little project and let her know what you've found."

"But..." she started to protest, but Ron already had her elbow, and they were on their way to the Operations Section.

They walked the short distance to Operations, where Rhodes was waiting, standing just outside Admiral Cook's office. Frances, never one to pay much attention to her appearance, realized she was even scruffier than usual, this being a Saturday morning, but if she had to brief Cook, the Admiral would have to take her as she was. Personally, she really didn't give a damn.

Once in the office proper, Ron made the introductions. Rhodes turned to leave.

Ron stopped him. "Mark, I think you should stay for this."

Mark looked at Cook, who nodded, so he took a seat to her left, facing Ron and Frances.

"OK, Frances, read them in."

"Yes, Admiral."

She paused to gather her thoughts. *Better to take a second or two before starting than to sound like an idiot*, she always thought.

"We have been working on the premise that the enemy is likely using SLIP technology to communicate. Forstmann knows of no other faster-than-light communications technology. They have built a set of scanners, four of which have been deployed so far, hoping to detect an enemy signal and then locate it using time difference of arrival."

She paused for Admiral Cook to ask any questions. Cook looked over at Mark, and when there were no questions, Frances continued.

"For months we've seen nothing, and then a few days ago we saw a message in the scanner data. It was not recorded, not that it would have mattered much because I doubt we could have read it anyway."

She paused again. "I requested that the other stations look at their data..."

"Were you able to determine a location?" Cook interrupted.

Frances looked at her a second before answering, "GJ 1061."

"Shit," she said, leaning back in her chair. She then looked at Harris. "So why so long to get this intelligence to me?"

"I understand your frustration, Admiral," he responded, "But understand, this is the first signal we have seen. It didn't look like what we expected. So, the software that we intended to kick in to record it and send notifications didn't trigger. It was only through Mrs. Wilson's diligence that we found it. Once she saw it, it took time to ask the other stations to look and report their times. She determined the source location literally minutes ago. I came as soon as I could."

Patty Cook nodded, sitting back in her chair, accepting his explanation.

"Do you know what the message says?"

"No."

"Will you ever be able to break it?" she asked, hopeful.

"We will get nothing more from this signal. Time and length are all we have. I probably shouldn't speculate, but personally, I doubt we'll ever read them. If we can get enough traffic, we should be able to create a map of their organization, but that will take time."

"And why am I only hearing about this project now?" she asked Harris, curious.

"We weren't sure it was going to work. I wanted to keep expectations down and keep the operational security as tight as possible. Now that we have results, it makes sense to bring more people in."

Ron's tone was empathetic, not regretful. They had really done pretty well with the information they had, and it was just damned unfortunate that there was a delay just at the time Fleet ships were in the area. He didn't like the situation, but he didn't create it, and he was making the best of the crappy conditions he could.

"We need to send an update to *Antares* and *Columbia*. What can we say?"

"Let's just say 'reliable sources' indicate possible enemy activity at GJ 1061 and leave it at that, OK?"

Cook accepted this, and Mark went to get it transmitted. Cook turned to Frances.

"That will be all, Mrs. Wilson, thank you."

"Yes, ma'am." Knowing a dismissal when she heard it, Frances left, closing the door behind her. She thought about waiting for Harris but decided against it and headed back to Fleet Intel.

"Captain Harris," Cook began, "Are we sure that this won't happen again?"

Ron sat a bit straighter in his chair. By referring to him formally in private, Cook made it clear that this was not a casual conversation.

"Admiral, I firmly believe that in time our engineers will refine this technique to a higher level of reliability. If you're asking me if we could still miss something like this in the next few days or weeks, the answer is yes. We have only just identified this signal, and it will take time for them to get to the root of it. Meantime, the other stations are actively watching for similar signals, and they will proactively report if they see something."

"That's a nice speech, Captain, but I have a fleet to operate, and I need to be confident that they are working with all the information possible."

"It's no speech, Admiral. It's our fleet, too. Mrs. Wilson is working long hours six or seven days a week on this. The rest of my staff is equally dedicated to this effort."

As he paused, Cook leaned back in her chair and nodded, looking out the windows at the blue sky.

"I would also point out, Admiral, that I came here the moment the location of the signal was identified. There was no delay from the moment we learned that to when you heard it. I think that speaks to your concerns."

She looked back at him. "I never lost a ship before, Ron. I don't want to make a habit of it."

Ron nodded and responded with a quieter, understanding tone. "Yes, Patty, I see that. I know people on *Otbara*, too. But, first, we can't be sure she's lost yet. Second, if she is, she won't be the last. We can't get through this war without paying a price."

"How long has this monitoring been going on?"

"Late March."

Cook's face reflected her surprise. "So, two months, and this is the first signal we've seen?"

Her skepticism hung in the air.

"Correct."

"And we still think this is a worthwhile effort?"

Ron now sat back and looked across at the Admiral. "Firmly. Don't forget that they just got a beating they could not have anticipated at Inor. Then *Dunkirk* slapped them again. Personally, I think they're deliberately being quiet while they try to figure out what they're up against."

"I see."

"There is also the potential that there is a range issue. Meaning, that they are too far away for the SLIP scanner to detect them. I don't believe that, but it is at least theoretically possible."

"And how will we know?"

"Well, this signal detection would support the idea that they are not so far away, but truthfully, only time and experience will tell us."

"So, you're telling me to be patient and trust you?"

"Yes, exactly."

"I'm not very good at either, Ron. You know that."

"I do, Patty, I do. But I need you to support this plan. I think it has the potential to crack the war wide open."

"Really?"

"Yes. If we can get a handle on their communications, even if it's intermittent, we may be able to identify where they are and where they come from. If we can identify their homeworld, we may be able to bring this war to a rapid conclusion."

"I like the idea of going for the throat," she said with intensity.

"Yeah, me too."

They sat for a moment, then Cook stood. Harris followed suit.

"Thank you, Ron. I am sorry if I was harsh before."

"I would have expected no less from Operations, Admiral, no offense taken."

"Good."

Cook extended her hand, and Harris took it, then he was out the door and headed back to his section. As he walked past Frances' office on the way in, he heard her voice.

"I am happy to see your head is still on your shoulders, Captain."

He stepped back and gave her a thumbs-up gesture, then walked on to his office.

## Chapter 12

Kapteyn Station
Midday, Saturday, May 7, 2078

The Fleet's newest star base was in the southern constellation Pictor, near the red sub-dwarf Kapteyn's Star, almost thirteen light-years from Earth and about ten light-years from Inor. Like most all red dwarfs, Kapteyn's Star is too faint to be visible from Earth, so it didn't get a name from the Greeks or Romans or even an obscure astronomical designation as part of Pictor. Kapteyn Station was much bigger than Tranquility II, with more space to provide rest and relaxation for visiting crews. Off-ship hotel space was available, and a small-town 'Main Street' of restaurants, pubs, and shops gave it a feeling of being back home. The sun in the 'sky' above Main Street was not the familiar yellow-white of the Sun but rather the yellow-orange of the dwarf star, a strange color to human eyes.

Carol was not on watch as *Antares* came into Kapteyn Station in the early hours of May 7. Commander Michael had insisted on bringing the ship in herself, even if 'bringing her in' really meant watching the Nav computer do it. Carol knew Dan Smith would be coming in on *Columbia* just a few hours after they docked, a happy accident of scheduling she was immensely grateful for. There had been so much on her mind, so much weighing on her heart, and she wanted desperately to talk to Dan.

It was almost 1300 before *Columbia* docked, but as soon as Carol thought they were within range, she sent Dan a regular text message from her phone: *Corner Bar, 1800.* He would know what she meant, and unless she heard back, he'd be there. As it was, he quickly responded *Wilco,* which made her chuckle to herself. *Funny how all those old war movies we watched all night come out in the way we talk sometimes.*

She was in the bar by 1745, anxious to be there when Dan arrived. This conversation was crucial to her, and she was still a little nervous about it. When Dan came, five minutes early, they embraced for a long time before they even began to talk. It was the embrace of old friends who had shared much and could not have been sure they would ever embrace again. Carol had already ordered wine for herself and the house IPA for Dan. He was particular about his beer, but at Kapteyn Station, there were limited IPA options. One, to be precise. Back at the University, their group had a reputation in the local pubs for strong brews, but try as she might, they all tasted like rat piss to Carol. Or, rather, what she imagined rat piss might taste like. They kidded her incessantly about her cold, dry whites and the occasional Moscato, but they made damn sure she had one while they were comparing alcohol levels and IBUs.

They talked about shipmates and war experiences for a half hour, killing two rounds. *Columbia* had begun the war standing watch outside Pluto's orbit, positioned between Earth and Inor. There was no real good reason to pick that spot, but in the initial days of the war, no one had a better idea, either. Once the details of the Inor attack became clearer, they pulled back closer to Earth. If the enemy could exit FTL within the Moon's orbit, there was not much point hanging out in the Kuiper belt.

"So, did you ask Linda?" she finally asked, excited about his future.

"I did, and she said yes."

"Smart girl. Is there a date?"

"Yeah, next summer at the Fleet Resort. We've booked a set of quarters, so plan to be there."

She smiled. "Unless the war has other ideas, I will be there."

Dan looked at her steadily as he turned the conversation to more serious matters.

"I was very proud of you, Miss Carol, after Inor. I saw Larry Covington shortly after, and he said the same. Michael was right to promote you."

She looked down, sheepish almost, smiling at the compliment in spite of herself.

"God, Dan," she said quietly, "I was scared shitless..." After a moment, she continued, "And I do mean literally: I didn't go for days."

That got them laughing again, but her face faded from the amusement back into a more somber expression. Dan let it settle for a moment and then asked the question her face was begging him to ask. "OK, Carol, what's eating at you?"

She smiled a little, revealing her stress. "I need to talk, Dan. I need your help to think this through. Old friends are the best, right?"

He reached across and took her hand, gave it a squeeze, and let go. "They are. And take your time. I have all night if you need it."

"I might," she deadpanned. After a moment, she continued, quiet, almost contrite. "I know Court's an ass. I know I was an ass to attach myself to him," she finished accusingly.

Dan inclined his head thoughtfully. "Yeah, I knew Court was a jerk from the start. I never quite got what you saw in him."

"I thought I could, I don't know, bring something positive out in him."

"Like a conversion?"

She frowned. "Nothing so spiritual. He was so smart and charming at first. It was hard to see what was behind the mask. But there was no changing him. Foolish, I know."

"We were all young, Carol. Don't be too hard on yourself."

"Young?" she responded angrily. "We only graduated last year, for God's sake!"

Dan held her eyes and responded quietly, speaking to both her heart and her head.

"All of that was before, Carol. You, especially, but all of us, really, are far older today than we were a year ago. Decades older."

She looked away for a moment, then back.

"I'm getting a little drunk," she observed, looking at her empty glass.

"I'll order another round!"

Again, she laughed, but the somber face quickly returned. "I have a problem, Dan, a real problem." She sounded serious, despite her three glasses of wine.

"Yeah?"

"I think I'm in love." The last two words seemed to catch in her throat as if she was afraid to let them out into the open.

"This is a problem?" he asked with a wry twist at the end.

"Dan! I think I'm in love with David."

Dan leaned back and smiled. It confused and annoyed her a little until he leaned back in and spoke quietly.

"Well, my dearest Carol, it's about time."

She looked at him in shock. "What?" she sputtered. "What do you mean—"

"When did you see him last?" he interrupted her.

"I haven't seen or heard from him. It's just, somehow, I just all at once knew. You already knew?" She didn't wait for an answer. "I hate this feeling. I am not some damn drippy female. Why am I sitting here blithering in a bar?"

He frowned as she mocked herself. He leaned forward again and spoke earnestly.

"Because this isn't about courage in combat or strength of leadership. It's about your heart, and facing what's in there can be harder for some than a firefight."

She looked away again, quiet, only focusing back when the pizza arrived. She killed a whole slice before speaking again. As Dan watched her, he could almost see her organizing her thoughts, prioritizing her feelings, and considering her options.

"I am afraid," she said intensely. "Imagine that. Terrified." Her eyes flared at the word. "I don't know what he'll say. We spent so much time together, but I don't know how he would feel about this."

Dan watched her for a moment, wondering if he should say what he was thinking or not. He decided he should. "Carol, I don't know anyone who's ever loved another person more than David does you."

She looked at him in surprise, pizza sauce running down the corner of her mouth. She suddenly felt it and grabbed a napkin to wipe it away before continuing.

"I thought he didn't feel like that about...I mean...I always admired him...and we got along great...but...he never said...never did...anything to say that...I didn't think I was, I don't know, smart enough or pretty enough for—"

"Carol!" Dan interrupted her. "You're selling yourself, and David, way short.

You're more than you say, and I think you know that. But David is, too. You need to give him a little more credit."

She started to argue, then thought better of it. She was calming down a little. "Do you know how long?"

"Last time he was as drunk as you, he told me the first day of Freshman year. I believed him."

"Oh my God. He'll be pissed you told me," she said, mock-threatening.

"Not if this works out like I think it will."

And again, they laughed.

"But he never did anything about it," she said, confused.

"Didn't he?" She just looked across at him, not understanding. "He invited you into the study group, right?"

"Yes."

"He sat up with you all night working on courses you had problems with?"

"Yes, but I helped him, too." She was starting to see where this was going.

"Right. When you had a crisis with Court or school or whatever, he was there to listen, to support you, encourage you?"

"Yes."

"What does that sound like to you?"

She didn't answer, so Dan went on. "David is methodical. He would not have approached you to start a relationship unless he was pretty sure you were as interested in him, too. You were with Rick, and he respected that. He would never have cut in on a classmate."

"That some unspoken male code of honor?" she asked sarcastically.

"No, it's just who he is: his personal code of honor, I guess. His sense of integrity, maybe. If I had felt about you like David does, I'd have cut in on that asshole without a second thought. But he couldn't do that, Carol. He could not risk turning you away from him. He had to be who he is and hope it worked out in the end."

"Will it?"

"You're asking the wrong person."

He waited for a response, but she only nodded slowly, ripping off another hunk of pizza.

"You know, Carol, we've seen a lot together. You and David are family to me. I have watched the two of you together for years, and I have believed for a very long time that you and he are two halves of the same person. You won't be happy with anyone else, and neither will he."

There was a long silence as she thought, her mind still racing as she erased another slice, and Dan sipped his beer.

"OK, so what do you do now?" he asked her quietly.

"Cut Court loose for good, then figure out how to let David know, and figure out how to get to him. Too bad there's a war on."

"That is an inconvenience, for sure. Where is he?"

"*Sigma*, with Commander Davis."

"Well, they're doing the random search like the rest of us. You should be able to get a SLIP to him."

"Yeah, if I could just figure out what to say."

"You're Carol Hansen, Carol. You'll figure it out," he said, starting to laugh.

She kicked his shin under the table. She set down her wine and slice and looked at him for a long time. "Dan, I'm not sure I would get through this without you."

He smiled and raised his glass. "To our hearts and those we hold there. May we both see them again soon."

She lifted her glass to his, tapped it, and responded, "Meanwhile, we fight."

Dan nodded. "Meanwhile, we fight."

*Columbia*
Kapteyn Station
Sunday, May 8, 2078, 0416 UTC

The lights coming on in his quarters shocked Dan Smith out of a sound sleep, his head still a little fuzzy from his evening with Carol Hansen. The XO was over his bunk, shaking him awake.

"Sir?" he asked groggily.

"Smith! Get your ass up. We are out of here in half an hour."

Smith blinked his eyes open, and the XO came into focus. "Half an hour?"

"Yeah. *Otbara* is overdue, and we get to go look for them. *Antares*, too. I need you on the Nav."

Now fully awake, he looked up at the XO. "Yes, sir. Be there in...uh...right away."

"Very well. Try to wake up in the meantime, OK?"

That said, the XO was off to roust a few more section chiefs. Dan got up, gave his face a quick wash at the small basin in his cabin, and started dressing. His roommate, the Weapons Maintenance Officer, rolled over and covered his head with his pillow. *Overdue*, Dan thought, *probably means dead.* With that ugly thought hanging in his head, he finished dressing, flipped off the light, and headed for the Bridge.

*Antares*
En route GJ 1061
Sunday, May 8, 2078, 0530 UTC

Carol woke up with a start, suddenly aware that *Antares* was underway and in a rush. Looking at her clock, she saw the early hour, her typical wake-up time, but today she had the day off, in port no less, with a brunch date with Dan to finish up their conversation. But obviously, they were no longer in port. She sat up on the edge of the bed to try to clear the confusion bouncing from side to side in her head. She had a small headache, too. *The wine,* she thought to herself.

"*Otbara* is overdue," she heard a voice say quietly, its Chula Vista roots still audible. "We're going to try to find her."

She finally shook herself fully awake and could process her roommate's comment.

"It's almost four days, so Michael decided not to roust you. We've been underway about an hour."

"Shit," Carol swore softly.

Marcia sat on the edge of her bunk. "So how did it go with Smith?"

Carol looked at her with a scowl not fully visible in the darkened room.

"Can't think about that now, Marsh. Did Michael come looking for me?"

Marcia shook her head, not that Carol could see it. "No. I heard them running around just after oh four hundred getting some of the division chiefs up, so I went out. George said to let you sleep, and he'd get with you in the morning."

"Good, thanks," she paused, "Four days...shit..."

"That's twice in five minutes, Hansen. You're going to spoil that choir-girl rep if you keep this up," Marcia kidded her.

Even in the dark, Carol managed to hit Marcia with her pillow. She got up, dressed, and headed for the Bridge before 0600 to see what she could do.

The time with Dan had gone well, even if she didn't have time to bring Doctor Marcia Soto up to speed, and part of her was thankful and relieved to have a clearer heart. But the rational part of her knew that the whole question of who to love and how and when might just be moot. They would have to live through the war for it to matter. *Or would they?* She suddenly asked herself, making the final turn into the narrow corridor to the Bridge. *Might it not be enough to love each other right now, even if it was only until one of them was gone?* No time for that, she quickly decided. *Meanwhile*, she repeated to herself, *meanwhile, we fight.*

Carol finished up a Conn shift for an officer who hadn't had any sleep. XO James George remained on the Bridge until Terri Michael came out of her duty cabin around 0900.

The day had that odd 'hurry-up-and-wait' feeling to it. They had scrambled to get off Kapteyn and underway as soon as possible. Now that they were moving, there was little for them to do for nearly four days. For Carol, those days could not move fast enough. They were running in low-EMR mode, so anything she wanted to say to David Powell would just have to wait until this mission was over.

*Antares*
GJ 1061
Tuesday, May 11, 2078, 2242 UTC

XO James George stood behind the Surveillance position as they exited FTL travel and the universe came back into focus around them. They deployed every sensor, and double staffs were making sure they didn't miss anything. It was only a short transit from Kapteyn, but it felt much longer from the loss of the expected crew leave time. Every member of the crew had been looking forward to the break. Terri Michael had tried to make the best of it, loosening some of the watch requirements and looking the other way at some games and parties. It wasn't the same, she knew, but it was what she could give them. A day from GJ 1061, the word went out that it was time to get back in line. Aside from some minor grumbling, the crew responded well. By twelve hours from their destination, they had the ship configured and ready to fight.

They digested the follow-on message from Fleet Operations: 'reliable sources' saying that there was enemy activity near their destination. They wondered what that term might actually mean but, in the end, decided it didn't matter. They took the warning seriously, and they would be on guard when they arrived.

The Surveillance display lit up almost immediately. The Surveillance Watch Officer, Ensign Jayvon Dean, turned to the command position.

"Multiple enemy ships, Captain. Working to resolve their positions."

Carol didn't wait. She immediately deployed the rotary launchers. "Captain, we are ready to shoot as soon as we get targets designated."

"Very well, Weaps." She turned back to Surveillance. "How long, Ensign?"

Dean paused a moment before responding. "A few minutes yet, Captain. They're pretty far away."

Michael quietly cursed in frustration, but she knew the young officer was doing all he could. It took time to integrate the passive data they were gathering and calculate an accurate position for the enemy. As she watched, the target list on the Surveillance display began to light up. Five targets. Jayvon got up and headed over to the captain.

"OK, we have good data on those five now, Captain. We're linked up with *Columbia*, so they use what we see, and we use what they see."

Carol had joined the conversation. "We're up with *Columbia* as well, Captain."

"Fine. Mister Dean, any evidence of *Otbara*?"

"Not yet, Captain. We're still looking, but it might take some time — if she's even here."

"Any indication the enemy is aware of us?" George asked.

"Too soon to tell, sir. We're still more than an AU away from them."

"Eight light-minutes," George said quietly to Terri Michael. "Too damn far."

"It is," she responded, "But we'll have to work our way in slowly. Meantime we need to check in."

She walked over to the Comm station. "First, tell *Columbia* that I am sending the check-in message. Then, send a flash to CINC and OPS...uh...On arrival, GJ 1061 detected five silver dots. We are monitoring and preparing an attack. No sign of *Otbara* yet. Will advise."

The tech quickly transcribed and sent the message.

"It's gone, Commander."

"Very well. Nav! Turn us thirty degrees right and ten down!"

If the enemy was listening on SLIP, she wanted to change course to throw them off. *Columbia* made a corresponding move, left and up, to also clear the area where they had transmitted. They continued for a long half-hour, cruising as quietly as possible and watching the enemy. The eight-minute delay was maddening to Michael, but she did not want to get them any closer until they had a better picture of what the enemy was doing. Finally, she walked to the Surveillance station.

"Show me what you have."

Ensign Dean pointed to the Surveillance display where she could see the five targets, each with a red circle around it. They were slightly more than dots but not large enough to see in any detail. They appeared to be in an ellipse, more likely, as Dean explained, a circle seen from near the edge, fairly close together.

"What's nearby?"

"There is a rocky planet near where they are, but I don't think they're in orbit. This star is so small, less than a fifth the mass of Sol, it wouldn't take much power to just hang there."

"Anything habitable?" Carol asked.

Dean shook his head. "No. The rocky planets, we've seen three so far, are all either too close or too far."

Michael looked at the display for a moment, seemed to make up her mind and turned to Comms.

"Get me a voice link to Commander Reynolds on *Columbia*."

In a moment it was up, and Terri sat in her command chair to talk to *Columbia*'s CO.

"It's Michael."

"Good evening, Commander," Dave Reynolds responded.

"We need to make a plan. These are pretty fat targets, but they sent us here to find *Otbara*."

"Some of us here are wondering if that's what they're hanging around," he said grimly.

"Yes, that thought had crossed my mind as well."

"If they have her or her crew, it could be a problem for us."

"It could. And they've had plenty of time to break them."

"Impossible to know at this point."

Terri didn't want to think about what might have happened, or be happening, to the *Otbara* crew.

"So, let's concentrate on what we do know. We have five targets."

"Yes, and I think we should strike them as soon as we can. I don't think this is a time to loiter and watch."

Michael paused a moment to consider Reynold's words. Moving quickly might work, but speed sometimes meant you missed something important, and that could get you killed, even in peacetime.

Without waiting for her reply, he continued.

"I will take *Columbia* right down into them, nail them with a volley, and then get the hell out. You could do the damage assessment from a few light-seconds away and then see what needs to be cleaned up. Once we're rid of these bastards, we can look for *Otbara* at our leisure."

Terri hesitated just a moment before deciding for herself that a quick strike was probably a good idea.

"That sounds reasonable. We'll be ready."

They agreed on the schedule and the course *Columbia* would take in and out. The only change was that Michael wanted to get *Antares* in place before *Columbia* dashed in.

"Conn, set minimum EMR. Nav, put us two light-seconds outside the enemy ship group, same inclination, before 0100."

The Nav officer looked at his commander for a long moment before turning back to his workstation and setting the course. Terri impassively returned his gaze. It took a minute or two before he could turn back to her.

"Ready, Commander."

"Execute."

Carol watched this exchange from the Weapons station, keeping her own deep concerns to herself. They were getting awfully close to those enemy ships. Close enough to get burned if they weren't careful. She got up and walked to the command position. Michael looked hard at her as if expecting an argument.

"Something to say, Lieutenant?" she asked stiffly.

"No, ma'am. I just thought it might be advisable to swap in some Spartans."

Michael's stern face eased just slightly. "Yes. Reload with half Spartans and half Lances."

"Yes, ma'am," she said quietly as she turned back to her position. She gave the orders, and the crew retrieved the rotaries and reloaded them with Spartan self-defense missiles and Lance attack missiles. During the short transit, Surveillance Officer Ryan Lewis arrived and began pacing nervously behind the Surveillance position, exchanging several intense conversations with Jayvon Dean. They came out of FTL exactly where planned, and the silver dots were no longer dots. The image processors made quick work of the new data, announcing on the main display what they were facing.

"Three Type IV's and two Type I's, Commander."

Carol had the targets identified and missiles assigned to each. With twelve Lances loaded out, she assigned two to each target. She turned again to the command position.

"We have good positions on all five, Commander. I've designated two Lances each, and we can shoot at any time. Minimum flight time profile."

A few minutes passed as they waited for *Columbia* to make its attack at 0100. Dean suddenly stood very still, staring at the Surveillance display.

"Something is happening..." he said, almost to himself. Terri Michael could see it, too.

"Nav! Turn ten degrees towards the enemy, and then give me 100 meters per second more." The ship moved slightly, then sped up. As they watched the visual display, they could see the enemy ships re-orienting, three turning in the direction of *Antares*, and the other two turning in another direction. Dean looked at the time: 0100 exactly. The Surveillance display lit up with white circles.

"Multiple IR flashes on the enemy ships, Captain. Look like Lance explosions to me."

*Columbia*
GJ 1061
Thursday, May 12, 2078, 0100 UTC

Dan had plotted the approach as the captain had requested, with the breakout from FTL just 1000 kilometers from the estimated position of the enemy ships. Their Surveillance crew, working with Antares, had resolved the enemy's position to about 100 kilometers. They had argued about how close to cut it, and Dan's caution had finally won Commander Reynolds over. It would not do to find themselves too close, or worse, to exit FTL beyond the targets. The Lances would strike in a few minutes, and unless the enemy was quicker now than they had been at Inor, those weapons would not miss.

The breakout occurred about 1100 kilometers from the enemy ships. They lit them up for a few seconds with radar to precisely define their position, a tactic Dan had opposed but Reynolds had insisted on, and then fired fifteen Lances as fast as they could. Columbia then shut down her radar and maneuvered, turning thirty degrees 'up' from the plane of the system and fifteen away from the enemy position.

Shortly after the radar went dark, the Surveillance display lit up with flashing red circles. Surveillance Officer Lieutenant Melinda Hughes called out, "IR transients from the Type I's, Commander. Missiles headed our way."

Reynolds paused a moment, considering his options. "How many?"

"Eight, so far."

"Weaps! Let's get some Spartans out there!"

Lieutenant Victor Shoemaker sweated as he managed the reload, filling one rotary with Spartans and the other with Bludgeons in case they needed to hit the enemy ships again. He dispatched all twelve Spartans as soon as he could and started another reload. As he did, the Surveillance display delivered more bad news.

"Eight more launches from another Type I, Captain," Melinda called.

"Weaps – let's get another load of Spartans out there!"

"Working, Captain."

As the reloaded launcher started to move back out, the Spartans already launched were intercepting the incoming enemy weapons, but something was very wrong.

Melinda saw it first. "That was too close! Captain! Those incomings must be faster than we thought!"

"Time for our strike?" Reynolds asked.

Victor looked at the counter on his screen. "Thirty-five seconds."

Reynolds, deciding he needed vision more than stealth, ordered the radar back up.

"Light the incomings up, Lieutenant Hughes, narrow band. Nav, I will need another maneuver as soon as—"

The explosion of an enemy missile somewhere aft cut him off. Dan, surprised but not immobilized, moved the ship slightly down and right and added fifty meters per second. There was a second explosion, the impact more forward this time. The ship status display was now on the main screen, and there were several sections now showing yellow: damaged, losing air, but not dead.

Melinda looked in surprise at her now-empty radar display.

"Radar's gone, Commander. Looks like the last hit took the—" a third explosion, now very close to the bridge, stopped her report.

"Smith! FTL now!" Reynolds yelled.

Dan reset his controls, set a 'good enough' course away from the enemy, and engaged the Forstmann Drive at full power. Two more explosions damaged the ship aft as they were turning, but as they bugged out, the Forstmann field's flood of anti-gravitons effectively redirected the last few threats, and there were no more hits.

Safe for now, the Bridge was a chaos of noise and activity. Weaps was shouting back at Reynolds, Comms asking over and over if they should send a report to Fleet. Damage alarms were sounding for the hits she had taken. Reynolds looked frozen, staring at the status display. After a few seconds, he seemed to regain himself. The damage control teams, composed mostly of maintenance and engineering staff, were already on the move. They could see which areas needed attention first, and the XO had already left the Bridge to supervise their work.

There were casualties, and the medical team was scrambling to get them out of the compromised sections of the ship and into treatment. After a minute, Reynolds collected himself.

"Comm, send to CINC, OPS, and Antares: Have taken five hits. Retiring FTL to evaluate status."

The Comm tech took only a few seconds to draft and send the message.

"It's done, sir."

"Very well." He sounded tired, more tired than one would think.

*Antares*
GJ 1061
Thursday, May 12, 2078, 0105 UTC

"Holy shit," Carol said under her breath, seeing how quickly the enemy missiles had crossed the short thousand kilometers to *Columbia*. If they could shoot that fast, it would change things, and not for the better.

"Any more launches from the enemy?" Michael asked.

"No, ma'am."

The Surveillance team zoomed the optical telescope's view to get details of the damage to the enemy ships. Two were clearly venting now, something that seemed characteristic of the enemy's construction. The working theory was that they were using fuel cells for power, not nuclear reactors, which everyone thought was strange. It might, however, provide some explanation for the size of the enemy ships. It would take an enormous amount of fuel to power a Forstmann drive in that way. The other three seemed intact, but they saw skin damage on all of them. The IR sensors were seeing a heat plume, again now typical of O2/H2 venting and then combining in the light of the star.

"Hansen!" Terri Michael called.

Carol got up and headed for the command position. Terri came down, and they walked together to the Nav station.

"OK, Weaps, let's get ten Bludgeon's loaded out on the port launcher."

Carol turned and signaled to her techs to get the launchers in and load the Bludgeons.

"Alex," Michael said, addressing the Nav officer, "I'll need a move towards the enemy, say, fifteen degrees. Stay on the plane and drop maybe fifty meters per second."

Alex Williams nodded his understanding.

"OK, we're going to drop ten Bludgeons with a five-minute delay. Then we'll maneuver—"

Conn officer Miho Ito interrupted her. "SLIP Message from *Columbia*, Captain."

"What does it say?"

*"Have taken five hits. Retiring FTL to evaluate status."*

Michael looked at Dean, who responded, "That matches what we saw. The surprising part was the time: something like forty-five seconds from launch to impact. I know Lieutenant Ballard will evaluate it later, but their stuff is faster than we had thought."

"Well, at least they're alive to retire. OK, back to our plan: we'll maneuver, then the Bludgeons will execute. Lieutenant Hansen, after the five-minute delay, let's set them for a minimum time course. Once they hit, I want another maneuver to take us up further out of the plane."

She paused to take a breath and think, then she looked directly at Alex Williams.

"Have an FTL retreat course ready to go. If I call for FTL, I'll want it immediately."

"Yes, ma'am. We'll be ready."

"How long, Carol?"

She looked over at the Weaps station. "We're almost ready, ma'am. Rotaries are moving back out now."

"OK, Nav?"

"I just need a minute to set the courses, Captain."

Terri looked around the group. "Questions?"

There were none.

"OK fine. Alex, when you're ready, tell Carol, and she'll drop the Bludgeons. Once that's done, we just follow the plan. Let's go."

A minute later, Nav reported ready. Michael watched as Carol launched the Bludgeons and gave Alex a thumbs-up. *Antares* changed course and slowed slightly. Dean kept an almost unblinking eye on the enemy ships. The Bludgeons would hit about eight minutes after their release, using their onboard Drive to strike at high speed. There was a timer counting down on the Weapons position, and Ryan would sneak a look at it from time to time. They were still almost two light-seconds away, so it was yet a moment after the time hit zero before the displays lit up. Their aim was pretty good, not perfect. They hit the two that had been venting again, and the gas release increased in volume. Two other ships took severe hits as well, they hit the fifth, but it was not badly damaged. Carol, standing at the Weapons station, looked hard at the images of the enemy ships.

"We hit them, all of them, but they're just so big," she said to her techs.

"Yes, Lieutenant. We seem to need a bigger club," one responded, just loud enough for her to hear.

Carol pursed her lips in frustration, pounding the back of the position gently with her fist.

Dean looked back and forth at his displays. He wished for radar, but he knew full well that it was too dangerous right now. The picture began to become clear in his head.

"Captain, I think they were trying to link up with the damaged ships."

Terri Michael and Carol Hansen came over to the Surveillance position. Dean ran the visual back and forth in time-lapse, and they could see what he was talking about.

"Rescuing survivors?"

"Could be, ma'am. If so, that would mean these are not robotic ships. There is someone aboard worth saving."

Michael nodded her agreement, then looked back at the main Surveillance display.

"Any evidence they've seen us?"

Dean shook his head. "No, ma'am, nothing. We've been watching for a radar or a laser detector, anything that they might use to see us. We haven't seen a thing."

"There's always the possibility that they have some other method," Carol added, having snuck up on the conversation. Michael turned and looked at her.

"Like what?"

"Star occultation, for starters, Commander. If they have a fine enough resolution deep field telescope, they could find us by the stars we block."

Dean nodded his agreement. "Yes, that's part of why Fleet said to never be up-sun from the enemy. Don't give them a silhouette."

Michael shrugged. "Or," she said skeptically, "they could have a completely different technology we know nothing about."

"Or that, yes, ma'am," Dean responded.

Carol looked at Terri Michael. "Do you want to shoot again, Commander? I have an idea."

"What?"

"I think we should try detonating the Bludgeons further out, so we get a wider dispersal of the pellets and maybe get more damage. The ships are just so big. We're not doing enough."

Michael considered the suggestion. "OK, three this time, and move the detonation point to whatever you think is best. We'll do a five-minute delay again."

She turned back to the Nav. "Get ready to maneuver again, Lieutenant Williams."

"Captain!" Ryan Lewis called out. "They're leaving, ma'am, and fast."

The three ships not venting were clearly on the move and accelerating away from the attack point. The two left behind were also moving, less quickly and in another direction. Michael frowned.

"Tell me they're not deorbiting into the star."

Ryan waited a moment before answering. "Yes, ma'am, that's our reading on it."

"Dammit!"

They watched as the still-venting ships began down a slow but steadily increasing path into the star. The star's heat would vaporize them within a few hours. Michael thought about chasing them down with *Antares* or smacking them with another volley, but they were already descending into the hellish fire of the star. Even this small red dwarf was plenty hot enough to destroy living tissue, so she decided to just watch. Any action she took now would reveal their presence, and she did not want to chance that. Even as crippled as they were, they might still have communications with the others and could call in trouble for *Antares*. *No,* she decided, *let them fry on their own.*

She turned to the Bridge crew.

"OK, folks, secure from Alert One, but set an enhanced watch on Surveillance. Hansen, let's reset to half Lances, half Spartans."

She walked back to the command position, still thinking.

"We're going to wait for the enemy to burn up before we try to look for the FDR. Meantime we'll hang right here nice and quiet. Conn, open the Bridge window covers."

Carol watched her techs complete the reload and secure the launchers. When that process was complete, she walked over to the Comm position.

"Anything more from *Columbia*?" she asked Miho Ito quietly.

Ito looked up and back over her shoulder and shook her head. Carol was worried about Dan, along with his shipmates, but no news was just no news and didn't really mean anything either way. It wasn't good or bad; it was just silence.

Regardless, she hated it.

*Antares*
GJ 1061
Thursday. May 12, 2078, 0345 UTC

With the ship off battle stations, Carol had little to do but was loath to leave, so she curled up on the floor in the far-left corner of the Bridge, just behind the Weapons position. It was a common cat-nap spot for officers and crew when they were not on watch but wanted to be nearby. She was thinking about Dan and *Columbia* and hoping Miho Ito would have something soon.

She had met Commander Reynolds once at Fleet HQ and felt an immediate dislike for him. Her impression was that he wanted to be tough but came across as brittle, perhaps a bit petty, with a tendency to insult and belittle. It was a sharp contrast to what she had experienced under Carpenter and Michael, both of whom led by example, by consensus when possible, but always without any sense of force or edict.

She knew *Columbia* would run off to a safe point, likely not too far, evaluate their condition, then either retire or return to fight on. Either way, they should know in the next few hours, and she wanted to be on the Bridge when it happened.

Terri Michael noticed her there and ignored it, as she did most of these kinds of small violations by her young officers. Jayvon Dean was sacked out in the far-right corner, not far from the Surveillance station. They were there out of care and dedication, and in this case, a nap was hardly a case of sleeping on duty. But it would not do for the captain to be sleeping on the Bridge, so she called her XO to take over while she got some rest in her Duty Cabin. She pointed out the sleeping officers.

"Let 'em be, James. They'll be awake as soon as we hear from *Columbia*."

He looked at the peaceful, expressionless faces, first Dean, then Hansen.

"Roger that. They look kinda young to me when they're asleep, you know?"

Terri smiled grimly. "They look kinda young when they're awake, too. Thank God they don't realize just how much they're risking out here."

"War has always been fought by the children, Commander. Hard to believe."

"Yes. OK, well, wake me if you need to. If *Columbia* comes back, see what Reynolds has in mind."

"Yes, Captain, will do."

James George noted their position, speed, and weapon status. He displayed the Surveillance video of the shrinking enemy ships on the main view screen. They could still see a steam trail from the venting hydrogen and oxygen gas, swirling away from the ships as they spiraled towards the star. Was there a crew on those ships waiting for their fate? Or had they already killed themselves to avoid the wait and the pain? He wondered but reminded himself that he didn't really care. The knowledge might be useful to him, but he felt no sympathy for the enemy, only a tactician's curiosity about his opponent. He walked to the Surveillance station.

"Any sign of *Otbara*?" he asked.

"None, sir. We're watching for anything on the visual or IR that might indicate her or her wreckage, but nothing so far."

"Can you tell what those ships were doing?"

"Intel was looking at that, sir, but we can't really say from here. We don't see anything in that area that looks like *Otbara* if that's what you were thinking."

George nodded. "Partially, yes."

He paused a minute and then headed back to the Conn position. He thought to call back into the Intel section and see what they were thinking but then took note of the hour and decided it could wait. It had been a long night for everyone.

## Chapter 13

*Columbia*
Deep Space Near GJ 1061
Thursday, May 12, 2078, 0400 UTC

*Five hits,* Dan thought, *they hit us five goddamn times.* There were four dead and ten wounded now in and around the small sick bay. One FPI engineer, two Weapons techs, and one kitchen tech were dead, all hit with pieces of shrapnel from the enemy missiles. Dan was carefully zipping a body bag around one of the weapons techs. Gwen Decker was a tiny, attractive twenty-something with a caramel alto voice that Dan would hear no more. He steeled himself as he and three others picked her up and placed her on a missile transport cart as gently as possible. They would use that to take her aft to the frozen storage compartment.

*I hate these bastards,* he repeated to himself.

Medical Officer Gerry Knight was on his fourth surgery already, two of which had been futile, including the weapons tech Dan was loading. Six more patients were waiting, triaged for severity. There was a lot of blood and barely-suppressed moans of pain but no critical wounds. Between surgeries, Nurse Ensign Lewis Park worked his way around those waiting, checking vitals and temporary dressings. Medical techs Mai Kubota and Jerome Calhoun alternated between the operating room and helping those still in the queue.

Time was, before the war, a ship like *Columbia* would carry two medical techs, and that would be all. With the outbreak of the conflict, the likelihood of battle injuries changed a lot of minds at Fleet, and by the time ships were heading out to find the enemy, their medical section included a qualified battlefield surgeon, a surgical nurse, and many times the supplies they had previously carried. Those decisions were saving lives today on *Columbia*.

The ship itself was in decent shape. They had around fifteen individual compartments that were damaged. Several were now open to space, and it would take the maintenance department a few hours on each to seal them back up. The rest had minor leaks that the crew repaired with the patch kits that were by every hatch on the ship. The kit included an oxygen mask with a hose that linked into a ship-wide system, an aerosol powder to locate the leak, and thick rubber patches with an adhesive on one side. If a section was hit, one used the spray, watched where it went, and then stuck a patch over the hole. It was a simple process, assuming they lived long enough to get the mask on. *Columbia* had also lost some of the thick stealth coatings where the ship was damaged, but they would just have to live with that until they got to a repair station.

The captain had asked Dan to check on sickbay and give him an update. That was over a half-hour ago. He now worked his way back forward and found the captain in his duty cabin. He knocked and entered when called.

"What the hell took so long?" Reynolds demanded.

"They needed an extra hand for a few minutes, sir. I couldn't just walk back out."

"So, what is the status?"

"Four dead, a few more seriously wounded, several more with minor wounds. Doc and the crew back there have it under control."

"Very well. That will be all."

It seemed an abrupt dismissal to Dan. No questions about the injured crew, just 'get out.' He closed the door behind him and walked the short distance to the Bridge. His fellow Navigator Ensign Stefania Tsikuda was standing the Conn. Dan climbed the three steps to the Conn station and sat down next to her. She turned from looking out the Bridge window to look at Dan.

"I felt the Drive go off. Where are we?"

"About thirty AU from the star," she answered, looking at her Nav status display.

"Anything from *Antares*?"

"No, but I suspect they're lying low and waiting to see what happens with us."

"Hopefully, they're finishing off whatever we left."

"Yeah, hopefully." There was obvious sadness in her voice.

"Stef, are you all right?"

She looked away, then out the windows, then back at Dan. "Gwen and I used to sing together..."

Her voice trailed off in pain and shock. Dan nodded, remembering their hangar-deck jam sessions, a favorite Saturday night diversion for the crew.

"Yes, I know, Stef, I'm—"

The sound of the ship phone ringing cut him off.

"Conn," she answered, her voice suddenly under control and textbook professional. As she listened, she wrote furiously on the command log in front of her.

"Yes, Captain, right away." she finished and looked back at Dan, her eyes now clear and alert even as tears were drying at their edges.

"We're going back. I need a course back to where we left."

Dan nodded and headed for the Nav workstation. She stood and faced the Weaps station to her left.

"Weaps...give me a load of half Spartans and half Bludgeons." Then, she addressed the Bridge in general: "We're going back as soon as Nav has the course in. We will need a double watch when we come out of FTL back at GJ 1061. You have not more than an hour, so get on it."

That last part sounded to Dan like a direct quote from the captain. He wondered if Stef even realized what she had said. It didn't take long to put in the course back to the vicinity of GJ 1061, and they were on their way in a few minutes.

*Columbia*
GJ 1061
Thursday. May 12, 2078, 0510 UTC

*Columbia* transitioned out of FTL fully loaded and with every sensor deployed. Stef was still at the Conn, watching the Surveillance crew look for the enemy. After a few minutes, Surveillance Officer Melinda Hughes came up to the command position where XO Barry Wood sat just next to Stef. The captain was now in his regular cabin, well aft, which struck Dan, still at the Nav workstation, as very strange, but he didn't ask Wood about it.

"They're gone, sir. Looks like two are headed into the star, and the rest we can't find."

"Any sign of *Antares*?"

"No, sir, but that's hardly a surprise. If she's out there, she's going to be quiet."

"And nothing of *Otbara*?"

"Nothing. But again, we haven't tried to activate the FDR or really scrub the system for her or her wreckage."

"Nor should we, sir," Dan spoke up, looking at the XO. "As long as those two ships are there, we should stay silent. Once they're gone, then we can signal *Antares* on VHF or laser and start looking for *Otbara*."

"What makes you think *Antares* is still there?"

Dan pointed to the display. "Because the enemy is gone, sir. If they had defeated *Antares,* they'd still be here."

"Hmm...maybe. In any case, I doubt Commander Michael would leave until she knew our status."

"Yes, sir. Right now, all she knows is that we retreated to lick our wounds. She'll expect us to either retire completely or return."

Wood nodded his agreement. "OK then, for now, let's get looking for *Otbara* passively."

They moved back to their workstations.

*Antares*
GJ 1061
Thursday. May 12, 2078, 0800 UTC

Carol had given up a few hours ago on waiting for *Columbia* to re-appear and gone back to sleep in her cabin. The best guess on the Bridge was that she was already back, or still making repairs before coming back, as they had not sent another message indicating they were leaving. The enemy ships were nearly to the star by now. They had driven themselves down close, and now gravity was finishing the job. Terri Michael believed that *Columbia* would remain silent, as she would, until the enemy was gone.

By 1130 the enemy ships were disappearing into the corona of the star. If they weren't dead already, they would be soon. Both ships had been saturated with heat and radiation for some time now, and nearly any imaginable organic creature would be long dead.

"Comm! Let's do a long-pulse VHF ping for *Columbia*. If they're around, they'll be listening."

"If *Otbara* is around, they'll hear it, too, Commander." Miho Ito offered, hopefully.

"Yes, that would be nice, wouldn't it?"

They sent the signal, an omnidirectional transmission on 121.5 MHZ, the old aviation emergency frequency. The message was relatively low power, but it went on for thirty seconds, long enough for a Fleet receiver to determine the direction and reply with a laser link. They would hold their position for a half hour, no more, and then maneuver to throw off any unintended interceptor's aim.

Shortly after the pulse finished, the Comm tech bolted upright in his seat.

"Laser link established, Commander. We have *Columbia*."

"How far?"

"About three seconds."

"Get me Reynolds."

The tech nodded and initiated the connection. Terri picked up the handset at her Command position.

"Dave!" she said with relief, "What's your status?"

The six-second time delay was awkward, but with patience, they managed it. They'd dealt with worse.

"Good to hear from you, Terri. Four dead. We took five hits, nothing vital, but some in the crew section. We're functional, though. I was about to send a ping your way when we heard yours."

Reynolds sounded guarded, as if reticent to speak openly.

"Sorry about the losses, but I am glad it wasn't worse."

"Yes, we're still getting through it here; they were good people."

He still didn't quite sound right to Terri. She turned the discussion back to *Otbara*.

"I was wondering if we should try to activate the *Otbara* FDR. We're looking, but we still have not seen any wreckage."

"Neither have we. It's possible she never made it here, that something else happened to them."

"Yes, I suppose it is, but I just naturally hate coincidences, you know? Can't be an accident that the enemy was here."

"Yes, that's true," he responded, still sounding passive.

"We will send the FDR call, so be listening, OK?"

"Yes, we will. I am going to investigate the area where we hit them. There may be something there."

"Understood."

She hung up with a nagging sense of something unsaid, something incomplete, but could not really make it materialize in her mind. She looked over at the Comm workstation, glad to see Miho Ito there.

"Lieutenant Ito, please look up the FDR activation for *Otbara* and send the signal."

Miho had never sent an FDR activation other than in a simulation, so she sat with her Chief Tech, and they reviewed the process. They verified that they had selected the right options, and the Communications processor sent the message.

Miho was a holdover from *Antares'* original crew since *Liberty's* communications officer had died on board. Before coming to *Antares,* she'd done a short tour on *Nippon,* her home country's cruiser. She hated to leave *Nippon* but *Antares,* a new ship, was a great opportunity for her. She was well aware that the last time anyone did this was to find the FDR of *Liberty,* a ship dear to many of her current shipmates. She knew that had to be weighing on their minds. But the best way to honor that, she thought, was to do her job as well and as unobtrusively as possible. There was no need to remind anyone of the pain associated with this process. Just get it done.

They waited six hours, maintaining their orbit and listening for the FDR. Carol had gotten up from her rest at about 1200, had lunch, and then was in the Bridge Weapons station before 1300. She remained there, waiting with everyone else, until 1800, when XO James George called them together.

"OK, it's been six hours, almost, so what do we think?"

They all looked at Miho Ito.

"Well, six hours waiting is three light-hours range. I checked, and that's beyond the activation range of the FDR. If it's out there, it should have responded by now. If it's further away than that, it won't hear the activation signal."

"Thanks. Thoughts?"

Surveillance Officer Ryan Lewis spoke up. "The enemy is gone, sir. Let's get the long-range radars up and see if we can find anything of *Otbara.* We might also find some enemy wreckage. "

"You're not worried about being seen?" Navigator Alex Williams asked.

"Not immediately, no. If they show back up, we'll just shut it down and run like hell."

The group laughed a little at that comment. Even the usually dour Williams smiled at the image. XO George looked at Ito.

"Lieutenant Ito, how long have you been up here?"

She looked at the clock. "Uh, dunno, twelve hours maybe."

"OK, you pass off your status to the techs and get lost. After you get me

*Columbia*, that is."

"Yes, sir."

"Lieutenant Lewis, go ahead and fire up the long-range radar. Let's see what's out there." George walked back to the Command position and picked up the handset. Talking to the *Columbia* XO LCDR Barry Wood, they agreed it was time to start actively looking for signs of *Otbara* and anything else that might be useful. They also decided to send *Otbara* a SLIP message in case she was nearby but remaining quiet for some reason.

```
ROUTINE 207805120900UTC
TO: OTBARA
CC: CINCFLEET
FROM: COLUMBIA
WITH ANTARES IN VICINITY GJ 1061
THREAT ELIMINATED
END
```

Ryan Lewis passed off the search task to the now-rested Ensign Jayvon Dean and headed for his quarters. He, like some others, was starting to lose track of the hours and days on and off duty. To a point, he didn't really care what day or time it was. He was the chief of the Surveillance section, and he'd make sure that they got the job done the best it could be. On the other hand, he knew if he were up too many shifts or didn't get a decent rest once in a while, he'd be pretty useless in a surprisingly few days. Commander Michael watched her crew's rest carefully and made an example of herself as well, passing the watch to XO George on a pretty consistent basis to stay rested.

Dean picked up the radar search from Lewis. He concentrated on the area where the enemy had been clustered. There was some wreckage around, but not enough mass to add up to *Otbara*. After an hour, he moved on, gradually working his way out from the enemy position.

But there was nothing. Big rocks, lots and lots of little rocks, but no trace of *Otbara*, her name Russian for 'valor.' It was a shame, Jayvon thought, such a mysterious end for a ship with such a noble name.

ISC Fleet HQ Operations Section
Fort Eustis, VA
Friday, May 13, 2078, 0800 EDT

Admiral Cook was not pleased with *Columbia*. Not pleased at all. The reports of a strike going badly at GJ 1061 disturbed her. This was a SAR mission, not search-and-destroy, and in her opinion, they should have just kept quiet and watched. But it was too late now to change any of that. *Columbia* was damaged but still on duty. There had been a loss of life, which she regretted. She needed *Antares* to investigate Beta Hydri, which they had not yet examined. It was a long way, and if they were going to get there and back with the supplies on board, they could not afford to linger at GJ 1061 much longer. She made up her mind before she arrived at the office and just stopped at Mark Rhodes' desk on her way in.

"Good morning, ma'am," Mark said as he stood and greeted her pleasantly, as usual.

"Good morning, Mark. Please cut an order for *Antares* to proceed immediately to Beta Hydri. I need them to get on with their schedule. Copy *Columbia*. They can keep searching for now."

"Yes, Admiral. Right away."

ISC Fleet HQ Plans Section
Fort Eustis, VA
Friday, May 13, 2078,1555 EST

It had been a long week in Plans. Joanne Henderson had been out of the office several times this week and most of the day today. It wasn't unusual for senior officers like Fiona or Joanne to be gone for significant periods. They sometimes briefed more senior officers, ship captains, or outside military or political representatives on the state of the war. It wasn't always comfortable or pleasant, but it came with the territory. They were both pretty good at sucking it up and not letting on to their audience how much they hated being there.

This time, however, unknown to the staff in Plans, she had been in CINC's office and then with the Chief of Operations. CINC had replaced Admiral Gerhard with Admiral Patricia Cook a month ago. Patty Cook had commanded *Freedom* and later served as XO on *Yorktown* before moving to staff work at HQ. She had most recently been the senior staff assistant to CINC Connor Davenport and so was handy when he decided to fire Gerhard. Davenport handed her a star and told her to get to work cleaning up the mess in Operations. It wasn't quite as terrible as Davenport had thought, but a few outright firings, demotions, and reassignments later, she felt that the section was working well.

Ben Price noticed that Joanne was gone more than usual this week. They had become close in the months since his wife had bugged out, finding in each other that most indispensable of relationships: a dependable friend. Neither wanted anything more from the other but what they already had. Just as it was, it was best for both of them. The Plans Division was working on improving the search load balance among the available ships and ensuring the crews got some reasonable time off, either home at Earth or at one of the starbases. That meant expanding the supplies to those bases as well as upgrading, as best they could, shipboard resources. More and better food, better entertainment options, more education, and advancement opportunities. The most significant downside of a randomized search was that ships did not necessarily follow the most efficient route through their assigned stars. This meant a longer trip, with some target star combinations that didn't make any sense to the crews. That time en route needed to be constructive, not just marking time. Joanne had started a project to find college or technical course curricula that matched the expertise of the officers or crew on a particular ship. With so many second-career technical crew members in the Fleet, they sometimes found that an enlisted tech or chief might happen to have a Master's degree in some other field.

Joanne returned to the office late in the day to find Ben head-down in his spreadsheets. He looked up to see her at his desk, a serious look on her face.

"Welcome back. What's up?"

Joanne looked at him for a second, then shook her head. "Not now. Eight?"

"Sure," he replied.

She paused, clearly something on her mind, then turned and headed out of the office. It was already past four, and he'd been there since before seven, so he wrapped up his spreadsheets and closed down for the day. Something was up, he knew. Captain Collins didn't look like her usual cheerful self, either.

Ben entered the bar a little before eight to find Joanne and Fiona Collins in their usual corner booth. He wandered down the bar and slipped in next to Joanne. They had the same somber looks he had seen earlier.

"OK, what's going on? You both look like somebody either died or is about to."

Fiona looked over at Joanne, who started to speak as the bartender delivered Ben's drink that he hadn't yet ordered. *Good to be a regular,* he thought.

"I'm getting a ship. *Intrepid,*" Joanne said flatly.

Ben looked from one woman to the other and back. "So why are we not toasting your good fortune?"

"I don't really want it."

"She's got a promotion, too," Fiona added.

"And you're not happy about that, either?" Ben asked, more incredulous than amused.

"I like where I am." Joanne hesitated, then continued. "Promotions are always nice, sure, but this one comes at a cost."

"Well, formerly-Commander-Henderson, I, for one, am happy for you even though I will miss your overbearing, annoying presence in the office."

Fiona and Joanne laughed a little at that. Fiona kept looking at Joanne. Clearly, something else was on their minds. Finally, Joanne spoke.

"Maybe not," she said evenly, keeping his eye. "Wanna come along?"

With that nugget dropped, she downed the last of her drink and waved for another. Ben now realized why Joanne had seemed so closed off all day. He leaned back, surprised but intrigued by the chance to go to the fleet.

"What did you have in mind?"

"Chief of Intel. It's usually a commissioned post, but I got Cook to agree to it if you're willing."

"You've been working on this for a while, haven't you?"

Fiona answered for her. "About a week. Cook has been dithering a little on which ship, but today finally made the call to send her to *Intrepid*. They need her."

Ben stalled for time to think, taking a couple sips of his drink.

"Captain Collins, I need your honest opinion."

Fiona nodded, inviting him to continue.

"Our friendship," he said, indicating Joanne, "is no secret here. Won't it hurt her credibility to assign me there?"

Fiona gave that some thought before she responded. "It could. There's no getting around that. Up to now, you two have served together, but you both work for me, so there hasn't been an issue. Now, you will be working for her." Fiona thought a little more, then continued. "Your friendship has been good for both of you and, frankly, for me. You will have to set that aside now. Can you do that?"

She looked from one to the other. Ben worked a little more on his drink, then turned to Joanne.

"We've worked together long enough by now; I think we can."

Joanne nodded her agreement.

"So, can I decline this? Can you?" Ben asked Joanne.

"*You* can. But orders are orders even for new Captains, Ben. I have to go."

Ben thought it over for just a few seconds, considering the options he had. He could stay in Plans, remain warm and safe like he always had, or he could get out on a ship and possibly into the fight that was going on all around them.

"Yes, I'll go."

He turned back to Fiona. "Captain, would it help you if I went a little later? That way, we wouldn't both leave you at once."

Fiona brightened as Joanne leaned back in her seat.

Joanne turned to Fiona. "Can we do that?"

Fiona nodded. "Patty'll go for it. I can talk to her. He'll need a couple weeks with Ron Harris' people anyway. It really would work better for Plans, so I'm sure she'll agree."

Another unordered round arrived from the bar.

Ben smiled as he raised his glass. "To Captain Henderson and the good ship *Intrepid*," he said thoughtfully.

They celebrated the toast and started talking about dinner instead of war. It felt really good, really comfortable, to have one more evening together. They laughed a lot that night.

A week later, Joanne packed up her desk and headed home. Monday, she would report to *Intrepid* and try to see just what kind of hand dear old Patty Cook had dealt her.

*Antares*
GJ 1061
Saturday, May 14, 2078, 0725 UTC

Communications Officer Miho Ito was on the Bridge when the message arrived. She was surprised at the contents.

```
ROUTINE 207805131330 UTC
TO: ANTARES, COLUMBIA
FROM: FLEETOPS
ANTARES IS RELIEVED OF SAR DUTY AND WILL PROCEED BETA HYDRI ASAP.
END
```

She forwarded it to the captain and the XO, who was at the command station.
"Message from Fleet Operations, Commander George. Orders to Beta Hydri."
George read the message and then called Terri. "It finally came, Captain. Proceed ASAP, Beta Hydri." There was a pause as he listened to her response. "Very well," he said, finally.
He looked back at Ito. "Get me *Columbia*, Miho."
"Yes, sir."
She walked back to the Comms station and activated the laser link to *Columbia*. The link came up quickly, but there was now about a four-second time delay each way.
"Commander Reynolds, sir, good morning, James George here."
Eight seconds seemed like a lifetime in a conversation.
"Yes, sir, as I am sure you've seen, we've been ordered to get back on schedule. We'll be pulling out in an hour or so."
Another eight-count.
"Yes, I will have Lieutenant Lewis send what data we have before we go."
Then, finally: "Yes, sir, thanks, and I will pass that along to Commander Michael."
He hung up.
"Pass what along?" Terri asked as she stepped up to the command platform.
"Thanks, and good hunting."
"Oh, nice," she said, sounding both skeptical and sarcastic.
She looked at her ship status display, then turned to the Weapons station.
"Weaps, let's get the rotaries in. We're leaving."
The tech acknowledged the order and pulled the launchers in. Navigator Alex Williams was at the Nav station.
"Alex! I need a course to Beta Hydri, leaving 0830."
"Yes, Captain, we'll be ready."
When it came time to leave, all the section heads were on the Bridge, ready in case of any problem. Alex took them up and out of the plane of the system before engaging the Drive at full power for Beta Hydri. It was over sixteen light-years,

so another two-week-plus transit between targets. Like most of the section heads, Carol was glad for some time to review her status and ensure that all was ready for whatever they might encounter at the next star, but she also dreaded the slack time that inevitably came after a few days of activity. But this was the job they had, and it was up to all of them to make the best of it.

*Columbia*
Vicinity GJ 1061
Monday, May 16, 2078, 1200 UTC

Commander David Reynolds knew days ago that the search for *Otbara* would end soon. When Operations released *Antares* to go on to Beta Hydri, he figured they had decided that there wasn't much point in continuing. And to be fair to CINC and Operations, they hadn't produced any evidence of *Otbara*. They had tried three times to wake up the FDR, but there was no response. They'd punched the enemy in the nose when they got here but took a slapping themselves. Reynolds knew he had letters to write. He'd work on those on the next transit.

They might never know what happened to *Otbara*, or they might learn someday in the far future. The distances were unimaginable, and a distress call in normal space would take years to get anywhere and might be too weak to detect in any case. *No*, he thought, *something terrible has happened.* But we don't know what, where, or even when. It was painful to contemplate leaving, but it was no surprise when the order came. The surprise was the destination.

```
ROUTINE 207805142200 UTC
TO: COLUMBIA
FROM: CINCFLEET
TERMINATE OTBARA SAR ACTIVITIES NLT 207805161600
RTB EARTH
END
```

Earth? Kapteyn was only three-point-seven days away, Tranquility II only nine and a half. Earth was *twelve* days away. The order coming from CINC and not Operations was also unusual.

"I'm screwed," Reynolds said to his XO as he got up from the command chair and walked back to his duty cabin.

The XO could hardly disagree.

*Intrepid*
Earth Orbit
Monday, May 23, 2078, 1200 UTC (0800 EDT)

Captain Joanne Henderson caught a shuttle up to *Intrepid* early Monday. It was just Joanne and the shuttle crew, which was fine with her. With only one passenger to deliver, the shuttle skipped the ShuttleLock and docked at the forward port airlock on the big ship. As Henderson stepped off, Executive Officer Lieutenant Commander Alonzo Bass was waiting. The previous captain, an older commander named Landen Ali, had departed the night before, leaving Bass in temporary command.

"Good morning, Commander," she said pleasantly, extending her hand.

"Good morning, Captain," he replied, returning a sincere handshake. She held his hand for a moment.

"I relieve you, sir."

"I stand relieved, ma'am, and glad to be so."

They began to walk down the passageway towards the captain's office.

"Will you be bringing on a new XO, Captain?"

She shook her head. "I have no intention of that, Commander Bass. I do have a number of concerns that we'll have to work through, but my initial assessment is that the XO hasn't been the problem."

They moved through the outer office into the captain's office proper. A young admin tech stood as they entered, but deep in their conversation, the officers didn't notice him. Bass closed the door behind him.

"Good to see you again, Alonzo. I can see it's been hard."

"Indeed, it has, ma'am."

"Joanne, while we're alone — we've been at this together long enough."

"Thanks. Honestly, Joanne, Ali was just out of his depth here. We've been stuck on the outer patrol line since it was set up, and frankly, the boredom got to the crew pretty bad. The Commander would not take action to improve their morale, and so lots of secondary problems start coming up."

"Like the weapons prep failures, sensor breakdowns, fistfights..."

"Exactly. I told Ali we needed to get some distractions out there — more media, more education, more of everything since they were getting no combat, no search work. We just sat there looking out at empty space. I mean, there are cargo or transfer shuttles that can bring us this stuff, or some of it we could get by data link."

"But he did nothing?"

"That's correct."

"OK, we'll deal with that. Also, we're not going back on the line. We're going out."

"That will be welcome news to the crew."

Joanne shook her head. "Nothing about that to them yet. We have to get this ship back together first." She passed a document over to him.

He read it quickly, then looked up. "This looks like fun," he said, deadpan.

"Yeah, it will be a shock, but I think they need one. We need to get this ship back in the Fleet as soon as we can. So, as it says, they get forty-eight hours to get their sections in order."

"If they make it...and pass...it will be a morale booster. If they fail?"

"If they fail, well, they're gone, Alonzo. This isn't trivial, but it's doable with some effort."

"Agreed."

"OK then, ready to be the deputy chief asshole bitch?" she asked, smiling only slightly.

"That is my job, Captain," he answered with a broad smile.

"OK then. Have all the officers in the hangar at 1300."

"Very well, Captain. Anything else?"

"Nope. Let's get to work."

After Bass left, Joanne came out to the outer office. Admin Tech Anthony Wallace stood again as she appeared.

"Technician Wallace, is it not?"

"Yes, ma'am. Welcome aboard, Captain."

She smiled. "Thank you, Wallace, you're the first. May I call you Anthony?"

"Tony would do fine, Captain Henderson."

"OK, good, thank you." She paused. "I know the usual protocol, but I do not want you interrupting your work to get up every time an officer enters. Your work is important to me and the smooth operation of the ship. Someone with a star or from outside, fine. But for the ship's officers, you can greet them from your chair."

"As you wish, ma'am." Wallace had expected to dislike the new skipper, but he was beginning to think the opposite.

"Fine."

"Any special requests, Captain? Coffee instructions? Schedule?"

She thought for a second. "No. I'll probably get my own coffee, but just in case, I take it dark roast with one sugar — real sugar. I will generally be on the Bridge by seven, then up here by maybe nine. I will establish set office hours later, but while we're still here in orbit, it will be hit or miss. What is your usual schedule?"

"Seven to four, ma'am. I take an hour for lunch around noon."

"That's all fine. Anything else on your mind?"

He seemed to hesitate before answering, unsure of whether to speak or not.

"Go ahead, Tony. Say what's on your mind."

"Well, Captain, a lot of the crew are nervous. We had a rough time on the line, and then they fired Commander Ali. They're not sure what to expect."

"That's good, Tony; they should be a little nervous. But, just between you and me, they're about to find out." She started for the door. "I am going to check the Bridge, take a look at the duty cabin, and then I will be in the hangar with the officers. You know how to reach me?"

"Yes, ma'am."

"Very well. Carry on, Tony."

"Yes, ma'am."

*Wow,* he thought, *this is going to be interesting.*


The lights in the hangar were bright, and the buzz of nervous conversation filled the space. They knew Henderson was here, some had actually spoken to her, but they didn't know what this gathering was about.

Bass preceded her into the hangar, calling the room to attention as he did. Joanne followed, moving to the center of the room, in front of the dozen or so chairs they had hastily arranged. As the officers stood, she turned to Bass.

"Commander Bass, what is the status of the ship's crew."

"We have 112 assigned, Captain, 17 officers, 9 FPI staff, 9 chiefs, and 76 ranks. There are 25 on leave, 3 in sickbay, the rest are present on board. All are accounted for, ma'am."

"Very well. Sit, everyone, at ease."

They sat, but there was very little ease in the room. She and Bass remained standing.

"When did those leaves start?"

"Two days ago. Most are seven days."

"Anyone scheduled to leave in the next two days?"

Bass checked his tablet. "Yes, ten."

"Let's keep them here for now, for a couple days, anyhow. If there is a family or another situation: birth, death, or marriage, that you feel is deserving of an exception, go ahead and grant it. Otherwise, they're staying."

She turned back to the officers, giving them her best disappointed school teacher stare.

"I won't dwell on your last stint on the outer patrol line except to say that it wasn't *Intrepid*'s finest hour."

She let that sink in for a moment.

"I am planning no firings or reassignments, not yet anyway."

She began pacing back and forth, something she did when speaking before large groups.

"On your NetComps you have a document from me which lays out the known deficiencies in each department. You have two days — forty-eight hours — to get your sections nominal. In my opinion, all you need to fix these deficiencies is yourselves, but if you find you need supplies or whatever, I will get it for you."

She stopped pacing and looked over the thirteen officers in front of her. She sat in the chair Bass had placed for her at the front.

"My eagles may be shiny and new, but obviously I am not. I've been at this for a while, both in the Fleet and at HQ. I know bullshit when I hear it, and I know what to do with it. People will say I am tough — bitchy even, sometimes — and they're right. But I am not arbitrary, or capricious, or *stupid*."

Her emphasis on the last word brought several heads up.

"Get with the plan according to the book, and we will be successful. I understand imperfection, but I don't tolerate incompetence."

She looked at her NetComp. "OK, it's 1325. At 1330 day after tomorrow, the XO and I will be knocking on your doors."

They stood as she did.

"Dismissed."

Lieutenant Larry Covington stood with the rest of the officers as Captain Henderson left the hangar bay with XO Bass. He wasn't sure he liked her hard-ass attitude, but he understood what she wanted. He liked the direct approach, at least: get it together or get gone. His classmate Ensign Rick Court caught his eye on the way out.

"Bitch!" he said, not quietly enough.

Covington looked at him. "Looking to get rank-locked again, Court?"

"How are we supposed to get all this shit done in two days? She's just gunning for me."

"Every section has issues, Ensign Court. You can't possibly think it's personal."

"Bite me, Covington. I was better than you at the U, and I'm better now."

Larry shook his head in disbelief at what he was hearing.

"Christ, Rick, will you never learn? Read the list and get it done, and you'll have no problems."

"Just another bitch thinks she's better than me."

"You mean like Hansen?"

"Yeah, the hero chick never had it better than she did with me, and she never will."

"Shut up, Rick. You're embarrassing yourself."

With a long eye-roll, Larry turned forward towards the Nav work area, where he had a relatively short list of deficiencies to work off. Court slammed his fist into the wall as he headed aft to the Maintenance workshops. His list was the longest of all.

Covington's promotion to lieutenant had come on schedule a year after his graduation, but Court's did not. His direct supervisor set him 'rank-locked' because of issues in his section and his behavior. He was turning out to be a problem officer, and XO Bass was not going to let him advance until he cleaned up his act.

Before long, he could be heard yelling at the chiefs and techs in his section. Their arguments that most of the list came from Ensign Court's own instructions were not well received.

## Chapter 14

*Antares*
En Route Beta Hydri
Tuesday, May 24, 2078, 1900 UTC

Carol sat at the small desk in her quarters and pulled up her messages on her tablet. She had an hour or so until she was due for another shift at the Conn. They were now ten days out from GJ 1061 and no longer under a minimum EMR restriction.

Among the usual mundane administrative communications, both Fleet-wide SLIP and local ship issues, there was a personal SLIP from Rick Court. His previous message had been yet another self-congratulatory, self-promoting treatise. She wondered all along what corners he was cutting that he didn't mention, as that was his usual technique at the University.

Now, she knew.

This latest message was an angry, accusatory screed vilifying *Intrepid's* new Captain, Joanne Henderson. On her arrival, she had apparently turned the whole ship upside down with a long list of deficiencies in nearly every department. But, in Rick's mind, she had done all that for the sole purpose of getting him fired. She had met Henderson a couple times, and she struck Carol as a good officer, tough maybe, but smart and honest.

Carol didn't understand why Rick was still sending her messages. She hadn't responded to him in months, but the messages kept on coming every couple of weeks.

After Inor, Carol knew she was a different person, as her emotional maturity paralleled her professional growth as an officer. Weeks ago, well before her conversation with Dan Smith, as her more mature assessment of her previous relationship with Rick crystallized in her mind, she likewise began to see who had been literally right in front of her all along: David. It was hard now to face what she had been blind to all those years. But she forced herself, literally sometimes in the mirror, to see with new eyes what David had actually meant to her.

She sat at her desk for several minutes, mentally composing and disposing drafts of the messages she wanted to send. Some of the early versions of the Court message were too harsh, a little too vitriolic. She wanted to be clear and direct, not cruel.

```
SLIP PERSONAL
TO: INTREPID/ENS RICHARD COURT
FROM: ANTARES/LT CAROL HANSEN

I PROBABLY SHOULD SAY I AM SORRY TO SEND THIS BY SLIP BUT I'M NOT.
IT CAN'T WAIT.
I WANT TO BE VERY CLEAR ABOUT THIS.
```

```
WHATEVER YOU MAY THINK THIS HAS NEVER BEEN GOOD FOR ME. WE'RE DONE.
I HOPE SOMEDAY YOUR ACCOMPLISHMENTS WILL MATCH YOUR AMBITIONS.

CAROL
END
```

Was it too harsh, she wondered? For Court, probably not. She sent it.

Next, she worked on what to say to David. Some versions were too soft, too gauzily romantic, and she knew that didn't really sound like her, nor did it speak in a voice he would hear. Leaning back in her chair and looking at the ceiling, she thought back to their time together in the eager pack of cadets that was their study group. She kept coming back to that day in October, the day David walked away and found he could not come back, the day he quietly stood at her side for that last time. She missed that calm, steady presence in her life. It occurred to Carol, as she looked back on it, that there may have been a chance at that moment to change her direction and in doing so, change his. Maybe, but she wasn't ready to see it at the time. *Enough mental hand-wringing,* she told herself, *just write the damned thing.*

```
SLIP PERSONAL
TO: SIGMA/CW2 DAVID POWELL
FROM: ANTARES/LT CAROL HANSEN

NEXT TIME I WILL STAY FOR THE SUNSET.

CAROL
END
```

Too obtuse? No, he would understand.

She sent it.

Time was getting short. Her mind was clear, and she felt confident by the time she left her quarters for the Bridge. She knew she had made the right decision. Her soul was now quiet and hopeful, her heart now firm in its resolve. Time would tell what might come of her choice. But she would trust time since it had brought her to where she could see what her heart needed her to see. And she would trust David because, well, she always knew she could.

*Sigma*
GL 887
Wednesday, May 25, 2078, 1820 UTC

There were no known planets around what was initially known as Lacaille 9352 before *Sigma* arrived. Afterward, there still weren't any. They found several dwarf planets, all icy frozen rocks well outside the tiny habitable zone. But nothing very interesting and no evidence of the enemy. Still, they spent their allocated five days cataloging the system's larger objects and watching for the enemy.

Ensign Leah Farley was responsible for the Communications systems on *Sigma*. She had a small group of operators who worked the Comms position on the Bridge and an even smaller group of maintenance techs that coddled and prodded the delicate SLIP, laser, and radio communications systems. She was short, not quite five feet, thin, but carrying around a sizable halo of very dark curly hair. Her fair complexion and bright blue eyes were something of a surprise against the dark mass around her head. She came from a prosperous family, a lawyer father and surgeon mother, and had earned her undergraduate degree in Economics at Penn State. She worked a year or two at a large management consulting firm before dropping her spreadsheets and entering the officer-transition course at SFU.

Navigation Ensign Travis Buckley, on the other hand, came from a small town in central Tennessee, the third and last child of a single mother who was a nurse. He got his Mechanical Engineering degree from Middle Tennessee State and went directly from there into the SFU program. Somehow the east-coast liberal orchestra-lover and the mid-south country music fan hit it off in officer training and were frequently together in their off-duty moments. Travis looked vaguely bearish with his height, full but neatly trimmed beard, and longish hair. He had that drawl in his voice that could fill a large room with no need for amplification. He also had a dry sense of humor that took Leah a while to fully appreciate.

Today Travis was dealing an after-dinner game of Spades in the wardroom, Leah on his left and FPI Lieutenant Tsubasa Kondo on his right. David came in for coffee, his work on the GL 887 census done for the day.

"Hey, Powell, join us?" Buckley asked.

David looked at the table, seemed to consider turning down the invitation, then said, "Sure. Haven't beaten anybody at Spades since the U."

"And so, the gauntlet is thrown!" Leah said, laughing.

They played for an hour, and David did well, but Travis was a new challenge for him. Farley and Buckley had been in an offset class for officer candidates who already had college degrees, which ran from January to December 2077. David was gone from SFU before they arrived, so they had known him only as the mysterious 'guy who left and never came back.' But they had some classes with Carol and other friends of David's.

"So, David, heard from Hansen?" Farley asked.

"Um, no. She's pretty busy on *Antares,* I suppose," he responded cautiously.

"She figured out she's in love with you yet?" Travis asked, just a touch of conspiracy in his voice.

"Excuse me?"

"You heard me. Has she?"

"Not that I know of. But she and Court are split up now."

"That shithead?" Travis said with disgust. "That creep is the biggest clump of human night soil I've ever met. Don't know what Hansen could have seen in him."

"Can't say I disagree," David said evenly.

Leah rolled her eyes. "Jesus, David, you're so cool about it."

He shrugged. "No choice, Ensign Farley. Sure, I think the world of Carol Hansen, most people do, but face it: she's an officer, and I'm not, and she's on *Antares*, and I'm here."

"And she's famous..." Travis let that line drop.

"Yeah, there's that, too. My guess is she hates that part."

"Court must be pea-green with envy!" Leah said.

"More like baby-shit green if you ask me," Travis responded.

David laughed pretty hard at that one.

The next morning he was at work in the Intel section, reviewing some of the questionable objects the FleetIntel spectra matching software had flagged. As he lined up the next suspect object's spectra against the *Liberty* spectra on his display, his phone buzzed quietly. Looking at it, he saw he had a personal SLIP message. He didn't get many messages, so he picked up his coffee, leaned back in his chair, and opened it.

```
SLIP PERSONAL 20780524
TO: SIGMA/CW2 DAVID POWELL
FROM: ANTARES/LT CAROL HANSEN

NEXT TIME I WILL STAY FOR THE SUNSET.

CAROL
END
```

He managed to set the coffee down without spilling it as he snapped upright, but just barely.

*Next time I will stay for the sunset.*

He could almost hear her smooth alto voice speaking in his head. His mind was suddenly racing, parsing and absorbing the meaning of those few words. He remembered clearly, and painfully their last moment together right before he went home that day, and his life changed.

*Next time* meant she wanted to see him. *I will stay for the sunset* could only mean that she wished that she had stayed with him then and not left with Court. *She said so much,* he thought, *with so few words.* He remembered the conversation with Buckley and Farley last evening. Had they known something?

He stood up and left the workroom without a word, leaving Abe and Sally to wonder what had just happened.

The Comms office was aft, just behind the hangar near the SLIP equipment. Most office spaces on Fleet ships were in the area the officer managed. Even in a world nearly devoid of 'paper' work, there was still a need for space for a supervisor to work uninterrupted and to have private conversations when necessary. Leah Farley looked up from her tablet as David appeared at her door.

"Ensign Farley, do you have a moment?"

"Sure, Mister Powell."

David stepped in and closed the door behind him. Leah's eyebrow raised slightly; her curiosity now engaged.

"What's on your mind that no one else can hear?"

"You're very perceptive, Ensign Farley. Good thing they put you in Comms."

She laughed, then asked, "So, what's up?"

David paused a second, then just passed his phone over to her. She read the message, her face showing surprise as she did.

"OK, so?"

"There's a lot of meaning in those words that only Carol and I would understand. Coming right after Buckley's comment last night, I wondered if she had said something to you."

"Don't believe in coincidences, Mister Powell?"

David shrugged. "Not really."

Leah leaned back in her chair, considering how to answer. "We only knew Carol for a short time, but everyone there knew how hard she and a few others lobbied the Administration to give you your diploma and your commission. She was adamant about that, relentless even. Court hated it — I once heard him ask her who she was really with, him or you."

"What did she say?"

"I didn't quite hear, but it obviously didn't satisfy Court. He stomped off all pissed off like he does."

"Yeah, I've seen that. Bulging eyes and long strides."

Leah laughed. "Exactly! Carol was someone everyone admired, even those of us who only knew her briefly. You were already gone, but you were still a presence in their lives. That group you started was a legend. The best students, best in the field skills, best officers, best whatever."

"I never thought of it that way. We were just trying to graduate," David said with a shrug.

"Well, legends do carry a lot of false glamor around the seed of truth."

They laughed.

"But she never said anything directly to us, Mister Powell. From what I know of her, she wouldn't have done that. It's too private. Still, it was obvious to most of us who knew her where her heart was going."

"Really?"

Leah nodded in response. "Really."

David rose to leave. "Thanks, Ensign Farley, you've been a great help."

"Before you go, Mister Powell?"

"Yes?"

Leah looked down at her work, then back up at David. She seemed to hesitate as if unsure she should say what was on her mind. Finally, she spoke. "From what

I see here on this ship, the legend is only half the story."

He looked at her for a moment, not sure just how to respond. "Thank you, Ensign Farley. That's very kind."

He left Comms and headed back to the Intel section. He had to respond to her, and he did not want to wait. If she was really reaching out to him, and he was pretty sure she was, then he needed to let her know right away that he was reaching back for her, too. It would have to be about the moment at the window. She had left with Court, and he had watched her go, still standing at the window. *There*, he had it.

```
SLIP PERSONAL 207805261950UTC
TO: ANTARES/LT CAROL HANSEN
FROM: SIGMA/CW2 DAVID POWELL

I WILL ALWAYS BE STANDING RIGHT HERE.

DAVID
END
```

*Antares*
Approaching Beta Hydri
Tuesday, May 31, 2078, 1100 UTC

Commander Terri Michael was ready for Beta Hydri to be just another star to check off her list. Beta Hydri was over twenty-four days from Earth, which is a long trip no matter how fast you're going. Terri reviewed the Fleet reports and realized they would be the first to examine this system. That surprised her a little, but re-checking the combined search itineraries, Beta Hydri was nowhere on the list. They had been searching for several months now, and Terri wondered about the enemy. Fleet had bested them three times now, which could not be encouraging. Would they move on, or would they push out to rid themselves of this new threat?

Lieutenant Carol Hansen, by now the well-established leader of the Weapons Division, was becoming more comfortable with what Michael would want and when. She had hit the books and the weapons stacks alike to expand her knowledge of their available weapons, their capabilities and limitations. Her energy and good humor earned her the respect of her fellow officers and the admiration of her crew. She would climb the stack, push a weapon into place, or help overhaul a faulty warhead with no reservations and no feeling that she would want to be doing anything else. Because, well, she didn't. This was the life she'd wanted, and she was glad to be so immersed in it. Her techs were hard-working, smart, and resourceful, and she felt as strongly about them as they did about her.

They came out of FTL as planned, three AU from the star, which is slightly larger than the Sun. Carol had the rotaries loaded, and every sensor was open and watching. It wasn't long before there was a shout from the Surveillance Station.

"Wait...is that...it is...a blue dot!"

A *blue dot*? Another Earth-like planet?

The Chief supervising the initial scan stood and turned to the captain. "There is a blue dot, Commander. Very high confidence."

Michael stood and called out, "Comms! Send a FLASH to Fleet: Blue Dot Beta Hydri. That's all."

"Yes, ma'am."

In a minute, the SLIP message was on its way. It would be a day and a half before it got to Fleet, but no matter what happened now, they would know. Michael turned slightly to the Weapons Station.

"Lieutenant Hansen, what's my loadout?"

"As requested, there are sixteen Spartans, twelve Lances, and four Bludgeons between the two rotaries. We have two Sleuths made up, with four more kits available."

"Deploy the rotaries."

Carol nodded her acknowledgment and indicated to Chief Guzman to open the magazine door and move the rotaries outside the ship, ready for firing. In a minute or less, they were out.

She turned back to the captain. "We're ready to shoot, Commander."

"Surveillance, where is this planet?"

"In the habitable zone, ma'am, of course, but we're still resolving the orbit. It's going to take a little while. We need to look at everything else, too."

"Roger that. Go ahead with your regular census routine."

She walked down off the command position and over to Carol. "Remind me of the range of the Sleuth?"

"Same as a Lance, ma'am: three or four AU. Beyond that, you're shooting at stuff that's not there anymore."

Senior Lieutenant Ryan Lewis, Surveillance Officer, joined the conversation. "Thinking about a Sleuth?"

"Yes, Mister Lewis, I was. Your thoughts?"

"It's not intended to examine a planet, more to check out a ship or something kinda the size of a ship."

Carol looked up at him. "I hear a 'but' coming?"

"But it might pick up a large civilization on IR or visual. There's only limited radio and radar detection, but if there's any industry or large population centers, we might see them. But, no guarantees."

Terri considered her options for a moment. "How well do we know where this planet is?" she asked.

Lewis smiled. "Oh, well enough that we can hit it with a Lance, Captain. Every minute we're getting more resolution. Give me an hour or two, and we'll have it close enough."

He paused a moment. "Carol, can we tell it to auto-find a target that big?"

She was intrigued by the question. "I am not sure what the limits are on that. Let me get with Chief Guzman and see what he thinks."

Michael had let the two junior officers talk but now leaned back into the conversation.

"Get on it. I want to launch as soon as we possibly can. This is the first Blue Dot we've seen, and I want to know what the hell is down there."

The Sleuth was a bit of a mashup device, and while the guidance and power plant were that of a Lance, which made the Weapons Section the experts, it had a new 'SpyHead' with sensors and data storage, and the Surveillance Section, along with Intel, were the experts on that.

It took a few well-animated, curse-punctuated conversations and reference document searches, but they finally determined that they could tell the Sleuth to fly past something as large as a planet. On the sensor side, they would just have to see what it looked like when it got back. That part settled, Terri turned back to Ryan Lewis.

"As I recall, we have some exploration drones aboard?"

"Yes, Captain, two surface-deployable drones."

"Put together some options for surface exploration, nothing too invasive, OK?"

"Yes, Captain."

"Can you have them for me by noon tomorrow?"

"Yes, that should be no problem."

"Very well. Congratulations, Ryan. Your team did well to find that planet so quickly."

"Thank you, ma'am. The software helps, but they work hard to see things for themselves."

"I can tell. Carry on."

"Thank you, Captain."

Lewis picked up the ship phone and called his deputy to set up the planning of the surface exploration. They had limited resources, but they would do their best to give her some reasonable options.

After some discussion, they decided to risk sending the Sleuth as soon as possible, FTL to about three hundred thousand kilometers, then around the planet and back. Even a civilization as advanced as their own would be unlikely to detect it. They would wait two hours to let Surveillance refine the orbit.

"Nav!" Michael yelled as the Sleuth discussion broke up.

"Ma'am?" came the cautious reply from the Navigation workstation.

"Get me the hell out of this orbit...make it a thirty inclination on the inside edge of the HZ...say...1.5 AU."

"Thirty-degree inclination to the system at 1.5 AU, yes, ma'am."

"How long?"

"How fast do you want it. Captain? We can go FTL and be there pretty quickly, but I'd be afraid that might be noticed..."

"Make it four hours."

"Yes, ma'am. Starting now."

Michael turned to return to the command station and noticed Carol looking at her with that 'I don't understand what you're thinking' look on her face. Michael smiled slightly, then walked over to her.

"I expect the enemy to be somewhere around the planet if they're here at all. If we're high and on the inside of the HZ, it means they will be fully illuminated, and we'll be lost in the glare of the star. We just need to avoid transits on the side facing the planet."

Lesson taken, Carol went back to her Sleuth preparations. Ryan Lewis was shortly able to give a more complete brief on the Blue Dot.

"We're seeing it at about half-phase, to the right of the star. So, roughly, it's 90 degrees to the right of our position relative to Beta Hydri. We can see clouds and oceans on the long range, but the resolution isn't that good yet. Looks to be about a 2.2 AU orbit."

"Which way is it orbiting?"

"Looks like we came in on the north side, so it's moving counter-clockwise from this vantage point." He paused. "We will be crossing the orbit in less than an hour, and I think that would be a good time to launch the Sleuth."

Carol nodded her agreement. "Yes, that makes sense."

Michael turned from Ryan to Carol. "Can you be ready in that time?"

"Yes, ma'am. I've already pulled in the port rotary and had the crew load the Sleuth. We can still send it any final command updates, but aside from that, we're ready."

"Well done, both of you. Proceed as you have proposed; you don't need a final release from me."

Carol nodded. "Fire when ready, yes, ma'am."

Right as planned, they dropped the Sleuth. It executed its flight plan, passing within a few thousand kilometers of the planet. Its sensors opened up after it came out of FTL, recording several hours of data as it passed over the planet. Emitting nothing and covered in its stealth sock, it slipped by the enormous blue marble like a long black ghost and moved on back towards *Antares*.

*Antares*
Beta Hydri
Tuesday, May 31, 2078, 1550 UTC

Senior Lieutenant Jack Ballard waited impatiently for Carol Hansen to get the Sleuth back aboard. They had made laser contact with the device and brought it alongside *Antares*. Once it was close, one of the Weaps technicians could bring it into the ShuttleLock using a joystick remote. Easy as pie. As Chief of Intel, it would be Ballard's job to take the data dump from the Sleuth and make something comprehensible out of it. He always preached the difference between information and intelligence, and he was now stuck figuring out the difference for himself.

Once the device was back on a maintenance cart and the ShuttleLock was re-pressurized, he, Carol, and Ryan headed over to it. Chief Guzman, as usual, beat them to it.

"OK, lady and gentlemen, with all respect, keep your goddamn hands off until we clear it."

Three sets of commissioned hands slammed into their pants pockets. Guzman grinned as he pulled back the stealth sock from the head of the Sleuth.

"OK, that's better. Lieutenant Hansen, let's have the checklist."

Carol was ready.

"Panel 102, open, switch propulsion master, off."

"Open, off."

"Panel 57, open, guidance master, off."

"Done."

"Panel 22, open, sensor master, off."

"22, open, off."

"Panel 35, open, remove data cartridge." Opening the panel, Guzman turned to Ballard.

"Here you are, Lieutenant Ballard." Ballard reached in, removed the cartridge, and dropped it in a clear plastic envelope. Ballard headed for the Intel section, Ryan following close behind.

Guzman looked at Carol. "Disposition?" he asked, indicating the Sleuth.

"Run diagnostics on it. If it's good to go, let's just put in a new data card, recharge the fuel cells, and put it at the back of the stack. If not, well, check with Mister Swenson and see what he thinks."

"Will do."

He pushed the cart carrying the now-inert Sleuth towards the passageway which would take him back to the weapons maintenance room. Carol waited a moment, impatient to know what was on the data card, wondering if the planet held intelligent life, even enemy life. Finally, she stepped off for the passageway, heading for the Weaps office and the report she was about to write.

Jack Ballard carried the data cartridge into the Intel workroom and unlocked the cabinet containing the Sleuth data reader. He opened the envelope and placed the cartridge into the reader. They turned the Intel computers loose on the cartridge as they set up the workstation for manual review. The display showed the visual, IR, and radio data in time sync. The whole pass around 'Big Blue,' as they had nicknamed the planet, only took about three hours.

The first few pictures were nice 'beauty shots' of the planet but too far away to yield any detail. As the probe moved closer, they were able to see the clouds more clearly and also see that there was quite a lot of ocean. As they were talking about how much it looked like home, a tone sounded, and an alert appeared on Jack's workstation.

"Computer sees something." He touched the flashing alert on the screen, and the corresponding image appeared.

"Oh my God, Ryan. Streets."

They sat for a moment in amazement. Without taking his eyes off the picture, Jack reached for the ship phone.

"Captain...Ballard here, Commander. I think you should come back to Intel...Streets, ma'am. Streets."

Slowly he hung up as more alerts began to populate his screen.

Terri Michael wasted no time in getting to the Intel workroom, with XO James George close behind. The original image was still up on Ballard's workstation, but now the computer was kicking off more alerts than he could keep up with. They all leaned in to see the next picture. There was clearly some kind of city or town along the shoreline. After about a half-dozen images, Michael straightened up.

"OK, I've seen enough. Jack, keep working these. I need some expanded versions of the best images. You'll brief the officers in the wardroom in an hour on what you've seen."

She turned to Lewis. "Where are we on the system census?"

"By schedule, it should be maybe 80%, but I will check with the techs."

"Fine. I need it done, and then I need it reviewed to make sure there is no enemy presence here."

"Yes, ma'am."

"I'll need your detailed status and a schedule for completion in an hour as well."

"I will be ready."

"Very good, folks, very good. Let's see what else we can find." Michael left the Intel section and returned to the Bridge, walking to the Comms station.

```
FLASH 207805311630 UTC
TO:   CINCFLEET
FROM: ANTARES ACTUAL
BETA HYDRI BLUE DOT SLEUTH EXAM SHOWS APPARENT STREETS.
PLAN TO COMPLETE SYSTEM CENSUS THEN ORBIT BLUE DOT FOR
CLOSER EXAMINATION.
END
```

She walked over to the Surveillance station. The techs were sorting through the other planets, asteroids, and small bodies that populated the Beta Hydri system.

"Anything interesting?"

The tech looked up at her. "No, Captain. All pretty nominal stuff."

"Very well. Keep at it."

"Will do, ma'am."

## Chapter 15

ISC Fleet HQ
Fort Eustis, VA
Thursday, June 2, 2078, 0030 EDT

The message from *Antares* arrived in Fleet HQ just before midnight as June 1st became June 2nd. It was a warm, typically humid night in Virginia. After calling Ron Harris and Chief of Operations Patty Cook, Admiral Connor Davenport walked the short distance from the Bachelor Officers' Quarters to his headquarters, dressed informally in a golf shirt and jeans. At this time of night, he just didn't give a damn about uniforms or formality. Harris caught a ride from base security and arrived a few minutes after the CINC. He also chose casual dress, an SFU T-shirt and shorts. They stood in the Operations Center, with the overnight watch crew looking on with amusement at their appearance, evaluating *Antares'* surprising discovery.

"Well, Admiral," Ron began, "she doesn't give us very much to go on here. Obviously, there is some kind of advanced species living there. How advanced, we'll have to wait and see."

"Beta Hydri. That's what, twenty-four light-years?" Davenport asked.

Ron nodded.

"Is it possible this is the enemy homeworld?"

"Can't know yet, sir, but sure, it's possible. I don't want to try to read too much into this. She's seen something she thinks we need to know about, but this is very preliminary. If she goes ahead and orbits, there will be a lot more data coming."

As they were talking, Chief of Operations Patty Cook arrived, having taken the time to get into uniform. Her short, sharp, dark appearance contrasted sharply with her taller, more shabbily dressed counterparts.

"Good morning, Patty," Davenport said.

"Hello, Connor, Ron," she said cordially, acknowledging each in turn, "What do we have?"

Davenport handed her the text of the *Antares* message.

"Wow, streets! A fourth intelligent species?"

"Maybe," Ron cautioned, "I mean, this could be the enemy homeworld."

Cook looked up sharply from the paper. "Do you really think so?"

"I think it's possible — I didn't mean to say that I think it actually is or even that it's likely."

"But you're reminding me, again, not to assume or jump to conclusions?" she asked, some humor in her voice.

"That is my thankless task, yes," he replied with a smile.

"Well, as usual, you're right. Still, either way, it's an exciting prospect."

"So, what do we tell Commander Michael?" Davenport asked.

Cook looked at him. "She is in possession of much more information than we have here. So, I think we need to trust her to do what needs doing."

Ron agreed. "From an Intel point of view, I can't tell her what to do because, much as you are saying, I can't see what she sees. Jack Ballard is first-rate, and she has a couple of bright stars there in Hansen and Lewis, too."

"And Jim George," Cook added.

"Indeed, an inspired choice on her part, I'd say," Ron finished.

"Stole him from right under my nose," CINC pretended to complain.

"Which you agreed to!" Cook pointed out, drawing a smile from the CINC.

"I did, I did. Once she started asking for stuff, I couldn't stop saying 'yes'!"

Ron smiled at CINC's self-deprecating manner but then moved the discussion back on topic.

"Back to the issue before us. My recommendation is to advise caution but let her proceed as she sees fit."

The Admirals agreed, and CINC drafted the message

```
PRIORITY 207806020700 UTC
TO:    ANTARES
FROM: CINCFLEET
CAUTION ADVISED BUT PROCEED OWN DISCRETION.
NOTIFY HQ OF SIGNIFICANT FINDS.
END
```

"Terse, sir, but I agree with the sentiment." Admiral Cook commented after reading Davenport's draft.

They each headed back to their beds, but there would not be much sleep this morning as each fretted over what *Antares* might find. It might mean trouble, or not. It might be dangerous, or not.

Ron regretted that there was no more he could offer ship commanders in these situations, but he wasn't there, and there was really no other choice than to let them do their jobs. The low bandwidth of SLIP communications was a recurring annoyance for him. He wanted to see what they had, have his team see it, and then give Commander Michael some solid advice. Just telling her to do whatever she thinks best seemed pretty lame to him. He hoped Terri Michael would understand.

He was the last to leave the Operations Center. As he walked out, he decided to pass on Security's offer of a ride and walk the half mile to his house. It was good to clear his head a bit, but it still felt like a long walk. He snuck in quietly, but Meredith was up, rocking in the living room, reading a book. As he came in, she set it down, took his hand, and led him down the hall.

ISC Fleet HQ
Fort Eustis, VA
Friday, June 3, 2078, 2020 EDT

It had been a typical day for Fiona, an early start followed by long hours. She lived less than a mile from Fleet HQ, and when the weather allowed, she would walk or jog it. This evening, it did not, and so she accepted a ride from one of the Fleet security techs that guarded the entrance. There were several senior officers that either came in early or left late, or both, and they kept a vehicle handy just in case.

Fiona rode the short trip in silence, speaking only to thank the young driver that brought her home. Annie, was it? Anna? Abby? *Shit,* she thought as she walked to the door; *I need to pay closer attention.* As she opened the door and stepped into the silent house, she heard the Jeep-equivalent pull away. They were always careful to wait until she was safe inside, and that was comforting. She flipped on the hall light and headed for the bathroom for relief, then she walked to the kitchen to see what was available for a meal.

She and 'Big Jimmy' Collins had separated a long time ago — over ten years. He had loved her best he could, but somehow, he just couldn't figure out how to be a one-woman man. Fiona finally gave him the boot after coming back from a week on her ship and finding him entangled with another officer's wife. They never did divorce. For Fiona, it just didn't matter since she had no intention of re-marrying. The same was true for Jimmy, but for vastly different reasons. He was fun at a party, that was for sure, but really not much more than that. Sometimes in quiet, solitary moments she regretted not having children, but she was honest enough with herself to accept that she loved the fleet as if they were her children, and she would defend them with an intensity, a ferocity, any mother would recognize. Besides, they would have been Jimmy's children, and that thought was usually enough to clear her mind on the subject.

She had consumed a coffee or two too many today, which left her with mild heartburn and feeling just a little edgy. Sorting through the refrigerator, she selected one of the prepared meals she kept on hand. She tossed it into the warmer, which read the barcode on the meal and took over the cooking. It was a huge breakthrough when someone invented meals and an appliance that could selectively heat different foods at the optimal temperature. When Fiona later opened the package, her salad was still crisp and cold, but the turkey and gravy were steaming hot.

Meantime, she poured a generous glass of Pinot Noir and flopped on her small sofa across from the flat screen. She was completely comfortable as a confirmed, unrepentant career Fleet officer and her small quarters looked it. She had just enough furniture to support the limited amount of time she spent there. On the infrequent occasions when she had out-of-town family to visit, she paid for their hotel, and they dined out. She started up the flat screen, but the news these days was just too infuriating, so she picked a favorite classic movie and settled back, trying to quiet her head and relax. Dinner would be ready in a few minutes.

Joanne was only gone a week or so, but Fiona missed her like a sister who had gotten married and moved out. *Intrepid* would be leaving soon, she knew. There was a job Fiona and Ron wanted Joanne to do. The first twenty Sentinels were ready for deployment, and *Intrepid* would be delivering the first batch of six. It was a different mission from the search vessels since there would be no time at each star to examine the system and look for the enemy. For this job, *Intrepid* would come in, establish the correct orbit, power up and validate the Sentinel, then push it overboard and leave. They didn't want to be there long, and they would not be sending the usual status messages. That worried Fiona a lot, but Joanne would not hesitate to call if they got into trouble. The longer *Intrepid* was silent, the better the mission would be going. But it had a strange feeling to it, and it made her nervous that there was some scenario she and Ron hadn't considered.

She was also dreading Ben Price's leaving. They had kept that quiet from the rest of the team to stave off the inevitable disruption it would cause. For now, the team was adjusting to the loss of Commander Henderson, and Ben was a big reason they were doing so well. She needed that to continue for another few weeks when they would have to break the news to the staff and accept the dislocation that would follow.

She was just starting to feel the wine when the dinner-ready signal went off in the kitchen. She sat cross-legged on the hardwood floor, eating from the container as she sipped from her refilled glass and watched *The Martian* for at least the twentieth time. She felt a strong connection to the captain, her difficult decision, and wondered whether she could have done the same. The rational, command-oriented part of her knew she would, but the Fleet-mother part had serious qualms about it. Movies have a way of mangling a happy ending, but in real life, Mark would have been dead in a few months, and it would not have been pretty. This evening, she was asleep before he made it to Pathfinder.

*Antares*
Beta Hydri
Friday, June 3, 2078, 2000 UTC

The message from Fleet HQ came back in just over seventy-six hours, meaning that they had taken only a couple hours to consider what she should do.

```
PRIORITY 207806020700 UTC
TO:   ANTARES
FROM: CINCFLEET
CAUTION ADVISED BUT PROCEED OWN DISCRETION.
NOTIFY HQ OF SIGNIFICANT FINDS.
```

So, Fleet HQ had decided she should do whatever she thought was advisable. That was fine with her. In the time since Terri had signaled CINC, her team had patiently completed the system census and determined that there was no detectable enemy presence.

They watched the blue planet with the long-range telescope and determined that it rotated in about forty-seven hours and was perhaps ten percent larger than the Earth. The planet's axis had only a small inclination. There were large ice caps both north and south. That they were larger than Earth's and nearly equal in size was another bit of evidence that the rotational tilt was small.

The towns were clearly visible now, but it was not possible to detect traffic from their current distance. Jack Ballard pieced together a few pictures and was starting to get an idea of how large the culture was. But, in the time since its discovery, the planet hadn't even rotated twice, so he had limited imagery to work from.

The officers met in the wardroom late that first evening and Terri decided to move into orbit around Big Blue. They would come in about halfway between the planet and its largest moon, smaller than Earth's and now nicknamed 'Little Gray.' Little Gray's orbit was around 500,000 kilometers, a little farther than the Moon, so they would come in at about 250,000 kilometers, minimum EMR set, and see what they could detect from a sun-synchronous polar orbit. There were two other small moons about a tenth the size of Little Gray, plus perhaps a dozen small rocks that they had detected so far. It was a surprisingly busy little system, Ryan Lewis thought, one to make the astrophysicists scratch their heads.

The approach was uneventful but nerve-wracking for the crew. Every Surveillance tech was on some sensor feed or another. The computer was post-processing every source, with the Intel staff watching for alerts.

Carol had *Antares* ready to fire. As they got closer, she wandered over to Ryan Lewis, standing behind the Surveillance workstation. He greeted her silently, still watching the feeds displayed on the large monitors above.

A tech looked up. "I can see the streets, Lieutenant. They're just coming into sunlight."

"Zoom that as close as you can," he replied. "Dawn would be a good time to get shadows and see if anything is moving."

The image grew large enough for all of them to see the grid. They thought they saw structures along the streets, and long shadows crossing, but no motion.

"Maybe they're late risers." Carol deadpanned.

Ryan suppressed a laugh and stuck to his monitors. The techs cracked up — it helped break the tension. After an hour of observation, Terri looked at Ryan Lewis.

"I need to know everything that's around us. Get the radar up and see what else is out there."

"Yes, ma'am."

She walked over to Weaps and pulled Carol aside.

"I've turned on the radar. Things may get a little hairy, so be on your toes."

Carol nodded her understanding. "We're ready to shoot, ma'am, as soon as Surveillance designates a target. I took the liberty of swapping in four Spartans - we can still attack if we want, but I thought we should be ready for defense."

"That's fine. All Lances?"

"Yes."

Terri moved back over to the Surveillance station. The radar picture showed satellites in low and high orbits.

"If any of those satellites maneuver, I need to know right away. We'll have to decide whether to smack it or bug out."

"Yes, Commander, will do."

The Surveillance station phone sounded again. "Lewis. Yes, she's right here. OK, Jack, we'll be there." He turned to Terri. "Ballard would like to show us something back in Intel."

Terri looked around the Bridge. "Hansen! Take the conn."

"Yes, ma'am." She spoke briefly to her techs and then walked to the command position.

"Nav, I have the Conn."

"Very well, Lieutenant."

She sat down, wondering what was happening back in Intel. A call from Ballard and a quick exit by the CO, XO, and Surveillance Officer were worrisome. She was quickly back down and standing at the Surveillance station, watching the feeds with the techs.

As Terri, James George, and Ryan Lewis entered the Intel workroom, Jack Ballard was just finishing his analysis. With a few (dozen) keystrokes he had it up on the large wall monitor.

"Captain, I've been grabbing frames every minute since we got close enough to discern the streets as the star rose. Watch this."

He played the two-hour sequence, which only took a few seconds. They could see the land get lighter as the frames sequenced, the shadows getting shorter. He played it three times. Finally, XO George looked away from the monitor to Ballard.

"OK, Jack, whatever I'm supposed to see, I don't see it."

Ballard smiled. "Well, Commander, in a way, that's my point. There's nothing. No motion, no vehicles, nothing on IR, nothing on UV. If this were Earth, there would be motion on the roads and IR plumes in the homes. Maybe some UV from lighting."

He turned back to the display. "We should see pedestrians, not well, but we should see that someone is there. There's nobody."

He paused. "And one more thing." He turned to a tech. "Put up that shot by the open field."

A picture of an open area near a large city appeared.

"You see the buildings, then there is an open area maybe a couple hundred meters across, then there are these shapes, they're white, but I can't resolve what they are yet."

Terri looked at Lewis. "How close would you need to be to be able to tell what those are?"

"We're at 250,000 kilometers now. I asked Nav, and the synchronous orbit for a planet like this is around 63,000."

Terri turned back to Ballard. "How far off the equator is this place?"

"Oh, 15 degrees or so. A synchronous orbit over the equator at the same longitude at 63,000 would work nicely, I would think."

She picked up the ship phone. "Conn... Hansen, this is the Captain. Get with Surveillance for the position of this, uh, settlement, and then put us in a synchronous orbit over it...yes, I understand...proceed immediately."

She turned back to Ryan. "You said there were high satellites. How high?"

"There were some at that general altitude. We'll be tracking them as we move closer."

"Please don't hit anything." Terri sounded like a worried mother giving her teenager the keys to the car for the first time.

"Yes, ma'am. We shall try our best to keep our distance."

"Yeah, please. I think whatever plan you had for exploration is shot to hell, Ryan."

"Yes, Captain, I agree."

"Soon as we get down to 63K, let's get a shuttle out and get a drone over this area. Keep it above 5000 meters. If there is anybody there, they won't see or hear it at that altitude."

"Will do."

She turned to James George. "Commander George, I'd like you and Lewis to fly it down. I can't have any screw-ups."

George nodded his understanding. "It's just an hour plus past dawn now, and it will take us four hours to get down. Do you want it delivered today in full daylight? It might be better to wait and launch it before dawn tomorrow."

Terri thought a second and then shook her head. "No, let's not wait that long. As slow as this thing rotates, there's still plenty of daylight. Deploy it high and offshore, and we should be fine. Maybe we'll have some convenient clouds to hide behind."

*Antares*
Above Big Blue
Saturday, June 4, 2078, 0200 UTC

Now that they were at a much lower altitude and hanging in orbit just south of the coastal settlement, the quality of their images improved dramatically. The white shapes were now in clear focus, and as they came to the realization of what they were looking at, a somber quiet slowly spread over the workroom. Where a minute before there were as many conversations as there were people, now there were none. They all watched as Jack nitpicked the image into complete clarity.

"Holy shit," he finally said, almost under his breath.

Carol Hansen, now off Bridge watch, was helping the Intel techs scan through the images. She also stopped what she was doing and fixed her eyes on the picture Ballard had put up on the primary monitor.

"Unbelievable. You should probably—" Carol said quietly.

"Yeah, on it." Jack interrupted her as he picked up the ship phone.

"Captain...Yes, ma'am. Could you come back here? We have something to show you."

Terri was back in Engineering talking with the FPI engineers, so it was a few minutes before she made it forward to the Intel Section. Jack just left the image on the monitor. Terri walked in, saw the image, and stopped in her tracks.

"Are those —"

"Skeletons, yes, ma'am, they appear to be."

At first, Jack said nothing more, letting her just take in the image.

"The drone imagery will be better, but from here they seem to be partially buried in the overgrowth."

He tapped and swiped, and a different image appeared on the monitor. Green and tan invasions marred the straight lines of what were now clearly streets.

"With the better resolution, we also went back and looked at the main part of the city. The city is also partially overgrown; there is vegetation that seems to be encroaching on the streets. The lighter tan color is probably dirt or sand or something like that."

"Still no motion?"

"No. Nothing visual, IR or UV. We could see a match from this distance, Captain. There's no one there."

"No one left alive, anyhow," Terri responded quietly.

"Also, we can see some craters, some other damage. Again, it's preliminary, but I'd guess they got the RFG treatment before whatever this scene represents happened."

He paused, changing subjects. "We started a larger area survey, and we can already see that this was a highly organized society. There is a regular sequence of larger concentrations, towns, or small cities, I guess. I can't tell exactly, but I'm guessing they occupied over 1500 klicks along the shoreline and a good distance inland as well. We're working on a set of survey images we can get more specific and build a map."

Carol pointed to an area inland of the towns along the coast. "Look here. Outside the cities, there are grids just like back home. Those have to be farms."

As they enlarged the area Carol had indicated, they could indeed see a lattice of fields formed by roads, and within each square, there were structures along one side.

"Farmhouses," Ballard finally said.

"Right. Or the equivalent, yeah. I'll bet the grids are oriented north-south-east-west, too."

A tech spoke to Ballard and pointed to another monitor.

"OK, we have the margins, finally." He swapped the ugly view of skeletons for a larger view of the entire coast. "We caught a break on the weather: clear and dry for quite a distance. The structures span about 2000 klicks along the shore and 400 inland. There is a large city, I guess it's a city, don't know what else to call it, right in the middle. Then smaller structures and concentrations every seventy-five klicks or so. We're guessing a little on the distances, ma'am, but give us a day, and we'll have a pretty good map for you."

"Where are we on the drone?" Terri asked.

"It's deployed and working its way down," Carol answered.

She pulled up a display showing the view from the front of the drone, its altitude, and speed.

"The XO and Lieutenant Lewis should be back aboard shortly."

"Jack, what have you and Ryan discussed about the drone?"

"Well, ma'am, we both feel we should stay clear of the larger cities for low-level investigation. Seems more likely to us that the higher density areas might be watched while the — suburbs, I guess — would be harder to monitor, if only because they're so much larger. The footage the Snooper will get is even better than what we can see from here, so we felt the Peeper would be better used to look at more common structures, residences, some buildings in the smaller concentrations, that kind of thing."

Terri nodded her understanding and agreement, then looked at the images of the skeletons for a moment.

"They died there for a reason, Jack. Those lines of skeletons mean they were defending something. Something important. Something worth dying for. I want to know what it was."

"We'll see what we can figure out, Commander."

"Fine. How much daylight is left?"

"About sixteen hours left in what we're calling Sol 1, Commander."

Terri thought for a moment and then looked around at the Intel crew. Now that they were over the initial shock of the skeletons, their discussion became animated, with plenty of opinions and pointing at new images. She looked at her watch. It was after 0230. She was surprised that it was that late and realized the excitement of this discovery was having an effect on all of them. But there would be mistakes if they went on too long and then a mental crash when they all ran out of gas.

"Can you all keep this up that long?" she asked.

They all said they could.

"These forty-seven-hour days are going to suck. Get some breaks, cat naps, or whatever, but as soon as the sun sets, get a full twelve hours off. No cheating! And then see what you can accomplish before it rises again. Lieutenant Hansen, you're with me."

They stepped outside just as Lewis and George were returning. Lewis went on inside, and George remained with the two officers.

Terri turned to Carol. "How long have you been up?"

Carol looked at the captain quizzically, then checked her watch. "About twenty hours."

"OK. James, get Lewis out here."

Ryan joined the impromptu conference in the passageway.

"I want you both to go get some sleep. Come back here in ten hours or whatever if you want. But when the sun sets down there, we're going to switch to a low-altitude polar orbit. I figure in twenty-four hours we can get maybe twelve or so orbits in. We will use that time to map the rest of the planet and to look for the enemy. If they did this, they might have left something behind to sound the alarm if anyone shows up."

"So, you need us loaded and ready in sixteen hours?" Carol asked.

"Correct. This—" Terri pointed to the Intel workroom, "—has to be primarily an Intel job. I appreciate you both helping Ballard out, but we have to get our regular jobs done, too. This is no less true for Commander George and me."

Ryan Lewis looked at Carol and responded, "We understand, Captain. We'll be ready."

"Very well. Good night."

## Chapter 16

*Antares*
Big Blue
Saturday, June 4, 2078, 2000 UTC (Local sunset)

It had been hard to sleep, but Carol was learning the technique of getting what she could when she could. She'd always been a sound sleeper but used to a regular schedule. Her time in the Fleet was starting to change that, and she found herself better able to get to sleep, but she was also more easily awakened. *Just part of the business*, she thought. After a few hours of helping out in the Intel section, she was again on the Bridge at the Weapons station.

The Snooper had been busy over the last sixteen hours. They had deployed it near the largest city, now called Capital City. Since the aliens lived on a more or less north-south axis along the coast, they decided to name the cities and towns by direction and order. So, First North Town was the small concentration just north of Capital City. First City South was the first larger set of structures south of the Capital.

The ideas of 'north' and 'south' are just arbitrary choices, so they established Big Blue's directions based on the pole around which the planet rotated counter-clockwise. Said another way, they made the planet rotate to the east, so the sun would rise in the east like Earth, giving them familiar directional references.

Terri stood at her command station. She had held a quick conference with the staff so they knew what she had in mind, and they were ready when she called for the changes.

"Comms, send the message."
"Sending, Captain."

```
PRIORITY 207806042000 UTC
TO: CINCFLEET
FROM: ANTARES
BLUE DOT SHOWS EVIDENCE OF POSSIBLE ENEMY GENOCIDE.
RFG CRATERS SEEN.
EXPLORING WITH SNOOPER ETC.
NO ENEMY ACTIVITY DETECTED.
EXECUTING LOW POLAR ORBIT BEGINNING THIS TIME DURING SITE'S
APPROX 24 HR LOCAL NIGHT FOR MAPPING AND SURVEILLANCE
END
```

"OK, here we go." She looked over at Surveillance. "Surveillance, secure the radar and stow the antenna. Conn, set minimum EMR."
"Radar is off, Commander."
"Minimum EMR set, Captain."
"Nav, give me a 1500 klick orbit. Proceed."

They dropped quickly into the new orbit, arriving in an hour or so. They had started at 250,000 kilometers, then moved to 63,000 kilometers and now were only 1500 above the surface. Terri thought about that altitude for a moment, then made a decision.

"Nav, roll us head-down to the planet. Conn, open the Bridge windows."

The windows opened, and there, passing seemingly just over their heads, was Big Blue. There was a lot of ocean and, so far, minimal land. But there were clouds and storms and obvious weather fronts and large areas of clear sky through which they could see the rich blue of the ocean.

"It's such a beautiful place," Terri said to herself quietly.

"Yeah, too bad everybody's dead," the Conn officer next to her responded.

Terri turned as if to scold the young ensign, but she stopped, knowing the ensign was right. The beauty of the planet only compounded the evil of the genocide by comparison. *Why,* she asked herself, *why did they do this? And why Inor?* The question weighed on her mind, as it did on others, but the lack of useful information precluded any real conclusion. Bringing herself back to current demands, she stepped down and went to the Surveillance station.

"Lieutenant Lewis, what's the status on the Snooper?"

Ryan picked up his tablet, then poked and swiped his way to the data. "Short answer is 'pretty good,' Commander. We dropped the comms when we maneuvered and set it to slow speed and minimum power use. It will wake up about an hour before local sunrise and start listening for commands."

"What's the power situation?"

"Also, good. We used zero fuel cell power the last day, and with the charge on board, we don't expect to use more than five or ten percent overnight."

"So, we can count on it for five local days, maybe more?"

"Maybe, ma'am. That might be a bit optimistic. Even moderate winds and bad weather would reduce that time. Today was almost perfect for us, with clear skies and very low winds."

She knew she was pushing the edges on the drone's capabilities, but this planet needed significant observation time. If she had to send the shuttle down to retrieve it and deploy another, that would be fine, too. But so far, it was working out well. She suddenly remembered Dean Carpenter smiling across the Bridge at her during an exercise when some plan of hers had come up a little short. He was almost laughing as he said, 'It's a play-it-where-it-lies world, Commander. What now?' *Yeah, Dean, it is,* she thought to herself. She realized that it had been a while since she had thought of Carpenter, specifically. The loss of *Liberty* was a still-present wound in all of them, something they shared but almost never spoke about. She felt a familiar pain in her chest as she thought of them, but she was better now about keeping that grief under control. She knew how to manage it and keep on working. She had to. She had a ship of her own now, one she cared deeply about, a ship carrying many who shared her feelings for *Liberty* and Dean Carpenter.

After three orbits they could see that Big Blue was almost a water world, with only about ten percent of the surface area dry land, in three continents all about the size of Australia, plus a few small islands. Terri wondered what strangeness they might find in the depths of that immense ocean.

The largest continent was in the southern hemisphere, perhaps a third of the way around to the west from the settled area. The weather was less clear there, but with IR to correlate with the visual spectrum data, they got a good picture of snow-capped mountains and difficult terrain. There were no apparent roads or other signs of advanced culture, just masses of thick vegetation at the lower elevations.

A third continent, the smallest but really not all that different in size from the others, was on the opposite side of the planet from the cities. It, too, had no evidence of occupation and, from their distance, appeared to have mostly scrub vegetation consistent with the tundra of the north on Earth. Unrelated to 'grass,' Terri expected, but a similar evolutionary response to a similar environment was hardly a surprise. *Then again*, she thought, *a completely different response probably would not have felt like a surprise either. Maybe I should be surprised that it's similar?* Terri was beginning to wonder if her flexible thinking and adaptive responses to these alien worlds were getting just a little too flexible and adaptive.

She shook off that thought and looked at the Surveillance display, watching as they methodically found, evaluated, and categorized any object within their view. The universe seemed to orchestrate an infinite set of variations on familiar themes when it came to the small bodies that orbited the stars they visited. The Surveillance techs would find something that looked a little like Ceres or a bit bigger than Io, but wait, it's different because it has or has not some minor attribute or another. They would bicker, argue, point, shrug, nod, and shake but eventually agree on how to classify a body, smile a little, and then move on to the next object in line. Jack Ballard's Intel processes were running ahead of this manual operation, looking for the tell-tale spectrum of an enemy ship or anything else that looked suspicious. How Jack had taught a computer to be 'suspicious,' Terri didn't know, but if it was possible, she figured Ballard could make it happen.

She maintained a nagging sense that the enemy might be here somewhere, in some form. If they did this, she thought, surely, they would leave something to tell them if someone else came around. There should be a tripwire or burglar alarm. *Or,* she thought, *maybe they don't care who sees this.* Could they be that shameless? Willing to be so flagrantly criminal? Her mind went back to the first quarter of the century when so-called Islamists openly murdered thousands in the name of religion. Or, further back, the Holocaust, the Spanish Inquisition, or the Crusades. All of these were public, plainly viewed examples of death in the name of something or someone they worshipped. They certainly weren't hiding anything at Inor. Could the enemy religion be at the core of all this? Could this be some kind of pogrom? She made some notes in her personal journal, planning to bring it up with FleetIntel when they got back. She would not saddle Jack Ballard with it, as he had plenty to think about already.

ISC Fleet HQ Communications Station
Fort Eustis, VA
Monday, June 6, 2078, 0321 EDT

Mark England was pulling yet another overnight. They played hell with his social life, but he enjoyed the work, and it had only become more serious over the last couple of months. His supervisor, Chief Diana Aviles, did her best to keep the rotating shifts fair, but for Mark, they seemed to too often conflict with the off-duty days of a particular data analyst in the Operations section. But there was a war on, and when on duty, he was part of the central nervous system of the Fleet. That meant something. Right before he was to take his lunch break, the SLIP receiver's subdued incoming-message tone demanded his attention.

```
PRIORITY 207806042000 UTC
TO: CINC
FROM: ANTARES
TOP SECRET
BLUE DOT SHOWS EVIDENCE OF POSSIBLE ENEMY GENOCIDE.
RFG CRATERS SEEN.
EXPLORING WITH SNOOPER ETC.
NO ENEMY ACTIVITY DETECTED.
EXECUTING LOW POLAR ORBIT BEGINNING THIS TIME DURING SITE'S
APX 24 HR LOCAL NIGHT FOR MAPPING AND SURVEILLANCE.
END
```

He sent it to the Operations Center and forwarded it to Admiral Davenport. He picked up the direct line to Operations Center.

"Torres"

"Commander Torres, it's England in Comms, sir. There is a priority from *Antares* you should probably look at."

"You read *everything*, England?" Torres asked, an edge of disapproval in his voice.

"At this time of day, we read everything above ROUTINE, Commander, in case it needs attention before the morning."

"Very well. I'll check it out."

Torres scowled as he hung up the phone. Something rubbed him the wrong way about Comms reading messages not addressed to them, but, as he thought about it, someone had to be there to handle these kinds of issues. He pulled the message up on a monitor.

"Dammit," he said to himself as he picked up the phone.

"CINC."

Connor Davenport was now staying in the BOQ most days, partly to be close to the HQ and partly to keep the middle-of-the-night disturbances away from his family. His phone rang.

"Yeah, Davenport," he answered sleepily.

"Harold Torres in Operations, sir. There is a priority message from *Antares* you should probably read. I can wait if you like."

"No, Commander, I'll look at it and call you back."

Davenport clicked off the voice connection on his phone and switched to the Fleet Messages utility. There was the message from *Antares*.

"Genocide? What the hell..."

He sat looking at the message for a minute, reading and re-reading it as if he could extract some additional meaning from the few cryptic lines in front of him. He had full confidence in Terri Michael and her crew. But what should they do? He quickly changed applications and set up a priority meeting with Intel, Operations, Plans, and Public Information at 0800. Usually, Noah Peters would do this for him, but he felt no need to wake his aide up in the middle of the night to do something he could easily manage himself. *Antares* was thirty-six hours away by SLIP, and a few hours to get his best minds together was time well spent. He called back into the Operations Center.

"Torres."

"Yes, Commander, I've set up a meeting at 0800 with the senior staff. Nothing more to do until then."

"Yes, Admiral. Shall I call you if we see anything more from *Antares*?"

"Only if it is something critical. If *Antares* follows up with more information, we can handle that in the morning."

"Very well, sir."

"Good night, Commander."

"Good night, sir."

ISC Fleet HQ - Office of the Commander in Chief
Fort Eustis, VA
Monday, June 6, 2078, 0800 EDT

The coffee cups on the CINC's big conference table varied in color, size, shape, and contents, but not in urgency. The thirty-six-hour communication delay from *Antares* to Earth was frustrating all of them. Ron Harris knew *Antares* was on to something important. A fourth inhabited world! There were a hundred questions he wanted to be answered. What were they like? Is this an enemy world? He and Fiona Collins had met several times to discuss redirecting additional ships to Beta Hydri after the initial report of a new culture. It would mean deviating from their carefully structured search plans, but maybe, in this case, they could justify that.

Then came the bombshell message this morning.

CINC arrived, placed his own barrel-sized coffee mug on the table, and called the meeting to order.

"Good morning. You all have the message from *Antares*. I'd like to hear your thoughts about what Commander Michael says."

He sat back in his chair, cup in hand.

Chief of Operations Cook spoke first. "So, we don't know how they came to that conclusion?"

Ron Harris leaned forward to answer. "No, but Jack Ballard is no fool, and neither is Terri Michael. If they say there's genocide, they have solid evidence for it. The presence of RFG craters would obviously support the idea that this is the same enemy."

"Who the hell are these...*people*?" Fiona wondered quietly.

"Assuming we're talking about the same culture as Inor, someone we're going to kill," CINC answered, his anger not well disguised.

"OK, so what do we do?" Fiona asked.

Ron sat back in his chair, looking off into the distance. "Commander Michael has deployed a drone. I wonder what else she's already done."

"Makes sense; she could get close-up documentation," Cook added.

Ron sighed in frustration. "The one thing I hate about SLIP, other than how slow it feels, is the low bandwidth. If we want to see her images, she has to bring them here."

Fiona shrugged. "Then we better get them back here."

CINC leaned forward in his chair. "Is there any guidance we can give her about how to investigate this? Do we have any relevant expertise?"

Ron shook his head. "Not really, sir. We're working to stand up the Exo-Biology and Exo-Technology groups best we can as we find qualified people we can clear. But they aren't yet operational. I would think we would want an archeologist or anthropologist for this job."

"If it really is a genocide, meaning they're all dead, we're looking at something akin to studying a long-dead culture here on Earth. Like the Sumerians or the Mayans or something," PIO Donna Wright offered.

Ron nodded his agreement. CINC looked over at him.

"See who you can find, Ron. Terri Michael's investigation, however far it goes, will only be the beginning."

"Yes, sir, Exo-Archeology Section. We'll get on it," he responded, one eyebrow raised as he wondered just how he was going to do that.

Donna smiled. "Now *there* is a title nobody ever thought they'd have."

There was quiet laughter at that. It did seem a little ridiculous, but the whole idea of a space war like they were in also seemed vaguely ridiculous to most laymen.

"We need more proof that the enemy at Inor also struck Beta Hydri," Fiona said.

"Agreed," CINC replied. "If we can't make that connection, then this is a tragedy, but it's not *our* tragedy, and we can't spend resources on it."

Fiona looked again at the message. "Did anyone else notice the twenty-four-hour night? She's talking about a forty-eight-hour day on this planet. That will play hell with their biorhythms."

"Maybe," Cook responded, "but it also means they have a lot of daylight to work with."

"OK, so let's think. The message is at local sunset, twenty-hundred UTC on the fourth," Ron started. "If we consider that Sol one, then sunset on Sol two is, what, six hours from now?"

"Sounds right," Fiona answered.

"And any message we get to her will be sometime after local noon on Sol three." Ron continued.

"Yeah, more or less," Fiona answered with a shrug.

"I hope they're managing these days better than I am. Don't forget it's three weeks plus for them to get back here," Patty Cook commented.

"So, on Sol three, we tell them to...what?" CINC asked the group.

"We can't really know how much data they're collecting. They have a couple of drones, and they're pretty competent folks. Let's give them three more sols after they get the message and then have them RTB." Ron suggested.

Fiona scribbled on her notepad, then looked up.

"OK, so, by my rough calculation, that's seven days and eight hours from now, so call them back as of June 14, 2000 UTC?"

"That will put them back here around July 7 or 8," Ron added.

"I can live with that," Patty Cook said. "They have enough supplies for that, but not much more."

Davenport had heard what he needed to hear. "Very well, then. Admiral Cook, please order them back as of Ron's date and time." He turned to Ron. "Do we have any guidance for their investigation?"

Ron shook his head. "No, sir, I don't. If this is the same enemy, I would caution them to be vigilant. Not much else I can say."

"Agreed. Anything else?"

Chief of Operations Cook had the message out soon after that:

```
PRIORITY 207806061400 UTC
TO: ANTARES
FROM: FLEETOPS
TOP SECRET
THERE IS AN URGENT NEED HERE TO FURTHER EXPLORE YOUR EVIDENCE
AND DETERMINE NEXT STEPS. THEREFORE ANTARES SHALL RTB EARTH
NLT 207806142000 UTC. EARLIER RETURN AT YOUR DISCRETION.
GIVEN THIS DISCOVERY MANY HERE SUSPECT ENEMY PRESENCE SO
CONTINUED CAUTION ADVISED.
```

```
TO KEEP LOW PROFILE WE ARE NOT SENDING ADDITIONAL RESOURCES.
REPORT IF YOU HAVE ADDITIONAL FINDINGS OR REQUESTS.

COOK
END
```

*Antares*
Beta Hydri (d) 'Big Blue'
Wednesday, June 8, 2078, 0225 UTC

The Comm watch supervisor brought the message from Fleet Operations to the Conn officer. Miho Ito read the message and then picked up the phone and called the captain. Miho remembered Admiral Cook as a friendly but demanding instructor at the University, with a sizeable collection of pithy Fleet stories and a hard-nosed teaching manner that brought out the best in most students. It could bring out tears in others, but Miho always figured that was part of the plan. The captain's arrival at her position brought her back out of her memories of University. Terri Michael read the dispatch twice, making sure she hadn't missed anything. She looked at Ito.

"OK, Lieutenant, what's your interpretation?"

Miho thought for a few seconds before responding. "They're giving us time to complete the initial assessment, then we must get the data back home for the experts to interpret."

"That's pretty close."

"Too bad SLIP bandwidth is so low; if we were using regular radio, even, we could transmit most of this in a few minutes."

Michael smiled. "But we aren't, so we'll just have to carry the data back ourselves."

"Understood, Captain."

"Frankly, I share your frustration, but since we're sending messages at many times the speed of light, it's hard to complain, right?"

Miho nodded.

The Comm watch supervisor, a young tech, joined the conversation. "Do you want to send a response, Captain?"

"No, I don't think so. We'll call home after we're on our way a couple days and far away from here."

"Yes, ma'am."

Terri waited a bit, looking around the Bridge. During the last daylight period in the cities, the drone circled Capital City, collecting stereo images in visual and IR for later study. They had sent the small exploration drone, what they called the 'Peeper,' to explore one of the smaller towns, suburbs as they called them, and had returned a remarkable image of what looked like a photograph of one of the inhabitants. Seen through a window of what was presumably a small residence, it was a breathtaking image of an animal that looked like a cross between a chimp or monkey and some kind of feline. It had patterned fur that was white and brown with areas of black, but the blue-and-green multi-colored human-looking eyes looked out from the image with obvious intelligence.

If she could send but one image by SLIP, she thought, that would be the one.

But here they were, past noon of Sol Three on Big Blue. She was disappointed that Operations had provided tactical instruction and guidance but nothing scientific or archeological. For that, they were apparently on their own. She counted heavily on her medical officer Marcia Soto and her young officer cadre: Hansen, Alex Williams, Jack Ballard, and Ryan Lewis. They pulled in Warrant Officer Denise Long from Reactor Ops as well, her physics degree adding to their collective expertise.

Terri wanted to do as complete a reconnaissance as they could, bringing back as much data and materials as possible. But she was an engineer and ship commander, not a scientist. From Cook's order, they had until after sunset on Sol Six, which was really a pretty decent amount of time. The brain trust had already figured out a tolerable work schedule that managed the two-days-per-Sol diurnal difference between Earth and Big Blue. They would wake up the drone around local sunrise and give it a flight plan. The techs and additional volunteer staff would work two twelve-hour shifts managing the images as well as analyzing the data from their own sensors. Ballard would supervise the first twelve hours of daylight, and Carol would pick up the next twelve. Once sunset hit, Carol would be off for ten hours, then split the next 16 hours between a shift at the Conn and analysis and planning. Then she would be off another ten hours until sunrise and another twelve hours in Intel. Each of the four worked a variation of that basic pattern, and each set aside time for their 'day jobs' as well as making sure they got enough rest. Terri Michael and XO James George were also splitting a much simpler twelve-on-twelve-off schedule on the Bridge.

Terri set a team meeting for 0800 the next morning, a time when they would all be awake. She would inform them then of the timeline and try to enable them to plan for the best use of their remaining time.

*Antares*
Big Blue (Beta Hydri (d))
Thursday, June 9, 2078, 0800 UTC

They gathered in the Intel workroom since breakfast occupied the wardroom. Jack Ballard put up a slideshow of images from the Sol before, the most striking of which was the portrait. They were still fascinated with the intense, blue-and-green multi-colored human-looking eyes. Carol half-expected the picture to speak to them.

"Heterochromic? Amazing!" Terri said quietly.

"So beautiful," Carol agreed.

Terri asked Jack, "Is that a photograph or a painting? Can you tell?"

Jack looked at the image. "We think it's a photograph, ma'am, but it's hard to tell for sure looking through the window."

Other shots revealed that there had been an RFG attack here as well, concentrated in the cities. Many of the larger buildings showed signs of fires, although it was difficult to know from a distance whether these were because of the attack or just happened later after they were abandoned. There were skeletons in the streets there, too. They watched in silence for a few minutes before Terri got the conversation moving.

"We have been ordered to RTB by twenty-hundred on the fourteenth."

Jack's eyes widened with surprise. "Wow, that's more time than I expected them to give us."

Terri nodded. "Yes, it's after sunset on Sol Six. I wonder if they actually took time to do the math, but it works for us. So, what are our priorities?"

Jack looked at his NetComp. "We need two more Sols to finish a good photographic survey of the ground, including out to the farms. So, figure that's the rest of Sol Three and all of Sol Four."

"Can the Peeper be working at the same time?"

"Some, yes, but it has to get back up to the Snooper to get recharged."

"Should we launch another drone to support the lower-level work?" Carol asked.

"We could," Jack answered, "but we only have two aboard. That would leave us with nothing."

Carol looked across at the captain. "I don't know what we would be holding them back for, ma'am. If we can dedicate the second Snooper to lower-level work, it would really augment the amount of data we can get."

Terri looked up at James George, leaning on the wall by the door. He gave a slight nod.

"OK," she said, "I see the value in that, but what about processing? Do we have the personnel to support a second vehicle?"

Jack nodded. "Yes, Captain, I think so. Most of what we're doing is monitoring the image collection and looking at the occasional interesting shot. We're not managing the drone on a continual basis. We can handle another one."

Terri looked over at Carol, who indicated her agreement.

"OK, anything else we need to do?"

Carol looked at Jack, who shrugged. The next move was up to her.

"I think we need to bring back some bones—"

Marcia Soto sat upright and leaned forward. "I don't think I can permit that," she said firmly.

"And some dirt," Carol finished.

"Like I said," Marcia let her objection fade out.

Terri looked from one roommate to the other, slightly amused at this disagreement. She adopted a conciliatory tone and demurred on reminding them that she was the one in command.

"OK, well, I can see the intelligence value of both. That's obvious, I think. So, Doctor Soto, what specifically are your objections?"

"That's equally obvious: contamination of us and the ship with unknown, alien organisms."

Jack challenged her caution. "But we have sealed sample containers, Doctor, which we would then run through the regular decontamination process. Isn't that enough?"

"Did you read *The Andromeda Strain*, Lieutenant? You're assuming that our regular process will kill any alien organism. I think that's likely, but it is not by any means a certainty."

"So, what about the drones? They're contaminated now, right?" Ryan Lewis asked.

"I was going to get to that. We can't bring them back aboard."

Terri put on her best 'time to get real' face and laid out the situation for all of them.

"First, let's remind ourselves that there is a war on here. Second, we never planned for surface exploration. Frankly, we were lucky the drones were even aboard. Third, there is no doubt that there will be follow-on missions to this planet. They've already ordered us home to look at our data. Clearly, they plan to review it and then come back with better resources for a more detailed examination. If we can provide bacteriological samples, even do a little of the research ourselves, then we advance that process by at least days and maybe weeks."

Soto nodded, surrendering. "I understand our situation, Captain, but I also take my responsibility for the health of the crew very seriously."

"Indeed, you do, and everyone appreciates that, especially me. Were we not in a conflict right now, I would agree with you, and we would leave everything behind. As it is, I have to accept some small risks to gain significant intelligence."

"Yes, ma'am."

"That said, can you work with Lieutenant Ballard to devise a decontamination process that will minimize our risk? We'll do the regular routine, but what else might we do that would lower our risk?"

"I can work with him. We'll figure something out."

"Can we do any work on the dirt on the way back? Cultures or whatever?" Carol asked. She was inviting Marcia to re-engage, to step back from her initial objections to even bringing the stuff aboard, and actually participate in its analysis. She was the obvious choice for that, but Carol wanted to give her a chance to do it on her own terms.

"In the isolation area, we probably could. I will have to do some literature research on environmental studies, but I believe we have such references available aboard."

XO George spoke up. "We should. I think we have most of the Library of Congress in there somewhere."

"OK, so, Sol Five?" Terri asked.

"I'd like to take the Snooper and one Peeper and get some detailed images of Capital City, up and down as many streets as we can in as much detail as we can."

Terri looked over at Ryan Lewis. "Lieutenant Lewis, you're as close to a weatherman as we have on board. What are you seeing?"

"Well, ma'am, we can see a front coming in from the west. We don't have any history with what that will do when it hits the land or the mountains to the east, but I would bet that we're going to see some wind and rain overnight from Sol Three to Four. It may linger, but as I say, I don't really know."

"Understood. Lieutenant Hansen, what do you want to do on Sol Five?"

"If we get the second Snooper down there, I would like to get out to the farms — or what we're calling farms — and see if we can tell what they were growing and what tech they might have been using."

"And Sol Six?"

Jack answered for the team. "Contingencies, Captain. We'll need a few hours to get the drones back by shuttle. Also, if we're going to do a sample return, it should probably be on Sol Four or Five, so we can manage any issues and not get caught by the deadline."

"But that means an extra shuttle trip, right?" she asked.

"Yes, ma'am, it does," he responded, not trying to conceal his smile.

"How soon can you get the sample return kit on the Peeper in the hangar?" the XO asked.

Carol turned her head to look at him. "I asked Chief Guzman about that, and he says a couple hours. He's got the Peeper off and the kit unpacked already. I just need to tell him to go ahead."

"OK, so we'll install the sample kit and launch the second Snooper today, hopefully before sunset, but that's not critical. We'll use Snooper Two to get low-level images from the area we've already started to explore. Carol, sample return is now your problem. I think we should get a water sample from the ocean as well, if that's possible."

Carol nodded her understanding.

"Then we'll work this plan over Sols Four and Five and keep Six for contingencies and retrieval, as Lieutenant Ballard has suggested. Any objections?"

There were none.

"OK, let's get it done."

They rose, the respectful quiet vanishing in the chaos of conversations as each went to their task.

*Antares*
Beta Hydri (d) 'Big Blue'
Tuesday, June 14, 2078, 1955 UTC

Terri Michael looked around the hangar where almost the entire crew had gathered. They were a determined bunch, she thought. There were Inor survivors, *Antares* plank-owners, new kids, and some solid contributors from elsewhere in the Fleet. She stood on a work table to get a little more height, and they gathered in a large circle around her.

"Well, Ladies and Gentlemen, we're done with Big Blue for now. You've all done wonderfully well during this phase of the investigation, and I know that FleetIntel will be chewing on those results for some time once we get back. Someone will be coming back here. There can be no question about that. Whether that someone is us, we will just have to see. I know all of you are invested in this place, as am I, and I will surely make the case that we are the best crew for any follow-up."

That got her some cheers and smatters of applause.

"But for now, it's time to go home. We've got just about enough supplies to get us there, so no more detours, OK?"

More laughter.

"I just wanted to say thanks and that I expect a quiet trip home, so get some rest, play some games, whatever. Keep your eyes open, but I think we can stand easy for these next three weeks."

"Thank *you*, Commander," came a voice from the crew.

She smiled. "Well, you're welcome. But don't forget that it's you that do all the work. I feel more like an orchestra conductor sometimes than a captain. If I cue you in at the right time, I know I can count on you all to make great music."

She took one last glance around.

"OK, dismissed. Now, how the hell do I get down?"

As she was saying those words, Jack Ballard began his shift at the Conn, ordering the Nav watch to move the ship out of orbit and proceed to Earth, best speed. It was an order fraught with mixed emotions for him. There was so much more to learn here, but they didn't have the right gear, the right expertise, and they certainly didn't have the stores to stay even a week more. They were up against a hard deadline, and there really wasn't any choice. Besides, orders were orders, and they followed them faithfully. He watched Big Blue receding in his aft visual display. It shrank rapidly as the Drive went to full power, and then they slipped into FTL mode. He flicked off the display and picked up his tablet, the Commander's test prep course software on the top of the stack.

*Antares*
En route Earth
Friday, June 17, 2078, 0021 UTC

Surveillance Chief SLT Ryan Lewis had the overnight watch when the Fleet message arrived.

```
ROUTINE 207806151200 UTC
TO: ANTARES
FROM: CINC
TOP SECRET
BRIEFING ON YOUR RESULTS SCHEDULED 071120781200UTC AT FLEET INTEL HQ
WITH CINC FLEETOPS INTEL PLANS PIO.
PREPARE COMPREHENSIVE REVIEW OF VISUAL AND OTHER RESULTS OF
YOUR INVESTIGATION, WITH EMPHASIS ON WHAT CAN BE PROVEN AND WHAT
STILL REQUIRES CONFIRMATION.
PREPARE YOUR TEAM'S EVALUATION OF NEXT STEPS TO BE TAKEN AT BIG BLUE
EXPECT EXTENSIVE QUESTIONS ON ACTIONS AND TECHNIQUES USED OR NOT USED
IN ORDER TO FULLY ASSESS RESULTS AND DETERMINE FOLLOW UP ACTIONS.
MEANWHILE, WELL DONE.
DAVENPORT
END
```

Ryan looked at the message on his monitor. "Oh, that sounds like fun," he mumbled as he forwarded the message to the officers who would need it most.

*Antares*
En route Earth
Friday, June 17, 2078, 0755 UTC

*Antares* was well on her way home, and Carol was about to finish a typically quiet late shift at the Conn. Many felt that the ships could run themselves, and to a great extent they did, but nobody in the Fleet really wanted to just sleep while under FTL. It was better, they all seemed to believe, to have the crew at their stations, ready to handle anything unforeseen,

As was her usual practice, Terri Michael made a circuit of the watch stations before taking the command chair. She made it look like a leisurely stroll, but in truth, she was checking each station's readiness, staffing, and situational awareness. This was an open secret, but the crew appreciated the informal attention. Still, Carol was surprised when Michael appeared at her side.

"Hansen, you're out of uniform."

Carol gave herself a quick once over but found everything in order. "Ma'am?"

Terri pulled a set of Senior Lieutenant's bars out of her pocket.

"Stand up, Hansen."

Carol stood as her captain removed the single silver bar from her collar and replaced it with the double bars in her hand.

"Congratulations, Carol," she said quietly in her ear, "You blew away the SLT test, so start studying for the Commander's exam."

Carol nodded slightly, and Michael reached out to shake her hand.

"Carry on, Senior Lieutenant."

"Yes, ma'am, thank you, I sure will."

A moment later, she was a little disappointed with herself for not having anything more profound to say, or even something modestly meaningful. But she was so surprised it was all she could think of. She had a promotion, again ahead of most of her peers. Sure, she'd pretty well aced the Senior Lieutenant Qualifying Exam, and she had more combat time than any of her peers, which counted heavily in the promotion scores. But she still wondered if she was really all that much better than the other ensigns and lieutenants around her. She was skeptical of that, which she knew was healthy, but the promotion system had just ground out one more for her, and she felt good about it.

Chapter 17

*Sigma*
GL 876
Sunday, June 19, 2078, 1030 UTC

Their target was GL 876, 10.2 light-years distance from GL 887. This is another red dwarf with massive, close companions. It's about a third the size of GL 887, which they had just left. Before *Sigma*'s arrival, there were four known planets, including a very close, very large terrestrial planet, spinning around the star in less than two days. Tidally locked, the side of GL 876 (d) facing the star is very hot, Venus-like, while the other side, the dark side, is viciously cold. The system is incredibly small by Sol standards, with four planets, three gas giants, and a large rocky planet, all within a third of an AU of the star, less than the orbital distance of Mercury. *Columbia* and *Soyuz* had both already checked out GL 876. Len Davis expected yet another routine no-contact visit.

Once again, they came in away from the plane of the system, pausing to examine it passively from a distance. *Sigma* was closer this time, only three AU away from the star. And David was again working on the data, spot-checking their automated review, and watching for anything else that might be interesting. He was keenly aware that this star was about the same distance from Earth as Inor. In his mind, this was a likely place to find evidence of the enemy. He was nervous, and Abe Jackson and Sally Gray could see it.

"Mister Powell, pardon me, but what the hell is eating at you?" Abe asked after a few hours of watching David's nervous pacing and finger-tapping.

"Dunno, Abe. Something about this system. I can't shake it."

Sally leaned back from her console. "You better shake it, or someone is going to be shaking you! You're making me a little nuts."

David laughed it off and promised he'd try not to be so agitated. But something dug at him, and he didn't really know why. It had been five months since the battle of Inor. *Maybe,* he asked himself, *did he just feel that they were overdue for a fight? Columbia, Antares,* and *Dunkirk* had engaged the enemy and won, but so far, *Sigma* had not fired a shot in anger. He decided to take a walk and headed for the Bridge, if for no other reason than to give Abe and Sally a break.

XO Rodriguez gave Lieutenant Boyd his second chance at Weapons, but she also delivered some fairly loud counsel on the treatment of subordinates. If he wanted to progress, he had to learn to work with his team. He grudgingly accepted that advice but implemented it by absence. He was almost never in the Intel Section, and David was at this point doing Boyd's job and very happy to do so.

The EMR covers were off on the Bridge, and the reddish star was plain, if small, against the black curtain of the universe. At three AU, they were too far out to see the terrestrial planet, but David could pick out the two closest gas giants.

Again, small from this distance, but obvious against the sky.

Lisa Briggs was also on the Bridge, having just done a status check on her weapons and loaders after some routine maintenance.

"So, out of your hidey-hole Mr. Powell?"

"Yes, Lieutenant, we just need a little natural light once in a while to keep rickets away."

They shared a smile at the old joke and stood side-by-side behind the Weapons console.

"This system gives me the creeps, Powell," she said quietly.

He looked at her with surprise. "That makes two of us. That's why I came up here. I needed to shake that feeling."

They stood together, looking out the windows for a full minute before he continued.

"So, what is it? The big rock in close? The small size of the system?"

She shrugged. "I got no clue. I just smell trouble somehow."

"Beautiful, though, don't you think?"

"Yes. I never really thought much about red dwarfs, but they are pleasant to look at, but not so red as I guess I expected. And these planets, so huge and so close. Strange."

"Indeed," he responded absently as he looked across the Bridge at the Surveillance console.

Lisa continued to talk about the system but gradually realized he wasn't listening to her anymore and followed his gaze over to Surveillance, where she could see a white circle on the monitor.

"What the hell?" she said quietly as she started to move.

David was already walking away. She followed. David moved in behind the tech and pointed to the circle.

"What is that?"

"Possible high-reflectance target. Still checking," the tech said without looking up.

"Do we have a long-range scope on it yet?"

The tech shook her head.

"Get a long-range scope on it," he said firmly.

She looked up at him. "All due respect, Mister Powell, I don't work—"

"Just do it. If Lieutenant Sanders wants to chew my ass later, that's fine."

He turned to the Conn officer. "Conn, I recommend we go to minimum EMR and inform the captain."

"Mister Powell, he just went to bed an hour ago. How about the XO?"

David shrugged his agreement and turned back to the Surveillance console. The long-range visual telescope was boring in on the bright object. It was still at the edge of resolution, only a few pixels.

Lisa stood next to him, watching. "Do you think—"

"Can't tell yet," he cut her off.

About this time, XO Linda Rodriguez arrived on the Bridge and headed for the gaggle around the Surveillance console.

"OK, so what's up?"

David pointed to the main monitor while still looking at the long-range telescope data.

"Can I get spectra on that?" he asked.

The tech nodded and started the process.

"Powell?" Rodriguez called him, finally grabbing his elbow.

"Sorry, Commander. We have a possible high-albedo target on the long-range visual scan. I suggested to the Conn that we go minimum EMR until we know what it is."

She looked over to the Conn officer. "Conn, set minimum EMR. Weaps! Let's preload half Spartans, half Lances."

Their beautiful view of the star disappeared as the EMR covers closed over the Bridge windows. Over at the Weaps position, Chief Dodson commanded the Fire Control System to load one rotary launcher with defensive Spartans, the other with Lance attack missiles.

"Where are we on the spectra?"

The tech looked over at the results. "Looks like iron-nickel-carbon, Mr. Powell."

"Motion?"

"Can't tell. There isn't much shift, so it isn't moving very fast relative to us, if it's moving at all."

David looked away, thinking. He caught Lisa's eye. She looked frightened as she stared back at him.

"I told you this system gave me the creeps."

David smiled, then turned back to the tech.

"OK, where is this thing, exactly?"

"Maybe a third of the way around to the right. Best I can tell it's outside the orbits of the planets — maybe a half an AU from the star — give or take?"

"So, that makes it say, three and a quarter AU's from here?"

"Sounds right."

John Sanders leaned into the conversation. "It would have to be pretty damn big for us to see it at that range." Sanders had come up when the tech called him with the contact report. David nodded.

"Yeah...makes me wonder if it's just a big iron asteroid." He turned back to the Surveillance Operator. "How does the albedo compare to what the *Liberty* data indicates?"

She worked for a few moments. "Hard to say. My guess is that it's less bright than the ships at Inor. If it's really where I think it is, we only see it like one-quarter lit."

"Or," Sanders pointed out, "it is a ship, but we're looking at it ass-on or from the side instead of head-on like *Liberty*."

"Shit." David turned again to the Surveillance operator. "Did this just fade into view or did it appear abruptly? Any IR transients associated with it?"

She ran the data backward, paused, forward slow, back, forwards again, then looked up at the group gathered behind her.

"Faded up, normal for something coming into view. No transient in IR."

"Thanks," Sanders said.

There was an awkward silence as the group thought about the problem. Finally, the XO broke the ice.

"Recommendations?" she asked, looking from Powell to Sanders and back.

Sanders indicated David should go ahead. "I think it's unlikely this is an enemy object, but I can't say definitively it isn't. Let's hold our orbit, keep our EMR down, and watch this thing for a while and see if it twitches. If we get better imaging, then we should be able to tell one way or the other."

"I agree," added Sanders, "We can probably stand down the Weaps."

Rodriguez shook her head. "Nope. We're keeping the rotaries ready. How long?"

"Unsure," Sanders replied, "Maybe, twelve hours?"

Rodriguez did not look pleased, but she gave them the time.

"It's not like we have a schedule to meet. But let's keep our guard up and keep looking elsewhere in the system. After twelve hours, we'll take a status and decide what to do. I'll brief the captain when he wakes up."

Sanders headed back to his quarters, but Lisa Briggs remained on the Bridge with David. After a few minutes, she leaned over to him, speaking quietly.

"If you scared the crap outta me for no reason Powell I am going to kick your ass."

He looked over at her, holding his expression neutral. "Does it help if I'm as scared as you are, Lieutenant?"

She smiled a little. "Maybe. Maybe not. We'll see."

She moved on off the Bridge and headed back to the Weapons area. David remained where he was, watching the long-range telescope's image of the object. It seemed to hold itself just beyond his mind's reach, just outside what he could confidently explain. He watched, hoping for another clue, some change that would tip him off to what it was he was staring at. SLT Jake Fleming arrived on the Bridge during the discussion, then headed back to the Weapons station afterward. Now, having noticed David was still at the Surveillance console, he left the Weaps position and walked over to him.

"Planning to stay the whole twelve hours, Mister Powell?"

David, his mind elsewhere, jumped in surprise at Fleming's question. "Oh, no, sir. Just a little while."

His eyes went back to the display. Fleming considered whether he needed to order Powell off the Bridge for some rest but decided against it.

"OK, but don't be here when I take the Conn in ninety minutes."

"Sure, sir. Will do."

The lead tech on duty tonight was Paula Johnson, a second-career crew member, like many of the technical staff. Aside from physical separation, space travel now had few physical demands greater than any other job, so Fleet had become open, even welcoming, to middle-aged individuals who wanted to contribute. Paula had worked in IT while raising a family and then decided, after a tough divorce, to join the Fleet. With her proven technical skills and maturity, she excelled in the surveillance role. On a few ships, spouses served together, but the Fleet's version of the Sullivan Brothers Rule prevented them from serving with their children, which could well have happened otherwise. The crew liked Paula; she was a stable, calming presence on the ship and someone whom the younger crew could look to as an example.

David watched for perhaps twenty minutes. Finally, he leaned down to Paula.

"Watch for changes in the intensity. If it's natural, it'll have some rotation, so we should see a regular cycle. Back home, Ceres rotates about three times a day. If it moves on its own, sound the alarm."

"Yes, Mister Powell, I was thinking the same thing." She hesitated a second, then spoke again. "Mister Powell, I meant no disrespect before..." She stopped, unsure of how to finish her thought.

"No offense taken. It's true, you don't work for me, but I couldn't afford to wait for Lieutenant Sanders to get up here in case it was closer than I thought. You're doing fine; keep up the good work."

"Yes, sir."

He leaned in closer. "I'm just a warrant. You don't have to call me sir."

She turned to look at him. "When we call you sir, Mister Powell, it has nothing to do with your rank."

She held his eye for just a moment more, then went back to her task. David was left looking at the back of her head, at the point in space where her face had been just before.

"Thank you, Paula," he said quietly.

Without turning her head, she responded, "Just how it is," only loud enough for him to hear.

David left the Bridge and returned to his quarters, entering as quietly as possible so as not to disturb his three sleeping roommates. He lay there for a while, looking at his tablet in the dark. *Where is Antares tonight?* he wondered. He hoped she was safe.

He thought about Lisa Briggs and how she kept turning up at interesting moments. Setting aside rank, she was an attractive, personable woman with an excellent sense of humor. He liked her very much. She was unattached. She was about his age. *In some other quantum universe,* he thought, *there might be more to that. But,* he concluded, *not in this one.* After more than a year of silence, mostly his own, he knew, he'd finally heard from Carol, and she was all he needed. Staring at the ceiling in the dark, he decided to let his friendship with Lisa remain as it was for now, but if she pressed him for more, he'd have to push back. He was never one to hurt anyone's feelings, let alone someone as kind as Lisa, but if necessary, it would be the right and merciful thing to do.

He drifted off, thinking about the sky outside that October window and how far away it was in both time and space.

*Sigma*
GL 876
Monday, June 20, 2078, 0420 UTC

David was up early, as he often was, whether he was on a ship or back home. He cleaned up and dressed for what he expected to be a long day. His night had been busy, full of dreams of Lisa and Carol and God knows what else. He'd slept, but he wondered to himself just how much rest he'd really had. He was back on the Bridge before 0500.

The object had neither moved nor had the intensity changed. Len Davis came on the Bridge about 0600, as the twelve-hour surveillance period Rodriguez had given them was running out. Sanders arrived shortly after the captain.

"So, Mister Powell, what do you think?"

"Still at the edge of resolution, sir. I really don't know. It could be a natural, tidally locked asteroid that just happens to look a lot like an enemy ship."

Sanders smiled. "Or it could be an enemy ship that looks kinda like a tidally locked asteroid."

David nodded. "Or it could be someone else's ship. The orbit is in-plane, which would seem to imply that it's natural. But again. It's too far to tell."

"Lieutenant Sanders, is there anything else around that arouses your curiosity?" the captain asked.

Sanders shook his head. "No, Captain, everything else we've looked at is clearly natural. We have not seen any other objects with spectra quite like this one."

"How many asteroids or dwarf planets have we cataloged?"

"Uh," Sanders flipped through data on his tablet. "About fifty. All pretty nominal stuff."

"Nothing similar to this object?" Davis asked, surprised.

"There are other irons around, sir, but nothing that fits what we know of the enemy ship composition as nearly as this one."

Davis turned to David. "Mister Powell?"

"Nothing to add to what Lieutenant Sanders said, sir. It's an outlier for sure."

Davis paused a moment, thinking, then turned to the Nav console. "Nav, get me a course to put us one million klicks behind that object in the same orbit."

He turned back to Powell and Sanders. "If we can't discriminate what it is from that distance, you're both fired."

It took a couple hours, but they settled into an orbit about three times the distance from the Earth to the Moon behind the suspicious object. The exact range was hard to know since they were keeping the radar offline. Whatever the exact distance was, they were close. Powell and Sanders stood side by side behind the Surveillance station as the long-range telescope focused in on the object. It came up clear now, craters and an irregularly shaded surface.

"I don't buy it," Sanders said quietly.

"Me neither," David replied. "Why?"

"If the numbers are right, it's something like five hundred meters in diameter. Asteroids that small aren't such nice neat spheres. It should be lumpy or potato-shaped or something."

"Are we getting any better spectra data now that we're close?"

Sanders looked over at the console. "Yeah, it's better, I guess. Still closely matches enemy ship material, but it's not as exact as other reports have been. Maybe they're trying to hide the construction with other stuff?"

The captain left the command chair and joined them. Jake Fleming and Lisa Briggs were also on the Bridge.

"OK, so what do you think?"

"We think it's a fake," Sanders responded. "The shape is wrong for the size. It's not normal for a body this small to be so perfectly spherical."

Fleming and Briggs looked at the captain. He didn't look back, but his expression became hard, determined. Davis had made up his mind. He walked over to the Nav workstation.

"Get us to ten thousand klicks. Take an hour and make sure we're in a slightly different relative position."

He walked back to the Surveillance position.

"We'll kill it. Once we get to ten thousand, assuming it's still quiet, we'll fire. I'll send the SLIP as soon as we shoot."

"What weapons do you want, Captain?" Fleming asked.

"It's a new type. Let's hit it with two Lances, center mass, five seconds apart. Load one rotary with Spartans, then the other with two Bludgeons and the rest Lances."

Fleming nodded his acknowledgment and went back to the Weapons position to set up the attack. Lisa gave David a long look before heading back to the magazine to brief the techs. David could see she wanted to say something, but she held back. He decided to try to catch her later and see what was on her mind. He knew she felt unnerved by this, as he did, but it wasn't something they could talk about with the captain present. It would have to wait.

David leaned in close to Sanders. "John, let's take that hour to recheck everything else in view."

Sanders looked surprised. "Losing your edge, David? First name?"

David frowned. "Just this once. Somehow, I feel like a mouse faced with a big perfect pile of cheese. I don't see the trap bar, but that doesn't mean it isn't there."

Sanders nodded and leaned over to his techs, asking them to go back and re-examine the largest objects they had seen. David turned and walked to the command position.

"May I have a word, sir?" he asked quietly.

"Yes, of course."

Len Davis came down the two steps, and they walked to the far-right corner of the Bridge.

"You may have thought of this already, sir, but I must express my concern that this may be a trap."

"I had thought of that, Mister Powell. But, go on."

"Have you considered, sir, the intelligence value of leaving it in place? Might we be better served by not killing it but watching it?"

"I have, but this early, David, with our limited knowledge of the enemy, I can't. It could be watching us just like we're watching it. Five or six of his best friends could show up any time now, and all we can do then is run. And run, David, is not something we're ever going to do, OK? We will strike anytime we have the chance. Is that clear?"

"Yes, sir, I understand."

"I appreciate your input, Mister Powell, and your view has merit, but this one we're going to crush as soon as we can."

"Sir, in that case, I recommend that you launch the Lances in delay mode, even a minute, and make a maneuver that takes us away from the launch point."

Davis looked at Powell for a moment before responding.

"I am beginning to see what Hansen was talking about." Seeing the shock on David's face, he continued, "She did extraordinarily well under hard circumstances on Inor, and she gave you and your study group at the U much of the credit."

"I, uh, I was not aware of that. But let me just say that Lieutenant Hansen gave as much or more to that group than I did."

"No doubt." Davis paused a second before returning to the subject. "I agree with your assessment of this object. It's a little too convenient. I had planned a maneuver, but I had not thought about a launch delay. We'll do that. Good work."

They left the corner, the captain returning to his position and David sliding in next to John Sanders behind the Surveillance position.

Davis called Fleming and the Chief Navigator Kameron McDaniel over and told Fleming to insert a fifteen-minute delay into the Lance attack. He then instructed McDaniel to use that time to move the ship out of the plane of the system and into a better position to observe the results of the attack. The runtime of the Lances would be about ten minutes, which gave McDaniel more like twenty-five minutes to be in position a few light-seconds from the target.

The time went by slowly as they maneuvered closer to the faux asteroid. David finally left the Bridge and went back to the Intel section to work with Jackson and Gray as they analyzed the data from the visual and spectral analysis. It sure looked like a fake to David, too round and too close to the enemy ships' construction to be an accident.

If it did turn out to be an asteroid, there would be a painful and lengthy well-deserved ass chewing from Davis.

The screens in the Intel section showed the same view in visual, IR, and UV. The radar was offline, as Davis wanted to be as invisible as possible. If this was a ship and not a natural body, they had not done a very good job of hiding it. The shape and the construction were just too obvious. The more David thought about it, and the more he and Abe and Sally reviewed the data, the more convinced he was that it was a fake. Sanders evidently thought so, and as the Surveillance officer, it was as much his call as it was David's. Or, more accurately, the missing Lieutenant Boyd's call. But Boyd was either in the Weapons office, or back in the magazine, or wherever.

The hour passed, the object was even larger on the screen, and they could see more detail. As the techs zoomed and scanned and re-zoomed and looked again, there were still no obvious tells, other than its incongruous size and shape, that it was not natural.

At 0930 UTC, *Sigma* dropped two Lances off her port rotary. She then moved out of the plane of the system, moving to a point where the target was thirty degrees below and ahead of her. The impact point would be visible from this angle, and they would have a good perspective to see what came off the object when the weapon hit.

At 0950, David made one last check that they had the right views selected. He finally sat down next to Sally and Abe, waiting for the attack to happen. He had the Bridge audio on in the Intel section so he could hear what was happening up there.

It was quiet on the Bridge. There was a time running on the central data monitor showing the estimated time to impact. The first Lance hit exactly in the middle of the object, as expected, leaving a hole perhaps ten meters across and sending a small amount of debris outward. The second passed through the hole and exploded inside. Then, they saw even more debris and gas exiting the hole. There now could be no doubt that they had hit an enemy facility of some kind.

Davis didn't hesitate. "Comms! Send the contact message!"

```
PRIORITY 207806201000UTC
TO: CINCFLEET
FROM: SIGMA
SILVER DOT
HAVE DETECTED AND ATTACKED FAKE ASTEROID ENEMY FACILITY AT GL 876
MORE TO FOLLOW
END
```

"OK, sir, it's off. Twenty-three hours thirty-eight minutes to Earth."

"Very well." Davis turned to Sanders. "What is it venting, John?"

Sanders turned back to the captain, smiling. "Oxygen, sir, and water."

The phone at the Surveillance position rang. Sanders picked it up.

It was David. "So, are we seeing the same stuff that *Dunkirk* reported? O2 and water?"

"Yeah, looks like it's bleeding to death. I don't see any Hydrogen yet, though."

Davis turned back to the Weapons position to his left. "Fleming, what's my status?"

"Full rotaries on both sides, sir. We replaced the two Lances already."

"Very good, thanks."

David was watching the IR screens in Intel, still talking to Sanders on the Bridge. "Anything on the IR?"

"Nope," John answered.

As they watched, whatever mechanism stabilized the fake asteroid began losing control, and the thrust of the gasses bleeding out into space began to have an effect.

"Captain! It's starting to roll." Slowly the ball began to roll. Within a few minutes, the opposite side had come around, and they could see that it was much the same as the side they had been looking at.

"Powell! Look at the IR," Sanders said.

There was now an obvious hot spot on the 'back' side.

"Anything else, like maybe nitrogen, coming out?"

The surveillance techs reviewed the spectra of the gasses and decided there was no nitrogen.

"OK, so, if it's a fuel cell coming apart, would we not see hydrogen as well?" Sanders asked.

David agreed. "Maybe the H2 tank is still mostly intact, or maybe that's where all the heat on the other side is coming from."

They watched the visual and IR displays for a couple minutes.

"What's the spin rate?" David asked.

"About one and three quarters a minute."

David let out a low whistle. "Holy crap...what is that in Gs?"

Sanders pulled out his NetComp. "Huh. About point nine. Less than I would have expected."

"But it is speeding up - as long as the gas lasts it's going to accelerate."

"I wonder if it's unmanned. With the damage we did, I'd expect something more interesting to be coming out."

"Yeah, me, too."

They continued to watch as the gas venting waned. It was now spinning about twice a minute. It had shed a few small pieces of debris but really less than they had expected.

"Ya know," David began, "If it's mostly tank space, there might not be a lot of debris. Maybe we busted open their tanks, but the crew and all the equipment might still be intact inside. Hell, they could still be alive for all we know. Even with the spin, it's only a little more than a G."

David rubbed his chin, looking off into the distance, something he did as he thought through a difficult problem.

"The *Dunkirk* object deorbited itself into the star. This thing hasn't done that." Sanders pointed out.

"Yet," was David's quick response.

Sanders nodded his agreement. David gave Sanders his best conspiratorial wink.

"Think we could get on it?"

"You're out of your goddamn mind, Powell."

"Amen to that!" Lisa Briggs piped in, having snuck up on the conversation.

"OK, well, maybe so. But it would be awfully interesting."

"Sure would." the captain commented. "Got any idea how to do it?"

David thought for a few seconds and then shook his head. "No, sir, I don't. Pity, though."

"Well," the captain said sadly, "maybe we can get a second mission out here with the right equipment and do that."

"That will take time, sir, and I'd bet it won't be here when we, or whoever, gets back," Sanders said.

The captain crossed his arms and looked at his young officers. He was impressed, perhaps more so than he had expected. They were smart, inquisitive, and demonstrated good sense. David was right that it would be interesting to get aboard that sphere, but he was quick to realize they couldn't do that and dismissed the idea himself without feeling like he had made a mistake. Not everyone could do that, Davis knew.

"So, what are your recommendations?" he asked them.

Sanders and Powell looked at each other. Then David spoke. "From an Intel point of view, sir, I would like to observe it for a while, maybe a couple days—"

Sanders interrupted him. "But the longer we sit here, the more we look like the mouse staring at the cheese, David."

David acknowledged Sanders' concerns. "No doubt, but if we pull back a little and stay low-EMR, even if he calls in his friends, we could bug out."

Davis looked hard at Powell. "If his friends come, Mister Powell, we'll kill them, too,"

Sanders and Powell exchanged looks, this time, John Sanders spoke first: "Sir, if I may, we have a wealth of intelligence already. I don't think we should risk that in a fight, especially if we're outnumbered."

"Noted, Lieutenant. I understand your caution. But as I said to Mister Powell earlier, I will strike the enemy whenever and wherever I can. Is that fully understood?"

They all said they understood. David looked at Lisa Briggs, her face impassive, but David could tell she was afraid. *No surprise,* he thought, *I am too.*

Davis scribbled out an update to CINC.

```
PRIORITY 207806201100UTC
TO: CINCFLEET
FROM: SIGMA
SILVER DOT
ENEMY SPHERE ATTACKED WITH TWO LANCES AND APPEARS DISABLED.
VENTING AS REPORTED BY DUNKIRK OBSERVED.
WILL REMAIN AND OBSERVE APPROX 48 HOURS THEN PROCEED
END
```

ISC Fleet HQ - Office of Commander in Chief
Fort Eustis, VA
Thursday, June 23, 2078, 0945 EDT

Senior Lieutenant Noah Peters worked quietly at his desk in CINC's outer office. It was a remarkably clean desk for someone working as a gatekeeper for the top admiral in the middle of a war. Peters kept his desk as he kept himself: well groomed, well-conditioned, neat, and prepared. Noah was of average height, a bit thin, with a light skin tone for an African-American. Peters graduated from Fleet University two years ahead of Carol and her group, and FleetPers selected him as CINC's aide for his exceptional organization and communications skills. If CINC needed to have something said just right, Noah knew how to give him the words. He could be prickly when necessary but otherwise maintained a friendly, professional demeanor. He had no close friends in the office, which he considered necessary because of his sensitive position, but in reality, he liked the emotional distance. No office dramas for him, no distractions, no favorites.

Months ago, CINC had asked him to look into the SFU history of a specific former student, now serving as a warrant officer in the fleet. His first call went unanswered, as did his first written request. They similarly ignored his second call. There was a war on, after all, and Peters had a good number of small and large issues he was chasing down for CINC, whom he admired greatly. *A good man in a very difficult position,* he thought, *too bad the wife was such a pain in the ass.* So much so that the boss was now residing on the top floor of the BOQ. So, the

Powell matter, as Peters had come to call it, moved at a slow pace. He finally sent a second request, upped the verbiage to make sure that the SFU administrators got his point, and copied CINC. The response was just three pages: a letter from the provost stating that Powell had been denied readmission based on existing regulations and two pages of transcript. That day he had walked into the CINC's office and asked him to call SFU.

"They're slow-walking us, sir. I don't like it."

Their response in a few days was a large file with reports, performance assessments, transcripts, and supporting details. Finally, he had the whole picture. It took him the better part of a week, working as he had time with his other priorities, to get through it, cull what was important, and create a summary worthy of CINC's review. This morning, he was finally ready. He picked up the phone.

"Sir, if you have time, I am ready to present the report on the Powell matter."

"Very well, come on in, Noah."

Peters sent the report to CINC's tablet, picked up his NetComp and his coffee, locked his desk, and went into the inner office. He sat across from the large desk that sometimes seemed to occupy half the room.

"I've sent you my summary, sir."

"Sure, go ahead, Noah."

"Well, sir, technically, yes, SFU acted within the letter of the regulation in denying him readmission," Noah reported deadpan.

When Peters spoke like that, Admiral Davenport knew there was more coming.

"Just say it, Noah."

"He got the shaft, sir."

The Admiral was surprised at the anger in Noah's voice. He leaned back in his chair. "Oh, do go on, Lieutenant."

"Grades - exceptional. Attendance - perfect. Attitude - excellent. Let me read from a letter from a senior flag officer: *At the annual Red Star/Blue Star Exercise Cadet Powell demonstrated technical knowledge and military judgment far beyond expectations. His continued participation in this exercise would be welcomed, and he should be considered for advancement well ahead of his peers.*"

The admiral's eyebrows raised. He leaned back forward on his elbows, thinking,

"Interesting. Who wrote that?"

"You did, sir, after the 2075 Red Star-Blue Star. Powell monitored the Intel shop for the losing side. Even as a cadet, he saw problems and was able to report them clearly. He was one semester short of graduation when he left."

"Even with all that, Noah, if, as you say, SFU was within the regs to deny him, how was he treated unfairly?"

"Sir, we both know that there is a level of discretion University authorities can exercise."

"So, they could deny him, but they also could readmit? It was a judgment call?"

"Yes, Admiral. I believe that they know they made a major mistake here, and that's why we had so much trouble getting anything out of them."

"Why didn't he appeal?"

Peters shrugged. "I don't know. Powell may not have known there was an appeal process. Sir, the Fleet was this man's one ambition from childhood. He had the physical abilities and the mental qualities required. I don't understand all of the issues with the father's suicide or what happened with the mother, but I feel like Powell was derailed just short of his goal, and there was no one there to get him back on track. So, he did what he had to for the family, duty-bound as he was, and then just took his medicine as a warrant. For him, the dream was gone."

The admiral thought for a moment. "OK, Noah, what would you have me do?"

"I discussed it with FleetPers. You can grant him a commission outright. Or, you can recommend him to the warrant officer board for commissioning in the regular process. Or, of course, you can leave things as they are."

"Terri Michael will crawl right up my ass if I do nothing."

"Honestly, sir, in that case, she will have to get in line behind me."

Davenport smiled. "Noah, I am glad you're willing to say what you think."

Peters relaxed a bit in his chair. "Sometimes, sir, I have to. Commanders in authority need deputies willing to tell them the truth."

"Which is why you'll someday be a Lieutenant Commander. So, I can do this?"

Peters nodded eagerly. "It's the last page of the document I sent you. Sign it and send it to FleetPers, and it's done."

"Good to be CINC sometimes, I guess."

"Yes, sir. Sometimes you get to do something really great amid this mess."

He signed. "So, how do we get this out to him?"

Noah consulted his tablet. "They're due at Tranquility II after GL 876. I am sure Admiral Whittaker could do the honors."

CINC smiled. "Yes, Brian would enjoy that. Draft a message to him with the basics and ask him to generate a commission for Powell. Where is *Sigma* now?"

"They should be at GL 876 for another few days."

"Fine, carry on, Noah. Good work on this."

"Yes, sir. Thank you, sir."

## Chapter 18

*Sigma*
GL 876
Saturday, June 25, 2078, 1225 UTC

Lead Surveillance Tech Paula Johnson jumped when the IR alarm sounded. It had been a dull day up to then, watching the presumably-dead enemy sphere rotate. She wasn't sure what they were doing still looking at this dead enemy object, but they sure kept at it. She looked at the alarm data and saw that the new contact was at a relative bearing of 170 degrees, almost directly behind them and 10 degrees above the long axis of the ship. She turned to the Conn officer to sound the alarm.

"New IR contact at 170 plus 10. Assess as enemy vessel entry."

John Sanders hit the general quarters alarm almost before she finished speaking. He slapped the controls on his console to close the Bridge EMR covers, all as he was standing to look at the Weapons station to his left.

"Setting minimum EMR. Weapons! Deploy the rotaries!"

The ever-present Lieutenant Boyd was standing the Weapons watch, but he was staring at the Surveillance display, unmoving. Sanders had to prompt him. Loudly.

"LIEUTENANT BOYD DEPLOY THE GODDAMN ROTARIES!"

Jake Fleming was just entering the Bridge as he heard Sanders' order. By the time he got to the position, Boyd, or perhaps the tech sitting with him, had activated the controls and the rotary missile launchers were moving out.

Todd Boyd, for all his good looks, cocky swagger, and dripping condescension, was frozen, pale, and terrified in his place at the Weapons station, staring at the target display. Jake Fleming grabbed Boyd, dragging him out of the position and leaving him in a ball on the floor in the far-left corner of the Bridge.

"Stay there, dipshit. Maybe you'll learn something."

Paula concentrated on the identification process. The Bridge around her was a chaos of activity as the primary operators entered, either replacing or supplementing the techs on duty. The section chiefs arrived to manage the work and to be a buffer between the command section and their functional area. It seemed a very long time to Paula and to her boss John Sanders, who remained at the Conn until the captain arrived. She watched the identification status evolve as the Surveillance processors crunched the data. They studied the light reflected off the object, considering the intensity and spectrum of starlight, examining the apparent rate of movement, the Doppler effect that the spectrum showed, *Sigma*'s own position and speed, and the intensity of the incoming light.

Finally, the contact display went from amber to red. *Shit*, she thought as she turned to the Conn station.

"Target evaluates to a Type I. Designated Echo-One."

"Range?" Sanders asked.

"Two point one million klicks."

She was calming down a little as Len Davis walked briskly from his main cabin to the Bridge.

"Captain on the Bridge!"

Davis moved to his command station and turned to the Conn officer. "Go ahead, Mr. Sanders."

"Ship is proceeding as before, sir, monitoring the object. We have a single new contact, a Type I, at 170 plus 10, range 2.1 million klicks."

Davis nodded his understanding. "I have the Conn. Thank you, Mr. Sanders."

He turned to his left as John left the command position to sit behind Paula Johnson and the other Surveillance techs.

"Weapons?" he called.

"One rotary each of Spartans and Lances. Rotaries are deployed, and we are ready to shoot." Fleming responded.

John Sanders and Paula Johnson continued to work the Type I, which had appeared almost behind them. As they watched the computer watch the contact, John suddenly became uneasy.

"It's not moving."

Paula looked up at the data display. "What?"

"It's not getting closer or going farther away or changing bearing. It's just sitting there."

He walked to the command position. "Captain, I really don't like this."

"Don't like what, Lieutenant?"

"It's pacing us, Captain. Same bearing, same distance, for the last five minutes."

"You don't think you're a little premature with that assessment?"

"No, sir, I don't."

Back in the Intel work area, David and Sally were looking at the spectrum of the object, verifying that it was a Type I. They were pretty sure about that. David did not miss the fact that the enemy was just hanging in one place, from *Sigma*'s point of view, and neither approaching nor retreating. He pointed to the data blocks on the Intel display.

"That can't be random. They're on to us somehow."

Abe looked at it. "Yes, Mister Powell, I don't think this is just luck."

Fifteen minutes after the initial detection, the enemy ship was still in the same position. David had seen enough. He picked up the ship phone.

"Surveillance," he said, some impatience in his tone.

"Sanders."

"Lieutenant Sanders, it's Powell."

"Getting nervous back there, Mister Powell?" John asked quietly.

"Damn right. What is the captain saying?"

"Nothing much," John answered.

Paula looked at him quizzically, only able to hear one side of the conversation, but he just shook his head.

"For now, we're watching it."

"Yeah, watching it watching us."

"That's possible."

"Possible? Come on, Lieutenant, either they have us dead on, or they're the luckiest goddamn navigators we ever saw."

"No arguments here, David." John looked nervously around.

"Well, meantime, we're getting some good visuals. With it just hanging there, Sally is getting some pretty detailed imagery on the high-res."

"I guess that's something. Assuming, of course, that we live to get it back to Fleet Intel."

"Yeah, assuming that, sure. How long is Davis going to wait?"

John looked around the Bridge. "I got no idea. I'll call you when I know."

They hung up, leaving David with a vague feeling of dread, a growing belief that something about this engagement was different and might not end well. Something fundamental had changed, and he wasn't sure what it was or how to deal with it. But it frightened him, and he felt no shame in that.

Davis stood at his command station, hands on hips, watching the Surveillance display, thinking. *Strike now? Wait? Leave?* He said he would strike whenever he had the chance, but this was a strange contact. Waiting might work, or the enemy might go ahead and hit them before he could attack. He could always bug out. The enemy was six light-seconds away, more or less, so he could get away if he wanted to. For now, at least, he had an out.

XO Linda Rodriguez arrived on the Bridge, having checked the status of the engineering staff aft, and stopped to give Lisa Briggs a word of encouragement in the magazine. She was perplexed by the quiet on the Bridge but moved smoothly to stand next to Davis.

"So, what are you thinking, Captain?" she asked him.

He shrugged. "Are they really on to us, or are they just lucky? Do I maneuver to shake them or just strike them where they are? Or do I just bug out?"

"Are you really asking me or was that all rhetorical?"

"You asked what I was thinking, Commander Rodriguez. And mind your tone, please."

"Sir, we have a wealth of information on the sphere. We need to get that back to Fleet Intel."

"I know, I know," he said quietly. "But if they're able to track us this well, we need to know that and just how well they can do it." He grimaced. "I want to think we're the predator and he's the prey," he said, pointing to the Surveillance display. "But right now, I am not really sure who is who. If I maneuver, am I telling him I can see him there, or am I confirming that his tracking is working?"

"They don't seem to care about being seen, Captain. Intel told us that before we left. So, I'm thinking they don't give a damn how well we see them. Maybe they just want to know how we're going to react to their stalking?"

They returned to watching the image of the enemy ship on the Surveillance display. It was the usual silver cylinder, in this case, seen from almost directly in front.

"This is getting creepy," Paula said to John Sanders. "It's going on too long, sir." She looked at the clock. "Thirty-five minutes that thing has been there."

"I know, Ms. Johnson, I know. We'll have to see what he wants to do. For now, we just wait."

After an hour, the captain called his Bridge officers together.

"OK, it's been an hour, and this contact isn't moving. Theories?"

Sanders spoke first. "They're pacing us. The range hasn't changed within the accuracy of our tracking, sir. That can't possibly be an accident. Somehow, they have us. And, they've had us since they came out of FTL."

Weapons officer Jake Fleming spoke next. "I know we don't have much experience with them, sir, but no one has reported this kind of behavior. I don't like it, and I think we should put a quick end to it."

Fleming's comment generated a murmur of agreement among the staff. Davis turned back to Sanders.

"You've been talking to Powell? What does Intel think?"

"Yes, we've spoken several times. They're in agreement that this is strange and threatening."

"OK, let's maneuver and see what happens. If it follows, then we'll strike. If not, perhaps we get on his tail for a while."

He looked at the Navigation officer. "Fifteen left, ten down."

As the discussion broke up, Davis walked to the Comm station and leaned in to dictate his message to Ensign Leah Farley.

```
FLASH 207806251330 UTC
TO: CINCFLEET
FROM: SIGMA
HAVE BEEN PACED REPEAT PACED ONE HOUR REPEAT ONE HOUR
BY TYPE I CONTACT VICINITY GL 876.
MANEUVERING TO DETERMINE IF CONTACT IS TRACKING.
WILL ADVISE.
END
```

*Sigma* moved quickly into her new orbit.

"If I were them," Linda Rodriguez began, "I would continue on course and wait to see what else we do."

Davis nodded. "Yes, don't tip your hand. When would you strike?"

"Me, I probably wouldn't. But if I were going to attack, I would strike as they cross behind us."

"OK, we'll see."

*Sigma* had turned left and moved nose-down, and after settling into her new orbit around GL 876, the position of the contact became 186 minus 18. David watched with everyone else, wondering what it would do. If it remained on the original course, its relative position should move across their stern from right to left if you were looking aft. Slowly it did just that, moving from 186 to 184, then 183, while rising slowly from minus 18 to minus 15. An hour passed, and Davis gave the order to stand easy at battle stations. They'd be ready in a few seconds if necessary, and that was all he really needed. Meantime they could take turns going to the head or getting a cup of coffee to ease the stress.

Another hour passed, and the Type I moved slowly back into its original position, 170 minus 10, and stopped there. Sanders' phone rang again.

"Sanders."

It was David. "Can you believe what you're seeing?"

"Not really, Mister Powell," Sanders answered, his voice low to not alert the captain.

"That prick has come right back to where he was and stuck there."

"Yep." Sanders was about to say more when the captain appeared at his station.

"Powell, the skipper is here. I'll call you back."

Sanders hung up the phone without waiting for a reply.

"Right back where we started, eh, Lieutenant?"

"Yes, sir. He seems to have his orders, and he's pretty good at following them. He is closer, however, sir. Looks to be about 1.2 million klicks."

"There's only one reward for being that good," Davis said.

"What's that?"

"Death."

Davis turned to the Bridge. "Bring the ship to alert battle stations."

He walked to the Weapons console, just left of the center of the Bridge.

"Four Lances, Mister Fleming, direct routing. I don't see any point in trying to hide where they are coming from."

"Four Lances, yes, sir. We'll be ready to shoot in about fifteen seconds."

"Proceed," Davis said, turning away from the Weapons station. He stopped at the Comm station and dispatched another message to Fleet.

```
FLASH 207806251545 UTC
TO: CINCFLEET
FROM: SIGMA
AFTER MANEUVER TYPE I CONTACT CLEARLY TRACKING THIS VESSEL.
ATTACKING CONTACT AT 1.2MKM RANGE.
END
```

Before the message was out, the Lances were already on their way. Davis stopped at the Nav station.

"Fifteen degrees left."

"Fifteen left, Captain."

"Enemy is shooting!" Paula called out.

Sure enough, there were several IR flashes around the enemy ship.

"Damn it! How did he know?" Davis asked no one in particular.

The Lances were accurate if they were well-maintained, and Lisa Briggs was one meticulous maintainer. All four struck the enemy ship about a half minute after it had fired.

"Four good Lance detonations on target, sir," Sanders called out after checking the results.

He watched the enemy track, looking for changes in the enemy's course. There were none.

"He's still right there, sir."

"Very well."

Davis was considering whether to launch a second attack when the IR alarm sounded again.

"IR contact 210 minus 15. Assess as enemy ship arrival." Paula called, again.

"Another one?" Rodriguez commented. Davis looked hard at her before responding.

"I understand your caution, Commander, but I'm going to do as much damage to these bastards as I can."

"Yes, sir. It's just—"

"That the odds keep changing? Yes, Commander, I had noticed that myself."

"New contact Echo Two evaluates to another Type I, sir. The range is 525 thousand klicks."

While the computer worked to resolve the new contact, Sanders and Paula Johnson worked the visual and IR sensors, looking for the incoming attack from Echo One. Finally, they saw them: six missiles passing aft.

"Captain, they passed aft of us. I don't think they're a threat."

"Stay on them, John. If they maneuver, we'll need to deal with them."

"Captain, Echo Two is pacing us, too."

This time Davis came down from the command position to stand with his Surveillance Officer.

"It came in at 210 minus 15, then after about two minutes, they maneuvered and have been at 212 minus 10, about 520 thousand klicks, for the last ten minutes."

"Jesus Christ, Sanders, what the hell is going on?"

"I wish I knew, Captain."

Davis went back to Comms.

```
FLASH 207806251612 UTC
TO: CINCFLEET
```

```
FROM: SIGMA
BEING PACED BY SECOND TYPE I CONTACT. RANGE 520 KKM.
STRONG BELIEF THAT ENEMY IS DETECTING AND TRACKING
THIS VESSEL
PLAN TO STRIKE SECOND CONTACT.
END
```

"Weaps! Put a Bludgeon in Echo Two!"

"Only one, sir?"

"Only one."

Fleming's techs worked the weapon assignment process, and then he pressed the Commit control.

"Weapon's away, sir, three minutes."

"Nav! Give me fifteen left again."

"Fifteen left, Captain."

The phone rang at the Comms station, and Leah Farley picked up. "Farley." Her eyes narrowed, then went wide with surprise. "When?" she asked, then finally, "Very well. I'm coming."

She shot out of her chair and walked to the Command position. "Permission to leave the Bridge, sir?" she asked, the urgency evident in her voice.

"Now, Ensign Farley? Why?"

"Something is up with the SLIP receiver, sir. My techs just called me about it, and I need to check it out before I say anything else."

"Your chief can't handle a maintenance issue?" XO Rodriguez asked with no small amount of skepticism.

Farley shook her head. "I don't think this is a maintenance problem, ma'am. My techs here can handle the position." She looked directly at Davis "Sir. If I may?"

Davis paused for less than a second. Farley was smart. He would trust her judgment. "Very well. Report back as soon as you know something."

"Will do, sir."

She ran out of the Bridge, sprinting aft to the Communications facilities.

Just as the Bludgeon struck the second enemy ship in the aft section, the IR alarm again raised its ugly cry.

"IR contact 345 minus 5. Enemy ship, designate Echo Three."

"This is getting ridiculous," Davis said to no one in particular.

"Echo Two is firing, sir. He doesn't seem very dead, Captain," Sanders called.

"How many?"

Sanders and his techs worked the data and were able to see each IR flash of the enemy's missile launches.

"Twelve."

"Weaps! Give me all twelve Spartans right now and reload."

Jake Fleming assigned and released the Spartans and began the reload process. Eight Spartans made the grade, but four missed, and there wasn't time for a second launch.

The first weapon hit just forward of the starboard rotary launcher, damaging it, and sending lethal shards into the magazine, somehow failing to detonate the ordnance stored there but killing everyone. Some of Lisa's weapons crew died outright from the shrapnel, and the rest suffocated in the vacuum of the shredded compartment. As if to add insult to injury, another passed right through and continued out the port side, exploding just outside the ship and pelting the port side with shrapnel. Yet another hit pummeled the hangar, blowing out the doors and destroying the shuttles and other equipment there, as well as taking six more lives. The ship whipsawed and shook from the impact.

XO Linda Rodriguez left the command position to evaluate the damage aft and direct damage control. She stopped to drag Boyd to his feet and push him out the Bridge door.

"Come with me, asshole," she sneered at him, "If you can't do any good here, maybe you can make yourself useful with me."

Boyd made no effort to hide the fear in his eyes as she hustled him aft.

David felt the shockwave move through the ship from the impact aft. He pulled up a ship status display and drew a quick breath. The hangar and magazine were red, showing a complete loss of atmosphere.

"Lisa," he said, almost involuntarily. She and her crew were almost certainly dead. He sucked down the pain and got back to work. The rest of them were still alive, so the magazine hadn't gone up.

The next strike threw Leah Farley and her Chief across the SLIP Maintenance Compartment, breaking the Chief's forearm and blackening Farley's left eye. Her ribs screamed at her from the impact with the wall-mounted steel work table. They slid and crawled their way back to the main SLIP receiver status display panel they had been looking at.

"How bad is it, Jeff?" she asked.

"Not good, Ensign. Broke my goddamn arm."

"Can you work?"

The Chief smiled. "If I can get a half an ensign to help, yeah, I'll manage."

"OK, yes, I think half of me still works. Show me what you saw."

Chief Shaw stood up and pointed with his good arm to a signal displayed on the receiver status panel.

"There."

"OK, so?"

"So, after every transmission, we have to check the alignment of the SLIP receiver."

"Right, the signal is strongest at the point of origin, so sometimes it can bleed over and shit on the receiver."

"Indelicate, for a lady Ensign, but yeah, accurate enough."

He pointed to a spike on the display. "Here is the transmission at 1330. I came in to do the usual check, and while I'm looking at it, this happens."

He expanded the display and indicated a small signal just above the noise level of the receiver.

"Did you have to realign the receiver?"

He shook his head. "No, it was fine. But this little piece of crap here caught my attention."

He paused to take a breath, then grunted in pain. He'd shifted his weight, and the arm had pressed against the wall of the compartment.

"Shit, that hurts." He blinked away the pain best he could. "Turns out that little turd shows up again. And again. Every 35 seconds, near as I can tell. Might be a fraction more or less."

"I've never seen anything like that."

"No, ma'am, neither have I. I don't know what it is, but it isn't right."

"You ran a self-test?"

Shaw rolled his eyes, the pain exaggerating his impatience with Farley.

"What am I, Ensign, a rookie? A moron? Hell, yes, I ran it twice and then a deep diagnostic. The receiver thinks it's OK, and frankly, so do I."

She smiled grimly through her own pain. Shaw was young for a chief but plenty competent. She liked him, respected his knowledge, and felt sure he would go a long way in Fleet.

"How far back did you see it?"

Shaw grunted as he swiped the display to the right, looking back in time. He was sweating now, and to Leah's eyes, he was getting very pale, but he pushed through the pain and concentrated on this display.

"First one is something like 1130...uh...." Shaw squinted to read the time stamp. "11:32:22 plus a few tenths."

"So, what happened at...oh shit."

The Chief eyebrows went up in reaction to Farley's comment.

"No," she said to herself, "that could not be it..."

"Care to share, Ensign Farley?"

"Kinda looks like a sonar ping, don't you think?"

"Oh shit!" he said, the realization coming to him as well.

"Like I said..." with her eye swollen almost shut and three broken ribs, she still managed to reach the phone.

"Intel," she said, wincing in pain as the ship rocked again. The motion knocked the Chief back to the deck, and he swore in pain.

"Powell." The connection took only a second. "David! It's Leah Farley in Comms. I think they're tracking us by the SLIP receiver. And I think they can do it from FTL."

She stopped to cough, which hurt like hell, and spat it out on the floor. Blood. *Well,* she thought to herself, *that can't be good.*

"Say that again?" he asked, incredulous.

"We see some periodic fluctuations in the—"

Another hit cut Leah's voice off, this one aft and squarely in the SLIP system.

The Navigation officer, Travis Buckley, called out the updated status. "Three more hits, Captain. The SLIP system is out. The other hits were to an empty crew area and the hangar deck, again."

Davis picked himself up off the floor and stumbled to the Weapons station. Jake Fleming didn't wait for Davis to ask.

"We're still functional, sir. Even the hit on the magazine didn't do any real damage to the weapons themselves. Freaking miracle, that one."

Davis turned back to Surveillance. "Who the hell hit us, John?"

"Echo Three, sir. They launched—"

Davis didn't wait for the rest of the answer. "Four Bludgeons, Echo Three, now."

Fleming dispatched the weapons as Davis made his way back to the Command position. His phone rang.

"Captain." He answered. There was a moment of recognition, then a look of sadness followed by anger.

"Are you sure, Chief?" He stood and addressed the Bridge.

"The XO is dead, and so is Boyd. They think Farley was killed when they hit the SLIP system."

He looked around, and his bleak expression rested on his Weapons Officer.

"Fleming, just in case, you're now the XO."

"Aye, sir."

"Fourth IR contact, sir. 070 plus 30."

Paula had found herself after the initial wave of fear. She was now steady and focused on working the problem in front of her. Sanders was grateful for her courage and her ability to do her job even under this kind of stress. They hadn't seen this sort of action before, and it showed. By now, they were all terrified, but they kept working.

"Range?" Davis asked.

"Not yet, sir," Sanders answered.

"They're firing!" Paula called.

"Fleming! Spartans!"

"On the way, Captain." The starboard rotary, full of Spartans, clicked through six launch cycles in as many seconds and then stopped.

"Six away, sir, but it jammed."

"Nav! Left 45, down 90, and full power on the Drive. I am tired of this sh—"

The six Spartans did as well as they could, but they were severely outnumbered, with multiple attacks coming from three different enemy ships. Four incoming missiles missed, but three missiles struck the Bridge in rapid succession, the last two detonated in the Weapons Section, putting that cranky starboard rotary permanently out of service.

## Chapter 19

*Sigma*
GL 876
Saturday, June 25, 2078, 1710 UTC

Back in the Intel section, the impacts tossed David and Abe Jackson to the floor. Sally Gray managed to stay in her seat.

"Christ, David, what the hell was that?"

David shook his head to clear it and looked at Sally. "We're hit again. But since we're not personally dead yet, let's see what we can do."

David pulled up the ship status display. It showed him schematics of the ship, side, and top views. Each of the modular sections of the ship was yellow, red, green, or black. Yellow meant danger, either fire or leakage. Red indicated sections that had no air. Black indicated sections where no data was available. Their section was green. Forward of them, the ship was entirely red. Nearby was mostly green with a few yellow areas. The starboard side was entirely black. The port side was mostly green, all the way back to the Engineering spaces, except for the Weapons section, which was red. Engineering itself was black.

"OK, folks, what does this picture tell you?"

Sally pursed her lips and frowned. "We lost a comm junction. Probably the secondary port crossover junction at section seventy-two."

David looked at her in surprise. "Very good. I agree. Abe, that junction is just twenty meters aft of us."

Jackson nodded and moved out the door.

David could see that the strike had destroyed the Bridge, which meant much of the officer cadre was gone. He switched to a display of available crew. There were no officers on the list. David stifled a gasp. The computer had just told him that no line command officer remained alive. Len Davis had been a good commander. He had allowed David plenty of freedom and listened when he spoke. Now Davis, Leah Farley, Lisa Briggs, John Sanders, all the rest were dead.

"Lisa," David heard Sally say quietly as she looked at the weapons magazine on the status display.

He nodded acknowledgment, "Yes," He then refocused on the task at hand.

David switched to a surveillance display to see what data he had available. Only the port IR and RF sensors were available. He selected the port IR, and the ship image was immediately replaced with a deep red picture of space to the port side of the ship. The course and speed of the ship appeared at the bottom of the screen. The margins of the sensor display were labeled with the relative bearings of the data displayed. Other than the stars, there was no IR or RF data. As he watched, some nearby debris moved quickly across the field.

Jackson came back in. "Got it, I think."

David reset the display and now saw that all the port side sensors were online. But he was more worried about the engineering spaces aft. He flipped back to the ship status display. Again, the image of the ship appeared, now with green throughout the engineering spaces. Weapons remained a solid, almost accusatory red. He picked up his ship phone.

"Engineering." A moment later, Engineering Lieutenant Kondo's voice was on the phone.

"Kondo."

"Powell, here, Lieutenant."

"Powell! Are you OK? Did you fix the port comm junction?"

"Yes, sir, we're OK. Jackson did the junction. Good job for a spook, eh?" David took a breath. "Looks like we're in decent condition starting about two sections aft of the bridge. Mister Kondo, you appear to be the senior surviving officer."

Kondo, his frown evident in his voice, said, "No, David, I will not take command. I am not a line officer. I'm an engineer for FPI, as you well know. I know you can do this, David. You have to do it. I can give you whatever speed and course you want, but you have to fight the ship, David. I can't."

Jackson, watching the sensor feed on his workstation, grabbed David's arm.

"I have a contact. It looks like it might be that 070 plus 30, Mister Powell. Looks undamaged."

Kondo, having overheard Jackson, asked: "What's your pleasure, Mister Powell?"

"I shouldn't be doing this, Mr. Kondo. You're in command here."

"Fine. So be it. Mr. Powell, my first order is to place you in tactical command and return to my engines. Now, I ask again, *what's your pleasure*?"

David sighed, shrugged, and finally yielded. "What's the status of the Drive?"

"Those last impacts caused the Drive to reset, so it's off right now, but we'll be back up shortly. The reactor is nominal."

"Get us turned towards Tranquility, slow, but hold the speed for the moment. We need to figure some stuff out up here."

"Got it."

David again punched at his workstation, accessing the command functions that the computer had granted him once Kondo put him in charge.

"Sally, I want you to set up an attack on that contact. What's the inventory?"

"The starboard rotary is offline, as is the reloader. We have the eight Lances and four Bludgeons on the port rotary. That's it. Slim pickin's for a big fight."

David shook his head. "Not that small. Let's give the enemy as big a headache as he gave us. Use a Bludgeon."

Gray nodded and began working the console to execute the attack.

"Abe, see if you can find that 345 minus 5 that came in right before we were hit."

"There was a 212 minus 15, too."

"Right, but really, we've maneuvered and been kicked around so much I don't know which way is what yet."

"And we only have the port sensors."

"Right. Keep at it."

David looked around in frustration. He was effectively a one-eyed fish, with *Sigma* able only to see what was to her left. As he spun his chair to look at another display, he suddenly stopped, slapping his feet to the floor so hard that Jackson and Gray jumped at the noise.

"Dammit." He said with a wry smile. "Why didn't I think of that earlier?"

Abe Jackson was about to ask what he meant when David grabbed the phone.

"Engineering...Mister Kondo, can you give me a four RPM roll without overstressing what's left of this ship?"

Back in the Engineering control room, Kondo thought about what Powell had asked.

"Yes, Mr. Powell, we can. We'll likely lose some of the loose pieces forward. You understand what I mean?"

David had a momentary vision of the remains of his shipmates being tossed out into space as the ship began to spin.

"I understand. But the decompression of the forward spaces must have done much of that already."

"True. I also have to say that much of the EM coat has to be gone, and we will be flickering if we do this."

The thick light and heat absorbing material that was the outside skin of *Sigma* was obviously shredded where she had been damaged. The secret to survival in space was stealth, and much of *Sigma*'s security blanket up forward was gone.

David set his jaw and answered. "I'd rather risk being seen than tolerate being blind. But let's make the roll one RPM. That should cut it down."

Kondo agreed. "Sounds reasonable. Shall we begin?"

"Please." David hung up and turned to his Intel crew again. They were both staring at him. "OK, OK, I know, it's nuts. But the computer indexes scan data to the relative position of the ship—"

"So, by turning like a pig on a spit, we get a 360-degree view," interrupted Jackson.

"Exactly."

Gray shook her head in admiration. "Brilliant."

"No, Sally, desperate."

Their desperation continued as the ship began to roll slowly. Within a few minutes, the tactical display started to register something intelligible. As they watched it take shape, Gray was setting up to attack.

"OK, so still four contacts. This one," David said, pointing to the display, "is venting. That's probably the one we hit with the Bludgeons. So, leave that one. We now have a 102 minus 2, a 95 minus 5, and a 220 plus 10. None of those seem all that disabled."

"So, what do you want us to do?"

David looked at the display, trying to implant their three-dimensional situation in his mind.

"The 95M5 is the closest. We'll hit them in distance order." He looked at the display for a few more seconds. "Sally, put a Bludgeon in that bastard."

"Will do. "

She worked the weapons controls carefully. They were relatively simple, meant to be operated under duress and in a hurry, but she hadn't seen them since her initial fleet training several years ago. As she worked, it came back to her.

"I have it, Mister Powell. Three minutes with direct routing."

"Shoot."

Sally hit the Commit option on the screen and the first Bludgeon deployed. She moved on to the next contact, the 220 plus 10, which seemed to be moving in their direction.

"I don't like this guy," David commented, "He's coming our way. Two Lances and a Bludgeon, Sally."

"OK," she said as she again worked the controls. She was getting more comfortable, so this setup took much less time.

"Ready."

"Go for it."

She looked back at David, who was head down, scanning forwards and back through the sensor feeds, looking for other contacts. "Go for it?" she asked.

"Just shoot the damn missiles, Sally."

She did.

"We should see the 95M5 strike shortly."

Despite the deterministic laws of gravity, Gray could not be sure when her attack would actually take place. Besides the uncertainties of range and final enemy course, the attack missiles varied their precise course and speed unpredictably, making them more difficult to detect and avoid. Jackson saw it first.

"IR transient at 95 even. Profile is a Bludgeon explosion."

David moved to look over his shoulder.

"Persistence?" The mark of a good hit was the persistence and especially increase of the IR trace after the weapon had exploded. David was pleased to see the intensity numbers move upward rapidly, reach a definite peak, and then begin dropping gradually. Somewhere over 500 kilometers away, an enemy ship was being incinerated.

"Oh, *yes*! Good persistence with sustained high level. Shift ruined. All leaves canceled." Jackson smiled to himself. It felt really good to get even. He might even regret his callous words later, but at the moment any sense of victory was welcome.

Jackson pointed to a new spot on the display. "New transient at the 210 plus 5 contact. Looks like a Lance." This time the trace did not rise dramatically to a peak. "No secondary. What did we shoot at them?"

Sally leaned over to see his display. "Two Lances and a Bludgeon. Maybe the Bludgeon is behind—" As she spoke, a third bright point appeared near the position of the enemy ship.

"Another Bludgeon. I think there may have been a Lance just before, but—"

The second ship exploded, just as bright as the first.

Jackson looked over at David. "Two for two, Mister Powell."

"Yeah, well, we're not out of this yet."

"Last target is now at 110 even, Mister Powell," Jackson offered.

"Two Lances, Sally. I want to hold back the last two Bludgeons just in case."

Sally dispatched the attack. The Lances hit, but there was no massive explosion.

David returned to his own console to watch the tactical situation. An hour went by before he was satisfied that they had destroyed two enemy vessels and forced a third to withdraw, damaged.

"Hey, Mister Powell, did you notice they never shot at us?"

David looked at Abe Jackson, the surprise clear on his face. "Huh. I was so busy shooting at them that I didn't think about it."

"Makes me wonder if maybe they couldn't see us?"

"Maybe. Ensign Farley called me right before we were hit. She thought they were tracking us with the SLIP somehow."

"But the attack took out the SLIP system. I checked on the comm systems, and there's no status on it at all. It's gone." Sally offered.

"What comms do we have?" David asked her.

"The laser seems OK, and the VHF is probably functional. We'll have to see. But that's it."

"So, if they suddenly lost track of us when the SLIP was destroyed, that would tell us a lot about how they were doing it, don't you think?" Abe suggested.

"It would. Interesting. Scary, but interesting."

After two more hours of slow turning with no new events, David called Kondo.

"Mr. Kondo, I think we are clear. Let's stop the rotation and get to T-II. What is the drive situation?"

"Not great, but adequate. Based on the condition of the ship, I think I can safely give you half of best speed to T-II. I kinda thought that would be where you'd go."

"Thanks, Mr. Kondo. Yes, let's go to T-II."

In a few minutes, they were accelerating away from the battle area, leaving a great deal of themselves behind. After another hour, David left Jackson to monitor the ship and walked, well, stumbled, back to his cabin. He sat on the edge of the bed for a moment. Two of his three roommates were gone. The Inor veteran Len Davis, strait-laced and honest Jake Fleming, Lisa — sweet, hardworking, funny Lisa who clearly had a soft spot for him, dead. That jackass Boyd, too. Paula, the dear Surveillance chief who had shown him how much the crew thought of him. Gone. All of them, in an instant, gone. Never one for tears, he held the pain inside. He saw their faces, heard their voices, remembered how they walked, their laughs and thoughts, how they led, served, or both.

For now, the waking nightmare was over. They had pulled the ship out, saving the rest of the crew, and managed a little payback as well. But payback would never be enough for David. He'd gladly trade all the enemy dead, let them just get away, if he could have any one of his shipmates back. But, as he was often heard to say, that is not the universe we live in.

After a few minutes, his mind began to slow down, and he took off his shoes and laid back on top of the bed. He concentrated on the fact he was alive, as were 42 others on his ship, and tried to focus on what he would need to do tomorrow to better their chances of living to see Tranquility II. Eventually, he drifted off, dreaming of a card game with Travis and Lisa and Leah, all alive and vital and funny again.

When he awoke, he felt a fresh pain that they were gone.

ISC Fleet HQ
Fort Eustis, VA
Sunday, June 26, 2078, 0830 EDT

CINCFLEET Admiral Connor Davenport was leaving the BOQ for the short walk to the chapel, planning to meet his wife and family for Sunday service. He made it home for a few days when he could, usually three or four times a month. But he met them for Sunday church and brunch weekly, so far without fail. Just as he stepped out into the bright summer morning, the FLASH message alarm sounded on his phone. Cursing, then correcting himself — it was, after all, Sunday — he opened the message.

```
FLASH 207806251330 UTC
TO: CINCFLEET
FROM: SIGMA
HAVE BEEN PACED REPEAT PACED ONE HOUR REPEAT ONE HOUR
BY TYPE I CONTACT VICINITY GL 876.
MANEUVERING TO DETERMINE IF CONTACT IS TRACKING
WILL ADVISE
END
```

Paced? They were being *tracked*? He stopped for a moment to think what he should do. *Sigma* was twenty-three hours away by SLIP, so whatever might happen to her had already happened. He had just less than a half-hour before the

0900 service with his favorite chaplain, Craig Erickson. The man had a way of making everyone in the place think he was talking just to them. It was spooky, but in a good way. Erickson was touching something important deep inside each of them. He decided to keep his Sunday morning schedule and set up a meeting with his senior staff, Cook, Harris, and Collins, at 1300. They could talk this over then. Regrettably, he thought to himself, it really could wait a couple of hours. They had no help to offer *Sigma* for at least twenty-three hours. Davis was on his own, like every other ship captain in the Fleet. When Davenport arrived at the chapel, he found Erickson and asked him to call out *Sigma* in his daily prayers.

After an hour of loud music, tough preaching, and quiet reflection, Davenport went home with the family for brunch. He enjoyed the noise and chaos of the kitchen as they prepared sausage, eggs, waffles, or whatever else his children, and a couple of small grandchildren, might want. The kitchen looked like a tornado victim as they all dropped around the large dining room table to eat. Cleanup could wait. He had just sat down when the alarm went off again.

```
FLASH 207806251545 UTC
TO: CINCFLEET
FROM: SIGMA
AFTER MANEUVER TYPE I CONTACT CLEARLY TRACKING THIS VESSEL
ATTACKING CONTACT AT 1.2MKM RANGE
END
```

He looked at it for several seconds, Marian staring at him disapprovingly. He looked up at her without responding. She didn't quite understand what war meant, he knew. He forwarded the message to his staff and put the phone away.

"Must you?" she demanded. "Today?"

"The war doesn't know it's Sunday, Marian," he said flatly. "I'll be going to the office at one."

Still glaring at him, she stabbed a waffle off the pile and dropped it on her plate. Connor could not help feeling that the poor defenseless waffle was taking a beating really meant for him. It made him laugh inside, but he suppressed the urge, and only a small smile crept out. He served himself some eggs, two sausages, and a bagel for a finish, then happily dove back into the loud family conversation going on around him. They were just starting to clean up when the third message came.

```
FLASH 207806251612 UTC
TO: CINCFLEET
FROM: SIGMA
BEING PACED BY SECOND TYPE I CONTACT. RANGE 520 KKM.
STRONG BELIEF THAT ENEMY IS DETECTING AND TRACKING
THIS VESSEL
PLAN TO STRIKE SECOND CONTACT
END
```

Ron Harris was in his office by noon, reading and trying to absorb the messages from *Sigma*. The last was perhaps the most frightening. Two contacts, both tracking them. Davis had given them no information on the outcome of his strikes. Fiona arrived shortly after he did, and they sat in Ron's office, trying to make sense of it.

"If we're being tracked, that might explain *Otbara*," the worry was clear in her voice.

"Yes, it might."

"We should be getting another update before long," she said, looking at the UTC clock behind Ron. It had been an hour since the last one.

"Let's hope."

They passed the rest of the time in small talk, heading for CINC's office when the time arrived. Chief of Fleet Operations Admiral Cook was already there, her face full of worry. CINC looked across the desk at them.

"It's now been, what, almost two hours since we heard from them?"

"Yes, sir," Cook responded. She turned to Harris. "So, what do you make of this tracking?"

"I have no idea, Admiral, I really don't. We've guessed previously that maybe we could be tracked by star occultations. After Inor, we talked a lot about that but didn't really arrive at a conclusion. Besides that, we've always been worried that there would be something we're emitting that we don't know about."

"Like?"

"Well, artificial gravitons, for example. But FPI tells us they don't buy that." He looked back across at Davenport. "Could the reactor be leaking something? We've checked and checked, and we can't see anything."

"And then there's the unknown," Fiona commented.

"Right. It could be something else we have no idea about."

"So, what should we do? What *can* we do?" CINC asked, clearly annoyed at the lack of information coming from his brain trust.

Cook spoke first. "We should get a message out to the Fleet that this might be happening. If they encounter an enemy ship that appears to be tracking them, they should drop whatever they're doing and leave."

"Yes, that would be sensible," Fiona agreed. "The longer we go without hearing from them..."

She had expressed what they were all worried about, but there was not much any of them could do about it.

"She could be damaged, sir, not necessarily lost." Ron offered.

"If they can, they'll update us soon," Cook said, a bite in her voice. "If they can't, I'll have to see what we can send."

Davenport nodded his agreement. "Meantime, get the warning out."

They broke up, each returning to their offices, wondering where they might find answers. There were no ships near GL 876. The best they could do was to send *Chaffee*, which was at Tranquility II, over seven light-years away. A week away from *Sigma*. Cook decided to wait and see what happened in the next day. If they didn't hear in that time, she'd see if *Chaffee* could make the trip.

ISC Fleet HQ Operations Section
Fort Eustis, VA
Monday, June 27, 2078, 0830 EDT

Cook looked across her desk at Ron. "They could just be incommunicado. They might not be dead."

"True, but we've heard nothing in almost a day after they went into action." His expression was hard. "The presumption should be that she's lost."

Cook's eyes flared. "I'll decide the presumptions, Ron."

"As you say, Patty, it's your call. You asked my opinion."

She leaned back in her chair and nodded in resignation. "Did you talk to Evans?"

"Yes. He's upset, as you'd expect. But he says you should tell *Antares*." About a third of the *Antares* crew, most critically her captain Terri Michael, were originally from *Liberty* and had been with *Sigma*'s captain Len Davis on Inor. They would take this loss very hard.

"They're pros, Patty; they understand what's going on. They'll be fine."

Admiral Cook shook her head sadly. "I was talking to CINC earlier. You remember that student that Hansen talked about? Powell?"

"Oh, right, sure. Dropped out, but Hansen wanted him commissioned."

"CINC decided last week to go ahead and promote him."

"That's good, I guess," Ron did not understand where Patty was going.

"He's on *Sigma*."

"Oh, shit. And Hansen is on *Antares*."

"Correct."

"It's going to be a very hard day on *Antares*. At least they're already on their way back here."

"They're still ten days out. I am going to wait one more day before I call *Sigma* overdue."

"I see."

"You don't agree?"

"I don't, but on the other hand, I don't see the harm in waiting another day. They'll still have time to digest it before they get back."

Ron left the Operations offices unsatisfied. His approach was more "get it over and then get over it," and he would not have waited to tell *Antares*. *Sigma* was already silent for almost a full day in combat. Sure, she might not be dead, but that did not seem very likely to Ron.

*Time will tell,* he thought.

ISC Fleet HQ Intel Section
Fort Eustis, VA
Monday, June 27, 2078, 1025 EDT

Frances looked across her desk at Roger Cox. She noticed that the young man needed a shave. His usually precise grooming habits had slipped a bit lately. *Probably my fault*, she thought. *I've been keeping him up too late. No matter*, she said silently to herself. *The work is more important.* And the work lately had been hard.

Frances had brought over two more experienced NSA analysts to help with the TDOA problem. To Roger, they were spooky legends with shady, possibly dangerous pasts. The truth was, Candy Hull was a grandmother of five who had never known any other life; her parents had met at NSA. She was tall, spare, severe looking, but with a fast wit and a broad smile. On the outside, Donald Curtis was just a dad of three boys, who could often be seen chasing them around the yard after work. Inside, he was a studious, attentive, insightful traffic analyst. Donald was of average height and slight build, and some said he reminded them of Sammy Davis, Jr. Donald wasn't sure that was a compliment, but he grudgingly agreed that there was a minor resemblance.

"So, Roger, what do you think?" Donald asked.

"Well, sir, based on what we've collected over the last week, six messages in all, I think we've found an enemy position."

Donald nodded. "Yes, I agree. How would you characterize it?"

Roger frowned. "I am not sure, sir."

"Take them one at a time, Roger, and walk me through it." Candy said.

He reshuffled the papers in his hand and started. "OK, message number one is about three seconds and locates to near GL 876." He flipped the sheet. "The next one is ten seconds and is located in deep space, somewhere 25 light-years in the south."

He paused. "I really wish we could read this stuff," he said sadly.

"So do I," Donald said agreeably, "But we really don't need to see the content if we can figure out which are questions and which are answers."

Roger nodded. "OK, we know the distance between the sources of M1 and M2 is about 30 light-years."

"Long way!" Frances commented.

"Right, it is. Based on that, M2 was sent something like two hours after M1 would have been received."

"Quick response. The message must have been important, don't you think?"

"Yes, that makes sense." He flipped pages again. "M3 is sent from deep space shortly after M2. It's also long, about eight seconds."

235

Candy leaned over, looking at Roger. "So, we have a ship calling into HQ, getting a response, and then HQ sends out some kind of fleet message?"

Frances nodded. "Yes, I think so. We haven't seen a response to M3 from anywhere, so my guess is that it was some kind of notification."

"Not yet, anyway," Donald corrected.

"Right, not yet. The delays still amaze me."

"OK, time to brief the boss."

Frances said as she picked up the phone.

"Cap - oops - Admiral Harris, sir, we have something to show you if you could come to my office."

Ron arrived shortly after. Roger and Donald led the discussion, bringing Harris up to date on their progress and the estimated position of what they began calling 'Enemy Station.' Harris was pleased, excited even, and promised to bring Frances to brief CINC the next morning.

As he stood to leave, Candy spoke up. "There's more, sir."

Her tone was serious, and Ron sat back down. "OK, go ahead."

Candy looked at each of her co-workers before continuing. "We're not sure what this means, Admiral. But Tranquility copied several sequences of low-level SLIP activity. It was not strong enough to show up here or at Kapteyn, so we could not locate it."

"OK, what do you think it is?"

"We don't know. There were three instances early yesterday, each about ninety minutes, where there was a short message every 35 seconds or so."

"I know you can't read the messages, but just how short?"

"Less than a second."

Harris sat back, thinking. "Any ideas?"

"None, sir. I was reticent to bring it up, but I think you should know everything that we're working on."

"Yes, that's fine, I agree. Strange." He got up to leave. "Keep on this periodic message. They must mean something. We just need to figure it out."

"Yes, sir, we'll stay on it."

"Very well."

Ron left, but the odd repeating message nagged at his mind. It reminded him of something, but he couldn't quite recall what it was.

*Antares*
En route Earth
Thursday, June 29, 2078, 0925 UTC

Terri Michael was checking with Dr. Soto on her cultures and other biological testing when her phone sounded that she had a new SLIP message. 'ANTARES ACTUAL,' it said. She found a quiet spot outside the lab in the passageway and opened the message. She gasped audibly as she read it.

```
PRIORITY 207805282200UTC
SECRET
TO: ANTARES ACTUAL
FROM: CINCFLEET, FLEETOPS

TERRI:
WITH REGRET MUST INFORM YOU AND CREW THAT SIGMA IS OVERDUE
AFTER ENGAGEMENT WITH MULTIPLE ENEMY SHIPS AT GL 876 MIDDAY 06/25.
WE ARE EXPLORING SAR OPTIONS AT THIS TIME.
SORRY TO TELL YOU VIA SLIP DID NOT WANT YOU BLINDSIDED ON RETURN.
WE WILL ADVISE YOU SOONEST IF ANY ADDITIONAL
INFORMATION BECOMES AVAILABLE.
STILL HOPEFUL.
COOK/DAVENPORT

END
```

She tried to pull back the tears forming at the corners of her eyes but failed. She wrapped her arms around herself as if in an embrace.

"Dammit," she said quietly to herself.

As she processed the initial shock, she knew there was one person that she needed to tell in person and without delay. Carol's quarters were not far down the passageway, so she made her way there, avoiding the eyes of the crew she encountered as she went. They looked at her strangely, but she could not tell them anything, not yet. She arrived at Carol's door and took a second to prepare herself before she knocked.

"Come!" came the voice from inside.

Terri opened the door and stepped in.

"Commander!" Carol exclaimed as she got up from her desk.

"Sit down, Carol."

"Yes, ma'am."

Terri closed the door behind her and sat in the other desk chair for a moment, saying nothing. Carol looked at Terri, at the closed door, then back at Terri, who was looking down at the floor.

"What's happened, ma'am? Just tell me."

She looked up at Carol, realizing that she had already seen through her own rigid expression and body language.

"*Sigma* is overdue."

She saw the same shock on the younger woman's face that she had felt herself. "David..." she said quietly.

Terri nodded her understanding. "Yes. Len told me a while ago that he was aboard."

For Carol, the tears came quickly and flowed freely, but without sound or sobbing. Terri gave her a moment to process what she had heard and let the first wave of shock and anger wash over her.

"When?"

"Message says they were engaged with multiple ships on June 25th. GL 876."

"Multiple? Why—"

"Would Len Davis fight when outnumbered? Good question."

Terri handed the phone over so Carol could read the message herself.

"SAR...where is GL 876 anyway?"

Terri shrugged. "I don't recall offhand. But we can't change course now. We're bingo on food and expendables as it is. No delays, no detours."

"Yes, ma'am, I understand. I would do the same."

"I know."

Terri regarded the woman in front of her. The wretched expression on her face was not what she would expect from the possible loss of a friend. No, this was something more, something much deeper. "Carol, I know it's none of my business, but—"

Carol met Terri's eyes, and she smiled a little despite the pain she felt. "Dan Smith said it best when we were at Kapteyn. David is the other half of me."

Terri sat very still, inviting the younger woman to go on.

"That's the only way I know to express it." Carol stopped to wipe her eyes and cheek. "I've only just come to realize it, but I think David's known all along."

Terri touched her gently on the shoulder, unsure of how to help her. She started to rise, to go back to her own cabin and process her own pain.

"I'll call the crew together at noon. That will give you some time—"

"I am not ashamed, Commander Michael." Carol's voice came with sudden strength, almost a defiance, which caused Terri to settle back into her chair. Carol's brown eyes were wide open, focused directly on Terri, even as they filled and overflowed. "I am not ashamed," she repeated. "I don't cry because I'm weak or afraid or can't do my job."

"I know that." Terri looked at the young woman, the young, courageous officer, with sympathy. "Carol, I once described you as 'all steel under the velvet,' did you know that?"

Carol shook her head. "No. When?"

"Before the walk on Inor."

"I really was afraid, then."

Terri smiled. "Any sane person would have been afraid. I was terrified. But you, you were brilliant. I took a risk putting you ahead of the other officers we had there, and you never, not once, disappointed me."

"Yes, ma'am."

"And as I sit here, I realize we are not that far apart in age, you know? Just a few years."

"Yes, I know."

Carol was again aware of the tears escaping her cheeks. She took a tissue to dry them. The flow was slowing down as she gradually brought her reaction under control.

"Well, Len Davis is *my* classmate, Carol, and *my* friend. I'm waiting until noon because *I* need it, not because I think *you* need it."

"Yes, ma'am. I know you and Commander Davis have a lot of history together."

"Indeed, we do."

"If he's gone then I am very sorry. He is a good man."

"Yes, he is. So, I think, is Powell. We will hold out hope for both of them — for all of them — until we know more, OK?"

Carol nodded.

"I meant what I said at Inor, and I would say the same today about the woman before me right now."

She rose, pushing the chair back under the other desk. "Try to get your head around this, Carol. The crew will be watching your reaction, and I need you to be strong."

Carol nodded her understanding.

Terri left Carol's quarters and made her way to her Duty Cabin, just behind the Bridge. She had her own pain to process and some kind of speech to prepare for the crew. She sat at her desk, still stunned despite her talk with Hansen. *So,* she thought, *Abuelita Santos, can you hear me from this far? What wisdom have you for me now?*

There was no way to sweeten this news, she knew, so maybe hard and fast like she told Hansen would be the right way to tell the crew. Perhaps she should give them the respect of treating them like adults and let them handle it the best they could. *Thank God we're only nine days out*, she thought.

*Little Teresa,* the grandmother in her head whispered to her, *you already know what is best, what is wise. Bitter news is tempered when delivered with kindness. You already know this.*

Chapter 20

Kapteyn Station
Tuesday, July 5, 2078

Ben hitched a ride to Kapteyn Station on *Gagarin*, which was heading out to replace *Stoykiy* (*Steadfast*), which had some problems with their IR sensors and needed a depot-level repair. He put the transit time to good use, learning and re-learning the internal specifications of the Sentinels. They were a remarkable invention, and he knew some of the folks in FleetIntel who had dreamed them up. Ben could hear their voices as he read some of the descriptions and process instructions. When it came time to deploy, Weaps would be responsible for getting them overboard, but it would be Intel, that is, him, that would be responsible for start-up and check out of the devices.

*Intrepid* was already there when *Gagarin* pulled in, but he suppressed the impulse to invite Joanne to a drink at *Uncle Vito's* on Main Street and instead reported to the ship in the usual way. He had also used his travel time to get up to speed on *Intrepid*, too, her general layout and how to get from most point 'A's to most point 'B's. Once past the duty officer, he made a fairly direct path to the captain's office. Only one wrong turn. Arriving in the office, he found the usual young admin tech, head down in some task on his workstation.

"Good afternoon."

The tech looked up. "Hello, Mister Price, the Captain has been expecting you. She said to go on in."

Price moved past the reception counter and opened the door. After his check-in with Joanne, Ben found his quarters easily enough. He was in a four-bunk room with three other warrants, all of whom worked in either Engineering or Reactor.

It didn't take long for one to needle the newcomer.

"So, Ben, word is that you and Henderson were pretty tight back in Plans."

Ben glanced around the room, which had become very quiet. Apparently, this was a pre-planned ambush.

"Yeah, we worked together, argued a lot, but we became friends. That's it."

"Oh, come on...*friends*? We all know you can't be a guy and be just friends with a woman."

Price looked at the instigator for a few seconds before responding. "Actually, if you're a grownup, you can."

"Ohhh, man, I just can't get it. You had all that right in front of you night after night and *nothing*?"

"All *what*?"

"All of her!"

"And what night after night? You have way too much time on your hands, and you're thinking up stuff that never happened," he said with finality.

"Bet it did."

It was a bait, but Ben was too savvy to fall for something this stupid. Finally, one of the others spoke up.

"Knock it off, Eric," John Meyers said.

"Shove it up your ass, Meyers. You're as full of shit as he is."

Ben, having dropped his bags in his locker, now turned and looked directly at the instigator. "Unless you're willing to formally accuse me and the captain of an illicit relationship, I suggest you shut your mouth and keep your fantasies to yourself."

Eric rolled his eyes and crawled back into his bunk. John stopped looking at Eric and caught Ben's eye. "Dinner?"

"Yeah, fine." they walked out and headed for the wardroom.

"I'm John Meyers, Reactor Ops."

"Good to meet you. What's with the asshole?"

"He's been ranting about you and Henderson ever since he heard you were coming. Seems he knows someone at HQ."

"Not surprising. I kinda expected something like this. I thought they'd wait 'till I got unpacked, though."

They laughed a little at that.

"Good job keeping your cool. He was really begging for a fight."

"Shit, if I had to beat up every asshole who didn't know what he was talking about I wouldn't have any knuckles left."

They turned the corner, went on into the wardroom and started working the buffet.

*Intrepid*
Kapteyn Station
Wednesday, July 6, 2078, 0830 UTC

Joanne looked around at her staff, now seated in the wardroom. They had turned out to be better than she expected, although some 'weeding' had been necessary. Fleet had beached Ensign Court, probably permanently. The maintenance Chief Tech was also reassigned. She regretted those decisions, slightly, as it likely meant the end of Court's career, but it was based on his obvious, measurable performance and not just on his shitty attitude. So far, no one had complained that he was gone. As the officers and warrants filed in, Ben took an inconspicuous position towards the far end of the table.

"OK," she said, "time to get started. I know you're all wondering about Mister Price and why we're here at Kapteyn. It's time to tell you."

She took a sip of her coffee. "After the last month of shakedown, I am satisfied that this vessel is ready for mission operations. This is not going to be a routine surveillance outing. We have a list of six specific systems which we will visit. We will be minimum EMR the entire time. Make sure we're clear on that. We will not be reporting our exits from each system. This is probably the stealthiest mission you have participated in. Or will. Mister Price?"

"Yes, Captain. FleetIntel has been working on an autonomous monitoring station, what they call a *Sentinel*. This station will collect IR, UV, RF, and SLIP data and report any events it sees back to the FleetIntel. These stations have the potential to give us information on enemy movements and location on a persistent basis without risking a ship. Once we plant one, we can stop visiting that system so often with crewed ships, which means the ability for us to cover more ground in less time. The first six Sentinels are now in our hangar. Our job on this mission is to deploy them in the six star systems FleetIntel has picked."

There was a moment of quiet, then the Weapons officer, Jim Kirkland, spoke up. "So, Mister Price, what is the procedure for deploying these things? How big are they?"

"Well, Lieutenant Kirkland, there is a draft procedure that FleetIntel has given us, but part of our task is to refine, fix, or otherwise verify it. Once you've had time to review it, I'd like to sit down with you and Commander Bass and see what you think of it. The Sentinels themselves are a meter or so in diameter, about three meters long."

"That will be fine. I would have liked a little more information to prepare for this, Captain."

"Understood, but until we were ready, and the Sentinels were ready and loaded, it was my decision to keep it quiet."

"Yes, ma'am, but I would remind you that the Intel officer works for me. I should have been told."

Kirkland was clearly annoyed, feeling both blindsided and diminished by being left out of the loop.

"I understand, Lieutenant. Nothing personal. This was my call, and you should know that Mister Price argued your point and I overruled him."

XO Bass leaned forward. "If it makes you feel any better, James, they only told me last week."

Kirkland nodded and smiled, appearing satisfied with her explanation.

"OK, well, that's settled. Our first target is Gliese 687, 15.1 light-years from here. From there, we'll hit L 143-23, 10.3, Epsilon Indi, 12.3, GL 674, 4.8, then Ross 154, 8, and finally Luyten 725-32, 15.5."

There were groans all around. Henderson just shrugged.

"Hey, I am just the messenger here! Call Ron Harris in FleetIntel if you have a better idea."

That got her a laugh, and not just a polite one. They were warming up to her.

"From Luyten, we go home, which is 12.5." She set down her tablet.

"That's almost eighty light-years to cover, so figure ninety days out at a minimum. With time to decelerate, checkout and deliver the Sentinels, then move on, we're probably looking at upwards of a hundred days."

She waited for a moment.

"I don't think the enemy has spies among us, really, but neither do we want to draw attention to this mission. Tell your families you're going out for 120 days on an exploration mission. Tell your crew to say the same. Depending on how it goes, it might well be that long since even Kapteyn is thirteen days from home. If we get back earlier, fine, maybe we can surprise them, but you know how it can go — we may get back here and get ordered somewhere else."

"How were these stars selected?" Kirkland asked Ben.

"I really don't know, Lieutenant. I have no particular information on that point. But looking at the pattern, clearly, FleetIntel thinks something is up in the southern hemisphere. At the outbreak of the war, when I was in Plans, we found that the southern sky had not been examined as carefully as the northern part, so this may reflect a reaction to that fact."

"I guess that makes sense."

"Yes, Lieutenant; for what it's worth, I was not at all surprised by this list," Henderson confirmed. She took one more look at the faces around the table and didn't see any more questions. "We leave in forty-eight hours. Spend that time getting your divisions ready for a long trip."

She turned to her Logistics officer, Ensign Bernado Medina. "Stores, I want provisions for 150 days, understood?"

"Yes, ma'am. That's a lot of cargo, Commander, but we'll get it."

"Anything you can get, Bernie, I'll sign off on."

"Yes, Commander. I'll see about entertainment and rec supplies as well."

"Great, we'll need it. Do you see any problem getting that much?"

"No, ma'am, Kapteyn is very well supplied. It should be no problem."

"OK, let's get to it. Dismissed."

They rose and filed out of the wardroom, sudden chaos of chatter filling the space and spilling out into the passageway as they went.

*Intrepid*
Kapteyn Station
Thursday, July 7, 2078, 1000 UTC

*Jesus, these things are ugly,* Ben thought to himself as he walked around the Sentinels in the hangar. When he first heard of them, he had thought they'd be more or less spherical, something like seagoing mines, but they were hexagonally boxy, with antennas and lenses sticking out here and there. He'd studied the drawings and system specifications, but they were far worse in person than they had seemed on paper.

They also weren't particularly stealthy, other than a coat of flat slate-grey EM-absorbing paint. End-on, they were a meter across and three meters long. They would sit in orbit about a half AU from the star, somewhat further out for the larger stars so they would not require any special cooling or other heat protection. The RTG would provide power and heat for the electronics. They mounted the IR on the opposite end from the RTG module since they liked it cold. Their orbits would be at a 90-degree angle from the nominal plane of the system. This would minimize the time they spent looking through the dust, miscellaneous rocks, and junk left behind by the process of planet creation.

There was a separate pallet containing the six plutonium RTGs that they would have to install and verify before launch. Those should last a good five years, according to the specs, possibly more. The RTG and electronics would be part of the star-facing section, with ion thrusters to permit the Sentinel to adjust its orientation when necessary. After release, the thrusters would establish the one-rotation-per-revolution condition, which would keep the hot end hot and the cold end cold. It was a slick approach, Ben had to admit, and he remembered the glee in some of the FleetIntel staff as they explained to him just how slick it was. Ann Cooper's infectious enthusiasm for her brainchild was hard to resist. Besides, it really was a pretty cool idea.

"So, Mister Price, what do you think?" came a voice from behind.

Ben turned to see the Weapons Maintenance Officer, Lieutenant Natalie Hayden. Taller than average for a woman, with light brown hair and a solid athletic build, Ben thought she looked the part for her job: stern, hard-working, tough.

"I don't know, Lieutenant. Are they as ugly to you as they are to me?"

She laughed, which surprised Ben a little. "Yeah, they're an aesthetic disaster, that's for sure. All bug-eyed and boney-legged."

He laughed at her bent-armed-spider-fingered imitation of the Sentinels.

"Hopefully, they work better than they look."

Ben nodded. She looked at the Sentinels and then back at Ben. "Kirkland asked me to work with you on the launch process."

"Still mad at me?"

She shook her head. "Nah, I think he's over that. Henderson talked to him again, and I think he gets that you had your orders. I actually asked him for this one; he's not that interested in it, and I am."

They talked about the pre-launch preparation, which made even less sense to Natalie than it did to Ben. They were both concerned about the RTG installation, as neither had any experience with them, and fouling the hangar with plutonium would be a fairly major inconvenience. They talked it over for a while and then finally just opened up the installation panels on the first Sentinel in line and looked at how the RTG would attach. Looking at the actual hardware was easier for both of them than deciphering the drawings in the manual. They then broke open the RTG pallet and looked at one of the units. There was a lot of pointing, and words like 'no' and 'yes' and 'what dumbass' and 'oh that's cool' and 'ok maybe' floated around the lively, echoic space for a couple of hours. When they finally pulled their heads out of the back end of the Sentinel for the last time, they understood what they needed to do. It was safe, after all. And really, not all that complicated once they have the steps in the right order.

"OK, Lieutenant Hayden, I'll write up the revised procedure and send it to you," he said with some relief.

"Fine, then we'll dry-run it again and see if there is more to do."

"Agreed. What about the actual release?"

Hayden had been thinking about that. "FleetIntel doesn't really tell us. They just say it should be released in the appropriate orbit, but nothing about how."

"Right."

"Well, the easiest and safest is probably to load them into a cargo shuttle, move the shuttle into the release airlock and take it on out. Then open the cargo doors and reverse the g-field in the cargo bay floor to push it out."

"That sounds not so simple to me," Ben commented, concerned.

Hayden shrugged. "Well, we really don't have any other method for putting it overboard. The docking port airlocks are too small. They're meant for people. Anything larger we bring aboard has to come through the ShuttleLock that leads into the hangar. We can't just open the hangar doors and shove it out, tempting as that might sound."

"OK, if that really is our only choice, then I would be happy to endorse that option."

Hayden laughed. "We backed ourselves into that one, didn't we?"

"Actually, I think I was doing the backing, but whatever."

"Since you're doing the final assembly doc, I will do the release procedure."

Ben nodded his agreement.

"So how long is the post-launch checkout?" she asked.

"A couple hours. We need to verify that it has its three stars for orientation and run a self-test of the sensors. This procedure seems pretty good. I didn't see any issues with it."

"That's all done with laser link?"

"Yes. Low power, close range."

"OK, I think we can live with that."

They parted ways, each to their own work area to write, or rewrite, the procedure they had worked out. Ben walked back to his quarters, opened his tablet, and started pounding away on the new document. He wished Ann Cooper had come along as she had requested. Ron Harris refused, believing that the Fleet would need to understand how to deliver these things and "so they might as well figure it out from the start." Ben understood that position, on one level, but on another, he thought having the designer close at hand might have helped them get through the process that much more quickly.

Natalie headed back for the Weaps office, dropping in on Jim Kirkland and closing the door behind her.

"OK, so how was Mister Wonderful?" he asked with his best snark in his voice.

"You should give him a chance, Jimmy. He's bright, knows his stuff, is flexible in his thinking, and does at least his part of the job. I like him. If you're smart, you'll get over whatever you think about what Henderson told him and get with it."

"Hey - whose side are you on here, anyway?"

"*Intrepid*'s. As always. This guy is not some concubine like we've been hearing. He's for real." She kept her voice even and sincere without being defiant or challenging.

"Maybe."

Natalie looked at her classmate, inclining her head skeptically. "No, Jim, not maybe. She brought him here for the right reasons, I think. Get over it."

"OK, fine, he's a freaking genius if you say so."

Shaking her head, she got up. "Never said that Mister Kirkland. It's just that he's not what you want to think he is, and you need to get past that if you want to think of yourself as a fair-minded officer."

"Yeah, ok, I hear you."

His voice made it clear that he didn't. She decided not to push this any further.

"I hope so, Jimmy. I spent too much time getting you through celestial nav to have you blow it now."

"Have you forgotten that you work for me, too?"

"Have you forgotten who also got you through Comparative Stellar Systems?"

She held his eye for a second before opening the door. "Get with it, Jim. At some level, we all work for Henderson, and you know where she is on this."

Kirkland slapped his pencil down angrily and looked away from Hayden.

"She disposed of Craig to get this — *warrant* — in his place. I don't like it."

"It's not like Craig was marooned or something, Jim. He got another ship, and I know for a fact she made it clear that this was for the convenience of the Fleet and wasn't really about him. He's fine."

"He's not here."

"I know, Jim, and you are going to have to manage that on your own. It wasn't personal, and Craig wasn't harmed by it."

Finished with the conversation, Hayden left and walked back to the Weapons Maintenance Shop just to check in, to make sure there wasn't anything needing her attention. There wasn't, so she returned to her quarters.

Stretched out on her almost-not-long-enough rack, she found herself thinking about Ben Price, who she realized wasn't nearly as young as he appeared. He was actually a few years her senior. She liked his easy, direct manner; how he could argue a point without being argumentative about it. They had gone back and forth pretty hard over the Sentinels, and Price had firmly defended his position when he was right and readily accepted hers when appropriate. He had a quick smile and a decent sense of humor. She now understood much better why Henderson had brought him here. She also now believed what she had heard, that Price and Henderson were good friends when they were in Plans, but not lovers. As she reflected on the man she had spent time with that day, she felt it would have been out of character for him to take up with Henderson in that way and from what she had seen of the captain, equally out of character for her. They were better people than most of the *Intrepid*'s officers had expected, and that was a very good thing for *Intrepid*.

ISC Fleet Shuttle Landing Area
Fort Eustis, VA
Sunday. July 10, 2078, 1430 EDT

Carol's return to Earth from *Antares*' trip to Beta Hydri could not have been more different from her arrival from Inor back in February. No cameras, no crowds, no snow. She just stepped off *Antares*' shuttle on a blistering, oppressively humid Virginia July Sunday afternoon. She was suddenly aware of just how dry and cool the ship's carefully filtered and sanitized atmosphere really was. The place smelled almost musty to her; the riot of pollen, flowers, the normal smells of human activity, the moisture off the James River, all conspired to give her a mild feeling of disgust. As funky as it smelled to her at first, it was good to breathe the real, wild, natural air of Earth again. She knew she'd adjust, and in a day or so, it would all seem natural, and it would be the ship that smelled sterile.

There was no transport available, so she and Jack Ballard hiked the two miles to Fleet Headquarters around Mulberry Island Drive. No one on the golf course seemed to notice them, something she was always glad of. Carol was happy for the chance to be in real sunshine again, and Jack made a good companion, serious when he needed to be but wry and funny when off duty. They'd spent enough time together on the Beta Hydri discovery to develop a close working relationship, and they were looking forward to this first meeting with FleetIntel.

"Carol," he said between breaths, "I'm sorry, very sorry about *Sigma*."

She didn't respond at first.

"I know, well, I know how that must hurt."

She stopped in her tracks and turned to him, her face hard.

"Yeah, hurt, that's a good word, Jack, but kinda inadequate. It's more like every day is a living hell now, where he's dead, and I'm alive."

He took the verbal slap well, keeping in mind how terribly wounded she must feel. "I am sorry, Carol, truly sorry. I just wanted to tell you I'm hoping for the best for both of you. All of us are."

She resumed walking. "Yeah, Jack, thanks, I guess," she said bitterly, "Let's not mention that again, OK?"

"Sure. I didn't mean to cause you even more pain, Carol. I just—"

"I get it, Jack. I do," she snarled. "But just shut the hell up about it, OK?"

He nodded slightly in response, and they covered the last couple hundred meters in an uneasy silence. They were just a short distance from the entrance when Carol put her arm around Jack's shoulder for a long moment.

"Sorry, Jack, still kinda raw over here," she said quietly in his ear.

He nodded and smiled slightly. "It's OK, Carol. Just know we're all here for you."

As they walked through the front doors of HQ, the duty Security tech looked up, then alarmed at who he saw, snapped to attention, dropping his notepad noisily on the floor. Carol and Jack approached the desk.

"Good afternoon, Lieutenant Hansen," he said in a shaky voice. "Welcome to HQ."

Carol smiled at him, biding time to read his name tag. "Really, Mister Orr, I'm just another looey here to do some work. You can relax."

The tech nodded, still nervous, and enabled their entry into the building.

"Yes, ma'am. It's just...you're..."

"Yeah, I know, famous. But don't think about that, OK?"

"Yes, ma'am."

Carol and Jack walked through the security point and headed for FleetIntel in the back of the building.

"Wow. You get that a lot?" Jack asked, surprised.

"Yes. Fame is going to damn well kill me."

Jack suppressed his shock at her uncharacteristic language.

"Well, hopefully not." After a moment he added, "I never really thought about that, how distracting it can be."

"Royal pain in the ass," she repeated, venom in her voice. "Just leave me alone to do the work. That's all I want, Jack, is for everyone to stop staring and let me do my job."

They walked the rest of the way, again in silence, arriving at the FleetIntel outer office. A young woman lieutenant sat at the desk. She looked up and smiled as they entered.

"Good afternoon, *Antares*!" she said pleasantly, extending her hand over the counter. "I'm Kathy Stewart."

Introductions complete, Kathy walked them back to Ron Harris' office.

"Hello, Jack!" Ron said, shaking Ballard's hand vigorously.

"Hello, sir, congratulations on the star." Harris frowned slightly, waving away the compliment, and turned to greet Carol. "Lieutenant Hansen, welcome. We're anxious to see what you have."

"Yes, sir, I think you'll find it very interesting."

"Is that Carol Hansen I hear?" came Rich Evans' voice from the hall outside. They embraced briefly.

"Hello, Commander Evans. Good to see you again."

"So, you brought us a puzzle, eh Carol?"

She nodded in response. "Sir, yes, we did."

"OK, well, let's go have a look, right?" They walked a short distance to a larger workroom with several sets of tables and chairs. They picked a table and arranged themselves around it, Carol next to Evans and Jack across from her, between Kathy Stewart and Ron Harris.

Ron opened the discussion. "Jack, I know you've been tasked with a briefing tomorrow. I just wanted to get with you and Carol ahead of time and get a general idea of what you have and what you think we need to do next." He looked from Jack over to Carol. "CINC is going to be asking me these kinds of questions, and I need to know what's in your heads."

"Well, sir, Carol and I have talked about that quite a bit on the way back."

He pulled his NetComp out of his side-bag. "So, let me go through some of what we found."

They put the display on the large wall monitor and Carol and Jack took turns presenting their data. They showed the initial pictures of the streets, then the detailed shots of the rows of skeletons. As they went along, they showed the portrait, perhaps the most evocative image of all.

"Wow," Rich said, "That is one beautiful person."

Jack smiled. "Yes, sir, and it's funny you should call it a person. We all had that same reaction: that this was a being we could relate to, that we could see sitting next to us and having a meaningful conversation."

"A sentient, sapient being," Ron commented.

"Clearly, yes, sir. An advanced society our enemy snuffed out."

"Makes me wonder what would have happened at Inor if *Liberty* had not been there," Ron speculated.

"Yes, sir," Rich answered. "But we don't know that is what they had in mind at Inor."

"Right, Rich, understood. OK, Jack, what else?"

Jack showed the images they had taken of buildings, with writing on each one. He displayed the lists of symbols they had isolated from the photographs.

"There appear to be these six which we see together in various groupings. Then there is a second, larger, set of forty or so that also appear in various lengths. But the two sets are always separate."

"Numbers and letters?" Kathy asked.

"Maybe," Carol answered. "But we're hesitant to jump to that conclusion. It's almost too easy to think that, but it does seem logical."

"Interesting," Kathy responded.

Jack looked over at Carol, who indicated he should continue.

"Sir, on to the biologic evidence."

"OK."

"Dr. Soto did some initial cultures and other medical work on the way back." He pulled up a new set of results on the wall monitor. "She found no pathogenic bacteria in the environmental samples, just stuff that looked pretty much like terrestrial bacteria. She did find some interesting small organisms in the water."

He flipped to a photomicrograph of a spiny, dangerous-looking organism.

"She recommends no swimming."

There was general laughter at that.

"What about the bones?" Rich Evans asked.

Jack again switched images. "Similar in structure to Terran organisms, and not much different from Inor. She wonders if calcium-based bones are just the universe's general-purpose answer to the need for something solid to build an animal on."

Carol picked up the discussion from there. "Well, three isn't really a very large data set, but Marcia was, as she put it, surprised at how few surprises she found." She turned to Ron. "The rest of the samples will be delivered here tomorrow."

"Good work, both of you," Rich Evans said.

There were no more questions, so the pre-briefing was over. Carol and Jack headed for the BOQ to get rooms for the night. *Antares* would be sending a shuttle down with the Beta Hydri samples in the morning. Dr. Soto was adamant that they be properly packaged, triple-sealed and the containers double-sterilized. Some said she had seen too many sci-fi horror films, but Soto just felt she was doing her job. Either way, she wasn't going to let those samples out of her sight until they were in a biologically secure facility.

Starbase Tranquility II
Near Gliese 1
Sunday, July 10, 2078, 1445 UTC

Technical Chief Leigh Meyers sat at her Comms terminal, unwrapping yet another stick of gum. Her crew sometimes wondered just how many she could fit in there and still breathe and talk. It was an amazing thing to watch sometimes. She stopped mid-stick as the VHF receiver flickered to life.

"Tranq...Two...Sig...ing."

"What the hell was that?" she asked the tech as she pulled an enormous grey mass from her mouth and tossed it into the trash, where it landed with an audible thud.

"VHF call—" the tech started to answer. She didn't let him finish.

"DF it and get the high-gain on it."

He looked at the receiver's signal pattern, swiveling the big high-gain antenna to the approximate direction.

"Best I can do, Chief, until they call again."

Leigh slapped the transmit button.

"Vessel calling Tranquility Two repeat your call."

As she let up, she heard it again.

"Tranquility...Sigm...ing."

Her eyes flared. Did they say *Sigma*? The tech refined his antenna direction.

"You gonna call them again?"

She shook her head. "If it's really *Sigma*, they're so weak they have to be a long way off. Several light seconds, anyway, so talking to them is useless until we get them in solid. They're trying to give us something to lock in on."

The receiver barked again.

"Tranquility Two, *Sigma* calling on one two one point five."

"Oh My God. Ted, call the Admiral and ask him to please get down here. Then call Lieutenant Leonard and tell him what's going on."

"The Admiral and *then*—"

"Just do it, Teddy," she pulled the microphone back to her lips.

"*Sigma, Sigma, Sigma*, this is Tranquility Two, we hear you on one two one point five. Say position and intentions."

A few seconds later, she heard the call again.

"Tranquility Two, *Sigma* calling on one two one point five."

Then again, a few seconds later.

"Tranquility Two, *Sigma* calling on one two—"

The voice cut off. Had they heard her?

"Tranquility Two, Tranquility Two, Tranquility Two, this is *Sigma*. We're about six light-seconds out. Planning arrival 0430 tomorrow."

A smile formed at the corners of the tough Chief's lips.

"They're alive, Teddy, *alive*!" she stopped shaking the tech by the shoulders and clicked the mike again.

"*Sigma*, understood. We're pretty excited to hear from you."

"Tranquility, we're pretty excited to be heard."

She had to laugh at that. Admiral Whittaker arrived during that exchange.

"How far?" he asked.

"Six seconds. They say they'll be here 0430."

"Crew report?"

"*Sigma*, this is Tranquility Two. Station actual inquires as to crew." There was a long pause.

"This is Warrant Officer Second Powell in command. All our commissioned line officers died in the last attack. We have forty-three survivors, all in good condition."

Whittaker nodded his understanding.

"Roger *Sigma*, forty-three."

She clicked off and looked back at the Admiral.

"Anything else?"

"No, just welcome home."

"*Sigma*, actual says welcome home. Good to hear from you."

Twelve seconds later, he responded.

"Thanks, Tranquility. It is imperative I meet with Intel immediately on arrival. We have news I can't discuss in the clear."

"Roger that, *Sigma*. We'll be ready." Whittaker was writing quickly on a SLIP message pad, then handed Leigh the result. "OK sir, we'll send it."

```
FLASH 207807101500UTC
TO:    CINCFLEET
FROM: STATION TRANQUILITY-II ACTUAL (WHITTAKER)
TOP SECRET
SIGMA REPEAT SIGMA REPORTED IN 1445 THIS DATE WITH 43 SURVIVORS
CW2 POWELL REPORTS ALL LINE OFFICERS KIA
EXPECT HER THIS STATION 0430 UTC TOMORROW
WILL ADVISE WHEN MORE DETAILS AVAILABLE
END
```

"Holy shit, sir," she said quietly.

"Chief," the old admiral smiled, "I could not have said it better myself."

"Gonna be a helluva story to tell, sir," Communications Lieutenant Ken Leonard commented.

Whittaker nodded. "It sure will, Lieutenant, and I can't wait to read it."

*Sigma*
Near Starbase Tranquility II
Monday, July 11, 2078, 0500 UTC

The lights of Starbase Tranquility II glowed dimly in the deep night of space. Placed strategically between Inor and Earth, it was far from any bright stars. Technically it orbited the red dwarf Gliese 1, but in fact, just a small Forstmann drive was all it needed to hold itself more or less stationary in space. Unlike Kapteyn, Tranquility was a sparse, functional place with no luxuries or conveniences. It did have full repair facilities, which *Sigma* was going to need.

Tsubasa Kondo throttled back *Sigma*'s drive well in advance, keenly aware of her battle damage. Two weeks of FTL travel had given David and FPT LT Kondo, and the rest of the survivors time to rest and make some repairs. Their consumables were not badly damaged, so there was plenty of food. The ship had a lot of no-go sections, but they managed to get around to where they had to and adapted to it the best they could. They were alive, headed home, and because of that, they could put up with quite a bit.

The SLIP system was gone, but they managed to fix up the VHF, and as they closed to within a couple light-seconds, high-speed laser-based video communications became possible. David opened the line to Tranquility, and soon the Admiral was on the screen. Admiral Brian Whittaker was short, five-feet-five or less, but his striking face and prematurely silver hair gave him a legendary personal presence, a presence that David could feel even over a video-comm link.

"Mr. Powell, you've done well," he said after David gave a summary of the fight.

Whittaker looked at some documents on his desk and then back at the video link. "I have some documents here for you, Powell."

Jackson and Gray exchanged surprised looks behind his back.

"Yes, sir?"

"Well, seems Terri Michael got CINC all worked up about you. We'll talk when you get in."

"With respect, that's a little cryptic, sir."

Whittaker smiled slightly. "This isn't the place." He nodded to the document. "When you get in, Mr. Powell, we'll talk."

"I need to see the Intel section as soon as I can, sir."

"Yes, I've heard a little about that from Admiral Harris. See Intel first and then find me."

The battle damage to *Sigma* made it impossible to bring the ship into dock. The survivors would have to take shuttles to the station. Once the station's repair crews had secured the worst parts of the damage, they would bring *Sigma* in, and complete repair work could begin.

"As you say, Admiral. With all the damage forward and midships, we're going to hold at ten klicks, sir. Oh, and I have no shuttle."

"Need a lift, Mister Powell?" Whittaker asked with humor in his tone.

"It's a long walk in a vacuum, Admiral."

"It is. Call in when you're ready, and we'll get someone out there."

"Thank you, sir."

The link terminated, and David got back to the business of running the ship. Now, as they were closing in, David watched the Nav display. 10.26 kilometers, it showed, then as he watched, the FPI engineers brought her to a stop at the appointed distance, 10.00 kilometers.

David exhaled and slumped a little in his chair, the weight now lifted. Sally reached over and embraced him. He reached a hand to Abe Jackson, who took it sincerely.

"An honor to fly with you," Abe said to both of them.

"And with you," David replied.

Their task was finally done. They had brought back a busted-up ship and some forty-three souls to the relative safety of the starbase. David's relief was tempered by the loss of so many, but he still felt good. He left the Intel space and headed for his quarters. He'd get some sleep before heading over to the station.

Chapter 21

ISC Fleet HQ Main Conference Room
Fort Eustis, VA
Monday, July 11, 2078, 0800 EDT

Fleet Public Information Officer Commander Donna Wright was pleased that the discovery at Beta Hydri had remained secret. She had expected someone to leak it any time after the first report of streets weeks ago. The conference room would not be very full today. CINC limited this high-level briefing to department chiefs and their deputies. CINC had insisted that they start with a small group and then decide how to roll the news out to the rest of the organization and to the public. It would be sensitive, he knew, and revealing that an advanced civilization, technologically less than a century behind Earth, had been wiped out would be frightening. CINC knew the mitigating factors, such as the small size of the culture, would be lost in the shouting.

The chairs in the front of the theater would hold the presenters: Terri Michael, Jack Ballard, Carol Hansen, and Marcia Soto. Others who had been involved, like Ryan Lewis and Denise Long, would also be in the room and available if needed. Jack and Carol had reworked the slide stack, working well into the evening after the pre-briefing with FleetIntel.

PIO Wright was in the theater a half-hour early, checking the setup and performing important quality checks on the coffee and bagels. CINC arrived early, Deputy CINC Yakovlev at his side. Operations Chief Patricia Cook and her aide LCDR Mark Rhodes were also there well before the start time. Everyone, it seemed, was anxious to see the Beta Hydri data for themselves. It was, after all, a shocking development. Ron Harris and his crew arrived just ahead of the scheduled start time, and Ron took his seat at the center front, facing the presenters.

Promptly at 08:00, Ron stood and motioned to the Security techs to lock down the room. After they had stepped out, he began with the required reminder of the classified nature of the briefing. He then turned it over to *Antares*. Terri stepped forward.

"Good morning. *Antares* is prepared this morning to present for you a complete summary of the discovery made at Beta Hydri. My role as captain in this process was mostly to cheer-lead and provide support and resources. The officers who will present today are the real experts, and we know what we know because of their intelligence, initiative, and dedication to their craft. Mr. Ballard?"

Terri sat as Jack Ballard took the podium.

"I am Senior Lieutenant Jack Ballard, Chief Intel Officer for *Antares*. First, as usual, Commander Michael throws too much shade on herself and too much sunshine on us. Her leadership was vital to our success."

He opened his folder, and the first slide was displayed. This was a long shot from orbit, the best image from *Antares* where the streets were clearly evident.

"This was the hook shot that grabbed our attention. That—" he said, indicating the web of streets, "—is clearly not a natural structure."

He went on to show a sequence of *Antares'* images, including some of the near-sunrise images that proved that nothing was moving. He showed a sequence of a single location in the 'suburbs' in visual, IR, and UV. He showed clearly that nothing was happening. No movement, no heat in the structures, no lights, nothing.

"Did you consider, Ballard, that these might simply be abandoned structures, and the inhabitants have moved elsewhere?" CINC asked.

"We did, sir. We looked up and down the settlement, and we found the same thing everywhere."

He paused for a breath and took a sip of coffee to stall for time.

"There is other life on the planet, sir. We detected some infra-red targets that we assess as small to medium animal life; say, foxes or dogs."

Jack went on to display the map he and his team had developed based on the images collected from *Antares*. He explained the city and town naming and how they had come to call the largest central city 'Capital City.'

"How did they get around?" Davenport asked. "If there are streets, that implies to me that there are vehicles to run on those streets."

Ballard nodded. "Yes, sir, there are wheeled vehicles. We saw several parked among the structures we believe are residences. We were not able to investigate that further."

Jack took a second to clear his throat and take another sip of coffee. "Here, sir," he said, looking at CINC, "is a view of what we call Main Street in Capital City."

The picture showed a long avenue pockmarked with wide craters. The buildings were damaged, and many were blackened as if by fire.

"As you can see, there is clear evidence of an RFG attack. We also saw evidence of Lazy Dogs."

He pulled up a picture of the pavement with the same pattern of small holes seen at Inor.

"Based on this, we concluded that we're dealing with the same enemy as at Inor."

"How wide-spread was the attack?" Fiona asked. "Some of us have wondered if they could carry out a full-scale, global strike with these weapons."

Jack nodded his understanding. "Yes, they struck the entire settlement, but I must remind you, Captain, that this culture only occupied an area that is something like 2000 kilometers by 400. It's not a global society."

He paused, still thinking. "Also, ma'am, we cannot put a timeline on the attack - we don't know whether they attacked everywhere at once or in waves. We just don't know."

"Very well. Thank you, Mister Ballard."

Ron Harris leaned forward. "What about weapons?"

Carol got up and stood next to Jack.

"At the Battlefield, we could see evidence of some kind of hand-held weapon mixed in with the bodies, something like a long gun, but when we tried to pick one up with a drone, it fell apart. So, we quit that and would make that a priority when we go back."

"When?" CINC asked.

Carol smiled her brightest at him. "When - if - whatever."

"Uh-huh," he grunted, turning to Cook. "Something you need to tell me, Patty?"

"No, sir, not yet," she replied, suppressing a grin.

Carol picked up the discussion. "Really, sir, whether it is *Antares* or someone else, we need to go back and get on the ground."

"Let's have the data before the conclusions, Lieutenant Hansen," Ron corrected her.

"Yes, sir."

Carol sat, and Jack continued.

"One other technology item, if I may," he said, switching to a different sequence of images. "This is one of a few shots we have of what looks like a space launch facility. We did see satellites in orbit, which we believe are for weather or other scientific purposes."

"Why not a military purpose?" Yakovlev asked.

"There is just the one culture on this planet, sir. We didn't see much that looked like military facilities on the surface, so that seems to be less likely."

Jack looked at Carol, who indicated that Marcia would be next. She rose slowly and took her place. Her first picture was of a skeleton partially covered by green overgrowth. She paused a moment to center herself, quietly cleared her throat, then began.

"This image is from what we have come to call 'The Battlefield.' There are thousands of remains in this area of just a few acres."

She displayed the second image, a larger scale picture revealing the rows of skeletons.

"Good gracious God," Patty Cook said.

Marcia shrugged. "Yes, ma'am, some divine intervention would have been nice. But it never came for these people." She shifted her attention back to the wall. "Here is a close-up. We got several good shots of hands and feet. It appears that they have four digits on each hand, three of what we would call fingers and an opposing digit analogous to a thumb."

She walked to the display, pointing to the lower part of the image.

"The fascinating part here is the feet. They have six of what we would call toes on each foot."

She turned back to gauge how well her audience was absorbing that.

"Terrestrial animals with four limbs usually have the same number of digits on each. This is very unusual."

"Any idea why that would be?" Yakovlev asked.

"No, sir. That would be pretty far out of my expertise."

"Very well. Please continue."

"Yes, well, I also processed some environmental samples for possible pathogens."

She turned to switch the slides on her display.

"My conclusions are only preliminary, of course. But, there was this little guy that caught my eye."

The picture was of a near-microscopic animal from the water sample. There were spikes and spines all along its body.

"I know I will be avoiding swimming with those."

She got some small laughter at that.

"The rest of the cultures were unremarkable. The samples are going to CDC for better analysis, but at this point, I don't see any problem sending in a team with SLUGs."

"Do you think the SLUGs are required? Could we go without them?" Ron Harris asked.

"Sir, I didn't even want to let the damned samples on the ship. So, yes, I think we should be using the SLUG sanitized breathing systems until we can somehow convince ourselves that the planet won't try to kill us."

Harris smiled. "Well put, Doctor. Noted."

"Really, sir, what I did was very preliminary. The CDC will be in a much better position to tell us if there is something there be concerned about."

"You don't sound all that convinced."

"Well, I'm not. Even if CDC's results are negative, the sample set is small. There is a whole foreign ecosystem that we have barely begun to sample. There's no way to know what else is out there."

She waited a moment for more questions. When they didn't come, she sat back down. Carol took the podium and pulled up a collage showing several collections of symbols as they had seen them on the outside of buildings in Capital City.

"These eight shots are of buildings on Main Street in Capital City. Notice that there are two sets of symbols."

She stepped aside, pointing to the groupings on the slides.

"There is a group of six symbols that always appear together, in varying orders and lengths. Those may be numbers, but we don't want to make that assumption without more research."

"But you're making it anyway?" Donna Wright asked, amused at the irony of what she was hearing. Carol moved next to the podium, standing informally and inclining her head before speaking. "Well, Commander Wright, it's hard not to do that. We think it's very likely those are numbers. But also, we know we're not the experts."

"OK, fair enough," Donna responded. "But I agree that seems kinda obvious."

"Yes, ma'am. The other group is about forty symbols. We can't be sure that's the whole set, but that's what we have seen so far. Our working theory, based on the language references available aboard, is that it's an alphabet. But again, we need a language expert to verify that."

Ron Harris shifted in his seat. "So, we need a language expert. Seems to me we also need an archeologist to figure out the culture."

"Yes, sir," she agreed, "That would make a lot of sense."

Jack rejoined Carol. "We've spent the whole trip back talking about this, sir." He pointed to the screen. "This is an advanced society. There are photographs. There are what look like addresses or names on the buildings." His voice was rising slightly as he spoke. "We believe there must be libraries, computer centers, other kinds of places where huge amounts of information would be found."

"So, what are you saying, Lieutenant?" CINC asked.

"Well, sir, I guess I'm saying that we really do want to go back. We want to get some SLUGs and some experts and get down on the surface and figure out what the hell happened to these people."

To emphasize his point, Jack switched to the portrait; its obviously intelligent eyes seemed to look out directly at them.

"These people, sir," he said, emotion in his voice, his body stiff with stress, "These people deserve an answer."

There was a long silence after that, CINC looking at the portrait. Emotionally demonstrative men don't typically rise to command, and CINC was no exception. But he was clearly moved by what he saw, and when moved, he was uniquely positioned to act. He stood and turned to Harris.

"How long do you need to get a plan together to go back?"

Ron shrugged. "Dunno for sure, sir. Maybe a month."

CINC nodded at looked at Terri Michael. "You up for this, Commander?"

Her smile said it all, but CINC also saw the excitement in her officers.

"We are, sir."

CINC grinned, something he rarely did, and looked at Ron Harris. "Ron, go find whoever you need: language, archeology, whatever. We'll find the money."

He turned from Harris to Cook.

"Patty, give *Antares* whatever priority she needs, get them outfitted, and get them back there as soon as we can."

"Yes, sir."

He took a deep breath, then looked around the room, meeting each eye in turn. "This remains Top Secret. Once the follow-up mission is complete and we have more answers, we'll release what we know to the public." Donna nodded her agreement.

CINC turned back to Terri. "This is exceptional work, Commander."

"Thank you, sir. I am blessed with good people."

"Indeed, you are."

He shook hands with Terri Michael, then the rest of the *Antares* personnel, giving each a firm grip and a sincere 'well done' or 'good work.' He then walked up the inclined aisle and out of the theater. He could hear the excited victory calls as the door closed behind him. It usually wasn't much fun being CINC, he thought to himself, but today was pretty good.

Michael would be up for another promotion soon, he knew, and with a growing fleet, he'd have to look at his organization. Was it time to create destroyer squadrons and cruiser divisions? Would adding another layer of command closer to the action make any difference? The time issues associated with the command structure in this environment bothered him. He didn't feel like he could maneuver the fleet in an optimal way. He felt like he was watching more than doing, and that would not do. Perhaps it was yet too early, he reminded himself. As long as we're searching for them, each ship working independently, more structure was probably unnecessary. Once we find them, on the other hand, and we start hunting them more directly, then we might want to diversify authority to exploit opportunities and avoid disasters.

He arrived back at his office, strolling through the reception area, and closing his door behind him, almost without consciously taking note of it.

Michael and Hansen had delivered again, he thought. They'd be famous, again, which they would hate, again. Ballard and XO George had also made huge contributions, and he reminded himself to not ignore that. It was sometimes too easy to give more credit to the 'celebrities' and miss what others had done. Terri would be furious if she thought he'd done that, he knew. The Fleet didn't give out medals, but he pulled out a notepad to start drafting letters of commendation for several individuals and a Fleet unit award for *Antares*.

As he was making his list of names, thinking carefully about what to say about each one, Noah Peters came into his office, unannounced and in a rush.

"Noah?" he asked, perplexed.

"There's a message from Tranquility, sir," he said as he passed the NetComp over to Davenport.

"You really need to read this." Noah handed the tablet with the message to CINC.

```
FLASH 207807101500UTC
TO: CINCFLEET
FROM: STATION TRANQUILITY-II ACTUAL (WHITTAKER)
TOP SECRET
SIGMA REPEAT SIGMA REPORTED IN 1445 THIS DATE WITH 43 SURVIVORS
```

```
CW2 POWELL REPORTS ALL LINE OFFICERS KIA
EXPECT HER THIS STATION 0430 UTC TOMORROW
WILL ADVISE WHEN MORE DETAILS AVAILABLE
END
```

CINC read the message, then grabbed Noah and ran back to the conference room. Terri, Carol, and the rest of the *Antares* personnel were still talking to Operations Chief Cook and FleetIntel Chief Ron Harris when they returned. They all turned in surprise as CINC and his aide came noisily through the entry doors.

"Sir?" Cook asked.

"*Sigma*!" he called as he half-ran down the aisle. "*Sigma*! She's not lost!"

He handed the message to Cook, who read it while Terri and Carol watched, wide-eyed.

"Lieutenant Hansen," Davenport began, "Your Mister Powell is alive and well. That's the good news."

"Oh my God," Cook said as she passed the tablet to Harris.

"But there is sad news, too. Powell reports all the officers were killed. He's got forty-three survivors."

"More than half the crew lost?" James George asked, mostly to himself.

"I am afraid so," Cook answered.

"Where are they?" Carol asked quietly as she sat down in the front row, next to Terri Michael. Ron Harris looked at his watch before answering.

"Tranquility. If they've met their ETA, they've already docked. My God, what kind of a beating did she take?"

Carol looked up at Jack Ballard, who was looking down at her, smiling.

"Welcome back," he said. She stood and hugged him tightly.

"Jack, I'm sorry about—" she started to say as she released her grip.

He didn't let her finish. "Forget it, Carol. Over and done and buried. I am happy for you."

She held his eye for one more second before turning to her captain, who had just received very different news. "Ma'am, I am so sorry about Commander Davis."

Carol reached over to embrace Terri. They were two women who had seen an awful lot together, from Inor to GJ 1061 to Beta Hydri, and now this whipsaw moment of loss and relief and loss again. Rank didn't mean much right then; they were just two people sharing a wartime cocktail of pain and joy. Finally, Carol let go and stood back, still looking at Terri as she sank into a seat in the front row.

"I think you have a message to send, Lieutenant?" Terri said, managing a smile over her pain.

Carol nodded and took a seat next to her captain. There was a flurry of voices around her, several side conversations both in the room and on the phone. She closed her eyes for a second and then started typing.

```
SLIP PERSONAL
```

```
TO:  SIGMA/CW2 DAVID POWELL
FROM: ANTARES/SLT CAROL HANSEN
JUST GOT THE GOOD NEWS FROM CINC.
THIS IS HOW IT WOULD FEEL TO BE A SINNER PAROLED FROM HELL.
MUCH SADNESS HERE FOR CDR DAVIS, LEAH, LISA, TRAVIS AND THE REST.
CAN'T WAIT TO HEAR YOUR STORY.
CAROL
END
```

As Carol raised her head from her phone and focused back on the conversation in the room, Ron Harris was talking.

"OK, this is good news, even if it's both good and bad." The side conversations died out. "But this doesn't change what we need to do at Beta Hydri."

They all agreed with him on that. He sat back down, clearly not finished.

"But there is something else you don't know. During the battle Commander Davis reported that he was being 'paced,' then he called it 'tracked.' That has to mean that he believed that *Sigma* was actively detected somehow."

There was a sound of surprise from the *Antares* crew, which had not heard of this before.

"I am hopeful that the survivors will have something more to say."

"Tracked?" Terri asked, now recovered and back in a commander's mindset.

"That's what he said."

"Amazing."

Noah Peters pulled CINC aside. "Have you told them?"

CINC looked back at him blankly.

"Powell, sir? The commission?"

Davenport's face suddenly lit up. "Oh, of course. No."

"Well?" Noah asked, prodding.

Davenport turned back to the *Antares* personnel. "Lieutenant Hansen, Commander Michael, may I have a moment?"

They walked a short distance away from the others. Noah Peters went with them.

"Sir?" Terri asked, uncertain about what CINC might have to say.

"I put Noah on that Powell issue you brought to me."

Carol looked at Terri Michael with shock. "You told them about David?"

Terri looked back at her. "I just passed on what you said to me and what you showed me on Inor."

CINC looked from one to the other, finally asking Michael, "You never told her?"

Terri shook her head and shrugged. "I didn't want to get her hopes up."

Carol was now wide-eyed, looking from one officer to another. CINC looked at her.

"I signed Mister Powell's commission a couple weeks ago. I sent it to Brian Whittaker at Tranquility since that was their next stop."

Carol closed her eyes, said a short prayer of thanks, then looked at CINC.

"Sir, you have no idea how much that will mean to him."

CINC smiled. "Actually, I think I do. But Noah deserves most of the credit. He's relentless. And were it not for Commander Michael, it wouldn't have happened."

"Thank you, Noah."

Noah smiled back at Carol, something he rarely did on duty. "Just doing the right thing, Carol, just leveling the scales."

Carol thought about following up on her message with congratulations, but she decided to wait until she heard from David about it. If there was some delay at Tranquility II, she'd be wrecking the surprise, and she wanted David to get it from someone like Whittaker, someone of authority, and not secondhand from her.

Carol sat back down a short distance from the others, trying to absorb what had happened in the last hour. Jack sat next to her, looking at her with a wry smile on his face.

"What?"

"Like I said, welcome back."

Chapter 22

Intel Section
Starbase Tranquility II
Tuesday, July 12, 2078, 0800 UTC

Lieutenant Steve Crawford considered the man across from him. This young warrant officer who had just brought in a beat-up half-dead ship had demanded to see him. Admiral Whittaker wanted to see him next, he knew, but David had insisted he see Intel first. He had sent a report ahead by laser, describing the tracking and his conversation with the Comms officer.

"OK, Mister Powell, I've read this, but let's go over it just in case. So, the Type I tracked you for over an hour?"

"Yes. I was stunned that Commander Davis let it go on that long."

"I can see why. Then, after he struck that one, there was another?"

"Yes, as you can see in the report, another Type I came in at like half the distance and was also locked on somehow."

"I see. Tell me exactly what Ensign Farley said."

David winced as he recalled the conversation. "She was in a lot of pain. I could hear her Chief kinda grunting in the background."

"Pain?"

"We'd been hit somewhere back there just before she called. Her voice was strained, and I heard her cough and spit a couple times. That wasn't like her. Seemed like it hurt her to breathe."

"OK, go ahead."

"She said they were tracking us with the SLIP receiver and thought they might be doing it from FTL."

David thought for a moment, remembering Leah's voice on the phone. "She said something about periodic fluctuations."

"Fluctuations in what?"

"I don't know. She was, uh, cut off at that point."

Crawford looked across at Powell for a moment. The man was entirely under control, he could tell, but also reliving something awful.

"Cut off?"

"Missile hit the SLIP facility while she was on the phone."

"Jesus, Powell." Crawford shook his head. "That had to be hard."

"Ever meet her, Lieutenant?"

"No, never did."

David leaned back in his chair, looking up, and put his hands in a pyramid in front of him. "Rich kid from the east coast somewhere. Ivy League degree in Economics, I think. Skinny little five-foot-nothing chick with this giant mass of dark curly hair." David moved his hands around his head as if to illustrate what Leah Farley looked like. "But inside, Lieutenant, inside, she was a giant."

"I can see that." Crawford tapped his finger on the report. "If this is right, she might have saved our asses."

David nodded. "I think she would have taken that deal, sir, so I hope we can make something of this. One more thing."

"Sure, what?"

"After Leah was killed, the enemy never fired on us again."

"Really?"

"Yeah, the whole battle was over before Abe Jackson pointed it out. It reinforced for me that they really were using the SLIP system to track us."

"I'll include that in what I send to FleetIntel. I can't send your whole report, but I'll get the important points across."

"Thanks."

"Of course. Glad to do it." Crawford stood and extended his hand across the desk. "The Admiral wants to see you, I think."

"Yes, he does. Any idea what that's about?"

Crawford smiled. "Only rumors."

David hesitated a second, but when Crawford didn't offer anything more, he left and headed to the Admiral's office.

Admiral Whittaker's Office
Starbase Tranquility II
Tuesday, July 12, 2078, 0845 UTC

Admiral Whittaker was even more intimidating in person than he had been over the video link. His perfectly tailored uniform showed a trim, compact, powerful physique that reflected the mind which managed it. He offered David strong Fleet coffee from a beaten-up stainless-steel pot. They sat separated by the Admiral's desk for a long moment.

"You left SFU in '76?"

*Uh, oh. Here it comes.* David thought. "Yes, sir."

"Why?" A simple, direct question, but not at all accusatory. Despite his discomfort and mild intimidation, David intuitively liked this officer.

"Personal reasons, sir." Whittaker frowned and leaned forward in his chair, elbows on the desk. He looked even harder at David.

"That won't cut it, Mr. Powell. Nobody drops SFU, in the top fraction of his class, six months short of graduation, without a serious reason."

"I didn't say it wasn't serious, sir. I said it was personal."

Whittaker nodded slowly, thinking it over. He leaned back in his chair and changed the subject, apparently signaling acceptance of David's non-explanation.

"Know Commander Teresa Michael?"

"I've met her, sir, once, as I recall. She was finishing up instructing about the time I was arriving."

"Nothing more than that?"

"No, sir. Excuse me, Admiral, but what's up with Commander Michael?"

"You're aware she was on the ground at Inor when *Liberty* was destroyed?"

David nodded. "Yes, sir, of course. She's a household name these days. She has *Antares* now."

"Correct. Seems that during their time on Inor, she was so impressed with a certain ensign that she made her a lieutenant on the spot. A classmate of yours: Hansen."

David sat up with a start. "Carol. Yes, sir, I think everyone saw that in the media reports."

Whittaker smiled slightly. "Yes." Whittaker paused, then looked away from the document and directly at David.

"Is she any relation to the reason you left the U?"

David blinked and looked back at the Admiral. "No, sir, really, no."

Whittaker paused a second, observing Powell carefully, finally deciding he believed him. "Well, as everyone knows, Hansen acquitted herself very well during the time on Inor. She seems to have given you some credit for that."

David was silent.

"So, once she got off Inor, Michael talked to CINC, who got the ball rolling at Fleet. They pulled your SFU transcript and your performance records. CINC signed off. You were already an ensign before you dragged that busted-up ship of yours back here."

David sat perfectly still for a long moment. He saw the admiral smile slightly, awaiting his response. "Sir?"

"You heard me, Mr. Powell."

"I am not sure I did, sir. Did you say 'ensign'?"

"I did."

"Thank you, Admiral." Despite his resistance, tears were forming at the corners of David's eyes. "I have wanted this ever since I was a boy. It's what I almost had. Long as I can remember, this was all I wanted."

Whittaker nodded sympathetically. "It's all I ever wanted as well. We're both damn lucky to get it. But I'm just the messenger for this. You should be thanking Lieutenant Hansen and Commander Michael. "

"I do, sir. I mean, I will, sir."

"But you're not going to be an ensign long." The Admiral had a wry smile, one David had the impression wasn't seen very often in the office.

"Sir?"

"Michael got everybody to wake up and smell the coffee about you, Powell. Seems pretty clear to me that she was right. After what you've just done with

*Sigma*, I'm going to finish the job. As of now, you're a lieutenant. Here are your commission and your promotion."

Whittaker carefully handed David two signed certificates, one his commission as 'An Officer and a Gentleman' of the ISC Fleet, carrying Admiral Davenport's signature, and a promotion to lieutenant, signed personally by Admiral Whittaker.

David took them as if he were Moses, taking the tablets from the hand of God.

"Sir, I'm not sure what to say."

"Well, you know old salts like me appreciate good manners. A thank you would be in order at this point."

"Of course, sir, yes, thank you, sir."

"Yes, well, I also have orders for you. You're going home to talk to FleetIntel, then to *Columbia*. *Chaffee* will take you and your data back home today."

"Today, sir?"

"To-day. FleetIntel needs that data as soon as we can get it to them."

"Dan Smith is commanding *Columbia* now, isn't he, sir?"

"Yes. Something of a mess there for him to clean up, I guess. Seems your class is everywhere these days."

"What about *Sigma*?"

"*Sigma* is a yard problem now, Mr. Powell. I've assigned a Senior Lieutenant to command while we patch her back up. Kondo will stay on as Engineer since The Drive was not damaged. Lieutenant White will ride back with you and assume command. The surviving crew is also relieved and will be reassigned."

David nodded his understanding. "They're a good crew, sir."

"No doubt about that. Good luck, Mr. Powell. We're done here."

David stood, saluted the admiral, and left the office.

In the outer office, a rail-thin six-foot female Senior Lieutenant stood talking to the Admiral's yeoman. She turned as David exited the Admiral's office and looked at him with very clear blue eyes.

"You Powell?" she asked in a voice that seemed a little too high for her size.

"Yes, ma'am."

She grinned crookedly at the formality. "I'm Peg White."

She extended her hand. The handshake was firm, almost painful.

"I understand you have just set the record for least time in grade for an ensign in Fleet history."

"I suppose so. Sure was a surprise to me!"

David's face reflected that he still hadn't entirely absorbed what had happened.

She nodded. "Well, in wartime all kinds of surprising things happen. Sometimes enterprising warrant officers even bring in a ship and crew nobody, but nobody thought had survived."

She kept him fixed in place with those eyes until the smile widened slightly.

"Come on, Powell. You need to stop at the Fleet Store and then escort me out to *Sigma*."

"Fleet Store?"

"Yeah. Last time I checked L-Ts wore silver bars, not the Rings of Saturn."

Peg White took him through the station to the Fleet Store, where he had to show the promotion to obtain a new set of insignia. That done, he stopped at the admin office for upgraded ID and received new pay information, account numbers, and new security access keys.

"I need a few minutes, Lieutenant White," he said as they left Admin.

"Call me Peg."

"Oh, well, OK, thanks. David."

"What do you need time for?" White looked at him quizzically.

"I need to send a thank you note."

Peg White laughed out loud and half pushed David further down the hall. A right, a left, a long corridor, and they were at the commissary. David sat as Peg drew a coffee, then sat across from him. He typed for a few moments, paused, continued, paused again. He re-read the final version three times.

```
ROUTINE 207807110915UTC
TO: ANTARES/CDR TERESA MICHAEL
FROM: LT DAVID POWELL
SUBJECT: COMMISSION

I AM SURPRISED AND DEEPLY APPRECIATIVE OF YOUR EFFORTS ON MY BEHALF.
I WILL DO EVERYTHING POSSIBLE TO BE WORTHY OF THIS HONOR.

PLEASE ACCEPT MY SYMPATHIES ON THE LOSS OF YOUR FRIEND LEN DAVIS.
HE WAS A GOOD MAN, AND I WILL MISS HIM.

BEST REGARDS,
LT DAVID POWELL
END
```

He hit the Send button and began a second message for Carol. The first part was easy, then it took him a long time to decide how to say what he wanted to tell her.

```
SLIP PERSONAL 207807110915UTC
TO: ANTARES/SLT CAROL HANSEN
FROM: LT DAVID POWELL
SUBJECT: COMMISSION

WHATEVER YOU DID AT INOR, WE BOTH KNOW YOU DID IT YOURSELF.
I'M NOT SURE HOW TO THANK YOU FOR MY RECLAMATION. BUT I PROMISE TO TRY.
COMING HOME VIA CHAFFEE ETA 29 JULY.
LOOKING FORWARD TO THE SUNSET.

DAVID
END
```

David's messages dispatched, they made their way back to the shuttle the

Admiral had loaned to the *Sigma* personnel, docked on the opposite side of the station. They talked as they worked their way through the busy passageways.

"I read your Fleet Action Report. What's your opinion of what went wrong?"

"Hard to say. They were tracking us for sure."

"That's pretty obvious," she said without insult. "Question is, how?"

David nodded grimly. "For sure. We think it might have something to do with the SLIP system, but I don't know what."

They navigated the rabbit warren of corridors and offices until they finally reached the shuttle port. FPI SLT Kondo was waiting at the airlock when they arrived, having made his own report in the FPI offices elsewhere on the station. David introduced Kondo to his new commander, and they boarded the small shuttle together. Kondo noted David's promotion.

"Well, *Lieutenant,* you'll have to take command with no arguments next time, eh?"

They laughed as they boarded the shuttle. The ten kilometers to *Sigma* passed in pleasant conversation.

Peg White watched the ship grow outside the forward windows. "Let's take a turn around her. I want to get a better feel for how she was hit." Peg instructed the flight crew to move up to the mangled bow of *Sigma*. She pulled her phone from her kit, swapping seats with the co-pilot, to get as close to those front windows as possible. The command pilot, a slightly overweight blond Warrant III, eyed her warily as they approached the ragged mess that was the forepart of *Sigma*.

"Stop here," she directed.

Like a coroner making an initial examination, Peg looked over the entire scene, then took some specific shots, adding voice annotations to each. The starboard side showed a distinct 'exit wound' where the blast had pushed the structure of the ship outward. Up forward, they saw the shattered Bridge windows, with only a few panes unbroken. The strike had pushed them outward towards the starboard. To port, they saw three clear 'entry' wounds. David would never forget the destruction forward and the ragged strands of wreckage that seemed to dangle in space. There was another entry hole, amidships in the Weapons area. As they came close, David looked at that wound for a long time, long enough that Peg White had the shuttle stopped near it. What had been a relaxed and talkative ride became very quiet. Peg waited a few moments to see if Powell would move on, but he didn't.

"Someone we cared about in there, David?"

He blinked back to his surroundings, looking away from Lisa's death and back at Peg.

"I cared about all of them, Peg."

She continued to look at him with some sympathy. "But you didn't stare at the other damage, so?"

She left the invitation open, and now the warrants who had started out matter-of-fact were also watching and listening. Finally, David relented and spoke.

"She was a half-year ahead of me at the U. Aboard ship we were friends. I think she would have liked it to be more, but...she deserved better than this."

"They all did."

"Indeed." After a moment, David asked, "Are we done here, Lieutenant?"

"Yes," she said, brightening her tone, "we are. Let's get aboard and complete the turnover."

They moved to the docking port, linked up, and boarded the now-quiet ship. Most of the crew had already left, and the ship was maintaining itself just enough to support the few still aboard. *Sigma* would remain in this low state as long as she was in the shipyard. They walked through the half-lit passageways to the Intel section, where the command console remained assigned. Peg connected to the central computer network and downloaded the ship's state to her NetComp. She reset the command console to her own control and did a few setups to enable the repairs to go forward. It only took a few minutes, and by the end, she was in command of *Sigma*, and David and the rest of the crew were electronically relieved. David last saw Peg White walking forward out of the Intel office to get a closeup of the intact bulkhead forward. She was already in full engineering mode, in charge, and impatient to get on with the task ahead of her.

Abe Jackson and Sally Gray had waited for David. Now fully relieved, they returned with him to Tranquility II. It was a very quiet trip. They embraced one last time as they docked. They'd each have a very different path from here, so for all they knew, this was goodbye for good. It was another hard moment.

As he stepped off the shuttle back on Tranquility II, his phone buzzed that he had a message.

```
SLIP PERSONAL 207807111500UTC
TO: SIGMA/CW2 DAVID POWELL
FROM: ANTARES/SLT CAROL HANSEN
JUST GOT THE GOOD NEWS FROM CINC.
THIS IS HOW IT WOULD FEEL TO BE A SINNER PAROLED FROM HELL.
MUCH SADNESS HERE FOR CDR DAVIS, LEAH, LISA, TRAVIS AND THE REST.
CAN'T WAIT TO HEAR YOUR STORY.
CAROL
END
```

He read the second line ten times before it really sunk in. *Like a sinner paroled from hell* is how she feels now that she knows he is alive. He thought about how much pain it must have caused her to believe that he was gone. He was again amazed at what Carol could tell him in just a few words.

Late in the afternoon, David walked down a long, dimly lit passageway leading to an open airlock beyond which was *Chaffee*, his ride home, and his new life. He carried a backpack of personal stuff and a duffel with his uniforms. He tried to walk at a steady, relaxed, officer-ish pace but as the hatch grew in his vision, he felt a nervous weakening in his knees and stomach. He fought back the feeling and managed to both not run and not fall as he came to the hatch. There were a young Marine and a very short lieutenant minding the access to the ship. As he approached, David nodded acknowledgment to the officer.

"Good afternoon, Lieutenant. David Powell reporting."

As she checked the access list on her tablet, she replied, "Good afternoon, Powell."

She extended her hand and gave him a firm, sincere handshake.

"I'm Rios. Congratulations on the promotion and on bringing *Sigma* back."

"Oh, so you've heard?"

"Duh, yeah. Mister Powell, you are gonna be big news back home. Big. News. I'd bet on that."

"I hadn't thought of that. I hope not."

She shrugged. "Well, whatever, you're in deck two, cabin fifteen. Happens to be vacant, so you get lucky."

"Thanks very much."

"Captain's gift. Or luck. Whatever."

"Either way, I'll take it."

"Karma, maybe, right?"

"Sure," he responded, secretly hoping this conversation would be over soon.

She flipped a couple screens on her tablet. "Captain says dinner 1800. He's not a stickler but don't be late."

"On time, will do."

She waved him on through the hatch, and he found his way to the quarters she'd specified. He flopped on the naked mattress and smiled at his sudden fortune. So much had changed so fast, so much had been lost and gained, he hardly knew how to absorb it. But every few minutes, he'd take out his phone and read Carol's message again. *LIKE A SINNER PAROLED...*

"Yeah," he said to himself aloud, "somehow that is never going to get old."

It would be a long, wonderful, torturous two weeks back to Earth.

Fleet HQ Shuttle Landing Area
Fort Eustis, VA
Saturday, July 30, 2078, 0800 EDT

David fidgeted nervously during the trip down from *Chaffee*. The data chips with the Sigma tracking data, the full FDR dump he made after the battle, and the after-action reports were in his backpack on the seat beside him. His duffel was in the cargo compartment. Ground personnel would transfer it to the BOQ for him after they landed.

His only job today was to get the *Sigma* data delivered to FleetIntel. He tried not to look at his silver bars, still so self-consciously shiny on his collar. He still could not quite believe they were there or how they got there. But here he was, and there they were. He tried, and mostly failed, to suppress a boyish grin about the whole thing.

But that's not what kept his knee bouncing rhythmically for two hours. *Antares* was still here, he knew, and he was pretty sure there would be a familiar face waiting for him when he departed the shuttle. What would he say to her? How would she react? He fretted about overthinking it and saying something too intellectually cool and about underthinking it and saying something kinda dumb. Maybe he should just let her speak first? Maybe he should trust his instincts since being himself was how he got here? Maybe he should just stop thinking about thinking about what to say?

Despite his impatience, he was somehow the last person off the shuttle. He was looking down at his feet as he stepped off the last step, not wanting to rush and fall flat on his ass at this moment, and as his last foot hit the pavement, he was broadsided by something very hard and very soft that was suddenly all around him. He reached around her and held her as close to him as she did him to her. They stood there, silent for a long time, as the shuttle crew walked carefully around them, amused at the reunion. They'd seen this kind of thing before.

"Carol—" he started to say.

"Well, yeah, who'd you expect?" she said brightly, and they let go a little as they laughed together.

She pulled back, locking his hands in hers, and looked at him, hard, as if studying his face. He was doing much the same. She wore a dark blue SFU polo, white shorts, and sneakers. Her hair was in a ponytail, her large sunglasses perched on her head. She used those frequently to hide her too-famous face a little. To David, she maybe looked a little older, a little tougher, but she was still more beautiful in person than his best dreams of her while they were apart. They turned to walk off the landing pad, arm-in-arm, Carol holding him very close.

"I'm sorry—" she said quietly in his ear.

"Sorry?" he asked, surprised.

"Yeah. Sorry to have taken so long. Too long, to see."

Now clear of the shuttle area, he stopped her and spun her in front of him. He slipped his hand behind her neck and pulled her forehead to his, her brown eyes just centimeters from his.

"I will never be sorry for whatever it took for us to be right here, right now. Never."

She smiled, and they turned and started the long walk around the golf course to Fleet HQ. David slung his backpack over one shoulder, his other arm over her shoulder, and Carol put her arm tight around his waist.

"You've got the data for Harris?" she asked after they had gone a little way.

"Yes. I need to drop it off then I should be free the rest of the day. I'll be at the

272

BOQ tonight."

"Harris will want a briefing next week."

David nodded. "No surprise there, we have a lot to talk about."

They walked on a bit more, savoring the moment, before David spoke again.

"So, what are the plans for *Antares*?"

"We're going back. Looks like we'll need a few weeks here to get ourselves together."

"I have orders to *Columbia*—Dan's ship."

She nodded in response. "I heard that from Cook the day CINC told me about the commission. It will be a good first gig for you. He knows you, knows what you can do."

"I hope so. It will be weird to see Dan as a Lieutenant Commander. Hard enough to see you as a Senior."

She shrugged. "I aced the test. I get extra credit for Inor. It's not a mystery."

David smiled. "You got it because you're wonderful, and you earned it."

"It's true. I am just that maaarvelous!" she said, laughing.

They walked together in the warm morning sunshine, either arm-in-arm or holding hands the whole two miles. She thought back to the last time she had walked this path, how much pain she felt, and how kind Jack Ballard was to her, despite her reactions.

"*Columbia* isn't due for several days," she said as they approached the HQ building, "and I am off until Monday."

"Good," he said quietly.

"Very good," she responded.

As they made the last turn off Mulberry Island Road towards the HQ building, she slipped her arm around David again and pulled him very close, and he returned her touch. They walked through the front doors of HQ, out of the hot, humid Virginia morning and into the very fresh air-conditioned space. The security tech looked up, and Carol saw a familiar face.

"Technician Orr, are you here *all* the time?" she asked brightly. Orr returned a wry smile.

"Just lucky, ma'am. So, who's this?"

Orr verified David's identity and sent them down the hall to the Intel Section. As they entered the Intel section, they found CW3 Kelly Peterson at the desk. She looked up as they entered.

"Good morning, Lieutenant Hansen."

She shook hands with Hansen, then extended the same to David, introducing herself.

"Lieutenant Powell, a pleasure. The Admiral tells me you have some data for us?"

David unslung his backpack from his shoulder and pulled a small case from one of the outside pockets. Opening that, he removed a plastic bag with two data chips.

"Yes, Ms. Peterson, here they are. This," he said, picking one up, "is the FDR dump I did right after the battle. It has the tracking data as well. This other one has all the after-action reports we could gather on the way back to Tranquility II."

Kelly took the chips, placed them in individual cases and set them aside.

"I will get those into Admiral Harris' safe for you."

David nodded in acknowledgment of what she said and turned to leave.

"Wait, Lieutenant! I have something for you and Lieutenant Hansen from the boss."

She passed over a small envelope. Carol took it and ripped it open. Her face brightened with surprise as she read it. "We're invited to a party at the Admiral's home, a cookout, today at six."

Kelly was nodding enthusiastically. She already knew all about it.

David wasn't very interested at first. "I don't know, Carol, I mean, I just got here."

But as he looked at Carol, she was clearly excited about the idea.

"Really, both of you, you should come. There's nothing like a party at the Harris' house," Kelly was shamelessly pushing and having fun with it. Harris had told her to encourage them as much as she could, but truthfully, she really wanted them to come.

David was intrigued. "Oh?"

"Oh yes, Lieutenant. Meredith, that is, Mrs. Harris, is a fantastic hostess. All of Intel and Plans will be there."

"Really?"

"Oh sure, Captain Collins and the Harrises are very close. Old friends, from what I understand. We have some kind of gathering about once a month."

Carol was now giving him a look he had not seen for a long time.

"OK, so what should we bring?" he asked, surrendering.

Carol waved the card. "Says here if you have a specific beverage you want, feel free to bring it. Otherwise, just come."

David turned back to Kelly. "Ms. Peterson—" he started to ask.

"Kelly"

"OK, Kelly, what does Mrs. Harris drink?"

"Norton. It's a historic Virginia red. She absolutely loves the stuff."

"Where can I get it?"

"Exchange has it."

"Expensive?"

"Not bad. The more expensive ones really are better, but don't pay more than $75."

"OK, then. Advise the good Admiral that we will be happy to accept his kind invitation." They turned to leave when David spun back around. "Wait...what's the dress code?"

Carol held up the card. "Civilian picnic casual."

"Say what?"

"Polos and shorts. Or whatever. Get with the program, Powell."

They left the HQ and walked to the exchange. They could have called for a car, but both of them were happy to be out in the open air again and in no hurry to be anywhere but together. They bought the Norton for Meredith, and David picked up some clothes for the picnic since all he had on hand were sweatshirts and jeans. They had a light lunch at the officers' club — in anticipation of the cookout later — and then got David checked in at the BOQ. Carol already had a room since she would be on the surface for several more weeks.

They walked the post for a few hours, glad now in the early afternoon for the occasional shade of real trees. They sat a few times on benches or steps of buildings or whatever patch of grass was handy, talking quietly about *Liberty*, Inor, and *Sigma*. And, of course, Beta Hydri. There were many details they hadn't been able to share in a SLIP message. Their talk was natural, comfortable, and intimate in a way it had not been at SFU. They were together now, and there were no longer any limits on what they said to each other. David felt like a man unshackled, able to express his true feelings freely for the first time. Carol talked about Marty Baker, the fun they had together, and how narrowly and horribly he was lost, and she survived. How close she came to the same nightmarish end haunted her more now than it had at the time. David talked about Leah, Travis, and Lisa and their kindness to him. He would never forget the look on Lisa's face as she left *Sigma*'s bridge and went back to the magazine for the last time. Frightened, but trusting him, Sanders, and the captain to do the right thing. He confessed a nagging doubt that he had somehow let her down, but Carol insisted there was nothing more he could have done. She made and, as usual, won the argument that, after all, Davis was in command.

As the afternoon started to wind down, they headed back to their rooms at the BOQ, showered, changed, and stepped off together for the half-mile walk to Admiral Harris' home. As they approached, they could hear the chatter of voices and followed that cheerful sound into the backyard. There were a couple dozen people there, with Ron and Meredith side by side somewhere in the middle.

"Carol!" Rich Evans called as he made his way to them through the crowd.

"Hello, Rich. This is—"

"David Powell!" Rich interrupted her, extending his hand. "Commander Rich Evans, Lieutenant Powell. Pleased to meet you."

"And you, sir."

"Come on, then," Evans said, taking David's arm, "Time to meet the boss, oh, and the Admiral, too."

They laughed as he pulled them to the center of the crowd. Evans made the introductions for David, Carol having already met both Harrises a couple weeks before. Carol handed over the Norton, which Meredith happily accepted.

"Thanks very much, Carol, so thoughtful of you."

"Well, truth be told, Mrs. Harris—"

"Oh, please, that's my mother-in-law. Call me Meredith."

"Yes, ma'am, as I was saying, it was David's idea."

David found himself pulled back into Meredith's circle to accept her thanks.

"Thank you, ma'am, for the invitation. This is really very nice."

Meredith nodded. "Yes, we try to have a normal moment every once in a while. We all need to have a little touch of home, you know? Something like we knew before?"

"Well, ma'am—"

"Jesus, what will it take to get you people to drop all the formalities?"

David grinned, understanding. "Sorry, Meredith. We're all indoctrinated to treat the spouse with the same respect as the officer. It gets to be a little Pavlovian."

"Ugh, boring. But the name rings a bell..."

They laughed together at her joke. David took his leave of her and found his way to the beer coolers. The variety was impressive, and he found a decent IPA he had heard of to try. As he was opening it, Rich Evans was again at his side.

"So, Powell, tell me about the tracking."

David looked around. "Here?"

"Sure. Everyone here is cleared, Powell. Don't sweat it at all."

"OK, well, it was pretty weird..." David went on to describe the enemy ships' behaviors, his conversations with John Sanders, and the last, short call from Leah Farley. As he talked to Evans, he could see Carol moving through the crowd, many of whom she had already met. She was in close conversation with an attractive woman in her thirties, and as they talked together, Carol looked across at him, and as their eyes met, she smiled slightly before she went back to her companion. He suddenly realized he was smiling a little, too, between the descriptions Evans was extracting from him. After a while, Evans cut him loose, apparently having heard what he needed to hear. David tossed his empty bottle in the recycle bin, got a fresh one, and then meandered back around to Carol.

"David! This is Lieutenant Ann Cooper. Inventor of the Sentinel."

"Oh, yes. Great idea."

"Thanks, but I had a lot of help!"

Their conversation quickly moved to less military matters, Ann talking about her young child and introducing her husband, Stan.

Before long, the scent of Meredith's unique burger blend and barbequed chicken filled the air. It was a long, generous buffet line. It was a prototypical American picnic, but the warmth and welcome that came with it erased any feeling of cliché or pretense. This was no act, no choreographed political affair. This was the real thing: generosity offered for the sheer joy of doing it.

They loaded their plates and wandered back outside, still talking to Ann and Stan. They found a table near the back of the yard. As the conversation continued through dinner, a pretty, slight, somewhat older, fair-complexioned redhead came over to join them.

"Hello, Captain Collins," Carol said.

"Good afternoon, Hansen. Lovely party, don't you think?"

"Yes, ma'am. Captain, this is David Powell."

"The *Sigma* David Powell?" she asked, the surprise clear in her voice.

"Yes, ma'am, guilty as charged."

Fiona sat down next to David, setting down her overloaded plate. She shook his hand, then reached around him for a brief hug. "Amazing work, Mister Powell, truly an incredible job bringing her back."

David, embarrassed, looked away, then back. "Just did what needed to be done, Captain Collins, no more than the next guy would have done."

Fiona leaned in close and spoke quietly in David's ear. "The next guy would have shit his pants, and you'd all be dead."

Carol heard about half of that and looked at David with a question in her eyes. He gave her a quick shrug before responding.

"Yes, ma'am, maybe so. Point is we made it, and it took all forty-three of us to do it."

Fiona touched his arm. "Congratulations, Powell, welcome home."

After dinner, they were back up and moving around the party, talking to a variety of Intel and Plans people and spouses. The late afternoon began to stretch into evening, a clear summer day leaning into a gathering dusk. Dessert was three different kinds of pie, all home-made by Meredith. For David, it was an event unlike anything he had ever seen since he joined the Fleet.

Many of the guests left early, especially those with children to get to bed, but Carol and David felt no inclination to be anywhere else, and their hosts were in no hurry to see them leave. It was a pleasant picture: tiki-torches and picnic tables, with dim lights strung overhead. It had a mystical, romantic quality to it that suited their mood.

After the rest of the guests had left, Carol and David stood at the railing on the edge of the deck, looking west at the sun as it sank lower in the sky. Ron, Meredith, and Fiona looked at the two young officers close together at the railing, two young heroes of different fights, and quietly moved inside, leaving them alone.

They had a clear view of the sun, and as it touched the horizon, Carol looked at her NetLink, confirming the time. David looked at her, wondering what was on her mind. She was now looking back at the orange, pink and purple sky, the sun sinking slowly away.

"Well, well, I finally made it," she said, with relief in her voice.

"Made it?" David asked, not understanding.

She turned to him. "I promised next time I would stay for the sunset," she said quietly, looking again at the sun and then back at him, her eyes now locked on his.

"Here I am, still standing here."

They leaned toward each other and kissed. As she leaned back, sliding her arms around him and resting her head on his shoulder, she could see her future, no, *their* future, as something as clear and bright and beautiful as the evening gathering around them. It was as if they had already lived it, and she was remembering the contentment of years together, the equanimity of a life lived as it was intended. Whatever the ultimate outcome might be for them, and in war, one could never really know, in their hearts they would always be just like this: together, silent, side by side at the end of the day.

### An additional note from the author:

I hope you enjoyed *Silver Enigma and* will go on to read the other two books in the series: *Silver Search* and *Silver Victory*.

Now that *Silver Victory* is done, I've gone back through *Silver Enigma* and touched up a few errors, revised some phrasing here and there, and added a comma or two where they had been missed before. Nothing about the story is changed, but it is without doubt a better version of itself. Again, I hope you enjoyed the ride and will leave a review or rating wherever you purchased it.

Rock Whitehouse
August 2020

### And Another Thing…

Welcome to the 2022 update of *Silver Enigma*!

My decision to release an audiobook of *Silver Enigma* resulted in quite a few changes in this version. I've added chapters, dropped the month/year sections, and fixed some of the remaining grammatical and punctuation errors. Hard to believe after so many readings that there were still some out there! I also rephrased some words and descriptions that I thought might leave the narrator speechless.

The story is, of course, the story, but this version has several small improvements that make it a better work, especially for the narrator.

There's also a new cover, one I think better reflects the story within.

Again, I hope you enjoyed reading *Silver Enigma*, and will go on to read *Silver Search* and *Silver Victory*.

*Assault at Zeta Doradus*.
*Status One*.
*SD*?

Rock Whitehouse

---

## Acknowledgments

This is my first attempt at a novel-length piece and believe me, that has been an education in itself. I have tried to dream up plausible future technologies and situations, combine them with some hopefully interesting people, stir gently, then set them loose in the real world of the stars around us.

The core of the story, David and Carol and the Inori and the surprise attack at Inor, were started in the middle 1990s and fussed with from time to time on nights when I couldn't sleep. I worked out the main technologies like the Forstmann Drive, SLIP, the 'sub-car' subterranean transportation system, the NetLink and NetComps at that time as well. The concept of the NetLink communication device on the wrist owes far more to the Dick Tracy two-way wrist radio than it does the iWatch. The inspiration for the NetComp tablets came from early tablet computers like the Grid and not the iPad or similar devices, although obviously current tablets like the iPad and the various Androids are the logical equivalents of the NetComp.

I gave a lot of thought to whether in 2078 we would still have devices something like smartphones and tablets and I have concluded that we will. Private communication requires something you can place between your ear and mouth, such that only you can hear, and you can speak softly enough to that only your conversational partner can hear. We've all heard that salesman in the airport on his Bluetooth headset who has no clue he's pitching to about a thousand people who really don't give a crap about his wonder widget whatevers. Could we do privacy with implants? Maybe. But I think we would be far wiser to keep ourselves analog and therefore completely unhackable. The question of tablet computers also mostly goes to privacy. We will always want to find and display information in a manner that is private. For both technologies, I see a lower limit on size, as our fingers can only hit buttons of a given size and our eyes can likewise only read a screen down to a pretty hard lower limit. You may feel differently, but I think remaining un-chipped is probably a good thing for us, both individually and as a society. But, of course, some new tech idea (VR contacts?) may make all this moot. Time will tell.

I have used that interwebby thing throughout the process, and if there is a site dedicated to nearby stars, habitable star systems, or concepts of alien life, I have probably been there, and I thank you for your help. I visited so many in the early phases of research I could not begin to name them all. There were several sites which I used extensively I want to acknowledge. If you are interested in any of the ideas or environment behind this story, these are a good place to start.

www.solstation.com
www.sci-fi-az.com
www.atlasoftheuniverse.com
www.projectrho.com
www.wikipedia.com
https://www.space.com/51-asteroids-formation-discovery-and-exploration.html
http://www.astro.gsu.edu/~thenry/PLANETS/paper.anderson.pdf
http://www.permanent.com/asteroid-mining.html
https://exoplanetarchive.ipac.caltech.edu/
http://www.thesaurus.com
http://www.kencroswell.com/thebrightestreddwarf.html

I generated many of the character names from one of two sites, character.namegeneratorfun.com and random-name-generator.info. Other names I created myself, usually from US Census data listings on first and last names summarized on behindthename.com and infoplease.com. The rest, I just made up.

I have been a sci-fi and military fiction reader all my life, and I realize that obviously shows through in this story. So, writers like Jerry Pournelle, Larry Niven, Robert Heinlein, Frank Herbert, Carl Sagan and to a lesser degree Isaac Asimov certainly have formed my thinking, along with later writers like Tom Clancy. I am a great lover of Ayn Rand's Atlas Shrugged (though not all of her philosophy - I am not an objectivist) and, of course, Tolkien's The Lord of the Rings.

My study with Lorain County Community College English professor Kim Karshner was, and continues to be, of great help to me. Her eye for grammar mistakes and awkward scene transitions made the work much better than it would have been otherwise.

I hired Jane Friedman (www.janefriedman.com) to review the query and synopsis, and her input was well worth the price. If you're a new author trying to get yourself noticed, I recommend her Greatest Courses course and her individual services as well.

I started the story using Microsoft Word, but that became unworkable about 60,000 words into it. I converted to yWriter (spacejock.com/ywriter), and that has been a great help. If you're considering working on fiction of any significant scope, you should at least give it a try

I have to thank my 'alpha' and 'beta' version readers. Starting with my good friend and former co-worker, and author, Dan, for his early encouragement and constructive comments about the technology and story. Also, thanks to another former colleague and sci-fi enthusiast (I think having a working Cylon in your family room qualifies you) Kevin for his feedback and encouragement. The ISC name is Kevin's contribution, getting me past the 'Terran Space Navy' which wa actually, pretty dreadful. Thanks also to beta readers Ray, Chris, Dina, and M for their encouragement and suggestions.

But I really have to call out our longtime friends Kert (engineer, ex-Na sub guy) and Jan (retired DOD contract administrator) for having the co read the first full draft. The two hours we spent over excellent food a (see www.thejailhousetaverne.com) was a transformational moment hear others talking about my characters as if they (the characters, real people was just astounding. It made me think this whole thin real. Without them, I don't think this work would exist.

Daughter Becky provided her direct, unfiltered feedback and 'abeulita' is one of her contributions. So much better Teresa's mind.

Finally, of course, my wife Carey has given me the imaginary territory, and I am enormously grateful to her reads every word, and her ability to spot missing or extr in a hundred readings was amazing.

Now, about that honey-do list...and on to book #

Rock Whitehouse
October 2018
email: rock@iscfleet.com
Twitter: @iscfleet

www.rock-whitehouse.com
www.iscfleet.com